STARTER KIT

AN INTRODUCTION TO THE BIZARRO GENRE

BIZARRO BOOKS
Portland * Seattle * Baltimore

Bizarro

www.bizarrocentral.com

BIZARRO BOOKS
205 NE BRYANT
PORTLAND, OR 97211

IN COOPERATION WITH:

WWW.ERASERHEADPRESS.COM
WWW.AFTERBIRTHBOOKS.COM
WWW.RAWDOGSCREAMING.COM

ISBN: 1-933929-62-6

Cover design by Carlton Mellick III
Figure model used for cover image: Erin Nolan
Edited by: Team Bizarro

Printed in the USA.

TABLE OF CONTENTS

DEFINING BIZARRO

1. Bizarro, simply put, is the genre of the weird.

2. Bizarro is the literary equivalent to the cult section at the video store.

3. Like cult movies, Bizarro is sometimes surreal, sometimes goofy, sometimes bloody, and sometimes borderline pornographic.

4. Bizarro often contains a certain cartoon logic that, when applied to the real world, creates an unstable universe where the bizarre becomes the norm and absurdities are made flesh.

5. Bizarro strives not only to be strange, but fascinating, thought-provoking, and, above all, fun to read.

6. Bizarro was created by a group of small press publishers in response to the increasing demand for (good) weird fiction and the increasing number of authors who specialize in it.

7. Bizarro is:

Franz Kafka meets Joe Bob Briggs

Dr. Seuss of the post-apocalypse

Alice in Wonderland for adults

Japanese animation directed by David Lynch

8. For more information on the bizarro genre, visit Bizarro Central at:

www.bizarrocentral.com

RAY FRACALOSSY

LOCATION:
(or lotion for short) Freehold, N.J.

STYLE OF BIZARRO:
New Absurdism

BOOKS BY FRACALOSSY:
Tales from the Vinegar Wasteland
mOsbURAnD (an ongoing project)

DESCRIPTION: Ray Fracalossy dreams of writing full-time, while writing of those trapped in full-time dreams. Humor is included at no extra cost.

INTERESTS: Absurdism, psychedelia, surrealism, spirituality, the metaphysical, coffee shops, pinball, the 1920's, U.F.O.'s, art nouveau, diners, krautrock, playing guitar, the science of dreams and daydreaming, sushi and raw bars, synchronicity, minimalism, potato chips, bizarre comic books, shots, being lazy, puns and wordplay.

INFLUENCES: Lewis Carroll, Danill Kharms, Daniel Clowes, C.S. Lewis, Roald Dahl, Barry Yourgrau, Shel Silverstein, Richard Brautigan, Alexander Vvedensky, polycarp kusch, D. Harlan Wilson, Valery Ronshin, Ernie Bushmiller, Edgar Cayce, Syd Barrett, Skip Spence.

WEBSITE:
www.myspace.com/rayfracalossy

FUN WITH DAN AND JOAN

Dan and Joan like to play. They pretend they are someone else. Pretend, Joan. Pretend, Dan. They have a dog named Spot. Spot likes to play too. Dan pretends to be Spot. Spot pretends to be Dan. No one pretends to be Joan. Joan pretends to be mother. "Mother, come see!" they say.

Mother comes out to play too. Mother pretends to be a bookcase. Spot takes a book out of Mother's mouth. Read Spot Read. "Oh Dan," says Joan to Spot.

"Yes Mother?" says Spot.

"It is time for dinner," says Joan.

"Oh boy," says Spot.

"We are eating Spot," says Joan.

"This is stupid," says Dan.

"Dogs can't talk," says Spot.

They pretend to eat Dan. Dan tastes good. Eat Joan. Eat Spot. Mother only eats books.

Father comes home. Father kisses Mother and Dan and Joan. Father licks Spot.

Father asks Mother, "What is for dinner?"

Mother says, "We are eating Spot."

"Really?" says Father.

"Really?" says Spot.

"Yes," says Mother.

Spot pretends to be a bird. He flies away. Fly, Spot, Fly.

Father and Mother and Dan and Joan pretend to be crab like creatures, and crawl to the sea.

A BODY IN MOTION

There once was a man with a fully functioning fully equipped body, and while you couldn't say it was still in pristine, straight from the factory condition (having aged a bit) it was operative, and suited him well, in many day to day activities such as moving and sleeping, eating and resting. But like so many things in these uncertain times, it was not to last.

First came his roaming eye, which usually only roamed for short periods of time, but eventually began to call out altogether. The other eye followed suit, and eventually, both eyes left the premises, and the eyes closed permanently due poor attendance.

Next his mind began to wander. It wandered deep into the woods one day, and no one has seen it since. It's believed to have gotten lost in a thought, and been unable to find its way back.

His lips, which had been warned on prior occasions to keep their distance, began to distance themselves even more, staying away from the body for good, feeling unimportant and unappreciated. His hands, which had struck previously went out on strike for good, and took the fingers with them, looking for better hours, higher pay, and an owner who didn't scratch their unmentionables quite so often. The man felt more betrayed by the loss of his hands than by his fingers, claiming he felt he could never count on his fingers anyway.

Next came the nose, which had run for years, but this time had run for good, and not looked back. Both his heels, his dick, and ass left in a huff one night, mostly due to a misunderstanding. They had found their names to be derogatory, and felt that the man had been picking on them all these years, and were fed up. The mouth and stomach became fed up as well. It wasn't based on anything. Mouths and stomachs just do that. It's their job.

The feet raised a big stink, and walked out leaving a note which simply stated, and I quote, 'These feet were made for walking, and that's just what they'll do.' End quote.

The skin, which had flaked off and peeled away until it could set itself up elsewhere, acted rather rashly, and sent for the other layers. The ears heard about the body mutiny, and decided to stick it out for a little longer. Sound advice, seeing how they'd been just hanging around for years. His teeth and hair had a falling out with the man. It was nothing personal, and purely genetic. His intestines crapped out on him one day, and his shadow disappeared on him gradually over the course of an evening. It was gone by the time the man had turned the lights off for bed.

So the man, or what was left of him, discouraged because he was unable to hold himself together, went to pieces. The ears, always open, sold the pieces for medical research the second they heard it was possible to do such a thing. The pair took the money they had earned and invested wisely. They managed to retire much earlier than expected, never having to rely on any sort of senior hearing aid like so many other ears they'd known had been forced to do.

THE INTRUDER

Last night I awoke in the early a.m. hours startled to find a poorly drawn two dimensional rendering of a man standing in our bedroom. The drawing looked like something done by a 4 year old trained in modern art. It looked to be a side profile, yet both eyes were clearly visible Picasso style, reminding me of a cubist rendition done in crayon. Its mouth was a meager squiggled line that extended off the chin into empty space. I couldn't tell if it indeed possessed a nose, or if the bulbous mass I thought somewhat resembled one was merely a sad attempt at a poorly placed ear. He was over near my wife's side of the bed in the process of leaning down to kiss her, if such a thing was possible considering its mouth. I watched as the drawing man's tongue emerged from his wavy crevice, and lapped the side of my wife's face. She stirred a bit, wiping his wet from her cheek, but seemed neither too bothered or excited by his efforts. I laid there trying to plan my attack. What sort of weapon did I have nearby that would be effective on a bad drawing? Who knew what strange powers this monstrosity might possess? I didn't want to make any sudden moves, thus giving him the upper hand (also ineptly drawn) and a chance to come at me.

His advances continued, and he began caressingly gliding his palm the entire length of my wife's body. The cad. Two more hands appeared, and began to search out even more erogenous regions. Was this some how a pay-back for the times I had gotten erotic thrills from the Sunday funnies? Had my lust for Blondie Bumstead and Aunt Fritzie Ritz caused this apparition to hunt me down in order to seek retribution and defile my wife? He began to lift the sheets off of her in an attempt to join us beneath them. I imagined a full scale grope session, its malformed crayon body bumping and grinding as it contorted against her helpless flesh. I was both disgusted, and I feel ashamed to admit, slightly aroused, but this was neither the time nor the place. . .well, maybe the place. There was only one option left open to me. The gun, baseball bat, rat-traps, switchblade, hand grenade, stink bombs, and mace that we kept near the bed as our own private arsenal would be of no help to me here. I thought of my mentors.

What would Salvador Dali do in a surreal situation such as this? And in a split second, it came to me. Yes! An Art Exorcism! I blessed myself with paint thinner and began.

Grabbing a copy of the New Oxford Art Review, I flipped to its most vicious art critiques and reading them aloud, watched in vanquishing splendor as the hideous visage grimaced and snarled, before turning into what looked like the remnants of a chalkboards ledge, which I gathered and later smeared on paper and taped to the refrigerator, as a symbol of my triumph! My wife claims to remember nothing of the incident, although she has of late developed an odd fear of modern art museums.

THE BIRTHDAY PARTY

Steve blew out the candles on his birthday cake, and wished for a pony. A pony knocked on the door. He asked for Steve. I told him he had the wrong house. Steve asked me who was at the door. I told him it was the repo man, here to take the cake back. Steve started to cry. I told him I was sorry, but that he should learn to manage his money better. At that point, a seven inch woman jumped out of the cake. She shook her head angrily at Steve, as if ashamed. She started to head for the door. I grabbed a quick handful of cake, and followed after her. We hopped on the pony, and rode off into the sunset together, stopping only occasionally for very odd sex. But it's alright. It wasn't really Steve's birthday anyway. It was mine. And I got my wish.

CORNFLAKES

While eating breakfast this morning, I am surprised by a bomb hidden in my bowl of cornflakes. I had already poured the milk in, too! I quickly examine the box, just to make sure A BOMB is not listed among the ingredients. It's not. I check the front of the box, uncertain if it had stated that for a limited time, a bomb would be included in each package. Nothing. No mention of bombs or weaponry of any sort. I sniff at the bomb. Should I just eat it? A bomb may very well be considered a delicacy in some countries. Hell, I've eaten stranger things.

I listen. It's still ticking. I'm not sure when it's set to go off. I eat quickly. When I finish off the last of the cereal in the bowl, I lick the remaining flakes from the explosive, and let out a sigh of relief. Mission accomplished, I think. Then it dawns on me that I'm still hungry. I look down at the bomb in the bowl angrily, knowing that just because I won the first round does not mean I will be so lucky this next time. I refill the bowl with cereal and milk, sweat beginning to form on my brow. I was so close. I had survived, but here I was tempting fate once again, simply because the only other clean bowl belongs to my roommate. I can't use it. We have an agreement.

Again I finish safely. As soon as I am through, I place the bomb back into the cereal box. I'm returning it to the grocery store where I bought it right after I shower.

I grab a fresh bar of soap and remove it from its package. A scorpion sits securely atop my lilac scented bar, clinging tightly to it. I seem unable to shake it free. I shower carefully, very slowly, with so much focus that I never hear my roommate return home. When I am through showering, I gently place the soap into the soap dish, dry off and dress. I return downstairs to unfortunately find my roommate sitting at the kitchen table nervously enjoying a bowl of cornflakes.

THE MAN WHO SAW GIRAFFES

Once there was a man who saw giraffes. Not in a social way, nor romantically. He saw them on the side, in his spare time as a hobby. At least that was the premise. He hadn't seen any yet. But he intended to. And each time he did see one, he would remove a marble from his marble bag, and drop it into his giraffe jar. The giraffe jar was in actuality an old cleaned out mayonnaise jar that someone familiar with both the man and his new hobby had presented him with as a gift, when the last of the precious mayonnaise was consumed as chicken salad. The man, thrilled with the gift, spent an entire day decorating the jar with glue and spray-painted macaroni and glitter. He then decided it looked much too girlish for a giraffe jar, and spent the next day returning it to its original state.

The man planned to use the old mayonnaise jar as a diary of sorts. He developed an intricate system in which each colored marble represented the grade of giraffe he had encountered. A red aggie meant the giraffe was beautiful, but not above gossip and over indulgence in sweets and liquor. A pee wee tiger's eye was for a tinier giraffe, the kind with that knowing look in its eye, and a certain lilt to its voice. A peppermint swirl signified the spying of an over-weight giraffe, the kind who, despite watching its diet and between meal snacking, and getting lots of exercise, still somehow found itself unable to lose the extra pounds. And so on. It was a system that was as breathtakingly intricate as it was mind numbingly complicated. It involved as much study into the world of marbles as it did knowledge of various giraffes and how to spot their distinguishing personality features.

And it was while in study that the man chanced to read about a giraffe of great scarcity. It was the Indian albino short necked-giraffe. There were rumored to be only two in existence. This presented the man with a great challenge. A challenge not only to find an Indian albino short-necked giraffe, but to find a marble worthy of representing such a rare beast. And so he set out on a quest to find the rarest marble he could. And each time he found one, he'd purchase it, admire it, and believe his quest was done until he encountered an even rarer atypical marble.

As the months went on, he became more and more fascinated with the marbles he was gathering, their odd colorings, their lava like patterns. So much so that he developed a system.

He began collecting leaves in a book. Each leaf would represent a different marble. A red maple would be for cat's eyes that were reflective, but also extremely lonely. A birch leaf was for a clear shooter that was equal parts brash and impulsive.

THE QUEST

I'm on a quest. She tells me that it's a scavenger hunt, but as my eyes scan the list, I think I'm being had. Most of it reads like a shopping list, apart from the inclusion of three high powered magnets and troll doll.

"What are the terms of this? What do I win? Is there a time limit?" I ask in rapid succession.

"Yes there is a time limit, and the prize won't matter much if you don't get going."

"Why don't you help me?" I enquire. "Between the two of us we could bang this out in half the time."

"Please!" she pleads with me. "There is so much at stake here. The consequences of you winning this thing may very well change the course of human history. That's all I'm allowed to tell you. This thing is big, very BIG!" She eyes me, then eyes the door again. Subtle, but I take the cue, and grabbing my jacket I begin to leave. I reach for the car keys.

"I'm going to need the car," she says.

"Isn't there a rush on this? It'll take me more time if I have to walk."

Not a problem she tells me. "It's part of the rules. No cars allowed." I nod in understanding. Some of these competitions can be quite strict. I hand her the car keys and edge to the door.

"Oh shoot! Can I see that list again real quick?" she shouts out.

"Um, sure."

I hand it to her, and she takes it, turns from me and scribbles something. After a short pause, she looks up, scans the room, and again her head goes down and I see her hand moving. I sniffle and scratch my neck, unsure of exactly what is going on here. She hands the list back to me.

"You may need to bring more money."

I look down at the list and see it now includes tampons and hoagie rolls.

"Are you sure this is for some intergalactic scavenger hunt? Because if this is just a grocery list, I have no prob. ."

She cuts me off. "You really better get going. Time is very short. Remember what I said about changing the course of human history."

I exit. It's a rather queer looking day outside. A haze covers everything, almost as if I were viewing the world filtered through a cigarette pack wrapper. I rub my eyes, and head down the block towards town. I walk as quickly as I can, convincing myself that I've been had until I turn a corner and see the supermarket parking lot absent of any cars. I pick up the pace a bit.

As I enter the automated doors, a chill goes up my spine. It is full of men, and they all have lists in their hands. I grab a cart and make a mad dash for aisle six. I'm quite certain the extremely short darker skinned man I passed while reaching for the last container of milk was a Venusian. Or possibly Peruvian.

THE SURPRISE PARTY

"Did we get you?"

"Oh, man did you ever!"

"No, really? You had no idea?"

"Are you kidding me? I was totally fooled!"

"How about me? How was my acting?"

"Oh my God! You totally fooled me! I totally thought you were ready to kick me to the curb. You seemed so happy when you met Paul! I thought you had really fallen out of love with me!"

"And what about me?" asked Uncle Phil.

"I can't believe you're not dead. You have no idea what a mind blower that is!"

"How about me? Did you really believe I was your daughter?"

"I was there when you were born. I was sure of it!"

Laughter continued as the party went on till the wee hours of the morning.

A CHILD'S GUIDE TO REAL SMALL PLANETS

As you stare up at the night sky on a clear night, you may wonder what all those twinkling lights are. Are they real small planets? The answer is yes, they are. You may wonder who put them there. Were they always there? You may also wonder if it is possible to shoot at them with a rubber-band. Perhaps you may have even already tried this. Were you successful? Can they also shoot at us with rubber-bands as well? Is that something you should worry about, the inevitability of one of these meteoric rubber-bands hitting you on the top of your head? Maybe wearing some sort of head protection is in order. Well I'm here to tell you your rubber-band fears are groundless. My, you have an active imagination! The truth is, while not being very fond of firing rubber-bands, they ARE big fans of water guns. This is where rain comes from.

You might be thinking to yourself, "Where do these tiny lights go during the day?" Possibly they attend the same school as your older brothers and sisters. Maybe they go to work with your daddy. Why do they only come out at night when we are all sleeping? Are they plotting against us? Is that something you should also worry about? Or are they sentinels, keeping a quiet vigil while we sleep? The answer is that they are always there. It's just that you see them better at night because of an eye phenomenon called night vision. Perhaps you've heard of it. If not, ask your mommy and daddy about it.

Many people wonder how the sun changes into the moon, and then back again in perfect choreography with the change from day to night. It's very impressive. Is there a man in charge of setting the moon ablaze each day? He must get up very early, like a farmer. Is he a farmer? And how does he put out the moon fire each night? Is it all done manually, with hoses and a giant blowtorch? Or does he just have to flip a switch, or push a button? Well, the answer is: God does it. He lights the moon on and off fire, of course under the supervision and watchful eye of a small group of farmers.

You might now be wondering about life on these other worlds. Do people cry there? Do they eat candy? Do they have cartoons? Do people on these planets get despondent, depressed, suicidal, divorced? Do they hate and murder and bomb and rape and destroy and pollute? Such very serious questions from such a small child. You must do very well in school! Your parents must be very proud. The answer is yes, they eat candy, including many of your very own favorite brands. After all, who doesn't like candy!

A fun experiment to try is to take a flashlight, and try to signal these planets. One flash means "We are here.". . . . . Two flashes means "Hello." . . . .Three or more flashes are considered very rude, and is the universal equivalent to passing gas at the dinner table. If you do accidently flash three times or more, be sure to shout out "Excuse me!"

THE DINNER PARTY

It was really nothing more than a casual get together of a handful of friends. Too intimate to be considered a party, yet with enough preplanning time to warrant bringing out the big guns. I made sure there was a decent assortment of food. I hoped I had risen to the occasion, as I nervously scanned faces for any outward cue giving the slightest sign of feedback. The evening built up speed with different dishes rearing their heads, each attempting to outdo the others.

"Wow, this stuff is good. Where'd you get it?" asked John, a great blissful satisfaction streaming from his face.

"I made it," I answered.

"You made it?" he asked questioning my abilities.

"Yeah," I answered, feeling both elated by his praise and stupefied by his innate lack of faith in my culinary capabilities.

"It's really good! Well alright, bro!"

A round of high fives and nods of approval followed, causing me to thrust out my chest, feeling ever more confident in the outcome of the remainder of the night.

They munched away, enjoying the end results of all my hard work.

Suddenly, in mid-chew, Tom, brows furled, let out, "You know what would have been better? It would have been better if you'd lied. You should have said you hit some kind of food lottery."

"Food lottery?" I asked.

"Yeah, and that all of this stuff was shipped from all around the world, and it contains rare spices, and gold flakes and stuff. Or you could have said that you had this whole affair catered from that place in Wellstown, you know, Feldman's, that high priced gourmet restaurant! It would have blown us away, you spending that kind of dough on us, and think how good you would have felt if we fell for it, knowing your cooking could pass for their stuff."

"Oh man, I haven't had good catered food in years, and I've been wanting to eat at Feldman's since the first time I heard people raving about them!" exclaimed John, suddenly changing his tune. "Rip off! That would have been cool."

"Wait, wait, better yet, what if you told us that some, like, I don't know, movie star or super model came to your door, because she had car trouble, and you helped her. No wait, check this out," he said, hushing their moans of disbelief. "In return, she cooked all this stuff up, but had to rush off for, like, a Hollywood premiere or something."

There was a sudden rush of approval over the mere suggestion of such an event happening.

"Better yet, she made all this stuff in the nude, just to thank you." added Brian, gaining an angry elbowing from his wife in the process.

"Oh dude, I would have been all over this stuff. I would have eaten the crap out of it," said Tom.

There was a general round of approval from all the gentlemen in the room concerning naked super model cookery.

They nodded with an assertive intensity, all smiles, and continued eating, still playing with the thought in their minds...

"Still, this stuff isn't bad," said John

"Yeah," said Brian, "it's not too bad." His head turned, anxiously eyeing the door awaiting the arrival of a food bearing goodess.

IT'S A JUNGLE OUT THERE

Once there was a man who because of bad judgment and human weakness had an indiscretion with a lady of the evening. That wasn't in and of itself the bad part. What was bad was the lady was not of the cleanest variety and the man found himself with a nasty case of the crabs. Annoying as that might have been, his real problem was his delay in seeking treatment. You see, the problem was compounded by the fact that these body lice had found an abandoned baby boy, and decided to raise him as their own. They named him Tarzan of the crabs, and taught him everything he needed to know in order to survive down there. Tarzan would swing from pubic hair to pubic hair, which as you might expect hurt the man a great deal. Things went from bad to worse when Tarzan, years later, became a sort of hippy cult leader, and started gathering followers who also took up residence in the man's pubes. This caused the man a great deal of discomfort, and he tried many over the counter remedies, as well as talc for the itching, but to no avail. Worse still was when the Mexican family of four moved in, figuring no one would notice they were there, and the price was certainly right. The man even got along quite nicely with Mr. Manuel, the father, but secretly wished he and his family would leave, as it made dressing and other daily routines both more time consuming and painful. Very painful. There was also Dave, who would occasionally park his van there when there was no room on the street. Certain nights, the man would be kept awake by a local band that had started using his pubic region as a rehearsal space. The man at this point was spending a fortune on talc, and constantly at the tailors (who also later moved in as well, because of location in terms of traffic, and also the view) getting his pants taken out yet again.

After a few years, and a trip or two to the doctors, all for nil, the man resigned himself to his fate, and opened up a pizzeria down there, which made quite a bit of money. He later went on the tour circuit as a motivational speaker, telling people his story, about how when life had handed him lemons, he made lemonade. "Oh, and also people," he'd throw in, "wash real good down there."

ME AND THE MARTIAN

I encountered an alien. A Martian to be exact. It was in the meadow near Laysman's Point out past the cow pastures, in a patchy clearing near the corn fields. How can I be so certain it was a Martian? There were certain clues, discovered only after considerable observation. Clue number one was the fact that he had three heads.

Clue number two was when he introduced himself by saying, "Greetings Earthman, I am a Martian."

We got to talking.

"I wasn't aware Martians were three headed," I told him.

"It doesn't always work in our favor," stated the middle head, "but by the same token, it certainly serves a purpose."

"How so? What purpose could three heads possibly serve?" I asked, unsure of which head to address the question to.

"My heads don't always agree on anything, but they somehow manage to work together enough to keep me in synch and sanely functioning, even if in the end I am so scattered I never quite end up accomplishing anything. You see, the one to my left is my spiritual head. It longs for enlightenment, doing charitable deeds, becoming closer with the Creator. And it might achieve its goal if not for the head on the right. He is the artist. He has an insane desire to create, but unfortunately, he is quite mad! He also has no self control, and can be quite lazy at times. He becomes easily bored."

"And you?" I asked, addressing the middle head, who was doing all of the talking.

"I am the liar. A fraud. I do all the things the other two cannot handle. I work for a living, I interact with people. But it is all a rouse. I do these things because I must, not because I find joy in them."

"So who has control of the body?" I said with interest.

"We all do, which is why Martians are a doomed race. We have not achieved enlightenment, created great art, or found peace in our daily existence because of the three way tug of war that is constantly raging. How we envy you one heads!"

"But you said it serves a purpose?"

"My artistic head gives us the joy of creating, but never feels fulfilled or connected or able to survive. My spiritual head gives me peace and a rest from the madness, but never achieves its ultimate goal. And I keep the body going and give it a sense of self worth, although I have no real meaning in my life save pure existence." I watched as the eyes of each head blinked one after the other. I wished I had an answer for him.

He began to walk away, so I took this as my cue to depart as well.

"Man," I thought during the walk home, "Martians are messed up!"

JEREMY C. SHIPP

LOCATION:
Loma Linda, CA

STYLE OF BIZARRO:
Minimalism

BOOKS BY SHIPP:
Vacation
Sheep and Wolves (forthcoming)
The Good People (forthcoming)

DESCRIPTION: Jeremy C. Shipp writes systemically-aware mind trips that transport you into the festering wound of civilization, guided by an occasional flicker of hope.

INTERESTS: Yard gnomes, coconut monkeys, using psychokinesis on plastic straws, parks, respect, and sporks.

INFLUENCES: Takashi Miike, Kurt Vonnegut, Hayao Miyazaki, George Orwell, Anthony Burgess, Arundhati Roy, Pink Floyd, and anime.

WEBSITE:
www.hauntedhousedressing.com

FLAPJACK

CHAPTER ONE

Wall #4's bumpy blemish showed me an environment capable of imperfection, and yet the Prisoners, AKA the Wee-the-People, AKA the Captivated Captivitized saw eternal only the wrongness of their own little selves. Of course, my thinker could produce not a one example to justify such sham-shame thoughts. These Wee ones never harmed each other. They had chances many, oh hai, but caused not a bloody scratch with their forenails. They were Hopper Lites (meaning wimps), the lot of them, just like me.

Once my cellmate Humpty ran his mind so far downwards, listing that and that and that his Sin, that I couldn't take it anymore, and I said, "I'm so sick and tired of your blubbering blubbery cheeks!"

He cried with crinklier eyelids. "I must be the worst man in the world to be yelled at by one of us."

"The Flapjack is filled with much worse!" You must keep in mind that rarely ever had I erupted such fury—the truth being I'd never known such a pitiful creature as this Humpty in my life.

His whimpering shrunk to a sniffle in a bug-flap. He stared at me, not with anger (as I expected, since I had just spoken blasphemy), but with fear. If Wall #2 wasn't blocking him, he might have kept walking backward until I twinkled out of sight.

My body trembled as my anger trickled down. More than anything, I wanted to alleviate his anguish, so I resolved to tell him the tippy truth. "It's not what you think, Humpty. I speak from experience. I'm from the Flapjack."

He laughed awkward through his nose, and mumbled something like, "Verily not."

"I know you don't believe me and that's fine for now. But I'm begging you to stop pleading so much."

"A prayer in the mind is worth nada," which was something I was beginning to understand about the Wee-the-People. They preferred speaking out loud—to walls, to floors, to anything inanimate. Speaking to other people was just as worthless as thinking to ones own self.

"Could you try to be quieter then?" said I.

Humpty stood from his knees. A sort of smirk tugged at his lips. "You've been so silent ever since you came here…I assumed you were a mighty careful man. I thought verily that you kept your body and mind tippy pure. But perhaps your lack of prayer has more to do with lack of care. Verily. I shall have to pray for you as well as I, as would any good-bearing man."

"I appreciate your concern, but praying isn't going to help either of us. If you verily care about my concordia, then allow me your ears for a short tiempo. I need to speak to a person."

"You're a strange man, Newton, but hai. I'll harken, for harmony's sake." His face then metamorphosized before my peepers, with a new exhibition of expression he had never shown before. Some might dub it interest or even curiosity. I, however, would call it waking up.

CHAPTER TWO

My first rememberable memory, I told Humpty, involved a thing which I at first mistook for an unwrapped candy-dandy, but was verily my sister's severed thumb. My father held the stained feeler close to my nose and said, "See this? Do you smell it, child?" Then he lifted me higher and higher and higher to his tippy reach, onto his shoulder, so I could say hello to the bloody beddy bye, where my sister wriggled. The tear on her face melted me, but my tearburst was silenced by my father's stone hand, and, "Hush child! This is your sister's time."

So I watched in silence, fighting myself, as my mother applied skin glue to my sister's wound. "Do you see what the Greens have done to her?" my father said. "Do you see?!?"

I opened my mouth and might have said, "Hai."

Gloria, my sister, only then seemed to notice me. She smiled a little, sickly sweet, as if to say, "I'm glad you're with me now, but I'm so sorry you're with me now." I was whooshed back down to the floor, and covered my sniffer, afraid my father would stick baby pinky back in front of me. But he didn't. Instead, my familia—my mother, my father, Granner, Gramper, Uncer, Aunter, and others—hugged Gloria. They said things like, "You're a real woman now," and, "The first one is the hardest."

Solus, I felt—being the #1 and only child in the room. The second youngest person was Gloria, who was at the time about fourteen. Far ahead than poor smally me. Soon, everyone said their goodbyes and left, except Gloria and my mother. I, of course, remained stuck to the ground, as if the bottoms of my feet had been ripped off and skin glue was applied before I landed.

"Take your sibber with you when you go," my mother said to my sister. "Do you feel dizzy when you stand?"

Gloria stood and shook her head.

"Good," said my mother. "Go when you're ready."

"I'm ready," my sister said.

So Gloria clutched my hand with her fivey, and led me into the hallway.

Just moments ago, I'd felt like I was in a monsterworld, where my familia wasn't really my familia. I'd felt like I wanted to leave. But now that I was actually leaving, I felt a thunder urge to run to my parents' beddy bye and hide under the coverings. My mother's words, "Take your sibber with you when you go," I took to mean that me and my sister were leaving eternal. So I released my tearburst and yanked to free myself.

She only held on mightier. "Sibber, stop. We're only going outside for a minuto, then we'll come right back."

I stopped struggling, though I didn't believe her verily. But the tranquility of her voice calmed me.

She pushed the sliding door with her foursies, very careful. We went into the backyard, and she led me to the sad drooping tree. We sat together.

She started to dig a hole with her fivey. "You can help me if you want."

So I did. Every scoop intensified the cold nothingness in my feelers.

"That's enough," she said. And she held out her foursies. Only then did I notice that she was clutching her separated part. She dropped it into the hole.

And while we covered it with dirt, we had a conversation something like this:

"It doesn't hurt too much, sibber," she said. "You don't have to feel sorry for me. Things like this happen all the time."

"How come there was blood?" said I. "The Body Fairy makes the parts go whoosh with no blood."

"Sibber. There's…no such thing as the Body Fairy."

When I breathed out, I saw a little fairy form in my cold air. "Then where do all the parts go?" Of course, I should have known the answer to that, considering what we were doing at that very momento.

"The Green familia does it, sibber. They cut us. That's what happened to all of mommy and Granner and Aunter and everyone's parts. There's no Body Fairy."

"But…why do the Greens do that?"

"Because we're at war with them. They cut us and we cut them."

"Why?"

"You don't have to worry about that now. Nobody's going to chop your parts until you're my age. So don't worry."

And the truth is, though it seems ridiculous, the momento I returned to the house, to my room, to my beddy bye, I did stop worrying. I went back to having a tippy unstressed childhood, except for the one little idea aft of my mind that Thumbelina the Body Fairy was dead and buried in the backyard under the crying tree. Crying, because I knew that one day my life would change.

CHAPTER THREE

I trotted downstairs in the white tunic, thinking blue, pink, blue, pink, and then pondering how little I cared. The living room ravaged my nose with hospital-smell, but the stinkeroo turned out to be emanating from the plastic wrapping around the furniture and tele and even the floor. My ceremonial place was in the center of the room, so there I stood. After they sang the Happy, Happy Self Day song (verily badly), my father said, "You are a boy." I closed my eyes and pinched my nose as they splashed me with smally paint balloons. My white tunic stained blue. However, this was not the same blue tunic I would wear for special occasions the rest of my life, as I'd first assumed. My father would soon give me a different wearable blue tunic, while my painted blue tunic would remain unworn eternal.

After I showered and the plastic wrappers were thrown away, we ate cake. I knelt beside my sister, and watched her grip the fork with the only three fingers on her right hand. Soon, she'd have to be fed by a man, like the other older women. By that time, she'd be married.

"Do you feel any different?" my mother said.

"Not verily," said I.

"You can start growing out your hair now. Aren't you hypered?"

I wasn't really excited, but I nodded my baldness anyway.

My father stopped fe[illegible] mother, and stood. "It's about ti[illegible] smally boy has a name, sure enough?" He walked behind me and placed a hand on my shoulder. "We have decided his name to be Newton."

"Hello Newton!" everyone said, but me.

My father continued, "As we all know, every given name has a double meaning. First, Newton is the name for someone intelligent, and we all must agree that my smally boy here is intelligent." (The familia agreed with yeses and nods.) "The second meaning is that he has a prox relationship with gravity."

Everyone laughed, and I smiled.

What they were saying, of course, was that I had a great frequency for falling—tripping, even when there was nothing on the ground to trip me. Ergo, I thought my name captured both my tippy and bottom traits. Though I soon came to understand that my lack of coordination didn't worry my familia one whittle whit. My father once told me, "Boys like you will probably never become a samurai, or gladiator, or wrestler, or knight, but you can still become a mighty crazy horse. Even wild randomness had its place in war, son."

Anyway, though the slight majority of children born with inward genitalia were made women, I was made a boy named Newton.

CHAPTER FOUR

You can imagine my surprise when Humpty interrupted me with, "And...and where was I during all this?"

"Where were *you?*" said I.

"Hai. What was I doing, I mean. Did I eat the cake? Did I throw those balloons at you? And if so, what did they feel

...e in my hands? What did the cake taste like?"

He continued on like this, in ramble. One might—if one hadn't seen the laetitia, the tippy happiness, in his peepers— have mistaken his words as spawns of sarcasm or teasing.

Obvious to me then, he didn't believe a word I was saying. But he liked the words. Verily. Enough to want to be a part of them.

"Hai, Humpty, you were there," said I. "Invisible though, you were at the time. Invisible to everyone but I. You were my best amicus for life. Eternal."

"And what do I…did I look like, if I may ask?"

"Oh tippy beautiful, Humpty. The most beautiful woman on the whole Flapjack. But when they looked at you, they couldn't see that."

"I thought you said I was invisible."

"You were, at the time of the party. Things would change in time."

"But things never change."

"Hai, verily they do not. But sometimes they can."

CHAPTER FIVE

My mother looked down at my bloody beddy bye coverings. "It's nothing to be afraid of, Newton. That's the blood of our ancestors. Let's go tell your father."

We went into the family room and my mother forced me in front of the tele.

"Haste, Newton, what is it?" my father said.

"There's blood on my bed," said I. For some reason, fear clutched my tum. I half expected him to yell at me or even slap me.

Instead, he happy-faced. "Newton, that's great!" He turned off the tele. After a biggy bear-hug, he said, "That blood came out to say that tonight you'll become a man."

I forced a smile, but I remembered Gloria's Thumbelina—though it was only women who lost parts. What then, would I lose?

That night instructed, dressed in the blue tunic my father had given me, I met the other men in the front yard. Before a word could pop my lips, they led me down the street to the house I'd passed mucho tiempos to and fro the gymnasium: the Green House. Mightily, I'd heard from my familia how ug this place was. Into the courtyard we went, and true enough, the stories reflected proper this wild place that zapped my peepers and nostrils. Bitter-stinking weeds where the grass should've been, some taller than I, swayed with the airbursts. Nearby, the forgotten forget-me-nots shivered. In the center court, a lady with red spots all over her clothes and skin froze in mid-step. Water was supposed to spurt from her mouth, but didn't. And even though she lacked feelers and toes and even ears, if I squinted my peepers, the vines that grew up around her formed new feelers and toes and even ears. My familia hated this place, but I wanted to sit by the lady and harken her silent stories.

Instead, my father led me toward one of the personal quarters that lined the courtyard. My Uncer and Gramper and some Cousers whooshed past, and entered first. By the time my father and I went inside, my familia had secured a young woman to her beddy bye. They gripped her wriggling arms and legs. They covered her mouth with tight cloth.

My father and I stood beside her. He held out a cutter. After my hesitation, he said, "Take it."

So I did. And as I did, the flank of familiarity caused a buzz in my mind. So known was this momento because I'd been preparing for it all my life. The games the young baldies played in the gymnasium ricocheted through my skull. Cutty me, I cutty you—cut, cut, to, fro, on, on, anon.

"Take a feeler, Newton," said my father. "The same feeler they took from Gloria.

Think about the pain she felt that night. Think about her tears. Think about the blood. Punish them, Newton, for what they've done. Punish them!" The words rumbled through his teeth, and I saw spit backflip off his lip onto the young woman's arm.

My vision crept from the spittle spot up to her peepers. She was mightily verily terrored. Hai, I did think about Gloria's pain, but the Red—the fury of my ancestors—didn't ignite in my own peepers. Instead, the spotted fountain lady awoke in my mind, and someone slashed at her viney feelers and toes and ears. With a cough, cough, cough, blood gushed from her wide-o mouth.

I dropped the cutter, whoosh, and the Red-spotted lady (as well as the young girl on the beddy bye) happy-faced.

CHAPTER SIX

Morning, and my courtyard sparkled clean, clean, clean with shimmer stones and flatty grass. Our fountain maiden gurgled in missing-bits ecstasy of spread arms. But nada of that mattered a whittle whit, because I stood outside the quarters of my parents and harkened.

"He's just not ready yet," said my mother.

"Verily so," said my father.

"These things happen, Maximus."

"Hai, but not in my familia."

"Don't give me that holier-than. Some tiempo is all Newton needs. A few weeks and he'll be ready."

"If he fails again…"

"He won't."

The words bit at me too ravagely, so I backed away. Without forethinking, I rat-a-tatted on my sister's door. Her hubber Francis helloed and let me inside.

"Salu, Newton," Gloria said, on the center-mat.

I knelt beside her. "Did you hear?"

"Hai."

Francis served her tea, completely—the way a man did for his fingerless wife.

"Why didn't you do it?" she said.

"I…couldn't," said I. "I don't know what happened."

Francis brought the cup close to her mouth, but she shook her head and he scooted away a little.

"You should've just done it and got it over with, sibber," she said. "It's not hard what you have to do. Have you thought about what I've gone through? Have you? Do you know what they've done to me!?!" Her face shook. "Cham the Greens!"

"Gomen, Gloria," said I, my blurred vision drowning in my tea cup.

"Sorries don't change anything," she said, and calmed her breathing, iiiiin ouuuuut. "I'm not mad at you. Verily, I'm not. But you're part of this familia. Whatever it is that stopped you last night, let it flitter, flitter away. Concentrate on the Red."

I tried—verily, I did, to find the Red, find the Red, find the Red. But when I closed my peepers, all I saw was Green, held down, trembling, and the young girl's pupils that vibrated in a way like bugs trapped behind glass.

CHAPTER SEVEN

Prox to sleep in my beddy bye that night, I saw my amicus eternal, clearer than I'd seen her for years and years and years. And let's say, for the sake of sakes, that her name was Humpty. Let's also say that she looked a little like the fountain maiden at the Green house, except her feelers and toes and ears were not made of blurry squinty vines, but feelers and toes and ears.

"Cheeks up, Newt," Humpty said, happy-faced beside my beddy bye. "So you didn't chop her. So what? It's not the end of

Flapjack."

"My father hates me," said I.

"Mayhaps, mayhaps not. But what matters is that I got what I wanted, true enough?"

"What do you mean?"

"Verily you're joking."

"Iie, I'm not."

She piggle-giggled (with a snort), and said, "I made you whoosh down that cutter, of course. I whispered those dreadful thoughts right into your listen-hole."

"Why?"

"What do you mean why? You know as well as I do, I hate all that bloody blood chop chop stuff. Cham it all to heckles."

"You didn't used to say words like cham."

"Hai, but I'm a growing young woman, true enough? You should see the size of my twiddly-wink."

"Sick, Humpty. Don't talk like that."

"Gomen, gomen." She bowed. "Anywho, I'd better be off and hit that dusty hobo, as they say."

"No one says that."

"You're obviously not yapping the right people. Well, sayonara, Newty-chan."

"Wait, where are you going?"

Before her mouth could pop another word, she whooshed into the floor. Verily, I hadn't spoken to Humpty and she hadn't spoken to me for a mighty tiempo. But she'd always known how to lift my cheeks. And even now, both of us grown and sprouting, she helped me forget my lack of Red, even when I felt—

CHAPTER EIGHT

Humpty the Prisoner's tearburst caused me to pause my tale. He collapsed to his knees and said, "Deserve I don't such a thing as this. Verily, verily, verily I do not."

"What is it you're talking about?" said I.

"These things are for the Flapjack, not Wee-the-People. Temptation has poisoned my concordia. I only hope I can purge your words from me. But will they shatter my honored nightmares and haunt me with laetitia dreams eternal?" He quivered on the floor.

"The story has only begun, Humpty."

"Humpty? Humpty?!? Who is that you speak of? I have no spoken name, for you have sucked away its purity."

"Then I shall have to tell my story to the void you have become, true enough?"

"Iie! Even a void knows its place."

"I see. So you'll never hear whether or not I ever became a man. You'll never hear how it was you became a real person who all real people could see. I suppose I'll count to three now, and then never, ever, ever speak again eternal. One mississippi, two mississippi, three—"

"Hold!" He pushed himself up and sat. "Mayhaps...mayhaps I'm meant to hear your story, then struggle to recover. Mayhaps this is a test of my concordia. Mayhaps you can continue on anon."

"Hai," and that I did.

CHAPTER NINE

The days following the mishap at the Green house felt like ground up wildflowers. Blooming rainbows burst and burst and burst into my mind, but every tiempo Humpty made me feel concordia and laetitia, my familia would hack away with a chop chop chop, wielding their sharper-than-sharp silences. For instance, when I walked into the dining room to dine, my familia would shush-up with a bug-flap. Oh, what a difference it would've made if they'd pointed their feelers or nubs at me and said, "A bloody Hopper Lite, you are!" or "Coward child, go cham yourself!" But no, my bloody Redless failure of a night was too titmouse even for open rabble-rouse ranting. So they kept their lips as tight lines. Lines that read: You are solus.

One night my Couser Betty helloed in my quarters.

"Salu, Betty."

She clicked the door behind her, and stood by my beddy bye. "Newton…I…"

"Betty, what's wrong?"

"I…"

In my thinker, I imagined she was going to boom a tearburst, but instead she roared like some trollbeast. She sat beside me. Her hands shivered and her face vibrated.

"What's wrong, Betty?"

"I…never had a sibber of my own," she said. "You've been the closest thing to a sibber I've had."

"Hai, you've been like a little sibber to me."

"I don't want to bother you, but there's no one else I can turn to."

"Don't worry about that, Betty. If there's something inside you that needs letting, let it out to me."

"Well…it's Uncer Matty. He used to…bounce me."

"What?" Uncer Matty was a man Uncer to the both of us.

"Hai, he bounced me. Cham him!"

"I'm so sorry, Betty. Have you told your parents?"

"You know as well as I do, it wouldn't matter if I did or not. They can't do anything to him."

"We have to stop him somehow."

"Stop him?!?" She laughed with gritted teeth. "He doesn't come around anymore since I reached the Red. He knows I'd bite his chamming face off." It was true. Betty had become a woman recently. Skin glue shined on her new finger-ghost. "So really, there's nada I can do, unless he enters my quarters. And he won't. He's a Hopper Lite at heart."

The words Hopper Lite thrashed me, and Betty must have noticed.

She clutched my hand. "I don't believe what the familia is saying about you. You may have dropped the cutter, but you're not like Uncer Matty. Even as a boy, you're a better man than him."

"I…I'd like to help you, Betty. But what can I do?" Hai, I asked the question, though I knew the answer.

CHAPTER TEN

Even then, my thinker and body were not animated by Red. Hai, I felt sorry for Betty in the tippiest, but, as pathetic as it seemed to me then, all I wanted was to forget Betty's pain. I wanted to grab Betty's hand and fly her into the dreambubbles above my beddy bye where Humpty lived. We'd play and play and play on the wildflowers, but no matter how many stomps we'd plant on the planties, they'd spring back up like a new spring eternal.

The only alternative to taking her to the dreambubble that I knew about was bloody Red cut cut.

"There must be another way, Newtrino," Humpty said, springing, springing, springing on the biggy marshymallow. "Why don't you ask those bloody blockbrained mommer and popper of yours?"

"Betty's right. Uncer Matty and them are the same gener. They can't do anything."

"So now you have to?"

"Hai."

"But you're a Hopper Lite."

"Iie."

"Just accept it and go eat some parsnips."

"Iie!"

The dreambubble popped, and for a while I labored to piece Humpty together again. But it was a puzzle of shattered butterflies and my feelers were too big. In other more thinkable words, no matter how verily Humpty was my amicus eternal, my familia was my familia.

So outside I went with heavy zombie limbs, but soon the nippy airbursts reached in my yapper and yanked the nightsickness right out. I tip-toe tapped into my Uncer Matty's quarters. Closer, closer, closer I slushed, careful as careful can be. But gravity played another one of its tricks, and my face slapped the wooden floor. I heard Uncer Matty rustle.

My face still pressed, I didn't know if he was looking down at me or not, but I didn't move. Somehow, all the bitter silence my familia had force-fed me seemed to radiate deep inside my gut now. I used this internal-quiet to transform into a waterless fountain statue, like the one at the Greens. Only this time, the statue was not beautiful.

After perhaps an hora, I convinced myself that Uncer Matty wasn't staring down at me with burning dragon eyes, and pushed myself up. I stood slow and awkward in a way that felt like a growing tree.

On the table by his beddy bye, a cutter smiled, reflecting white moon-teeth. I touched it and didn't pick it up for a long while. Still, Red didn't urge me on or thank me. No one lifted the cutter but little me.

I peeled away Uncer Matty's beddy bye coverings, then his body's coverings. I wanted Humpty to speak to me then. I wanted her to break out of the fountain maiden outside the door like a chicky from a shell, and then run in and save me. But I heard not a word. All I saw were Uncer Matty's peepers that stayed straight black lines. Lines that read Betty's answer to my question: "Chop that tinkerdam twiddly-wink of his, so I can give it a proper burial."

CHAPTER ELEVEN

"Why do you hold?" Humpty said in his smally Wee-the-People voice.

"Because that's the end of that tale," said I. "I'm trying to decide where the next story of my life begins."

"The end, you say? That it was not."

"If I were speaking a prayer, then hai, it would not be the end. So hear this amen and calm yourself: amen."

"That's not enough."

"Praise be my suffering, amen. Is that better?"

"Did you chop him or didn't you?!?"

"If you hadn't noticed, Humpty, the stories I've been telling you have been going in the order of my life. Therefore, the next story I tell you will be an older me than before. I will either be someone-who-chopped-my-uncer-in-the-past, or someone-who-didn't-chop-my-uncer-in-the-past. Don't you think you'd be able to tell the difference between those two people?"

"I..."

"Rhetorical questions are answered by those who ask them, Humpty, so rest your yapper."

He rubbed at his forehead like he was trying to erase something. Finally, he said, "I'm sorry."

"What about?"

"When you were in your Uncer's room, you wanted Humpty to come in and save you. I'm sorry I...I'm sorry that Humpty wasn't there for you. I'm sure she would have helped you if she could."

"Verily so."

CHAPTER TWELVE

In the dining room, Red swirly-whirled in Uncer Matty's peepers as they did everyever he and me were prox. My familia perceived his peepers as two cycloid mirrors that reflected my own Redness, where things looked even less mighty than they verily were. So sat Newton the Red Man, Hero of and to the Familia.

On the left of me knelt Betty, (that being her chosen place now), and on the right knelt Venus, a young woman with outside genitalia—the newest dinner guest of my father, though of course he invited her not for his own self.

"Can you help me with something, Newton-san?" my Uncer Edo said from across the table.

"Hai," said I.

"My thinker wishes to acquire a new cutter, but I'm halted between the Bane and the Lance. Which model do you prefer, nepher-san?"

The differences between those blades I neither awared nor cared, but "The Bane," said I, the false prophet.

"Hai," my Uncer Edo said. "An older model, but proven mighty."

"Newton-san speaks wise," my father said, anod. "Hai, there is a place for new innovations, but when it comes to war, it is trust most important to familia. I trust the Bane as I trust my son."

"Verily so. I shall take Newton-san's advice," my Uncer said.

After a few momentos, Venus fumbled with her teacup, though she was only missing two feelers on that hand. She set the cup down and turned to me. "Newton-san, could you help with my drink? My familia uses a different sort of cup, and my poor touchers can't seem to get a hold of this one."

That wasn't true, of course, but I obliged. I brought the cup close to her lips and she sipped. My familia watched and one of my Uncers—I know not which—made a hissy-whistle to tease me.

Verily, part of why I served Venus her tea was because Venus and my familia expected such, but the other part had to do with my own horndoggy throbby. To serve a woman meant also to serve oneself.

"Thank you," she said. And in my freakshow thinker, those words implied gratitude for the dreambubbles whooshing out my peepers that replaced her missing parts with those I'd chopped from the beautiful Green butterflies quivering under a bloodmoon.

CHAPTER THIRTEEN

"Iie," Humpty said, his arms and eyeroofs diagonal.

"Pardon?" said I.

"Mayhaps you did chop your Uncer, but chop the young Greens, you did not. Return and change your words."

"That I cannot."

"Words can be changed as stains can be cleansed."

"Hai, speak I mutable words, but the events their own selves remain stone. Mayhaps you don't believe this to be my life's tale, but that it is my tale, you can't deny. Unless you believe my form and manner projected from your mind."

"Impure notion! I am my own self. You yours."

"Then allow me my own words."

Slow, he uncrossed himself and was open like a day-flower once again.

CHAPTER FOURTEEN

One might expect that acceptance would bring with it a lesser need for Humpty, but iie—the tighter they embraced me, the more I suffocated and yearned for fresh fairy-air. Night eternal, Humpy and I trotted through misadventurous meadows, but that was not enough. I needed tippy tippy tippy more, like a spiral-bearing druggy on neon brain-worms.

Viz, nearly all my semi-wake horas I spent at the comper in my quarters, talkathoning with Humpy through the rat-a-tat pecking of my touchers.

Often we spent our tiempo in the teahouse of my mind. There, mucho men thronged about the smally geisha, who wore patterns of open wounds and heroes of old and shimmering blades.

"These women are mightily ug, true enough?" Humpty said. She sat at the table thighs aslant, like the men about.

"They're considered tippy beautiful by most," said I, and watched one such man hold a hanky close to a geisha's sniffer so she could sniffle out.

"Professional amputations a beauty makes?" Humpty said. It was true. The geisha had their entire arms and legs removed at a very young age to become less and more than any other woman.

"There's mas to their art than missing parts, Humpty. They're trained to speak the words a man wants to harken."

"Shock! Men desire to harken a woman's words? Why then do they hum when I open my yapper?"

"I'm only playing the devil's advocate."

"Advocate or avocation did you say? I cannot hear you mighty what with the chitchat and razzmatazz swarming."

"You'll never get betrothed with that attitude," said I.

"And what would I do with a hubber? Do I not have feelers and feet unbroken to serve my needs and wants?"

"Verily so."

"Then slow yourself to spew me pity, for I stink enough from sleeping in a tree."

"You're jesting, true enough?"

"Iie. I ran away from my familia before our enemies had the chance to chop me, and I've slept in a tree that day eternal, with a moat and traps circum. And if they manage to breach those barriers, everyever I'll have sharpened parsnips to pitch at their chumming faces."

I laughed, then turned my happyface down. "Does such a life not make you feel solus?"

"I have you."

"Verily so."

And I noticed two things then. One: a group of men were standing circum Humpty, pointing feelers, hahaing, speaking words like ug and mannish. And two: Humpty didn't care.

CHAPTER FIFTEEN

And Humpty the Prisoner said, "If Humpty cared not what spawned in the thinkers of others, then why is it you could not be the same way?"

"There it is," said I. "The question of questions."

"That's all you give me? Another bland statement drowning in abstraction?"

"I see. So you wish to be served answer after answer after answer as a man would serve a geisha, true enough? That sounds very unHumptylike to me."

"Even Humpty my thinker imagines would at tiempos grow weary of your riddles."

"My riddles?!? You name the question born from your own mind: Newton's Problem? Take some responsibility."

"And how does one go about doing that?"

"Start off by naming your own brainchild after yourself. Humpty Junior or Humptina, if you like. Then answer their questions when they ask you."

"What if I know not what to reply?"

"Make it up as real parents do. The important thing isn't that you're right, but that they shut up their yappers. Otherwise, how will you ever sleep?"

"I don't think I'm ready to be a

brainparent."

"Well don't look at me. I have my own children to feed."

"I say I'm not ready!" He repositioned to his knees and locked his feelers.

"Pray not! To hear a parent's worries brings only suffering and greater agitation to a child. But worry not, for I have a known remedy. Allow me to continue my tale, and soon your child will fall to sleep. Then you'll have tiempo to your own self once more."

He nodded, and for both our thinker-children, proceeded I in lullaby.

CHAPTER SIXTEEN

An e-Hermes soared into my comper vision and proclaimed, "Salutations and congratulations! Your Site has just become one of the tippy hundred on all Flapjack." My Site, you see, had been—for quite a mighty tiempo—devoted lock, stock and bottomless barrel to the Humpty-and-me Semi-goodtime Adventures in Mundane Land. Not that I verily cared to make our talky intercourses public, but I had nada else to put on my Site, since this specific composing gobbled all my Cultural momentos. Being of the tippy one hundred Sites was assumed to be a thing of an honor, for every site had matched space, matched accessibility, and matched advertising, and therefore the only course to pop-fame was through word of yapper. Hai, the news of hundredthness forged a flabbergast gasp, but I stored the info at the aft of my thinker as mucho achievable. My familia never mentioned the Site—they probably didn't even know its pop-fame—until that day my mother, with dazzled peepers, enlightened me about a visitor waiting. So to the living room I trekked and found a woman kneeling on the center mat. She, who I knew to be Ambrosia, probably the tippiest adored person on the tele, tickled at me with the biggyest peepers on the Flapjack. Every year, they appeared to grow larger and larger, and many assumed she accomplished this with surgical tinkerings, but others asserted that they grew by their own accords. Every phenomena about her—her clothes, the way her pupils danced, her trembles—spoke the same words: "I need you."

Across from her, I sat, a mighty distance away.

My father trotted forward and said to her, "Mayhaps you would like some tea?" and he reached for a cup.

To this, my mother coughed in the archway, and my father stumbled backward as if he'd been shoved.

"I would mightily enjoy some tea," Ambrosia said, then peeked at me for a momento. "Mayhaps Newton-san would do me the honor?"

"Hai," said I, and repositioned to her side, while my mother yanked my father to the archway with her glare.

The cup to her yapper, she appeared to have only the strength to part her lips a slit. I tilted the cup and she sipped. This was the official fantasy of many Flapjack men, as polls identified, but the momento to me felt not so much like a dreambubble, but what I imagined a twisting stab in the gut to feel like.

"You're probably wondering what I'm doing here, true enough?" she said.

"Verily so," trembled I.

"Your Site brings me to you. Or pulls me, rather. Like a black hole." Her words flowed from her in gentle gusts. "I'm sure you know it has reached the tippy hundred. It's only a matter of tiempo before it reaches the tippy ten. By then you'll have actresses all over you."

"It's nice of you to say," said I. "But verily it's not my future you speak."

"Oh, but it is. I have a seventh sense for these things. The cause of my present pop-fame is that very sense. I seek out the rising treasures before their sparkle shines for all to see. This all means, of course,

I'd like to take your stories to the tele. I'd like to play Humpty. Such a funny character, she is, and yet so tragic. It's the role I've been looking for. Dreaming of."

"It's...the tippiest honor for you to give me such praise—" I could hardly believe myself to be saying this, but it came out without a hindrance. "—however, Humpty is a woman with all her parts. You are not."

Her peepers thinned like a curtaining stage. "That I am well aware. My voids can be hidden."

"From the tele-eye, hai, but not from the thinkers of the spectators. They know of your missing parts. Your ghosts of female beauty will not be forgotten. Anyway, Humpty's parts must be seen. That is who she is."

"Newton-san." She nuzzled her stump against my hand. "Your Site has been a mighty source of pleasure to me since I discovered it. This pleasure I've shared with mucho influential and powerful people. Surely you won't forget all I've done for you."

"Forget, I will not. And though it pains me to speak the words, they are the words. A woman with missing parts cannot play Humpty." I lowered my peepers. "Gomen."

"Iie." She stood and grew taller than me. "The sorry one is I for you. Mucho days and years you'll spend regretting those words to me. A missed opportunity rots the thinker like fruit in the sun. Time only brings bitterness and worms."

After she whooshed out the archway, my parents took her place at my side.

"Newton-san," my father said. "Is your thinker aware of who that was?"

"Hai," said I.

"You could have found an actress to court," my mother said.

"Hai," said I.

They continued on and on and on, and I hai-ed and hai-ed and hai-ed, but what my thinker really boomed was iie, iie, iie. A fruit will rot verily, my thinker spat within, but through that bitter, stinky, buggy ugliness a seed is borne. And no matter how many fruits my familia or Ambrosia or anyone else sliced with their cutters, the trees would always keep growing eternal in that Magic Green Forest where Humpty lived, throwing parsnips at even the biggyest, loveliest Red eyes.

CHAPTER SEVENTEEN

"The power of you," Humpty the Captivated Captivitized said, more real-appearing than I'd ever seen him. You see, most of the tiempo, the white-tuniced Wee-the-People fused into the pallor of the prison walls and floors, with their exposed skin tucked together in balls of sunken faces and conjoined feelers. Fact, the first tiempo trekking the halls, peepers blurry from tearbursts, I viewed mere invisible no-ones, whose existence only solidified in vinegar prayers. But now Humpty stood as a man of lines, sharpened and glowing with a beyond-the-barrera expression of self. "The power of you to protect Humpty is verily mighty."

"She is my amicus eternal," said I.

"But this power traverses the border of your strength for self. That I do not understand."

"Unimportant."

"Unimportant, you say? My thinker supposed all brainchildren should be cared for, not exposed upon a hill to wither away amongst the elemental virulence."

"My advice signifies not abortion but contortion. Ask not from where the power came from for me to protect my amicus, but rather: would I, Humpty, like to feel that power my own self? And if so, how?"

He sighed. "Such spoken shackles you burden me with."

"Mightier than the cage circum?"

"In a way."

"Then mayhaps it is tiempo to question the relevance of these walls."

"Relevance? Is not existence relevance enough?"

"You tell me."

"Iie." He sat again. "This is your story and not my place to speak of unknowns. So continue with your chatter-chains and bind me to your words. But if I suffocate, I will curse you in death."

"Fair enough."

CHAPTER EIGHTEEN

As Ambrosia foretold, my Site did cultivate in pop-fame to the tippy ten. But actresses did not swarm the household. I assumed Ambrosia had alerted her colleagues that I would not consent to a partless woman, which intimated, in fact, every.

Days after my tippy tenness, a male visitor awaited me. He happy-faced when I passed through the arch, in a way like we were old amici. At the tiempo, my thinker played with the idea that mayhaps we had known one another at the gymnasium. His form I felt I recognized, or should recognize, but was unable to with the tiempo allotted—being the walk over.

"Salu, Newton-san," he said.

"Salu," said I.

"Mayhaps you recognize me."

The truth bit my neck. "Oh, hai!" I spoke louder than I wished, but attempted to suppress my embarrassment. "You're on the soap opera. One my mother watches day to day. You're a new character, true enough?"

"Hai, that I am. You're probably wondering what I'm doing here."

"Something to do with my Site?" said I.

"Verily so." He sipped his tea. "It's a terrible thing what Ambrosia has done to you. Terrible."

"And what thing is this?"

"Blacklisted, she's made you. To join with you now is married to crossing Ambrosia. Most telepersonalities fear getting prox to you."

"But not you, I see?"

"Oh, fear surges through my veins. Not due to our proxness, but the proposition I've yet to release."

"Proposition?"

"Hai. I..." By then, I noticed his body moved eternal. He tinkered, or tapped, or twiddled, or twitched at every momento, like a tree haunted by an incessant breeze. "I would like to take you to the tele myself. I, my own self, would play Humpty."

Shock! This I did not expect, and surely I thought my face reflected it. So I looked down, rearranged my features, and looked up once more. "You realize...you'd have to play a woman."

He nodded. "Hai, but I see no other way, if your Humpty is to keep her parts. These parts are important to you, I deduce, judging by Ambrosia's fury."

"Hai."

"Of course the spectators will always know she's being played by a man, but I'm not a well-known personality. Most televiewers have never even looked upon me. So that should aid imaginations in their thinkers' creation of Humpty, true enough?"

"That it would. But would the tele verily show my stories?"

"Fact. I've personally heard mighty a few directors expressing a desire to bring them to life. They simply have been unable to find the means. Means I am, or could be, with your sanctioned nod. So what say you, Newton-san? Shall Humpty meta to flesh and blood or remain silenced in the realm of shadowscript?"

CHAPTER NINETEEN

"Hitherto, I would have interrupted you this momento and demanded an answer to that question," Humpty the Prisoner said, in a proud sort of manner.

"But you interrupt me with a statement in the stead?" said I. "This you consider an improvement?"

"I simply wished to inform you of my progress."

"And what exactly is this progression you speak of?"

"I...know not."

"You vowed to speak nada of unknowns, did you not?"

"I told you I would not, but vowed nada."

"And what's the difference between speaking and vowing?"

"Vowing lives in fragility, my thinker imagines. Promises can shatter, where speaking cannot. What you say is what you say, endpoint. I shall pledge nada."

"Nada at all?"

"Well...except to harken in return after my own words are released."

"And I vow the same. So with these promises, we are bound, true enough?"

"Verily so."

"I suppose we now live in fragility then, if what you said is correct. And I also must suppose your life of old was mucho mightier, when you pleaded to faceless forms in void-of-vow solitude."

"You...suppose in the wrong. If you were to disappear, more fragile then than now, I would feel."

"Then I shall continue with the story, and mayhaps I will not fade away."

CHAPTER TWENTY

"What say you?" said the Director to me. "Which one do you prefer?"

For the past mucho horas, the Director, the new Humpty, and I had harkened to could-be Newton after Newton after Newton. And of them, I said, "None."

"None?" the Director said.

"Hai. They...they speak the lines as if the lines are tippy important. They speak nothing of the unspoken."

"Your meaning escapes me."

"Newton-san," Humpty said, on the other side of me. "If you wish to play Newton your own self, you can marry in contract your body to the story. Then the only way the creators can bring the tale to the tele is if you are Newton."

"It...is so," the Director said and coughed. "Such things have occurred in the past, but more often than less, such an attachment entails a clear path to cancellation."

"Fear not, Director," said I. "I will not force my own self upon you, as many men would. But I do ask for the opportunity to audition. The choice then will be verily your own. You may have the tale of Newton and Humpty whether you choose me or do not."

"So be it," the Director said, like a burped baby.

To the center mat, I stood with Humpty. And let me say that though this was an audition for the tele, it meant to me tippy more. This was a test of sorts, and I forgot the Director even existed. I found myself floating in a dreambubble once again. A group of young men passed by, and did the expected.

"Does it ever bother you?" said I.

"What?" Humpty said.

"Their pointing and laughing. They speak such terrible things."

"What is so terrible about what they say? Tell me their words."

"I cannot."

"You can. You're simply a Hopper Lite who fears even inflicting welcomed rudeness."

"You want me to say it? Very well. They call you mannish."

"I care not."

"They think you are the ugliest woman on the Flapjack."

"Hai, but do you?"

Nada, said I. Nada, nada, and more

nada, for that was all I could say. A nada formed from words never spoken to my familia; from the muffled screams of the Green butterflies I chopped; from my own imprisoned tears. A nada that replaced the waterfall of the broken fountain maiden. And a nada especially made of Humpty's ugliness. For even if the whole of Flapjack proclaimed Humpty the ugliest woman of all, I knew I had the power to drown out all their voices, if I allowed myself to open up and set free the hidden words. But nada, said I, and the words remained hidden. But I heard them, inside, loud as a lie.

CHAPTER TWENTY-ONE

"My thinker resolves to interrupt you with a question this tiempo," said I.

Humpty trembled as one who had seen a spirit, or realized he was one. "I would rather you continued with the story."

"And had I not rathered the same thing every tiempo you interrupted me, I might honor your request. So here's the question: did I get the part or didn't I?"

For a mighty tiempo, he stared forward, frail. Then he grew mighty once more. "Whether you did get the part or not, I know not, but that is not the real question to be asked."

"Which is?"

"Did you or did you not pass the test? Your own test."

"And did I?"

"Your peepers say hai."

"As speak your own."

CHAPTER TWENTY-TWO

The Tele Adventures of Newton and Humpty was no difficult over-and-undertaking, but there existed no mightier gift than feigning such. Pop-fame blessed me like a magic stone, illuminating everyever my familia's peepers became prox, and spat out a sparkly ray with hypnotic powers. "Newton the Telepersonality is too busy for familia business," said the stone, in their thinkers. "Leave the boy be, you smally somebody." And chopped I no more women and touched no more cutters. I did, however, play-chop women-shaped comper forms, and touched improper cuttery props. And so the Redness of my life meta-ed into a reddish hue which could be peeped by fans (including my familia) wearing thornless rose-colored spectator-spectacles.

Mucho tiempo I spent at Humpty's home for the practice of lines, or at least such was the (mayhaps unneeded) justification. He was my amicus after all.

"What is it about these stories of mine?" said I, to him and my own self. "Why rise when others fall?"

"Humpty is a woman who lacks the lacks of womanhood," he said. "She hasn't the common personality of anyone you'll meet eternal."

"And yet those who gaze her with fervent peepers dub her ugly. Who would care for ugliness so mightily?"

"And who would so mightily create such ugliness?"

I preferred not to lie to him, so silence swallowed us.

Finally, "Does it feels strange?" said I.

"What?" he said.

"Wearing pink for the tele."

He sipped tea with more-than-usual shaky feelers. "I don't focus on my own self. Such an activity would beget too many unanswerable questions."

"Such as?"

"What does it mean to be a man wearing pink? How can an unadorned man once called handsome be then made a treasured but horrid woman?"

A dreambubble I knew this was not.

The real Humpty hacked on such self-spawned question marks until answers vomited forth, no matter how bitter the bile.

CHAPTER TWENTY-THREE

The question of Humpty's popularity did not release her stranglehold. There was mas to her attractive unattractiveness than simple rarity. I began to wonder—

CHAPTER TWENTY-FOUR

"I know the end already," Humpty the White said.

"The end?" said I.

"The answer to that question of questions."

"Release your thinker then, amicus."

Humpty stretched his legs out on the prison floor, as if preparing for a dash. "Humpty intrigues the thinker due to the questions she spawns. Not the questions she asks, but the questions of we. Why do I live in a cage and not in a tree? Why does Humpty feel laetitia with her parts in tact? Why do you think she's beautiful?"

"True enough, you capture the end, and your words have shattered this story like a parsnip through a window. I can no longer tell it."

Humpty's face tightened. "Forgive my insolence! A word and I'll smash my head upon the wall to dislodge this parasite!"

"Hold. That specific story was rather boring anyway, with all the self-analysis and hubbub. It's better obliterated, so that we may continue to a mightier image."

CHAPTER TWENTY-FIVE

I helloed and entered Humpty's quarters, to find him in his beddy bye, dressed in his pink tele-tunic. The desire to run twirled me, but my hello must have flicked his thinker, for I heard him stir.

"Newton, I..." he said.

My yapper exported nada.

"I wear it sometimes," he said. "It...aids in getting into character."

"Of course," said I. "Shall we practice the lines anon?"

"Hai."

We stood prox and spoke the words.

I realized (or mayhaps could no longer deny to my own self) that neither of us acted a whittle whit. The acting took place outside of our tele life, when we read not the lines. His want was to wear a pink tunic. His want was to be a woman. He was Humpty, but had to pretend to be someone else. Because Flapjack demanded the lie. And on that day, I acquired my first real enemy.

CHAPTER TWENTY-SIX

Humpty the White stared at Wall #4 for mucho heartbeats. Then, "Wee-the-People have always venerated the Flapjack for its freedom. But who is the freer? At least my own people can be who we think we are."

I happy-faced. "Brainchildren grow up so fast, do they not?"

"Verily so. And did you go to war against the Flapjack? Is this what brought you to me?"

"Hai and hai. But I fear your thinker has been misled by my terminology. My battles involved no blood, no Red, no cutters."

"Good. I have no taste for such matters."

"You lie like a child, but I appreciate

the intention. If only I could bestow upon you a mightier adventure than what occurred, but it was a tippy snoozy process of sitting at the comper, searching, searching, searching. Years I spent trying to understand my enemy. The mightiest shock burst from the fact that the answers were all out there, broken apart, as shame-sham shards. Piece them together was the only task, and not a difficult one. I own not an extraordinary thinker. Anyone could have learned what I learned. The vomity truth is that no one wished to see past the walls of their cage. The question now is: do you wish to see? Do you desire the truth of Flapjack?"

"I...do. However, I would appreciate if you would speak not the truth to me direct. Place it in a dreambubble, if you could."

"I can."

CHAPTER TWENTY-SEVEN

To understand the Flapjack, said I to Humpty, I required answers. And so I gathered ingredients from all over the Flapjack to summon a mighty wizard. At last the day came when I mixed everything together in a biggy black cauldron in the most mysterious section of Magic Green Forest, at the spot of Humpty's nestplace.

The cauldron erupted with fire, then the Wizard whooshed, adorned with a tunic of Red. "You shake me from a biggy slumber, smally boy," he said. "This had better be tippy important."

"I wish to know about the Flapjack," said I.

His laughter boomed, and the leaves vibrated circum. "You summon me for a knowledge that will bring you only mightier gray-thoughts?"

"My outcomings are not your concern."

"Verily so. What you wish, I will give you."

So we both sat on leafy mounds, though in truth he hovered a bugspace above.

"Of the history of Flapjack, what do you grasp?" he said.

"Not mucho," said I. "My people lived once as groundlings, but crafted the Flapjack and rose above."

"And do you know the reason for this crafty crafting?"

"The progression of technology, I assume."

He laughed loud, but not leaf-shaking. "Twas the progression of understanding which birthed the Flapjack. You see, smally one, mucho tiempo in the before, civilization grew to be mightily conscious of the causes of human behavior. Every action of every human spoke of their genetics, their environment, their past. Many humans expected a more enlightened society to be borne with such knowledge. Verily, humans were tippy capable of living lives of laetitia and balanced authority. But occurred, this did not. The civilization of old fought back like an angered trollbeast. Ideological strangleholds squeezed tighter with this war for and against modifications. The Flapjack was created by the Merican sect that fought the hardest against the Enlightenment of Understanding."

"Is Merica not a mythological place?"

"Twas real. This Merican sect hugged an ideology which justified the taking of resources from all over the planet. But this sect realized that ideologies could not last eternal. So they replaced their ideology with an automated resource abductor. The Flapjack, this is. Your culture has meta-ed much over time, in texture, however one thing holds eternal. Your machines abduct resources from the humans on the surface, killing more than many. You use mas energy than all the groundlings in combination, and you are one percent of the population. That is your truth."

CHAPTER TWENTY-EIGHT

"I will have to burst the dreambubble if I'm to continue," said I.

"Continue," Humpty said.

CHAPTER TWENTY-NINE

The knowledge I had acquired bansheed to flee, and so for the next teleshow, spoke I not the lines Flapjack expected, but the lines of my real self.

"Something blazes within, Humpty," said I. "A force wishing to be freed."

"What?" Humpty said.

I held her shoulders. "You're the most beautiful woman I've ever known. I love you." I kissed her.

Humpty's jitters meta-ed to fleshquakes, and he stumbled back.

Faced I to the tele-eye. "The things done and the things not done, this is our choice. We must meta the ways that pop the dreambubbles of our whispery hopes. We must meta that which spreads suffering to those below. We know our energy spawns from the ground, but do we ponder the how to the Flapjack's forever-flap? We fire no weapons. We press no buttons. Direct, we do nada to the groundlings, but can disconnectedness illusionate as a comfy-warm void of responsibility? Iie. The mechanical feelers that ravage the lands below animate these lives of ours. Let these feelers serve as metal ghosts of murdered history, so that we may harken the need to fall to grace once more."

I turned to Humpty.

But only a handsome man stared in reply.

CHAPTER THIRTY

"The worst part was not that a machine took me from my familia to this prison," said I. "The worst was that my words meant nada to them, unquestionable."

"But Humpty harkened your words. Mayhaps he will—"

"Mayhaps nothing. He was not the real Humpty. The words will not meta him."

"But they have meta-ed me!"

I happy-faced. "Verily so, and I finally understand how and why. The Wizard could not explain to me why this prison exists, but you have enlightened me."

"How could I enlighten you before my own self?"

"These things happen." I pressed my feelers against Wall #4 and its imperfection. "This prison hangs below the Flapjack like a cancer. A great population lives in this prison, and are born in this prison, and expire in this prison. You and your people are here because your genetics dub you mas viable to destroy the Flapjack's automated consumption. The ideological forces of this space force those tendencies to dormancy, and keep you all subdued. Viz, the Flapjack wins. Those who would fight are stuck here. There's no hope. I fear that's the end of the story."

"Iie!" He stood. "As I still live and breathe, your amicus eternal I will be. And together, we will smash this chumming place until the Flapjack falls to the forests, where we may live among the trees once more!"

"Now that sounds like the real Humpty."

"Humpty, I am."

JORDAN KRALL

LOCATION:
The quasi-industrial wasteland of Central New Jersey

STYLE OF BIZARRO:
Pulp Bizarro

BOOKS BY KRALL:
Piecemeal June
The Longheads
Fistful of Feet

DESCRIPTION: Jordan Krall writes fun, fast-moving bizarro stories that are a blend of grotesque surrealism and violent crime fiction, soaked in a wide variety of bodily fluids.

INTERESTS: Cats, drinking, UFC, playing games (chess, RISK, poker, Scrabble, pool), haunted places, making electronic/experimental music, sleazy go-go bars, watching for UFOs, Elvis, the 1960s Batman television show starring Adam West, pretending to be a marionette, Japanese spider crabs, impersonating a nonexistent person named Henry Price, toys and television shows from the 1980s, gambling.

INFLUENCES: Jim Thompson, William Burroughs, David Lynch, Tom Atkins, Terry Silver and the Quicksilver Method, Elmore Leonard, Dadaism, crime, H.P. Lovecraft, Lee Van Cleef, gialli cinema, Shaw Brothers, Takashi Miike, Spaghetti Westerns, Alfred Hitchcock, motels, Arthur Spooner, film noir, Barry Gifford, the films of Charles Bronson, Clive Barker, prison movies, alcohol, Buddhism, The Karate Kid Trilogy, Silver Shamrock Novelties, squid.

WEBSITE:
www.filmynoir.com

THE LONGHEADS

CHAPTER ONE

The donkey on the hill laughed loudly through its Halloween mask.

It stomped its feet, shaking the snow off its fur, and let out a small, deep-throated giggle as well as a squeaky fart. The donkey turned toward the sunset, its eyes filling with pure light, and then dropped dead in the same way it had lived: joyful and filled with gas.

At the bottom of the hill, the city of Thompson, New Jersey bustled, despite the heavy snow and bitter cold. It acted out its routine like an oversized ant colony. Each man, woman, and child went through the motions of good citizens, despite the underlying hum of several factories that pumped noxious smoke into the air, adding cancerous spice to the falling snow.

Tommy Pingpong sat in his car with the engine running. Jake should've been out ten minutes ago. *What the hell's taking him so long?* Tommy knew he was taking a risk idling in front of the building like that. Sure, the cops didn't patrol often but when they did, they were a bitch to get rid of. Despite that worry, he stayed, looking at his watch every thirty seconds and glancing up to see if Jake was on his way.

Fifteen minutes. *Shit, where the hell is he?*

Finally, through the snow flurries, he saw Jake run out of the building, almost tripping over his own feet. Opening the passenger door with a frantic pull, Jake plopped down in the seat, out of breath. "Just drive," he coughed.

Tommy put the car into gear and stepped on the gas. The car's tires lost traction for two seconds but then regained control and moved quickly down the block. Jake turned his head and kept his eyes on the back windshield. A thin blanket of snow covered most of the window. "I can't see a thing."

"What happened? Who's following us?" Tommy's voice was calm though inside he was as frantic as his friend. He knew that he had to balance out Jake's emotional outbursts with a good amount of composure.

Jake kept looking though he could barely see through the snow. "I don't know. Everything got fucked up. It wasn't my fault, no fucking way."

"Yeah, okay, calm down. What happened?"

Turning to the front, Jake moved the rearview so he could keep an eye out. "Everything was going great. I was telling Aaron the whole plan and he seemed into it or at least that's what I thought just by the way he was acting. But then Peachy walked in and everything got fucked up."

"Christ almighty," Tommy whispered. *Okay, I'm not going to freak out. I know damn well Jake's a paranoid motherfucker. Stay calm...stay calm.*

"How the fuck was I supposed to know Peachy would be out already? He was supposed to do at least half of his time."

Tommy nodded his head. "Yeah, well, apparently he got out early. So go on, what else?"

"I was nervous to begin with, then he walks in and just stares at me, fucking smiling at me. I lost it. I don't even remember what the fuck I said. I just ran out." He ran his hands through his hair.

"What'd Aaron do?"

"He looked at Peachy and then he said something like 'I'll have to think about it'. That was it. They smiled at each other and I just fucking ran out."

Tommy threw his hands up. The car jerked to the right. He put his hands back on the wheel. "And you RAN out? Jesus Christ..."

"I've been in those situations before, I know what that fucking means. I'm not a complete idiot, you know. Trust me on this, will ya?" Jake looked at Tommy, waiting for an acknowledgement. Tommy kept his eyes on the road, careful not to get into an accident on the snowy, congested streets.

"Jake, I trust you." As it came out of his mouth, he realized that his tone betrayed the message even though he believed that statement whole-heartedly. "All I'm saying is that you might have, MIGHT HAVE, over-reacted. Look, is Peachy a back-stabbing prick? Yes, but that still doesn't mean that he'll cause problems at every step of the way. You could've stayed cool, kept talking to Aaron. Now they both know you're fucking freaked out. There's no doubt now that someone's coming after us. Even if it's just to ask why the fuck you ran out."

Jake sighed. "I don't know, man. You know that creepy sonovabitch better than I do. Doesn't he still blame one of us for that shit?"

A year and a half ago Tommy and Jake worked a job for Peachy. The job went south and the two of them got pinched. By sheer luck, they were let go because the witness couldn't, with one-hundred percent confidence, identify Tommy and Jake as the culprits. They were released soon after.

However, someone had left a dirty diaper behind at one of the job sites and a dirty diaper at a crime scene meant only one thing to the Thompson Police Department: Peachy was behind the whole thing. With as much diligence as they could muster on a weekend, the cops cornered Peachy at the local pool hall where he was showing his fellow patrons how far he could stick the pool cue in his ear without damaging a single brain cell. He was arrested without incident but had squealed on Tommy and Jake as soon as he was taken into the station. Since they had already released those two and didn't want to make it appear that they had made a mistake, the cops ignored Peachy's accusations and charged him for the whole thing.

In Tommy's opinion, the two of them had every right to be pissed at Peachy and not the other way around. They could have ratted him out but choose not to do so simply because snitching could ruin your reputation fast. Peachy, on the other hand, betrayed whatever trust they had between the three of them. To Tommy, however, all was forgiven. He never liked holding a grudge; it got in the way of executing a successful job.

Jake got more frantic. "When I was running out, I totally got the feeling that they'd be coming after me. I really think Peachy's gonna come after us."

"Yeah, probably, after you ran out of the room like a goddamn rat off a sinking ship."

"Whatever. You always blame this shit on me. I'm sick of it."

Tommy rolled his eyes. "Jesus Christ. I just don't want any fucking trouble, that's all. Sometimes you overreact, okay? That's it. Doesn't make you a bad person or anything and it doesn't mean I don't take you seriously. Now, is there anything else I need to know? Before Peachy came into the room, did Aaron say anything else?"

"No, he just nodded. He looked like he was into it. Until Peachy walked in. Then there was some weird vibe, I'm telling you."

Though Tommy was doing his best to restrain himself and act like the calm half of the partnership, he felt himself falling deeper and deeper into a whirlpool of aggravation. "Fuck!" He slammed his fists on the steering wheel. If Peachy was again in Aaron's good graces, even more so than Tommy and Jake were, then the two of them were fucked pretty good.

Jake got defensive. "Why'd you make me go in there by myself, anyway? If you were so afraid I'd fuck things up, why didn't you do it your goddamn self, huh?"

"I did the last meeting. If Aaron was normal and let us both in, we wouldn't have this problem but when we deal with him we have to alternate." Tommy wasn't too crazy about Aaron's eccentricities. He never allowed a meeting with more than one person who didn't belong to his organization. The fact that Peachy was there in the room with Aaron and Jake also gave Tommy some worry.

Their relationship with Aaron Jeffords was strictly business related. Because of that, there was always the chance that there would be a falling out. No personal attachments meant no assurance that Aaron would think twice before putting a bullet into both of their skulls. Now with Peachy involved, Tommy was worried that everything might turn to shit.

"What're we gonna do, man? What?" Jake trembled, partly from the cold (the car's heater hadn't worked since Tommy got the car ten years ago) and partly from the stress.

"Okay, listen. We'll stop at a payphone and I'll call Aaron, try to test the waters, see what his reaction is. I'll explain that you overreacted and hopefully I'll be able to smooth things over."

Jake's eyes widened. "What good will that do? I told you, it wasn't an outright threat. It was sneaky the way they looked at each other. He'll just lie to you, tell you everything's okay and that he was shocked when I ran out, whatever, but really he'll just be bullshitting you. Next thing we know, both of us are in the river swimming with the Thompson squid."

"I'm going to have to take that chance. I'll make it clear how we feel about Peachy, don't worry. There'll be no confusion about that. This way, if he is bullshitting me, he'll know that we're fully aware of things and that we'll be on our toes since we know Peachy's somewhat involved."

Tommy slowed the car down easy, not wanting to skid into a telephone pole or one of the many pedestrians on the sidewalk. As he parked the car in front of an alley, he looked to his right to see if he was close enough to the curb. His eyes caught something in the alley.

"Christ almighty, what the hell is that?"

Jake looked over. "What? Where?" He followed Tommy's finger.

"Looks like a longhead but what the hell is he doing?" Tommy asked, not sure he wanted to know the answer. Ever since the war ended, he was made uneasy by the fact that a small fraction of the troops came back looking like *that*. Their skulls were vertically elongated, the skin stretched close to its breaking point to where it was translucent and one can see straight to their skull. One of the odd things about the whole situation was that all the longheads ended up moving to Thompson, forming a small ghetto at the south side of town. They took up with desperate prostitutes and had children who came out looking like even more sinister versions of their fathers.

The longhead in the alley was dressed in a cowboy costume and standing on a soapbox. In his arms was a strange contraption that looked like a combination of a manual meat grinder and cappuccino maker. His right hand furiously twisted a lever while his left held it tightly to his chest. Out of the top of the machine came spurting long, curly strips of what looked to Tommy like pasta.

"Tommy?"

"Yeah, Jake?"

"Is that longhead making...pasta?"

"Yeah, Jake, I think so."

They stared at him for five minutes totally forgetting about Aaron and Peachy. Watching the pasta drop to the snowy ground made Tommy think of footage he once saw from the war of a troop getting disemboweled by a guerrilla fighter who used only a set of sewing needles. The troop's entrails fell to the ground with the same wet clunk as the pasta.

"Tommy?"

"Yeah, Jake?"

"Can we go to another payphone?"

"Yeah, Jake, I think we can."

They drove off, Tommy keeping his eyes on the road and Jake keeping his eyes on the alleyway, hoping to God that he would not see that longhead again.

CHAPTER TWO

Aaron grinned at Peachy. "What the fuck was that about?"

"What're you looking at me for? I didn't do anything. The bastard got scared, what's that gotta do with me? You're the one who said I could sit in on this one."

"Yeah, I wanted you to sit in so you can patch things up with those two assholes."

"So why didn't you invite *both* assholes?"

"I didn't want things to get crowded in here. You know how I feel about that. Things get too crowded, I start to get jumpy." Aaron took a cigar out of his front pocket and lit it. "Why do you look so bulky?" He pointed at Peachy's pants.

"Diaper."

Aaron stifled a laugh. "Oh yeah, I forgot."

Peachy blushed and had a seat in the chair across from the desk. *Motherfucker didn't forget. He knows I shit my pants. At least I don't have a squid fetish..* He leaned forward, cupping his hands as if to tell his boss that he was ready to get down to brass tacks. "So, what are we going to do about this?"

He could tell Aaron wasn't listening. His boss was too busy looking at the cigar smoke, his eyes a heavily sedated green haze of preoccupation. He ignored Peachy's question and instead asked his own.

"Peachy, do you know why I really invited you to the meeting?"

"No…."

"I had a dream last night." Aaron got up from his chair and came around to the front of the desk. He leaned on it like he felt a real boss was supposed to do while he looked down at Peachy, his long-time employee. "I had a dream that changed my life. For better or for worse, I don't know. It was about my stint in the war. I told you about that, right?"

"Yes, you've talked about it a little."

"Well, I probably didn't tell you the bulk of it for fear of having you think of me as a coward or an asshole or something. Anyway, I had a dream about it again last night. I actually have these dreams quite often, but most of the time half of my body is a squid while the other half is completely covered in sunburn. So yeah, I have these war dreams a lot, you know, in between the ones where I'm screwing Chesty Morgan and that one about taking a nap in a fruit stand but anyway, let me go on." He puffed at his cigar. "I was in battle, the rest of my fellow troops having gone deep into the shit, fighting their little patriotic asses off while I stood there, watching the sun in the sky as it turned into the face of Barbara Stanwyck. You know Barbara Stanwyck, right? I'm not that old, am I?"

"I don't think I know her, no."

"She was an actress from when I was a kid. Beautiful, beautiful woman. I was looking straight at the sun, being blinded by her face but also by the rays of sunlight. I swear I even felt the heat in this dream, like my skin was going to burn off. Then my troops came back, half of them were blown to bits, being brought in on wheelbarrows, donkeys, and I think even an elephant. Their eyes were falling out of their faces and their cheekbones were all busted up. But the ones that weren't wounded were even more disfigured. They were the longheads. That's one thing I never told you about my tour of duty. I was there when that shit happened. I've felt guilty about that every day since. I should've been one of those longheads. I choose not to go in there and all those boys came out looking like….*that*." He made a face of disgust.

Peachy's eyes bugged out of his head in shock. He never gave much attention to what he considered just mutated freaks of war. In fact, he never gave much thought to politics in general and for all he cared, the country could blow itself up along with the rest of the world. But to think his boss was intimately involved; that was incredible. *I guess there's more to Aaron than just money and squid-smelling.* Peachy nodded his head and listened as his boss went on.

"And so I realized this morning as I shook myself out of the dream that not a single thing I do can make a difference. Whether I was a longhead or just a short head, nothing really matters, not a goddamn thing. I might as well be a longhead. Get it? Do you get what I'm saying? I was looking at the sun, at Barbara and the men came back. So even in the sunlight, where everything is lit up, illuminated or whatever, I still was blind to the fact that I was pretty much the same thing as them. What I was doing and what they were doing were the same. But still, I still feel that gnawing guilt, you know? The feeling that my life deviated from its predestined path. But now, I don't know."

Aaron sucked on his cigar and exhaled. A few puffs of cigar smoke enveloped Peachy's face and he coughed.

Peachy felt uncomfortable. He knew he had to act sensitively but it was something he wasn't used to. "I'm...sorry...about everything. But what's this got to do with anything? I mean, business-wise."

"What I'm trying to tell you is that whatever you choose to do, it'll be done. What's done is finished. That path I've always thought was there in front of me, it doesn't exist. Everything is done, over with. So with those two assholes," he rubbed his cigar in the squid-shaped ashtray, "you can do what you like."

Peachy contemplated this. Not many people can say that they have received philosophical lectures from their boss. Still, though, he didn't feel like it was something he would like to hear on a daily basis. After all, the more time one spends with Aaron Jeffords, the more one becomes used to all of his habits and routines. He couldn't count the number of times he had to sniff Aaron's squid collection or ride the albino pony that was kept locked up in a large closet in the office. If it wasn't for the large sums of cash, Peachy would have left years ago.

He still wasn't sure though. "Are you serious? I can take those fuckers out?"

"Yes." Aaron opened his drawer and took out his pony harness. "Now, if you'll excuse me."

With a smile, Peachy got up, adjusted his diaper, and left the room.

CHAPTER THREE

A few blocks from where Tommy and Jake were scouting for a new payphone, a man clad in a trench coat, black leather gloves, and a fedora hat stood outside of a go-go bar. He had been standing in the snow for an hour, waiting for Ms. Isabella Martino who was known mostly by her stage name, Sweetie Martini.

Despite the warnings from her coworkers, Isabella left the bar without an escort and started to trot her way to the bus stop. Her car was in the shop and it was only a ten minute bus ride home even with one stop before hers. She couldn't wait to get home and curl up next to the window with a good book, with complete view of the snow-covered streets. Having worked a five hour shift most of which was spent on her feet, dancing and gyrating, she was more than simply exhausted. Isabella wanted to spend as much time lying down as possible.

Isabella never planned on becoming a stripper but she knew perfectly well that no one does. Little girls don't dance around in their rooms to bad rock music, pretending to be on stage in front of sweaty old men or obnoxious frat boys. When she was a child, Isabella was like many girls her age; she dreamt of getting married, having a huge wedding, and perhaps pursuing a career in a myriad of fields.

She learned quickly, however, that life doesn't always work out as planned and sometimes people have to do things that they aren't proud of simply so they can eat and pay the rent. Her father's brutal murder at the hands of Terry Silver (war veteran, millionaire, and organized crime boss) left her with little faith and even smaller hopes for herself.

As she was walking past the alleyway next to the club, the man who had patiently waited for her all of that time grabbed her hand. He whispered something into her ear and led her to the alley.

"So you knew my father, then?" She smiled, recognizing the handsome face of the man who wore black gloves.

He answered in a frantic whisper as if it pained him to get the sound out. From inside his jacket he pulled out a straight razor, opening it like he had practiced so many times before, although in those instances he had been nude and standing in front of a full-length mirror.

There was a quick horizontal whoosh of his arm and Isabella's throat exploded in a fountain of deep red squirting that stained the snow both on the ground and in the air. Crimson snowflakes sparkled like tiny rubies in front of the man who was now breathing heavily and whispering bittersweet verbal abuse.

Isabella's body fell to the ground, landing in the soft snow like a stuffed animal on a shag carpet. The man looked down the alleyway and saw that everyone who walked by was distracted with their own lives, be it business or pleasure, and didn't as much as glance down the alley. Grunting with joy, he turned Isabella on her stomach and ripped her jacket and dress off, revealing her pale, bare back.

He dropped the razor and took out a black permanent magic marker. With delight similar to that of a child in art class, he meticulously sketched a comic strip across the back and upper buttocks of Sweetie Martini. The comic wasn't an original idea; the man had memorized it from a book he had found, a book he had stolen after he killed its original owner, Terry Silver.

Two strips of five panels in black marker, colored in only by the hues of stripper skin. In this grim adventure, Fauntleroy Le Roux was on the bloody trail of Little Bing Bong, the Apocalypse donkey. Even with assistance from his stalwart side-kick (ex-boxer Mushy Nebuchadnezzer), Le Roux ultimately fails and in the tenth panel, the world is brought to its knees by Little Bing Bong.

The man looked down at his work and was satisfied that it was an exact copy of the original. He capped the marker and put it back in his jacket pocket. Through the whole ordeal, the man's fedora hat had stayed on and he could now feel a puddle of sweat forming on the top of his head. He felt like an infant with a warm, soft spot in its skull.

He dragged Isabella against the wall and positioned her so that anyone walking down the alley would have full view of the comic strip. They would therefore be able to admire his artwork not only for its esthetic value but also for its soon-to-be historical significance. He looked at his work once more, memorizing the image, and then ran off with his mouth open, catching snowflakes on his tongue.

CHAPTER FOUR

"I think we'll stop here, see if Red Henry is around," Tommy said, pulling the car over to the right, nabbing a spot right in front of Kreese's Bar and Packaged Goods. It was a place well-frequented by people just like Tommy and Jake, citizens of Thompson who wanted to keep a low profile but still be able to get what they needed when they needed it.

Red Henry Hooper was their firearm supplier. If there was a clean gun somewhere, Red Henry could get it, though often it was attached to a ridiculous price. Still, Tommy knew he could rely on him to keep quiet even under the most pressing of circumstances. Not to mention the fact that Red Henry had helped save Tommy from an unfortunate fate at the hands of some very angry haberdashers.

"Do you even know if he's there?" Jake asked, "Why don't we just stop at the barn, pick up a couple of shotguns."

Tommy shook his head. "That's in the complete opposite direction and Peachy knows about that place anyway. If you're so worried about him, the barn should be the last place you wanna go. I want to get a drink and use the phone. I'd rather sort this shit out with Aaron before running ourselves out of town for no good goddamn reason."

"Okay, let's go then." Jake opened the car door even before the car stopped moving. He jumped out onto the sidewalk, put his hands in his coat pockets, and waited at the doorway of Kreese's, trying to stay out of the way of the barrage of snow flurries that twirled over the sidewalk. Once Tommy was out, Jake walked into bar.

As soon as he entered, they smelt the squid.

There weren't many places in Thompson where you could get a one-dollar shot of whiskey with a squid chaser. Bits of the marine animal were blended together with egg yolk and extra virgin olive oil and then stuck in the freezer to make it ice cold. Among the regular patrons of the bar, it made a delicious first drink and an even more delicious last drink of the evening.

Those who have had the drink had often likened the experience to being beaten about the abdomen with a sac of warm jello. One patron even went so far as to call it "the most sexually arousing liquid seafood in the world" immediately before choking on an unblended piece of squid. That quote was now carved into a piece of wood and hung over the bar.

Tommy made eye contact with Kevin, the bartender, and mouthed the words "Is Henry around?" Kevin pointed to the back room. As Tommy and Jake made their way, they saw an amorous couple in one of the booths, sharing a huge pile of bacon cheese-fries. The man looked up at Jake and coughed. "You lookin' at somethin', son?" He took his hand off of his date's ample breast, picked up a handful of bacon cheese-fries, and slowly covered the woman's face with it, as if the grease was soap and the fries were a washcloth. The woman had no reaction.

Jake looked at his partner but Tommy just shook his head and pushed him into the backroom. "Just ignore that shit," Tommy said as they made their way into Red Henry's back office.

"Well, goddamn, if it isn't Tom Pingpong and Jake Waite. To what do I owe the pleasure?" Red Henry talked stern and fast. His mouth seemed to move two steps ahead of his words.

"What's happening, Red? How's things?" Tommy extended his hand and Henry took it, providing a short but vigorous handshake. He gave the same to Jake.

"Can't complain. Just came back from visiting my P.O. who is, I might add, a complete asshole. Tells me I gotta stop hanging out at Kreese's. Part of my parole, he says. Well, fuck him, that's why I say. A man's gotta eat, you know? A man's gotta pay rent. What's he think I should do? Flip burgers? Man's a fucking idiot, thinks I'm gonna live a straight life so I could rot in some halfway house."

Tommy nodded his head in agreement. "I hear you, man. There's no disagreement there. Speaking of which, I was looking to buy a piece, nothing big, just something to get the job done."

"Close range?"

"Nah, I'm not expecting it to get that intense. I don't have much cash on me right now."

"Well, how much do you have?"

"Only two hundred and change."

Red Henry scratched his face. "Sorry to break this to you, buddy, but I'm almost completely sold out. Slim pickings, know what I mean? I only got a 9mm, about fifteen years old. Nothing fancy or anything but it'll do the job at close range."

"Last time we talked you had a pretty big inventory. You were practically begging me to help you unload it. What happened?"

"Ah, you know I keep my mouth shut about that sort of thing. That's why I can stay in business, people know I'm not gonna name names."

Tommy gave an open mouth smile. "You seriously going to pull that shit on us?"

The three of them laughed and Red Henry sat down at his well-worn, second-hand mahogany desk. "Okay, to tell you the truth, I don't even know any names. I was honest to god cleaned out by a bunch of longheads. In a little over two weeks I must have sold thirty or forty pieces, all to those longhead bastards. The one I'm sellin' you is just an old spare I keep around for myself."

"That's fucked up. You think anything's going down?"

"Not that I heard. And usually I'm first or second on the grapevine so I wouldn't worry about it. You know those guys are just paranoid war vets, anyway. Probably scared as all hell and hiding in their bunkers, waiting for the end of the world."

Jake tapped his fingers impatiently. "So, let's talk price."

"Well, you said you have two-hundred. That's a fair price."

Jake shook his head. "Oh, no, that's before we knew we'd be getting a piece of shit." He turned to Tommy. "What do you think?"

"Jake's right, Henry. I'll give you one-twenty-five."

The three sat in silence for a minute while Hooper chewed on his fingernail. Behind him was a window frosted with snowflakes. Still, Tommy could see clear enough to notice someone looking in from the building next door. It was a longhead, naked and standing on a velvet couch. He was holding a candle which he moved slowly from right to left, tipping it over just enough to let a few globs of wax fall to the floor with each movement.

"Jesus Christ." Tommy got closer to the window and Jake then followed. Red Henry turned around in his chair.

"Well, would you look at that? Now he's got a candle." Red Henry chuckled.

Jake looked wide-eyed at him. "What do you mean? What did he have before?"

"A snapping turtle. Thing must have been a foot long. That guy was just holding it by its feet, dangling it over the floor. Felt bad for the turtle but I wasn't just about to go knock on the door of some longhead. Especially not right after I sold him a gun."

Tommy squinted. "What the hell is he looking at? Us? What the hell is wrong with him?"

"Who the fuck knows?" Red Henry leaned forward in his chair and opened up the desk drawer and pulled out a gun that looked as if it was dragged under a truck for at least three blocks.

"That's an ugly piece of shit, you got there, Henry," Tommy said.

"Take it or leave, Pingpong." He put the gun on the desk and waited as Tommy took out the cash from his pocket.

After the quick transaction, Red Henry got up from the chair and ushered the two out of the room. "Now, if you'll excuse me, gentlemen, I gotta go pick Susie up. She's been out there all night and Christ knows she probably spent most of the money already. Boys, if you follow one piece of advice, let it be this: never marry a whore."

Tommy gave a wry smile but Jake didn't have a reaction. His mind was on Peachy.

As the door was shut behind them, they walked toward the bar to get a drink. Before they could reach it, however, a fat man in a raincoat blocked their path.

Tommy let loose the fakest smile he could muster. "Detective McMadigan, how nice to see you."

"I'll be a son of a bitch. You drink here, too? I had *no* idea." The cop laughed and the sound that escaped his throat was filled with cigar-phlegm. He was a round man with a face full of dull, gray stubble. His shirt was stained with red wine and yellow spittle, combining to form tentacled shapes over his overwhelming gut.

"What can I do for you, Detective? You see, my friend and I here are in a rush to catch a movie." Tommy, without realizing it until it was too late, felt his jacket pocket where he had put the gun. He was relieved to see that the detective didn't notice. He was too busy eyeing up Jake.

"Who's this goofy looking bastard?"

Jake started to sweat. He had heard about Detective McMadigan but never had the displeasure of running into him. From the stories that Tommy and others have told him, the cop was partial to a whole slew of odd behaviors. On any given day he may show up at an ex-con's apartment and force him to dig out his stash of girly magazines or ask the guy's wife to strip while he played his harmonica. She'd then be subject to a wide range of mental abuse mostly involving being nude and forced to recite old Honeymooners routines. It's well known even in the police department that Detective Shawn McMadigan is behind the prostitution ring that moved in downtown. It catered to those who liked to live on the wild side of Thompson. McMadigan made sure to provide customers with anything they desired be it born-again housewives addicted to prescription pain medication or bald hookers with dwarfism.

"This is Jake Waite." Tommy turned to his partner. "Jake, this is Detective McMadigan. I'm sure I've mentioned him a time or two."

McMadigan put his hand out and smiled, yellowish saliva sliding off his dull teeth. Jake reluctantly shook the cop's hand and was pulled forward. The detective put his mouth close to Jake's ear. "If you stick with this guy, then I know you're looking for trouble, my kind of trouble. If I gotta teach you, that's fine by me. Ever get gang-raped by a group of angry cops?"

The twinkle in the cop's eye was disturbingly pornographic in nature. Jake looked into the speckled orbs and saw himself being torn apart by sheer force of McMadigan's cannibalistic penis. He saw its teeth, its gaping mouth, and its mucus-filled nose. It was joined by three others, all belonging to members of the Thompson Police Department, their nightsticks being no match for their throbbing rods of power-drunk retribution.

Jake pulled away and headed for the door. The detective's face turned angry and shouted. "Hey, I'm not done with you."

Digging into his pocket, Tommy took out a twenty-dollar bill and discretely handed it to McMadigan. "We really have to catch that movie, detective." He rushed out the door before the cop could do anything, though he knew that with a greased palm, Detective McMadigan would probably save his abuse for another day.

Once outside, Tommy ran to catch up to Jake who was walking down the sidewalk, away from their car.

"Christ, Tommy, that guy is a psycho."

"Yes, I know. I told you about him. What the hell did he say to you?"

"What did he say to me? He fucking threatened me with a gang-rape! Thanks a lot for giving him my name, too, by the way. Real fucking smooth."

"Shit, he's a cop, man. Getting your name would be easy as fucking pie for him, anyway," Tommy stopped walking. "Shit!"

Jake stopped two footsteps ahead and turned. "What?"

"Forgot to use the phone."

As they both stood there cursing, Tommy felt a tug at his coat. He looked down to see a bald dwarf in a blue velvet coat. "Hey, baby, wanna date?" Even without a hair on her head, the woman was quite attractive with Russian facial features and a pierced nose that added a touch of feminine brutality to her allure.

"Uh, no thanks," Tommy said, not finding the sight of the woman even the least bit surprising. Where there was Detective

McMadigan, there was a dwarf hooker. From Tommy's experience, that's just the way it was.

"How about you, honey, thirty bucks, half and half." She moved over to Jake and sucked on her finger. Her crude gesturing made Tommy so queasy that he knew that he'd vomit if she touched him.

"Maybe some other time," Jake said. He made eye contact with his partner and shook his head slightly to the left. The woman saw this and stuck up her middle finger.

"Fuck you both, then." She walked away and moved on down the sidewalk where she was accosted by a longhead dressed in an old moth-bitten business suit. The longhead looked at the dwarf, looked up at the sky, and then slapped the woman in the face before running off past Tommy and Jake, almost knocking them down.

"Jesus Christ, man. Tonight's just getting worse and worse." Jake took out a pack of cigarettes. "Hey, you know who McMadigan reminds me of?"

"Who?"

"Orson Welles in that movie *Touch of Evil*. Ever see it?"

"No, I don't think I have. Any good?"

"Yeah, it's pretty fucking good." He took a drag and blew the smoke upwards, looking at the stars in the process. "Okay, well I'm still worried about Peachy. Do we go to a phone and call Aaron like you wanted? I think we should just get the hell out of town for a few days. Let things simmer down."

"Despite the fact that I think you're overreacting just a little bit, I guess I agree with you. Let's go back to the car and get going."

They walked back the other way, toward their car, passing another alleyway. If they had looked down that alley, they would have seen the longhead who had slapped the dwarf. They would have witnessed him sitting on a large snapping turtle and using one hand to shave his head with an electric razor, his hair falling off of his elongated skull like burnt wheat. If Tommy and Jake had looked down that alley, they also would have noticed that the longhead's body was slowly shrinking to about the size of a dwarf.

CHAPTER FIVE

Peachy drove down Main Street blasting the radio. His head bopped to "She's Lost Control" as he nearly skidded into a group of teens who ran across the street throwing snowballs at each other. He muttered a curse and then looked past the kids and saw Tommy and Jake getting into their car.

"Oh yes, you cocksuckers, I got you now." He gripped the steering wheel and then felt his stomach bubble. His bowels exploded, letting loose a storm of diarrhea into his diaper. The deluge was far more than the diaper could hold, so much of it leaked out down his legs. "Oh, Christ, not now!"

He looked down at his lap to make sure he wasn't leaking shit onto his car seats and didn't see the ice patch that was clearly evident on the road. The car slid horizontally into a parked car that had been parked behind Tommy and Jake's.

A fat man came running out of the bar. "Son of a bitch! Get the fuck out of the car!"

Peachy opened his glove compartment and pulled out his handgun that had been carved from an elephant's tusk. It had been a gift from his great uncle who was a world traveler and was known within the underworld as Bootlicker Benny in reference to his tendency to steal the shoes of his rivals' wives. His uncle had never endorsed the nickname but he had never rejected it either.

Peachy gripped the gun in his hand but hid it in his sleeve as he stepped out of the car.

"I'm so, so sorry," Peachy said, smiling and trying to sound like a remorseful driver. Then he saw who the fat man was and the smile quickly dropped into a frown.

Detective McMadigan smiled sinisterly. "Well, if it isn't Mr. Keen. You're in a world of shit, now, aren't you?" He put his hands on his hips and nodded his head. *Oh, I'm gonna have a whole lot of fun with this motherfucker,* he thought, *and after I'm done with him, he's gonna need more than a diaper.*

With one slick motion, Peachy swung his arm up and unloaded three shots, hitting McMadigan twice in the torso and once in the neck. The detective fell backward, barely able to register what was happening. His last living thoughts were of an elephant with diarrhea spearing him repeatedly with its tusks.

Screams echoed through the streets as the terrified pedestrians ran to take cover. Peachy ignored them and went back into his car. His mood quickly darkened as he realized that more shit had leaked out of his diaper and had formed a trail along the street.

After getting back into the car and pulling away, he ejected the *Joy Division* cassette from the car stereo and continued the ride in silence. In honor of his great uncle, he kissed his warm, ivory gun and pretended it was a boot.

CHAPTER SIX

"Hey, Tommy, how about we stop home?" After being threatened with a law enforcement gang-bang, he was less worried about Peachy.

"First you want to get out of town, then you want to go home? If Aaron's got someone after us, first place they'll look is our place. Then the barn. We'll stick with the original plan."

Jake leaned back. "Okay."

The car swerved to the right and Jake grabbed the dashboard. Tommy groaned and slammed on the brakes. "Would you look at that shit?"

Walking across the street, through the slush and ice was a longhead.

"It's another longhead. Yeah, he's walking his dog. So what?"

Tommy pointed. "That's not a dog."

The longhead was walking a snapping turtle on a leash. The animal was wearing snow boots that were obviously made for an infant. While Tommy and Jake watched, the longhead stopped at the sidewalk, unzipped his pants, and proceeded to urinate on a parking meter. The passersby ignored him as they do whenever they see a longhead. To acknowledge them was to bring thoughts of war, guilt, and consequences.

"Just drive, man, just drive," Jake said, making himself look away from the scene. Out of the corner of his eye, he saw the snapping turtle take a step into the stream of piss. It splashed off of its shell in large droplets that mixed with the downpour of snowflakes.

Tommy pulled away and went one more block. He slowed down in front of the movie theatre. "I have an idea." He pulled into a side street and parked the car. "Let's see a movie."

"Are you kidding me?"

"Nah, listen, we'll hold up here, keep our eyes on the door, and see if anyone's following us. What's a better hide-out than a big, dark room?"

"I don't know. A big, dark room out of town, maybe?"

"I'm just saying, if we go out of town and Aaron gets wind of it, it'll look like we got something to hide which isn't the case, am I right? So, this way we're not doing anything but watching a movie."

Jake nodded his head reluctantly. "Okay, fine."

They walked around the corner and up to the ticket booth. Tommy looked up at the marquee. "Hey, which movie do you want to see?"

"What's the difference? We're not

actually here to see a movie."

"Oh, whatever, just pick one."

Glancing up at the titles, Jake was surprised to see that they were all old movies. "Let's see…*Ball of Fire,* um, *Remember the Night... Flesh and Fantasy*….Never heard of these." He directed his statement toward the ticket seller.

"We're running a marathon. All Barbara Stanwyck pictures. We're also showing *Clash by Night*." The ticket seller was a lanky bearded teenager who, Jake thought, looked happier than he should've been to be working on such a cold night in an unheated ticket booth.

Tommy took out the remaining money from his pocket. "Two tickets, then."

"For an extra five dollars, would you each like a Barbara Stanwyck Halloween mask?"

Jake made a face. "Are you serious?"

The teenager smiled, revealing a bright overbite. "Yes, very."

"No thanks, no masks." Tommy handed over the cash and took the tickets.

As they walked away, he heard the ticket seller mocking them, speaking in a faux-Spanish accent, "Masks? We don't need no stinkin' masks!"

Tommy and Jake stepped into the theatre but not without taking one last look out onto the street to see if anything looked amiss. From what they saw, the Thompson night was close to a normal one.

The theatre lobby was large; it reminded Tommy of a church foyer, albeit one with movie posters and a floor sprinkled with popcorn. He stepped up to the snack bar and turned to Jake. "Want something? I got a few dollars left."

"Just popcorn, I guess."

The girl behind the counter had both her hands in the popcorn machine. She was making hand-washing motions, sticking her arms deep into the popcorn. Tommy caught her eyes. "Can I have large popcorn, please?"

She looked at him, eyes grey and blank. "We have no popcorn."

Jake and Tommy looked at each other. "What're you talking about? There's popcorn right there!" Jake pointed.

"We have no popcorn, sir." She continued washing her hands with the warm kernels.

"What the fuck is wrong with you?" Jake's voice echoed through the lobby. Tommy grabbed his arm.

"Let's just go into the movie. Forget about it."

Jake slammed his knuckles into the popcorn machine and pointed to it with his middle finger. "Crazy bitch."

He followed Tommy towards the theatre. As they walked, something caught Tommy's eye. A small group of men walked past them and made their way to a small hallway off to the side where only the employees were allowed.

"Oh, shit, I forgot about this place." Tommy gestured toward the men. "Totally forgot. This place is fucking loaded."

He led Jake toward the hallway and heard the popcorn girl shout.

"You can't go in there, sir."

Tommy held his hand up. "Really?" He kept walking. Once they got to the door, they could hear the low thump of music, like a rapid heartbeat through the walls.

"What the fuck's in here?" Jake asked.

"Gambling. Been here once, years ago with Joe Gurney. It's pretty wild."

He opened the door and walked slowly in, cigarette smoke confronting them like a cloud. Through the smoke, they saw five tables set up in a circle each with a different casino game being played. In the middle of the circle was a small stage where tall, skinny women gyrated. All of the dancers were dressed in cowgirl outfits and wore Barbara Stanwyck masks, obviously the same ones that Jake and Tommy passed up at the ticket booth.

The music was a noisy cacophony

of metallic clanging and bowel-churning bass. A syrupy voice oozed out of the speakers. "*It's the smiles that keep us going, don't you think?*"

"Neat place," Jake said sarcastically.

"It's actually not that bad. Let's have a seat." As soon as he started walking, a short man dressed in a tuxedo approached them.

"You don't belong here, assholes."

Tommy smiled. "Don't worry, I've been here before."

"I've never seen you, so get the hell outta here. Hit the bricks." He stuck a thumb out and made a backwards motion with it.

Jake took a step back. "Okay, okay, we're leaving." He walked out the door and realized that Tommy wasn't following him but instead was looking past the short man over to the stage where a new dance was starting. The women took off their masks and began rolling around on the ground like worms. As they writhed, they violently caressed their exposed breasts.

"Tommy, come on!" Jake was relieved when he finally saw his partner turn around and walk in his direction.

They walked past the popcorn girl who was now smearing a melted chocolate bar on her hands. "I told you. You can't go in there," she said, not looking up from her hands.

Tommy and Jake ignored her and went into their theatre. As soon as they walked in, they were shocked by how cold it was. Though it was freezing outside, there was no heat in the theatre. Goosebumps appeared immediately on their skin even under their coats.

"Fucking cold as hell, man." Jake stated the obvious and Tommy just nodded, looking at the screen as Barbara Stanwyck smiled. The film flickered for a moment and between Stanwyck's lips, Tommy saw the shape of a longhead as if it was climbing out of her throat. It morphed into something that looked like a furry inkblot with four legs.

Barbara's forehead was a huge, blank slate on which Tommy envisioned a plethora of grotesque geometric shapes that moved with every utterance of dialogue.

Jake tapped him on the shoulder. "Let's get a seat with a good view of the door." He started walking to the corner of the room, where they could see the entrance easily and have a clear path to the emergency exit.

Tommy was still looking at the screen, entranced, as if Barbara Stanwyck herself was performing a bizarre point-of-view seduction for him and him only. She licked her lips. She touched her forehead, forcing the kaleidoscopic forms into a whirlpool of silent violence.

Jake slapped him on the back of the head. "Tommy! What're you doing?"

"I don't think I wanna stay here," Tommy put his hands up to his face. "Let's just go." He turned around and headed out of the theatre.

Jake followed him out and they walked past the snack bar attendant who was picking her nose with her wet, brown index finger.

"Tommy, what's the matter?"

"I'm just really fucking confused right now."

"About what?"

They reached the door to go outside. Jake looked out and noticed that there were more people than he expected there to be considering the weather and the near certainty of frostbite and car accidents. Thompson wasn't exactly a substantial metropolitan city. It was caught in a limbo that was not uncommon in New Jersey. Too small to really be called a city, but too impersonal and urbanized to be called a town. Suburban streets were cut in half by strip malls, factories, and the occasional run-down park.

As soon as Tommy opened the door, a gust of wind combined with a wall of frosty daggers attacked their faces. Jake closed his eyes and for a split second imagined that he was in a sandstorm, lugging his body through a desert as if his brain was simply a corpse-mover, delivering flesh and bone to a destination that was clear across the treacherous landscape.

Tommy walked out and then leaned against a parking meter. He coughed and looked at the sky. White streaks were now flashing across the pinkish hue beyond the hill. Through the noise of voices and car engines, he heard the almost-subliminal sound of the factory down the street. The rumbling ambience made him mindful of the fact that he indeed could be in much danger and that he was only a fragile sentient form standing in the cold, waiting for something that was beyond his present knowledge.

Jake put his hand on Tommy's shoulder, shaking him out of his quasi-meditative state. "Come on, let's go."

They walked back to the car. Nearby, a longhead wearing a Barbara Stanwyck mask was sitting on the roof of a 1966 Plymouth Barracuda. He held a match in his right hand and staring straight ahead, he made it disappear and appear over and over, performing wintry sleight-of-hand for an audience of snow flakes and car-exhaust-stained slush.

CHAPTER SEVEN

Several blocks from where Tommy and Jake were getting into their car, a woman was answering a quiet knock at her door. Dressed in a robe under which she wore a brand new negligee, the woman looked through the peephole and saw that it was her lover, Willy Packard.

She opened the door and ushered him in. "My husband will be out all night. He's working a double," said Mrs. Sara McMadigan.

Willy planted a short but wet kiss on her lips. "I still feel weird, though, doing it in your house. Why couldn't we stay at my place?"

"Because it's too cold and I didn't feel like going out. You wouldn't want your little sweetie to get sick, would you?" Mrs. McMadigan wrapped her arms around Willy and returned his kiss.

Sara had met Willy when she was a secretary for Dynatox Industries. He had been a fisherman for most of his life but when his wife went missing (she was believed to be abducted by either squid or octopi), he gave it up to work with computers. As soon as they met, there was an obvious mental-sexual connection and the affair began when he bought her a lunch of tuna salad and oysters. They've been screwing ever since.

Sara and Willy walked together into the living room and sat on the couch. Sara had set down two glasses of scotch. Willy grabbed one glass, handed it to her, and went to pick his up. When he did so, he glanced up out the window and saw something in the window of the neighbor's house. He dropped his glass and the scotch spurted out of it all at once, silently splattering the carpet.

"Shit! Sorry!" Willy looked around for a napkin.

Sara giggled. "Don't you worry about it. I don't mind stains on the carpet. They remind me of blood, makes me remember when I was a teenager."

Willy made a face. "What do you mean? Why?"

"You know I used to work on a boat, helping bring the squid in. Almost every day someone would cut themselves open because they weren't paying attention, just slicing open the suckers and their own hand in the process. The floor of the boat had splotch after splotch of blood and squid guts or whatever it is that squids have inside of 'em. I remember this one sleazy guy who used to always try to get me to bend over in front of him. Ray! That's what his name was. Anyway, one time he cut his hand open and there was this HUGE blood stain on the floor of the boat." Sara took out a cigarette from the pack on the table and lit it. She took three drags before she began talking again.

"Well, he went right ahead and took out this turtle shell and started draining his blood in there. Then he went around asking us if we wanted our fortunes told. I couldn't help noticing, too, that all the while he's doing this, he has the biggest erection I'd ever seen."

"He was naked?" Willy laughed.

"No, no, he was wearing pants but you couldn't miss it, I'm telling you. After that, I just didn't mind stains all that much. If I spill some juice or some wine on the carpet, I just stare at it and try to see my future or someone else's."

Willy pointed to the stain. "Well, what do you see here?" He kissed her neck. Sara tilted her head and looked at the carpet.

"That's fucking weird."

"What?"

"I just thought of my old neighbor from when I was growing up in Brooklyn. I haven't thought of her in years. Barbara something. God, she was like a big sister to me." She got down on her knees and put her face closer to the stain which was now fading, sinking deeper into the carpet fibers. "Yeah, I can almost see her face, her nose especially, she had a big nose."

Willy looked down at Sara and then out the window again. The person he saw in the house next door was still there, standing on some sort of stool, waving a flag. While his married lover inspected her stain, Willy got up closer to the window. At that distance he could see that it was a longhead dressed in a Viking costume. Willy couldn't see what sort of flag was being waved but he could see that it was being moved with fervor and passion as if the man on the stool was actually marching in a parade and not standing in his room alone.

"Honey, come look at this," he said. Sara was still on her knees.

"Wait, I see something else, I think. There're some dog hairs in the carpet and they're adding shapes to Barbara's face. Come here, Willy, I want to know if you can see it, too." She put her cigarette out in a squid-shaped ashtray.

Willy stared at the longhead for another few seconds and then walked back to Sara. "That guy Ray really did a number on you, huh? Having you stare at carpet stains. Shit."

"Oh, who cares? Just come down here and look at this."

Willy grabbed the bottom of Sara's negligee and pulled it up. "I'd rather look at THIS." He caressed the backs of her thighs. Sara stiffened and turned over. Willy fell into her and they made love on top of the Barbara-stain.

Afterwards, they leaned against the couch, smoking. Sara nuzzled into Willy's neck. She pointed to the piano. "Can you play something for me?"

"Sure can, honeybunch. What would you like to hear?"

"I don't know. Anything. I love anything you play."

Willy got up and sat on the piano bench. "You make a wonderful audience, you know that?" He smiled, cracked his knuckles, and took a fake bow. "Ladies and gentlemen! Mr. William Henry Packard!"

Sara giggled and lay on her stomach facing Willy who was sitting naked in front of the piano.

Willy started pounding on the keys, his face contorted into humorous expressions. Then his face faded into seriousness.

The piano made no sound.

"What the hell is this?" He turned to her. "Sara, what happened to the piano?"

"Nothing, no one uses it but you. It hasn't been played since the last time you tried teaching me how to play."

Willy got up from the bench and opened the piano. He nearly fell backward when he saw that the inside of the piano was filled with long, wet strips of pasta. "Jesus Christ!"

"What?" Sara took a look inside. "Oh my God!" She fainted and fell sideways, hitting her head on the coffee table, dying instantly. Blood oozed out of her skull, covering the scotch stain with a fresh one.

Willy's eyes bugged out of his head in shock and horror. "Sara? Sara?" After checking for a pulse and finding no signs of life, he quickly got dressed. As he scurried out of the apartment he took one more look out the window. Willy thought he saw the longhead pointing and laughing at Willy though he wasn't so sure he was willing to trust his own eyes.

Before closing the apartment door, he saw Sara's new stain on the rug and thought that it looked a lot like a turtle shell.

CHAPTER EIGHT

"Stupid cop." Peachy shook his head, still thinking about McMadigan but not necessarily regretting what he had done. The detective had made a pastime of screwing around with ex-cons and Peachy was fed up with having to supply the cop with impromptu urine and stool samples at the drop of a hat. *That's the last fucking time I take a shit for that asshole.*

The car moved slowly down the street, windshield wipers barely moving fast enough to keep up with the snowflake assault. Peachy looked out the passenger window as he drove and his eyes caught the movie theatre marquee.

"Hey, watch out!" a voice called out just in time for Peachy to see five teenagers in the road with snowballs in their hands. He swerved to the left, sending the car straight into an empty fruit cart that sat in front of the Thompson Produce Shop.

Shards of wood and snow piles flew off of the cart as he hit the brakes. The car skidded and then stopped, hitting a brick wall. "Christ almighty," Peachy said, stepping out of his car, praising every god that he could think of that he was wearing his seatbelt. He took a step out and yelled a few half-hearted curses to the kids who returned the sentiment. If there was one thing he had a soft spot for, it was kids. *Ah, to be young and carefree. Lucky little bastards.*

Then Peachy saw the body.

A middle-aged man dressed in a tattered suit and a long beard lay against the wall. He had been sleeping in the fruit cart and was killed on impact when the car hit. "Oh, you must be fuckin' kiddin' me!" Peachy looked around and saw people walking over to him to see if he was okay. He quickly grabbed hold of the body and dragged it a few feet away and covered it with the pieces of the cart.

"Are you alright?" one voice shouted. Peachy ignored him and went back to his car. He dug out his gun and then jogged down the street.

"I'm calling the cops!" another voice yelled.

Peachy kept going until he saw Scooter's Go-Go-Rama. He hadn't been in there since before being locked up and he was getting erotic stirrings despite the stress of the evening.

His stomach rumbled so he clinched his ass cheeks, knowing what to expect. A wet squeak escaped followed by a spurt of liquid shit. *Should of brought an extra fucking diaper*, he thought. He walked down the alley next to the go-go bar and started to take down his pants when he saw the body.

At first his mind didn't register it as a body because he saw the comic first. The drawings were so vivid, so bold, that Peachy couldn't help but respect it as a piece of art and not just magic marker scribbling on the back of a corpse.

Pants down to his knees, his dirty diaper drooping with the weight of diarrhea, Peachy read the comic strip three times. He was no fan of comic strips, comic books, or art in general but this adventure of Fauntleroy LeRoux entranced him with a bittersweet vertigo. His head swam in an increasingly psychotic state, his brain cells screaming the apocalyptic hymns of Little Bing Bong.

Down the alley, a group of longheads watched intently. One of them grunted and Peachy looked at them. They laughed and continued pissing into empty wine bottles. Deep yellow urine filled each and every one. When the last longhead was done, they muttered words that Peachy could not hear and then as quick as it takes for one's eye to register a snowflake falling to the ground, the urine in the bottles became deep red wine.

The longheads proceeded to get drunk while Peachy pulled up his pants, half mad with visions of jack-ass eschatology. He ran onto the sidewalk and then across the street, stumbling to the ticket booth of the movie theatre. The words *Barbara Stanwyck Film Festival* swirled off of the marquee and into his brain. He didn't know what Stanwyck looked like but he sensed her as if she was a long-lost lover who was present in spirit only.

"How many tickets?" the teenage ticket seller asked. He gave a face, seeing the diaper sticking out of the top of Peachy's pants.

"I don't know…what are you….unveiling tonight?" Peachy slurred his speech and felt the sudden urge to wag his tail that is, if he possessed one.

The guy pointed to the sign in back of him. "A bunch of classic Barbara Stanwyck movies. Are you interested?"

"Give me a minute," Peachy replied, wanting so much to take his elephant tusk gun and beat the ticket seller to a bloody pulp and then use those pieces of pulp in a display of snowy, blood-soaked divination.

He settled on buying a ticket.

"For an extra five dollars more, would you like a Barbara Stanwyck Halloween mask?" He held up the mask.

Peachy looked at the seductive features of the mask and felt his heart flutter a warning.

"Shove it up your ass!' Peachy said. With a grunt and a curse, he fell backwards into the snow and crawled away from the theatre.

"*You* shove it up your ass!" the ticket seller laughed while he started rolling a joint.

CHAPTER NINE

"Hey, pull over for a second," Jake said. He tapped the window with his knuckles.

"What for?" Tommy slowed the car down.

"Just pull over."

A parking spot opened up in front of the liquor store so Tommy pulled right in. "Okay. Now what?"

Jake gave a half smile. "I'm starting to think you might've been right."

"About what?"

"About this whole situation. I mean, why are we running? It's like we turned into a bunch of paranoid assholes all of a sudden."

Tommy stared at Jake. "What the hell is this? I told you that you were overreacting from the get-go. Christ Almight. I can't believe this shit."

"I know. It's my fault, I'm sorry. I've just been on edge for a few days."

"Why? What happened?"

"I have no fucking clue." Jake ran his hands through his hair. "It's this town, it's messing with my head or something."

"I know what you mean." Tommy didn't elaborate but instead looked out his window.

Jake shouted. "Oh my god, isn't that…?" He pointed to the sidewalk where a man was pulling his hair out of his head, ranting and raving. His skin was blotched partly from the cold and partly from years of hygiene neglect.

"Holy shit, it's Pastor Timothy. I haven't seen him since he threw that rock through the window of the soup kitchen." Tommy laughed. "That fucker is crazy."

"Yeah, was he that nuts when he was preaching? I can't imagine any church would put up with that shit."

"My parents used to just say he had a nervous condition or something. Anytime he'd do something fucked-up, they'd tell me that we have to forgive him because God forgave him. I just think he's a hateful son of a bitch."

"Are pastors even allowed to hate anything?"

"Apparently."

"I thought religion was supposed to make you nice." A flash of memory illuminated Jake's mind. He remembered a kind uncle from his childhood who used to point to the grass and say "That's God" and then point to the sky and say "That's God". Before Jake could ask any questions, the man would point to a stray cat and say "That's God, too." Jake would then be treated to an ice cream cone which was, much to Jake's surprise and delight, God as well.

"I don't know. I guess for some people it's something to make them nice and compassionate. I think Pastor Timothy just hates a lot of things, figures God wants him to. Figures if they don't believe the same things as he does, they aren't worth giving two shits about. He's just miserable and thinks that he might as well be since he's going to heaven to live in paradise."

"That's one of the most fucked up things I've ever heard." Jake thought again of that compassionate uncle who spent most of his free time helping feed the homeless, mentoring orphans, and helping nurse sick animals back to health. All of this without having gone to church. His good deeds had outshined his lack of religious showboating.

That all ended, however, when the uncle was eaten alive by squid after being thrown into the Raritan River by an angry mob of religious conservatives. They thought that his time would best be spent raising funds for the church rather than helping the needy. After all, Jake's uncle was the mayor and what else should a politician do but support the church?

Tommy and Jake watched as the disheveled man screamed while lighting a book of matches on fire. "The Lord your God is a devouring fire, a jealous God!"

Jake scoffed. He remembered his uncle reciting a scripture from the bible....*Love is patient, love is kind, it does not envy, it does not boast, it is not proud, it is not rude...*

Pastor Timothy spit onto a woman's face, a woman he suspected of being a homosexual and, even worse, a democrat. Witnessing this, Jake thought again of his uncle... *For God so loved the world, that he gave his only begotten son.*

"Ah, I guess having a son coming home a longhead doesn't help either." Tommy reasoned. "That's gotta do some psychological damage to a man."

Jake felt a tang of compassion. "Shit, I guess that explains some of it. But still, what's the point of religion if it ain't gonna help you deal with shit?"

Pastor Timothy was scratching the skin off of his face, throwing the flakes of flesh into the air like confetti. "Hear what the Lord thy God has spoken! If anyone comes to me and does not *hate*," the pastor said, gritting his teeth, "his own father and mother and wife and children and brothers and sisters, yes, even his own life, he cannot be my disciple, says the Lor-" Pastor Timothy was cut short by a snow shovel to the face wielded by an elderly drag queen.

"Ah, shut your pathetic little piehole. The hell I'm hatin' my parents for any god!" the drag queen shouted as Pastor Timothy fell backward, his yellow teeth coming straight through his lower lip.

Tears started to stream from the pastor's eyes. "My son, my son, the pagans killed my son," he repeated over and over.

Jake looked at Tommy. "This town's fucking weird, man."

"No kidding. But it's not as weird as Fisherville, let me tell you. That place is a fucking zoo." He laughed and looked at his watch. "Shit, I feel calmer now that we're not going fucking crazy running from nonexistent assassins."

Jake laughed, reclined his seat, and continued to look at the scene out on the sidewalk. "Man, let's just sit here and enjoy the show. But I do think we should give Aaron a call later, like you said."

"Sounds good." Tommy and Jake sat for a few minutes, watching Pastor Timothy and the drag queen arguing over who got to keep the shovel.

"You hit me with it, look at my lip, I'm a wreck, I should be able to keep the shovel!" The pastor was insistent about it in between mumbling about his son and how the pagans were destroying the country with all of their talk of peace.

The drag queen wasn't having any of it. "Oh no, you don't. It belongs to my girlfriend and the hell if I'm gonna let some impotent fire and brimstone cocksucker take it home so he could shovel heavy metal albums onto his little bonfire!"

Jake laughed at the drag queen's argument and then dug in his pocket. "I'm going outside for a few minutes, have a smoke. Want one?"

"No thanks."

Outside the car, Jake smoked and watched the crowd that was growing around the shovel debate. Inside, Tommy leaned his head to the side and stared at Jake. *Man, he put on some weight. Should I tell him? Nah, he'll get pissed. Maybe I'll tell him we should join a gym together.*

His eardrums crackled as a gunshot rang out. Instinctively his head went down and as he did so he saw that Jake did the same thing. Then he realized that Jake didn't go down to protect himself. He had been shot.

CHAPTER TEN

Tommy crawled over the seats and out the passenger side door. "Jake! Jake!" He could see that the shot wasn't fatal. It had grazed the side of his stomach. Despite being scared and face-first in a slushy pile of what looked like snow, motor oil, and dog shit, Jake was okay.

"Can you move?" Tommy asked him, pulling him up.

"Yeah, I can. What the fuck was that? I knew someone was after us. Christ!"

Tommy held Jake and started him walking. "Let's fucking go, NOW." They started running, not bothering to look back at where exactly the bullet came from. They had an idea about who it was but weren't in any sort of rush to confirm their suspicions.

Even with the snow and the screaming crowd on the sidewalk, they managed to make a good run for it. They made it to the corner and slipped up the side street.

Up the street Peachy stood clad only in his dirty diaper, brandishing his ivory gun. His thoughts alternated between thinking about those two assholes and creating new adventures of Fauntleroy LeRoux. Peachy created an alternate ending of the comic strip, one in which Little Bing Bong does not usher in the apocalypse and mankind does not have to learn the ultimate truth about their existence. Peachy loved ignorance and he didn't want to know any more than he had to.

Through his quickening madness he heard Pastor Timothy and started to agree with the man. Maybe this life *was* a shithole. Maybe he should just put his faith in God so that he can spend an eternity in paradise. Who would want to be happy *here* and *now* on earth when you could be happy forever in the ambiguous heaven of God? "Damn straight, pastor, you have a point." Peachy sniffed the muzzle of his gun. "I'm livin' this life for my soul and my soul only. God damn everyone else." He giggled.

Pastor Timothy looked over at Peachy. "Oh yeah, son, you smell that? Smells like the burning flesh of sinners, don't it? Sweet smell, it is." He looked at Peachy's diaper. "Does your momma know you're out here in the cold?"

Though his mother had been dead for over twenty years, Peachy said "Yes, she does," and then walked down the street toward Tommy and Jake. He thought he heard police sirens but realized it was only the humming of the Dynatox factory down the street.

The snow got heavier and blinded him for a minute. Every snowflake became a weak hand of resistance that pushed him away from his goal. Tiny white hands, cold with rebellion, slapped Peachy across the face, across the stomach, across the legs. It melted against his skin and soothed his diaper rash.

Meanwhile, Tommy and Jake stood against a brick wall. Tommy took out his gun, opened it up and thanked God that it was loaded as he had never checked after buying it from Red Henry. With a deep breath, he cocked his gun and turned the corner.

Through the blinding snow, Peachy was stumbling toward him in the middle of the snow-covered street. Tommy quickly aimed and pulled the trigger. The bullet ripped into Peachy's kneecap and it exploded like a piece of oversized ravioli. Despite the wound, he didn't go down but instead used his good leg to stay standing like a scarecrow.

Tommy turned to Jake. "Get up! Get the fuck up! We gotta go!"

Jake was pale and mumbling.

"The bullet barely hit you, Jake. Come on, you're alright. You'll be fine. We gotta go NOW!"

With a cough, Jake motioned for him to get closer. Once Tommy was in earshot, he started talking in a gargled voice. "You know, my dad was in the war. He wasn't supposed to have another tour of duty but he wanted to go. He was patriotic, you know?"

"I didn't know that, Jake." Tommy didn't like where this was headed. Besides, they didn't have the time to go into all of this.

"He came back alive. Mom and I were happy he didn't come back a longhead, you know, but the thing is, he just wasn't the same. He didn't have that spark that we loved, didn't care so much about life, about living things. It was like he became an inanimate object during his tour or something." He coughed up blood and wiped his mouth.

"Oh shit, Jake, shit, man.." Tommy whispered, using his own jacket to wipe away the blood. Tears gathered in his eyes. "Fuck, man, let's go." He couldn't hold it in any longer; he started crying.

Jake smiled. "After three months, dad died. Doctors told me and mom they didn't really know why. Said he just gave up. Never heard of that before, you know, someone just giving up and their body listens. My dad didn't believe in heaven even though he went to church every week. I was there when he died and know what he told me? Know what his last words were?"

Tommy thought it was a rhetorical question but Jake stared straight at him as if expecting an answer.

"I don't know, Jake, what were they?"

"He said to me 'Son, none of this is real. Not a goddamn thing. We're all the fucking same. All just ants waiting to be burnt by the sun.' That was it and then he closed his eyes like he was going to sleep but there was no snoring, no fidgeting. He was just gone."

Tommy turned his head and sobbed into his hands. He'd heard many stories about Jake's father but never this one. He knew Jake's father was a dependable, loving father who always provided for his family. Even though he was disappointed in Jake's criminal path in life, he had never turned his back on his son.

Jake's head fell back. Tommy could see that the life was slowly leaking out of his body. He bent down and gave Jake a long, soft kiss on the lips that tasted like copper and salt. "I love you," Tommy said, "Don't go."

A barely audible bubble of speech escaped from Jake. "I love you, too." He coughed. "Thanks for the laughs." And then, like a snowflake on a stove, he was gone.

CHAPTERELEVEN

Aaron Jeffords stood in his office looking out the window at the pink, snow filled sky. He shook his head when he saw the image of Barbara Stanwyck appear and noticed that her breasts were much larger than they were in her films. Her cleavage was a long, deep black lightning bolt across the sky. Aaron longed to smother himself in it, lapping up the breast-sweat. He imagined her drooling down her chest causing him to drown in her abundant saliva.

He leaned back, picked up his phone, and dialed his attorney.

"Hey, Bill, Aaron Jeffords here. Yes, remember what we were talking about earlier today?"

"Yes, of course I do. What about it?"

"Is everything in order?"

"Uh, yeah, Aaron, why? What's the matter? Aaron!" Bill shouted.

Aaron hung up the phone. He opened up a desk drawer and took out a gun. He turned to face Barbara, mentally sinking in between her massive, fiery breasts. The sky behind her became a mixture of pink and black swirls. She lifted a foot and Aaron could see her wrinkled soles that were as large as a mountain. In an instant he could smell her foot stench through the windowpane. Aaron sniffed up as much of the smell as possible and then put the gun to his head.

Lord, I'm on my way.

He pulled the trigger with no hesitation. Blood spurted and pieces of brain fell like dice onto his desk. His skull, however, stayed connected to his body in one piece albeit a bit disfigured. He now resembled a longhead. The gun dropped to the floor, smashing a spider that had come out to witness the sight of Barbara Stanwyck outside. Aaron's body fell forward and was held up against the window by his misshapen forehead.

CHAPTERTWELVE

Pete and Randy dragged their sleds up the hill, laughing the whole way up. They were quite grateful that this early snowfall had come. School would surely be cancelled the following day and that would mean more sledding and more snowball fights.

When they reached the top, Pete saw something that nearly made him faint. A dead donkey, stiff yet bubbling from corpse-gas, was lying in the snow.

"Holy shit! A pony!" Pete yelled.

"It's not a pony, jack-ass, it's a donkey!" Randy was quick to correct his friend.

"What's wrong with it?"

"Duh, it's dead." Randy walked closer to it, still holding onto his sled. His eyes flickered with adolescent creativity. "Let's put it on your sled and send him down the hill."

"Why my sled? Let's use yours!"

"Mine's brand new. Your sister gave you that piece of shit so who cares what happens to it?"

"Fine," Pete gave in, knowing that arguing was futile when talking to Randy. He brought his sled over to the donkey and the two of them held their breaths and heaved the donkey onto it. "We're gonna get in so much trouble. Man, I don't want to be grounded on a snow day."

"Oh, don't be such a pussy. No one will find out. Trust me."

They positioned the sled so that the donkey would be sent flying down a path that ended just to the left of Main Street.

Randy took a deep breath. "On three, okay? One..two…"

CHAPTER THIRTEEN

Even with his kneecap blown off, Peachy was able to stagger down the street toward Tommy. *I hit one of them, I know I did.* He saw the two of them run away and felt his self-esteem lower just a bit. *I used to have better aim.*

From around the corner, Tommy stuck his gun out and sent three shots in Peachy's direction. Two of the bullets missed but one hit him in the other kneecap, sending him to his shredded knees. With the diaper on, it made Peachy resemble an ugly infant playing in the snow. He dropped his gun.

Tommy looked at Jake one last time and then came out onto Main Street. He aimed his gun and was ready to finish Peachy off when he heard a ruckus down the street. Through the thick snowflakes he saw a small army of longheads stomping up the street, shooting the guns that Red Henry had sold them. One by one, they slaughtered the citizens of Thompson in a macabre parade.

After seeing this, he knew that Peachy was the least of his worries. Then he saw the bastard pick up his gun. Before Tommy could react with his own firearm, a brown and red blur sped past him and smashed into Peachy, slicing him in two.

"What the fuck…" Tommy questioned as he now realized that the blur that had turned Peachy into a quivering mess of flesh and diaper was a dead donkey on a sled. *You gotta be fuckin' kidding me.*

Tommy took another look toward the oncoming assault of the longheads and decided his best bet was to go over the hill into Fisherville. He would have liked to take Jake's body with him but knew that he didn't have the time. Besides, he knew that whatever consciousness or soul that had been Jake was now far away from his corpse.

As he raced upwards, slipping and sliding in six inches of snow, he looked up and saw the shimmering image of Barbara Stanwyck in the sky above. Tommy froze. His testicles retracted and his heart skipped a beat. Barbara winked and jiggled her breasts which appeared to be three sizes too large for her body. Her nipples were dots of pink fire and her teeth were glistening bubbles of starlight.

He continued running and when he reached the top of the hill, Tommy fell down to his knees. He chuckled, realizing that this was exactly the position Peachy was in when a speeding donkey on a sled killed him. This thought made him cut short his rest and sent him down the other side of the hill. *I hope Joe Gurney still has that shack in the clay pits,* he thought. His friend Joe used the shack for bootlegging and it would be, in Tommy's opinion, a great place to hide out for a while.

Thinking back to his childhood, Tommy decided on a better way to go down the hill. He ran a few feet and then jumped onto his belly, sliding down the rest of the way. The freezing cold seeped through his jacket and shirt. He smiled and thought that Jake would have found all of this extremely hilarious.

CHAPTER FOURTEEN

Inside Laruso's Italian Eatery, the killer in black gloves sat at a table, his magic marker sitting beside a bowl of pasta. His mind was divided between the pleasurable taste of the food and the fracas outside on the street. Also in his mind, in a small corner that had always been reserved for obsession, was the remembrance of the musky stench of Sweetie Martini's armpit sweat as he tore off her clothes.

The man eating pasta stared out the window, watching as a group of longheads came to the door of the restaurant. He shouted to Dan, the owner and cook. "You better leave now," he said. Dan nodded and went to hide.

A group of four longheads came

through the door. The one standing in front was dressed in a wrinkled military uniform. He walked up to the table where the man was eating pasta.

Instead of the frenzied manner in which they attacked outside, the longheads calmly took the man to the floor and proceeded to beat his arms and legs to a pulp with the butts of their guns. The man did not fight, did not say a word.

A living torso with crushed bones and flesh for appendages, he flapped around a little bit and then stared at the ceiling remembering his years spent in the military.

"General Entwistle, you awake?" one of the longheads asked. He looked around and saw his attackers gathered around him. His mind flashed jagged slivers of light and memory.

Now, General Entwistle remembered everything. He had brought the troops to the city and ordered them to attack. Meanwhile, he stayed back, out of harm's way, with his good friends Sgt. Aaron Jeffords and Sgt. Dario Martino. They played cards and ate pasta while their men fought a fierce battle.

Many hours later, the troops came back. The walked their own trail of tears, gnashing their teeth and dragging snapping turtles that had attached themselves to the soldiers' hands and feet.

The turtles were the least of their problems, however, for the men came back with freakish elongated skulls which made them resemble pale clones of Frankenstein's monster. It was as if the soldiers were crystal clear reflections of a funhouse mirror.

General Entwistle scolded the men for not winning the battle and forced them into the worst hospital tents he could find. There they sat for weeks, being fed stale rations and being shown the same three Barbara Stanwyck films over and over. The men requested new movies, ones that were current but General Entwistle reserved those for himself. After viewing the same films for weeks, all of the longheads had memorized the dialogue. They chanted it like scripture, reworking it into their own stories of existential revelations and horrific revenge.

So now, he found himself on the floor, unable to move, finally facing the cruel, elongated arm of fate. One of the longheads took out a bizarre contraption and strapped his head into it.

General Entwistle felt a strap and a buckle being closed around his skull and felt metal rods being forced against his temples. He stared at a painting on the wall of the restaurant: a vibrant mural of modern Venice. He wanted so much to visit there. Even without arms and legs, he thought, it would be rather pleasant. I could hire someone to carry me around. *Maybe a nice big, Amazonian woman with huge tits. I can sit on top of them and she can walk me around the city.*

The longheads cranked the contraption that they had attached to the general's head. It took five whole minutes of vigorous cranking until finally they had made him into something even more grotesque than themselves.

Entwistle spent the last fifteen minutes of his life thinking about snapping turtles and how nice it would have been to be able to visit Venice with his good friends Aaron and Dario. A minute before he died, the face of Barbara Stanwyck appeared over the wall and he watched her swim in the canals of Venice while her breasts bobbed in the water like oversized cantaloupes.

The longheads watched as General Entwistle expired and when it was all over, they started to convulse. The veins on their heads bulged like raging underground rivers which then exploded in a spurting display of biological apokalypsis. Floating rivers of blood shot through the air like ketchup angrily squeezed from bottles. The longheads dropped dead on the floor.

Dan Laruso came out of the kitchen closet where he had been hiding and took a look at the scene in his restaurant.

"This is gonna be a real pain in the ass to clean up," he said, grabbing the mop and bucket.

CHAPTER FIFTEEN

The donkey corpse still lay on the sled, Peachy's entrails dragging close behind. The falling snow had covered it with a thick layer of glistening whiteness that reflected the streetlights.

A wet bubbling sound erupted from the donkey's stomach along with a rip that echoed down the street, tickling the ears of each and every longhead. Out of the corpse of the hairy sled-rider came a baby donkey, half-dead with fright but with a resolve that was above and beyond that of any trauma victim.

It took only a few seconds for Little Bing Bong to get his bearings and when he did, he stood on all four legs and let out a hee-haw that shattered windows and brought goose bumps to everyone within a half mile radius. The sound even made the remnants of Peachy's kneecaps slide into the gutter where they were eaten by a three-legged stray cat.

Little Bing Bong made his way down the street, ignoring the longheads and the slaughter of the citizens of Thompson. He started up the hill and when he reached the top, he looked into the eyes of Barbara Stanwyck. His donkey consciousness debated the idea of jumping off of the hill and into her cleavage but his reasoning skills told him that he'd never make it. Instead, he settled on bowing his head, mentally supplicating for a boon of some kind.

After ten minutes, Barbara responded favorably to the donkey's petition and lifted her feet up and let loose a fierce brevibacterial wind of snow and sole dirt. Little Bing Bong closed his eyes and inhaled through his large donkey nose, filling his lungs with the revelation and blessing of Barbara Stanwyck.

At the bottom of the hill, a large crowd of longheads gathered, staring up at the animal on the hill. They were silent, focusing their minds on every snippet of dialogue from the Barbara Stanwyck movies they had watched. Every line was not only recited mentally but was studied and meditated upon.

Barbara's foot brought another gust of wind and the longheads watched as each and every snowflake now reflected a different scene from the very films they were thinking about. The sky before them became a holographic universe of black and white memories, a seemingly infinite array of twinkling Barbara-clones encased in frost.

Little Bing Bong shook the snow from his fur and snorted in donkey-laughter. He looked down and saw a cardboard Halloween mask. Lacking the appropriate appendages to pick it up, he kicked it instead and watched it flip up into the air and get carried by the stink-wind that was still emanating from Barbara's feet.

And so Little Bing Bong, the Apocalypse donkey, stood on top of the hill that rose above Thompson, New Jersey, and for the first time in his young life, felt a tinge of bittersweet sorrow. He knew that something was going to happen to the world, something so massively absurd that it would erase any semblance of normality that had previously existed in any form whatsoever.

And so he watched and waited.

And waited.

Little Bing Bong was finally sucked up through the air and into Barbara Stanwyck's mouth where he swam in her yellowish, gelatinous drool.

CHAPTER SIXTEEN

Willy Packard ran out of Sara McMadigan's apartment building and stumbled down the steps. While dressing, he neglected to pull up his zipper and now a cold rush of air enveloped his penis, tickling it with icy fingertips. Though the feeling wasn't unpleasant, he zipped his pants.

The street was quiet except for the

always existent hum of the Dynatox Factory that reverberated through the town like an inexhaustible gong. Willy took a look down one end of the street and then the other.

No people.

He started walking until he got to Main Street and stopped when he saw all of the corpses.

"Whoa. What the fuck happened here?"

He walked slowly, careful not to step on anyone as he took a look at each person. Some people he recognized. Mike Barnes from the hardware store. Jessica Andrews from the pottery shop. John Lawrence, Willy's mailman. Even Officer Freddy Fernandez was lying in the snowy gutter, his torso riddled with bullets. Willy shook his head. "Goddamn."

His stomach growled so he walked farther down the street and saw that the lights were on in Laruso's. Willy walked in and saw that Dan was mopping the floor which had streaks of gore across it. "Jesus, Dan. What the hell happened?"

"The hell if I know, Willy."

"I hope it's no trouble but you mind if I sit down? Maybe have something to eat?"

Dan gestured to the empty tables. "Sure thing, have a seat. What can I get ya?"

"Hmm," Willy wondered. He knew the *fettuccine alfredo* was delicious but he'd also heard good things about the *insalata di polpo*. Not being able to make up his mind, he asked for both. "Can I have a glass of your house red wine, too?"

Dan nodded and went into the kitchen to prepare the food. He grabbed a wine glass, picked up a bottle of wine and poured a full glass. *Good thing some winos left these bottles outside,* Dan thought, remembering the weird looking drunks who were hanging out in the alley next to the restaurant.

After Dan had cooked up the food, he walked into the dining room. He saw Willy sitting at the table and almost dropped the plates.

Willy Packard was sitting, hands folded, at the table wearing something on his face. Dan slowly walked closer and quietly placed the plates on the table.

"Are you okay?" Dan asked.

Willy Packard laughed loudly through his Halloween mask.

MYKLE HANSEN

LOCATION:
Portland Fucking Oregon! W00t w00t!

STYLE OF BIZARRO:
Cranio-rectal Subterfuge

BOOKS BY HANSEN:
Eyeheart Everything
HELP! A Bear Is Eating Me!
The Bored, Bored Princess
21st Century Typewriting
Book of Lists
Rampaging Fuckers of Everything on the Shitting Planet of the Vomit Atmosphere

DESCRIPTION: Comedy as cruelty, as therapy, as surgery.

INTERESTS: Architecture, anarchy, bicycles and sound. And other peoples' asses.

INFLUENCES: Donald Barthelme, Jim Thompson, Martin Amis, Alice Donut, the UNIX operating system, Black Cat Firecrackers, coffee.

WEBSITE:
www.mykle.com

MONSTER COCKS !

Tue Aug 05 20:37:52 PDT 2008:

Life is short, cruel, and uncertain, but this I know: I have got to have a larger, longer, thicker and more satisfying penis—AS SOON AS POSSIBLE!

I have MALE SEXUAL PROBLEMS. No sex whatsoever, for instance, is an enduring PROBLEM of mine. I understand now that my enduring virginity is just a symptom, and the PROBLEM lies elsewhere. I get it now, what it's all about. But it came slowly. It took a lifetime of lying to myself about the secret importance of so-called chivalry and sensitivity and being "special" and "different." And waiting, alone. And jerking off, which is actually kind of difficult for me— not at all like it is for Rod Girder, star of the original MONSTER COCKS and narrator slash producer of MONSTER COCKS TWO through NINE, all of which I own, all of which I have watched, alone in my hiding places, all of which are available for immediate download from www.monstercocks.com. All of which describe an existence the exact opposite of mine.

We live in a futuristic wonder-world where a larger, longer, thicker, more satisfying penis is available for immediate download. So why should I stew in my SEXUAL PROBLEMS? The Old Me used to try to jerk off while watching Rod Girder swing around his monster cock on laptop DVD, while imagining myself as "Lightning" Rod Girder, while imagining Rod Girder's co-stars Andrea Assbury and Lana Liason as duplicate copies of Angela Fine from Payroll—who is six feet tall and has skin like milkshakes and huge, delicious-looking breasts and who wears a side-slit skirt and heels around the second floor and is so totally sexy and totally nice at the same time—and the Old Me would imagine her moaning, in a lust-crazed version of her sweet, gentle voice, how big and satisfying and adequate of a penis I have, smiling at me, feeling for me what I feel for her, then closing her eyes and riding out one of the screaming, squirting, squeezing, hair-bending five-minute orgasms that Rod Girder Productions claims as their unique selling point. That's what the Old Me used to fantasize about doing, as recently as earlier today.

And then, right after the Old Me finally achieved one frustrating little mouse-sneeze of an orgasm, but before he wiped himself clean and reactivated the card-key and unlocked the door of the Off-Line Backup Vault and returned to the Trouble Center; after the fantasy and the shame and the desire annihilated one another in their mutual impossibility, leaving a little puff of bitter smoke and burnt flesh at the spot in the Old Me's brain where rogue neurons of hope once dimly fired, but just before the Old Me trod a long circuit of shame back to my post in the Trouble Center, through the coffee/soda/yoga/Pilates area, through the marketing/communications/weightlifting area, past the ladies' room, in the sad and perhaps creepy hope of accidentally bumping into Angela Fine, literally or figuratively, in the halls; between then and then, the Old Me used to shed exactly one and one half tears from each eye, for a total of three.

The first tear was for myself, because I am so pathetic and small and weak and ashamed. I am also pale and pasty and scrawny, although better to be skeletally thin than morbidly obese like IT supervisor Glenn Lotz. But Glenn is shameless in his slovenly fat decrepitude—he slaps out a caffeine-driven disco rhythm on his breasts and thighs like a feisty manitee as he clomps down the halls, disgusting and terrifying the conspicuously fit and healthy non-IT employees of our international sportswear company— while the Old Me knew far too well what his problems were, and struggled constantly to hide, to become invisible.

The second tear was for Angela Fine, because she is beautiful and pure and nice, and staples pictures of kittens to the pay envelopes of the entire IT department every Friday because she believes that little things count. If I were her lover I would be the most dedicated, kind, brave, understanding, sensitive lover any woman ever had. I would give her cunnilingus every morning, and fix her car, and rub her back and change all of the light bulbs in her house on a regular schedule before any of them ever actually burned out, and I would defend her home from thieves and her heart from loneliness and her body from violence and her laptop from viruses and unstable Microsoft updates. Because that is what a beautiful, perfect creature of Angela Fine's caliber—a caliber of one, a class unto herself—deserves.

But Angela Fine does not get what she deserves. Instead, Angela gets:

1. A new pair of wide-rimmed glasses, slightly tinted—not nearly as flattering or sexy as the small, black-rimmed librarian glasses she used to wear, yet still gorgeous in context and incredibly lucky to be on her face—with which, aided by mascara, she disguises a swollen black eye; and

2. A small, perfectly round scab just beneath and behind her right ear, approximately 8 millimeters in diameter; a kind of scab the Old Me knows well from his awful childhood; the kind of scab you get when your sadistic, abusive boyfriend or stepfather stabs you with a cigarette, as punishment.

(I am a keen observer in general, and a particularly keen observer of Angela Fine.)

The third tear is for my penis, with its Peter-Pan-like immunity to puberty; my withered disappointment, my runty pig, my tragic appendage. My third thumb. My problem.

It's late. After a relatively mild day of Trouble in the Trouble Center (87 tickets closed, 93 opened), my co-workers have gone home to their medium-and large-sized homes, to relationships based on mutual adequacy, and I have come here, to my secret sanctum in Retired Hardware Five, next to the loading dock, across from the lacrosse field. Retired Hardware Five is the mausoleum where we honor and dispose of our formerly beloved equipment, equipment that we could not live without until it was superseded by the even better equipment of the ever-encroaching digital future. Racked up on the walls all around me, lights unblinking, are 714 still hard disks that will never again spin, 220 dark monitors that will never again glow, 11,071 unplugged male and female ports—DB9, DB25, RJ45, 13W3, IEC, IDE, HPPI—that will never again feel the satisfying hookup of the cable-ends they were born to mate with. Some of them never even got the chance; dead virgins, gone to waste.

Spread before me on an empty server rack are the cardboard boxes I have downloaded, containing the crystallized essences of the New Me: the packets, the bottles, the instructions, the testimonials and the solutions to my MALE SEXUAL PROBLEMS.

The first cardboard box was shipped Priority 3-Day from the Cayman Islands by UPS. Inside, nestled in fresh styrofoam peanuts, is a white plastic bottle of yellow pills, labeled ENHANCEMENT PLACEBO FORMULA in a font that is discreet yet medically suggestive. This is MEGADIK—a proven herbal formula which complements the human growth hormone secreted by my pituitary gland. (If I even have a pituitary gland. My glands are a constant letdown.) Dosage instructions are not included. I take three, and wash them down with Diet Fresca.

The second cardboard box, liberally stamped RUSH with smeary red ink, was shipped 2-Day Express by FedEx from the Cayman Islands. Inside, another small plastic bottle, very similar to the first, maybe even identical, containing similar yellow pills, one might even think the same yellow pills, but with a different label on the bottle, actually an only slightly different label, but just different enough for me to recognize it as a completely different male enhancement technology altogether: XtraHuge++, a naturally occurring erectile tissue conditioner from Korea. (Apparently they have huge dicks in Korea. Dicks bigger than their necks. Rod Girder did a special segment about it in MONSTER COCKS WORLDWIDE. Rod Girder endorses XtraHuge++, as does his sometimes co-star Mitch Morecock.) The included instructions, in broken English, accompanied by gratuitous close-ups of some really extremely large, veiny penises entering the mouths of stunned-looking women, are clear. DOSAGE: ONE CAPSULE PER DAILY.

I take three, and wash them down with Diet Fresca. My problems are immediate and severe.

The Internet knows all, and the Internet provides. Without eBay, I would have no polyvinyl Anime figurines. Without Google, I'd know nothing of Rod Girder, or the Monster Cocks cinematic cycle, or how to fix and deploy the complicated IT systems that IT must deploy and fix. And the Internet, in its kindness and wisdom, has been trying for years to grant me a larger, longer, thicker and more satisfying penis! But the Old Me wasn't ready, the Old Me fought the truth. The Old Me blocked and deleted those unsolicited offers before they hit my Inbox. The Old Me, afraid of the truth, afraid to be free, afraid to be loved, employed an ever-evolving arsenal of anti-penis-enlargement tools: blacklists, graylists, SPF and MX records, honeypots, carefully honed lists of keywords like `V|1gr@` and `$e><ual` and `+ur6idid+y`, ASCII insinuations of unspeakable acts ... unspeakable because they never happened to me, so why speak of them? The Old Me engineered and deployed a best-of-class mail-filtration system to purify the inbound and outbound ones and zeroes of our international sportswear company network, to stem the rising tide of Internet sewage: realistic Rolex replicas, anonymous investment opportunities, cut-rate Canadian Cialis, weight-loss miracles, eternal youth, ultimate fighting power, and a million other excellent improvements to the sad, lonely life of an unloved Systems Administrator. Every morning for four years three months and eleven days, the Old Me said no, and flushed away the Internet's fecal onslaught with one bitter keystroke. But today the New Me said YES.

In the third cardboard box, shipped Priority One by DHL from Moldova, is a ziplock bag, containing six smaller ziplock bags, each of which contains one day's pharmaceutically-impregnated WONDERCUM PLUS-PATCH. To achieve maximum results, I am to apply this patch to my penis, in the direction of preferred growth, before I go to sleep each night. As I sleep, my penis will busy itself with self-improvement, and in the morning I can remove it, or, optionally, move it to my scrotum and enjoy it for the rest of the workday. After six days, effects should be noticeable and pronounced, or I am entitled to request a full refund.

Oh, to be noticeable! Oh, to be pronounced! Oh, for Angela Fine to gaze upon me, not just in the chaste way she gazes upon kittens, hamsters, injured birds and members of the IT department, but in the hot, hungry, confused and ashamed way she gazes at the groin of that asshole who beats her.

That asshole with the monster cock —who she loves, instead of me—who beats her.

The Old Me denied this inescapable, ultimate human truth: the penis is the source of all male excellence! Strength, vigor, determination, chest hair and charisma flow outward from this central organ. Yes, it suppresses brain function somewhat, but I don't care. Until I have a larger, longer, thicker and more satisfying penis, my love is useless torture! Angela Fine, perfect as she is, has FEMALE SEXUAL PROBLEMS. She needs, craves, and I daresay deserves a large, long, thick and satisfying penis. As a woman, a sexual being, an earth goddess, this is her birthright and her handicap. Women (I once denied but now admit) are hypnotized by large concentrations of erectile tissue. They are drawn to them, like moths to a light bulb. To ask otherwise of Angela would be to misunderstand her beauty, and yet ... Angela's needs are so very extreme, they could destroy her. Because the most satisfying penis she has found, the penis whose orbit she is powerless to exit, is mounted on an abusive, mullet-wearing, coke-dealing, Camero-driving piece of Nazi surf-trash ... a man so dumb, his name is actually Rock. A man so stupid and evil that, given that great gift that is the adoration and attention and body and sweet love of Angela Fine, he does what with it? He beats her!

But I swear, with my hand upon the collected RFCs of the Internet Engineering Task Force, that I will grow a better penis for Angela, a perfect love penis of supernatural strength! And when I'm coaxed forth from the desert of my loins this artificially-irrigated wonder genital I will present it to her as a gift, a human flower, a symbol and a token of my pure, undying, laser-like love.

Peering into my underpants, I apply two WONDERCUM PLUS-PATCHES from box number three to my miserable third thumb—one lengthwise, one across. Together, they envelop it completely like a tiny tennis ball. Box number three mocks me. Bring me box number four.

I'm not stupid. I know what "placebo" means. I have taken six pills and applied two patches and I don't feel any larger or any more satisfying. Boxes one through three are garbage, rip-offs, trash. These patches on my penis offer only nicotine. I know this, because the same Internet that gave them to me also gave me the largest, longest-running and most satisfying online forum for the Internet penis enlargement community:

www.cocksmiths.com

Cocksmiths.com readers have tested MEGADIK and found no measurable enlargement. WONDERCUM, while causing some swelling of the testicles, produces less than 4 millimeters of increased manhood on average, well within statistical fluctuations. The jury is still out on XtraHuge++ (a mixture of Ephedra and horse semen) but early results are not promising. The Old Me spent perfectly good PayPal on this snake-oil, knowing it was snake oil, for the same reason the rest of the Cocksmiths.com readers did: we're all extremely desperate. There's no oil we won't rub on our sad little snakes.

But that was the Old Me. Inside box number four lies the New Me, waiting to uncoil and inflate. Box number four holds a new treatment—new like yesterday, bleeding edge, but very promising indeed. So promising, in fact, that this week the cocksmiths.com on-line forums are shuddering from the shock of the new, crumbling under gigabits of enthusiastic testimonial traffic and startling photographic evidence of the results from this new and promising treatment. They've been knocked off-line three times this week. They're soliciting donations to pay for the added bandwidth consumed by the high-resolution, un-retouched before-and-after evidence. No one's sure what it is, or even where it comes from, but they're calling it the miracle we've waited for. They're calling it the cure.

They're saying it hurts. I don't care. Open the box. Peer inside. No pills, no patches, no suction pumps. It's a device, a sort of gun, steel and beige plastic, with a duck-billed maw on one end and a pistol grip on the other—plus a tenth-generation photocopy giving a single illustration of the device in use. The device doesn't even have a name, as such—it's available through a single non-English website with an unlisted IP address, shipped from somewhere in southeast Asia. But online, they're calling it the Monsterizer.

The Monsterizer implants, subcutaneously in the target organ, a tiny gold pellet, which mysteriously Just Works. We don't know how yet, it's too new. The cocksmith.com forums, when not off-line, are abuzz with theories. Newbie members like dickcheney think it's a targeted hormonal release, some kind of steroid, but more experienced cock-smiths point out that those things have been tried and don't work except for side effects. Highly respected member goldenrod13 and some other old-timers have proposed it's a chip, RFID-style, talking to the penis and organizing its growth. Based on something they do in Iraq, with limbs, they say. Technology. And like all good technology, how it works doesn't matter unless it's broken. I don't need to know. It works by stimulation. Magnetism. Voodoo. I don't care. I peel back the patches, free up a parcel of my little peninsula ... pinch as much flesh as I can grip with the spring-loaded tongs ... close my eyes ... pull the trigger.

HURTS!

Wed Aug 06 11:10:05 PDT 2008:

Today is the first day of the rest of my penis! It's amazing, impossible, miraculous, uncomfortable. It's like painful swelling, basically. I'm running a slight fever and I itch like crazy. But user goldenrod13 said the first day was like this for him. The first new day. User small_paul said the same thing. I've seen pictures of their dicks so I know I can trust them.

The Trouble Center is knee-deep in the following trouble this morning; aggravating WADSLAP breakdown in Shenzhou office kills trans-pacific VPN, delays final selection of Malaysian footwear shipment two hours before some arbitrarily pre-determined summer fulfillment cutoff moment. Shenzhou office's hot-spare WADSLAP is mysteriously absent, probably embezzled. Upper-mid-sportswear-management shits their sportswear, demands immediate solutions to impossible problems: blood, sweat, spit, bailing wire, bales of cash, helicopters full of replacement WADSDLAP airdropped over Shenzhou, time travel, human blood, whatever we've got. Just Do It.

While IT panic builds, I calmly peruse the logs. A bitter argument has broken out between the two WADSLAPs, concerning whose turn it is to shift the transmission window. Shenzhou calls Virgina "out of sync". Virgina calls Shenzhou "non-compliant." Every seventeen seconds they scream at each other, break up, re-sync, bicker, scream some more. While Greg Lotz oozes the pale gelatin sweat of stress and barks through the phone at Shenzhou in a pidgin of swearwords and TLAs which we both know Shenzhou doesn't grok, and the NetOps grunts and the Chad Squad try desperately to look busy, and upper-mid-management sharpens their axes outside the Trouble Center doors, your humble sysadmin:

1. quietly determines that the WADSLAP manufacturer released a patch this morning,

2. theorizes that Shenzhou may have promptly installed that patch, particularly after last week's pidgin & TLA tirade from Greg Lotz re: prompt patch installation,

3. remote-installs the same patch on the matching WADSLAP in Virginia, and reboots.

Instantly, the warring WADSLAPs come to their senses, renew their marital vows and engage in immediate hot data coitus. Several hundred iterations of the same footwear order march in single file across the virtual private urethra of their love, and fifteen minutes later it's Shenzhou's problem.

I did that with my new penis! The Old Me would have panicked, hidden, perhaps wept when mid-upper-sportswear-manager Phil Tong burst into the Trouble Center, his morning coffee running down his tie, clutching an ink-stained printout, calling the IT department 'clueless trolls' and dialing our manager's manager's manager on his iPhone. The new me didn't even blink.

Phil Tong, I'm guessing, has a very small penis. Not as small as mine, but smaller than most. I know this because I know what kind of pornography he downloads. We have the same tastes.

Phil Tong is always bitching about IT, decrying the competence in IT, demanding IT heads on mid-upper-sportswear-management platters. He needs to feel larger than he is, larger than someone else. IT fills this role for him. We are a department of the kinds of people who fill that role. Greg Lotz, Chad Day, Chad Wankel, Grunt Number One and Grunt Number Two: misfits, nerds, social failures, Information Technology professionals. We wipe the asses of machines so we won't have to talk to people. Phil Tong threatens us because we don't fight back.

Thirty-seven minutes and fifteen seconds ago, I scooped up a virulent sample of child pornography from the external spamstream and installed it on Phil Tong's laptop. For eleven minutes and thrity-three seconds I strategized how best to anonymously notify Human Resources how Phil uses company hardware to pursue his dangerous perversion, but then I relented. My new penis is a forgiving penis. One day it will crush Phil Tong's penis, but for now, let them live together in peace. For now, let Greg Lotz issue a technical debriefing to a grateful but still panicky boardroom, while I visit the soccer/rugby executive changing booth, for the third time today, to adore my beautiful new penis in the full-length mirror.

Wed Aug 06 12:23:40 PDT 2008:

Hello, little monster. I swear you're bigger than you were two hours ago. Once you were a thumb, now you are a fat big toe, long and red and laced with busy veins, a toe to kick someone's ass with. Right where your knuckle would be is a hot white raised bump, where the subcutaneous golden seed works its magic.

Directly behind you is Jack Stalker, who needs to get a grip. This could all go wrong, Jack. This could be a localized infection disguised as male enhancement. A crippling injury, a rip-off. If that happens ... you will want to kill yourself, Jack. It will be the last straw. Only, if that happens, you won't have the nerve. Because then The Old Me will be back, and he'll just dig a sub-basement in the basement of his soul, carry his things downstairs, and cry a few more tears.

Only I can kill the Old Me.

Phil Tong is waiting outside the soccer/rugby executive changing booth. He glares disapprovingly at me. I know, and he knows, that this booth is reserved for executive changing. But he knows, and I know, that sysadmins are everywhere always, scurrying underfoot or suspended overhead, pulling wires, testing hookups, installing repeaters and base stations and HVAC and AC and whatever other technology is necessary for executive changing in the digital age. Making things work. Phil Tong and his management ilk need us to do these things, and he hates that he needs us.

"What's the story, Jack?" demands Phil Tong impatiently. "Stalking something?" He puts two fingers against his temple to massage the constant headache that I and my coworkers are, to him.

"I'm done. Just tying down some D-Links. It's all yours."

"D-Links?"

"Yes. In the crawlspace. They were dangling."

"Is that what you do all day?" he snidely demands, surely expecting me to whimper or run away. I do neither. In truth, Phil Tong hasn't a clue what we do all day, doesn't know what a D-Link is, so I could say yes or no or "one, one, zero, zero," and it would all be rot13 to him. But before I can deliver more than a shrug, he rolls his eyes, shoves past me and shuts the door.

I see he brought along his laptop. I

don't think he's here for soccer/rugby.

Wed Aug 06 20:15:40 PDT 2008:

I wasn't even trying to bump into Angela today. (I wouldn't have been holding a Diet Fresca, obviously, if I'd been trying to bump into her.) I've been preoccupied, busy ... I was on my way to kick the printer in receivables—every day before 16:00 PDT it must be kicked, squarely, in the side, for historical reasons—and it was 15:42 PDT already and I had lost track of time in the cocksmiths.com chat rooms, exchanging my first excited reports with a group of disbelieving noobs, who called me a bullshitter and demanded photographs of my penis in a way I found slightly offensive, and then actually receiving a private chat request from goldenrod13 himself (!!!) at 3:57pm PDT, which is, in the context of cocksmiths.com, a kind-of-big deal, when suddenly my phone buzzed to remind me that it had buzzed twice earlier to remind me to kick the printer in receivables before 16:00 PDT, and it was already 15:58 PDT. So I switched my chat mode from "Available" (icon: large erect penis with bow tie) to "Be Right Back" (icon: droopy penis next to cigarette), and headed towards Receivables at a trot. Passing the drink/snack/shuffleboard area I felt thirsty, dry and hot—as I've felt all day—so I grabbed a quick Diet Fresca as my phone buzzed a more insistent, throbbing vibration to inform me it was already 16:00 PDT and I had better move it. And the friction of my jeans as I ran towards Receivables wth the drink in my hand, plus the itching of my new penis, plus the vibration of the phone in my pocket, suddenly it all at once started to well up and grip me in a crazy combined feeling of well-being and energy and strength, and I just ran, faster, and felt it surging stronger, and I closed my eyes and turned the corner and crashed right into Angela Fine as electricity gripped my knees and strange, hot juice erupted into my underwear, as I spilled diet Fresca all over her and her paperwork as she spilled paperwork and coffee all over me and my penis, as we tumbled to the floor together in one glorious, disgusting, humiliating pile-up of orgasm and shame.

And then, up out of the ashes of yesterday rose the Old Me, supplicant and snivelling. Oh God, I am such a stupid nothing. Oh God, Angela Fine thinks I'm such a loser. Oh God, her hair smells like a beautiful, ripe peach. Oh God, she's staring at me, oh God, that is some extremely hot painful coffee. Don't look at my crotch! No, please look! I can see her bra! I'm a pervert! It's pink! I'm an idiot! Did we just have sex? Am I on fire? This pleasure, this pain ...

Angela Fine grasped my shoulders as we struggled to our feet together, diet Fresca dripping off her wide-rimmed glasses. She stared, with great concern and concentration, directly at the site where my large, long, thick, satisfying penis will soon spring forth for her. "Oh gosh, Jack, are you okay? I'm so sorry! I don' t know how I did that!"

"No no no! It's me, I'm sorry, I'm stupid. I was, there's—oww! Hi!"

"Oh no!" She bit her finger in concern. "Go pour some water on it!"

"No, I gotta go kick the printer. It's okay, I'm hot. You're hot too. Hi Angela!"

"Jack, this could be serious! Like that lady at McDonalds!" Her face a perfect circle of sweetness and worry, and right then and there I fell in love with her a second time, superimposed on the love I already fell, double down. All the world's goodness shines out of Angela Fine's brown eyes. "I'm just so sorry!" she said.

"I gotta go!" I said. "Will you talk to me some more when I'm not burning?"

"Jack, please be okay!"

"Going! Sorry! Bye!"

And the Old Me hauled ass right out of there, ran all the way back to Retired Hardware Five in shame, and disrobed to find my poor, guilty-looking new penis, head hung low, bashfully awaiting punishment like a little potbellied piglet who's wet the carpet.

I cradled it in my hand. How could I stay angry at that precious little life, staring at me with its hamster eye, trembling in shame. My own penis. Fruit of my loins!

I decided then and there to call it Lassie.

I changed into a different pair of pants, dirty but at least not sticky, and walked jauntily back to Building One, re-living that anxious, intoxicating moment over and over: that hot instant of the smell of her and the heat from inside me, inside Lassie, and the aroma of diet Fresca and coffee and photocopies and Angela Fine staring at my crotch. It makes my knees weak, even now, just thinking of it. Oh, Angela!

And then I returned to the Trouble Center with my head in a cloud of Trojan Condom advertisements ... and caught hell from Greg Lotz, passing along the hell he caught from Receivables, for not having kicked the printer.

Therefore: now it is 20:43 PDT and Lassie and I are on month-end tape swap duty in Ice Station Zebra, the climatized server room in building six, as punishment, subbing for NetOps grunt number one so he can go do something at eight. The rest of IT has gone home. I pull a backup tape out of the jukebox, hand-label it with an anti-static pen, and insert a fresh tape in the open gap, slowly, gently, lovingly. I do that one hundred and forty four times, and every time the tape transport swallows my offering I think of Angela. It seems so unreal.

The second seed is planted. goldenrod13 says I must be careful. He says there's such a thing as too much. For him that may be true. But my problems are immediate, and severe. The Old Me must die so that Lassie can live.

Thu Aug 07 09:08:07 PDT 2008:

Yes! Yes! Yes!

This is the most unreal, amazing thing that has ever happened to me. This is better than every Rod Girder film combined, this is real. Lassie woke me up this morning, squirming, tapping, wriggling me awake. He's already five and one thirty-second inches long, and almost four and three quarters inches in circumfrence! That's literally twice as long as he was two days ago! At this growth rate my penis will be ten inches long in three more days! After that .. I don't know, that would be more than enough to show to Angela. This, frankly, is more than I've ever dreamed of. The Monsterizer is real, it works! I'm sorry I ever doubted you, Monsterizer! Lassie, I love you.

Lassie's burning has subsided, although the itching remains severe. I can touch him now. In fact I can't stop touching him! He really is like a rambunctious puppy, so excited and full of energy. This is what a penis is supposed to feel like! Finally we are together, a boy and his penis, exploring a new world! I've been showing Lassie new places all day: a loaf of bread (soft, crumbly), a jar of peanut butter (exciting, messy), a cup of diet Fresca (cold, sticky), the hot-swappable drive bay of a Hewlett Packard RL3000 information server (mildly shocking.) So many places exist for a penis to go, if that penis is just long enough to reach. A beautiful new world of openings.

The Monsterizer, I predict, will change human civilization forever! Computers are nothing compared to this. Rural electrification, running water and sliced bread are nothing. I declare small penises extinct! Nobody with a credit card and Internet access need ever experience smallness or inadequacy again. All men shall be giants! A new era of peace and adequacy dawns worldwide as we put aside our petty squabbles, shed our insecurity, and hump our way to global understanding! I'm awed to be present at this pivotal moment in human history, an early settler on a rich new continent forested with large, long, thick, satisfying penises.

Lassie really wants to run free. Every time I pass a female employee in the halls, Lassie twitches at his leash. Young, old, married, fat, Lassie doesn't care. What a nut! It's a big responsibility, raising a monster cock, teaching it right from wrong. The women have no idea.

Or maybe that's not true: one visual merchandiser, a red-headed older woman named Wendy, brushed past me in the photocopy area/Hall of Sports Heroes, and Lassie nearly jumped out and bit her.

And she looked. I saw her look. And I think I saw her smile.

Thu Aug 07 19:44:23 PDT 2008:

Today the Trouble Center was hip-deep in the following kinds of trouble: The east coast is in the grip of hysteria due to a wave of unexplained killings. Virginia state sheriffs are soliciting tips from the Internet. The Internet is flooding their on-line tip-server with tips, and by sad coincidence our Virginia BGP box is co-located not only with that tip-server but also with a major CNN.com news mirror; ergo, the fiber into that co-lo is hosebagged by hysterical suburbanites finking on their mailmen, ergo only a spluttery dribble of ones and zeroes remains for the other co-lo residents, including our newly launched online yoga-and-breakdancewear store. Ergo, urban sports product manager Phil Tong is livid. (What else is new?) Dollars, he says, are dropping on the floor in Virginia, and we in IT, he says, have our heads up our asses.

And also: today the Internet caught a cold. Spam & virus counts just doubled, overnight, everywhere. That's both scary and amazing—it's as if every asshole in the world suddenly sprouted a second asshole. Some new cabal of sleazy h@xx0rs has announced their arrival, some shift in the Russian cybermafia power structure has admitted mean new players to the game of viruses and spam, and they are busy, busy beavers. Everything is slow. Everything is late. Many things are offline—cocksmiths.com, for example, but also our main corporate Web site and two of our main B2B sites—but they'll come back when the storm passes. My spam filter is holding. The firewall is solid.

And also: the Hewlett Packard RL3000 Information Server is down. Information Receiving is hot for information, but Information Services can't keep it up. Information Receiving demands a vendor tech on site within the hour, and I don't think I want to be around when he gets here. (Silly Lassie!)

And more: backhoes, dead drives, interruptions in the Uninterruptable Power Supply, managers who cannot grasp a spreadsheet no matter how wide it is spread. Trouble, trouble, trouble. Solve, solve, solve. 72 tickets closed today, 137 opened. It never ends. As long as there are things and idiots, idiots will break things.

But I don't mind, and neither does Lassie. We've got each other, and we've got the future. Stiff black hair is sprouting on my chest, I feel my pores clearing, I feel my voice deepening, my mane thickening. Energy and power and strength are coursing through me. I grow studly!

Is it normal for a penis to jump around so much? Lassie is so enthusiastic! It reminds me of once, when I was little, visiting my cousin Sam in Eau Claire, Wisconsin, when Sam's pet ferret Mister Bonzo climbed up my leg and ran around in my pants. That's what I keep mistaking this for, whenever Lassie starts twitching like this. Mister Bonzo ferret bit my penis, but if he tried that today he'd have a fight on his hands. Lassie has Mister Bonzo outclassed. You little monster!

Tonight, in my secret sanctum, surrounded by my polyvinyl figurine collection and my Xbox and my movies, Lassie and I are posing for photographs, to show all our friends at cocksmiths.com what we've been up to. Six inches! That's an inch longer than this morning! And as we struggle with lighting and focus and finding the right pile of de-comissioned hardware to bring the camera to loin height, I am posing, in my mind, not for the obnoxious, naysaying, possibly gay noobs on the forums, but for my princess, my perfect love.

Angela, Angela, Angela Fine. Lassie and I will make you mine.

Fri Aug 08 08:09:10 PDT 2008:

Angela, Angela, Angela Fine: Lassie and I will hunt down the abusive bad news cokehead surf-Nazi who dares to call you 'sweet-cheeks' and shove his own cock down his throat!

Why do you go back to him, Angela? Why do you allow him to debase you? Is a larger, longer, thicker, more satisfying penis really worth the pain?

I am a keen observer of you, Angela. From my window in the Trouble Center I observed you in the basketball/parking court this morning, dropped off by your concerned girlfriend Estrella after a brief but tender hug, and I observed you limping, just slightly, with your head hung low and your tender hand touching a tender spot on your side, as you limped through the entrance and on up to your second floor desk, there to staple pictures of kittens to our pay envelopes in pain, and draw smiley faces on our Friday Party notices in pain, and brighten our workplace with the smile that hides your pain.

Fury! Aggression! Black feelings the Old Me and his three thumbs never knew are pumping through the New Me like hot poison! Lassie turned nine today, incidentally. Nine inches of seething hatred for that bastard asshole who's named after Earth's stupidest material. Lassie's two white eyes squint angrily when I take him out for lotion. His happy-go-lucky personality is gone today, Angela. Lassie wants blood!

Fri Aug 08 17:55:23 PDT 2008:

Today the Trouble Center weathered the following shit-storm of trouble: general utter total breakdown of everything Internetty and/or located on the entire east coast! All last night, heaping boatloads of spam throttled everybody, particularly and interestingly yet unfortunately including some newly deployed ConEd power futures trading bullshit system, triggering a truly stupid and preventable over-delivery of megawatts at major crossover points in the eastern seaboard's electrical grids, and boom: PCB-laden shrapnel rains down from telephone poles all up and down the east coast. Blackout! Three of the four major handshake centers go dark just like that, their redundant power is up but the telcos that feed them are down. Giant holes in Blackberry coverage, so upper-management can't even call to complain. All because of spam! Plus: killers run loose in the streets, still.

Meanwhile, here on the west coast: overloads, under-supplies, and an onslaught of refugee data from Virginia. Everything distributed must now be consolidated, here. Ice Station Zebra is about to boil over, and business-crazed couriers fresh from private jets keep bursting in here demanding uploads to Shenzhou. Shenzhou claims everything is fine but nobody believes them. Tickets and tickets and tickets of Trouble flutter down from on high. Glen Lotz exudes the odor of the damned, and dutifully conveys to us the screaming babble of a terrified upper management. The Chad Squad builds up emergency flotation devices from hot spares, as Grunts 1 & 2 jury-rig an emergency data center in the Footwear History Library, as I re-route configurations and re-configure routers until my fingertips are numb, and I suddenly remember that none of this compares to you.

Meanwhile, the rest of the company decided it was time for Friday Party. That's where I found you, Angela Fine: in the outdoor picnic/bungee area where our international sportswear company division throw its employees the same party every other Friday. The mood was nervous, habitual, bleakly festive. Sportswear professionals picked at high-fiber hors d'oeuvres, or dangled tentatively from the Bungee Mesa, or warded off the shock of the crazy news with light beer and cheap jokes. You sat alone on a bench, smiling absently, staring out into the parking lot with a look on your face that even I, keen observer, could not fathom, nibbling on a carrot stick in a way that ties Lassie in knots, and twisting fretfully at the cap of your non-twist-cap beer.

I opened that beer for you, Angela, with my trusty pocket tool, as I would open for you all beers, all boxes, all bags of chips, all cartons of milk, all doors, all windows, my savings account, my checking account, my mint-condition polyvinyl anime figurines, my heart, my soul, the fly of my trousers, everything I have, for you, if you would just let me. I opened your beer, and handed it to you, and spoke my most heroic word:

"Fixed."

"Oh, Jack! I'm—" was your three word reply ...

... before the HORRIBLE NOISE. The wretched, bastard CANCELLATION of all other sounds, the primal metallic GRUNT of the oversized air horn of the rectal-black Camero of the square-headed, cop-mustached, surf-Nazi coke dealer who beats you, who honks at you from the basketball/parking court and beats you, who yells "Hey sweet-cheeks! Let's move it huh?" and HONKS his horn at you again, HONKS HONKS HONKS his horn at you, in front of your entire department ... and who also, incidentally, beats you.

I observed you keenly. I watched your mind parse his dial-tone, in discrete procedural steps:

```
   If A(ngela),
  then B(oyfriend);
If B(oyfriend), then {
   C(ock),
   C(ruelty),
   C(amero)
  }.
```

"Have a nice weekend, Jack," are the other five things you said to me in your desperately cheerful voice as you gathered up your purse and put down your beer and walked out into the parking lot of your ongoing abuse and boarded the muscle car of your destruction.

I screamed, but you didn't hear me. You heard tires squealing and jock-rock blaring from the stereo. I threw the rest of your beer at that Camero, but you didn't see the foamy broken glass. It didn't reach you ... I throw like a girl.

I tried to chase you, but was restrained by the Chad Squad:

"Jack Jack hey! Hey Jack. Woah Jack. Don't crash."

I couldn't form words, only angry moans and spittle in my throat, as a cloud of uncombusted Camero exhaust blew back over me like piss.

"You're crashing, Jack. Reboot!" pleaded Chad D.

"Here, eat chips," begged Chad W. "Salty goodness! Drink Fresca ... stabilize ... stabilize ..."

Chad and Chad sat me down and fed me and watched me and held my hand, addressing my malfunction, while the iron bands of hatred around my head and my penis slowly loosened and fell away.

"Sorry ... sorry guys ... inappropriate freak-out, sorry."

"Fuck of a day, man," said Chad D. "Too many tickets. Too much trouble."

Sat Aug 09 00:23:11 PDT 2008:

We stayed late, cleaning up the mess, filing the files, flushing the routes, stabilizing the patient. The patient will live. The Internet, I'm not so sure. This is the Worst Storm Ever, easily, but all over the world, sysadmins and NOC workers are laying hands on the Internet, massaging it, keeping it up. The porn, as we say, must flow.

Today, sixty-one percent of legitimate Internet traffic is pornography. Those pornographers pay their bills and attend trade conferences and have customer relations managers. Their explicit depictions of sexual acts are legitimate, solicited traffic. To a significant degree, pornography subsidizes all other solicited Internet traffic. But today legitimate, solicited traffic is down to just over thirty-one percent of overall packets. The rest is spam.

At the end of the twentieth century, humankind pooled billions of dollars and millions of hours of genius-engineer-sweat, in an unprecedented spirit of cooperation and market freedom, to create the capstone of human progress we call the Internet: a vast intelligent self-healing network of digitized ideas, speaking directly to all mankind, connecting us all to one another at the speed of thought ... and the Internet, in gratitude, constantly and tactlessly urges all humankind to enlarge its penises, enhance its breasts, lose its unsightly fat, attach vibrating pleasure toys to its genitals, ingest all kinds of drugs, and gaze endlessly into its bottomless pool of explicit multimedia pansexual exploitation, the greatest horde of pornography that has ever existed.

Maybe the Internet is hot for us. Maybe it wants our monster cocks.

I got home sometime after midnight. Chad and Chad offered to give me a lift; I tried to convince them I'd rather ride my bicycle. I took a long shower at the Olympic skatepark/pool, waiting for them to give up on me. When I came out I didn't see them, but to be safe I got on my bike and rode out Victory Drive, down Victory Circle, left on Victory Expressway, left on Sportsmanship Boulevard, up the unused multi-use path, and back to Retired Hardware Five, where I slipped through the deactivated fire exit, unseen.

I live at work. Why not? Work is my life. Retired Hardware Five is storage enough for me, my movies, my collections. And my Lassie. Lassie is happy here, I think. And all this retired hardware, that blinked and beeped and toiled for us, and told us everything it knew ... I don't know, I just feel it deserves to be remembered. Kept company. Honored, somehow. I still find it beautiful.

I used to have an apartment, but I never went there. And then I got a little too overextended into polyvinyl figurines, a bit maxed out ... I stopped paying the rent and I stopped going home, and life has hardly changed in the six months since.

I'm burnt out. Today's anger and hatred and tension are just a few loose embers knocking around in the ash-pit of my heart. I want sleep ... but Lassie won't let me. Lassie wants to play.

I can't, I protest. But Lassie insists. Poor Lassie ...

Okay. I haven't watched Monster Cocks Six in a while. I cue up the DVD in my trusty lap-mate, stretch out on my styro-peanut beanbag bed, and release my pet from his cage ...

Lassie! You startled me, you're so huge! You've been busy! You're really on your way to Monster Cock status! Rod Girder would be proud of you! So heavy, so thick ... how long? Eleven? No! That can't be right ... eleven! That's enormous! The implications ... I'm reeling! I think you've made it into the top tenth, the top twentieth maybe, of all penis measurements worldwide. I really wish cocksmiths.com would come back up. People need to meet you. You need to come out and shine.

Menu screen. Flying logo. Credits. Fade in ... I'm Rod Girder, welcome to my world ... blah blah blah, asses, a swimming pool, more blah blah blah, Lana Liason raises an eyebrow, a brief attempt at acting as she slips off Rod's loose-fitting trousers and gets slapped in the face by his half-hard meat. Suck suck suck, etc ... yawn. Lana Liason is slightly cross-eyed. She's a big fake. She bleaches her eyebrows in a way that's so slutty it's revolting. She looks nothing like Angela Fine. No porn star comes close. I start to rub some lotion on Lassie anyway, but he rears up and wriggles away from me, peering at me with his two little white eyes. Sometimes he looks like a real snake, a scary cobra ... but he's not scary, he's my Lassie. C'mere, Lassie. You like this stuff, it soothes the itch.

Lassie doesn't want that. Lassie wants something else.

What is it, Lassie? What's the trouble? What do you want?

No.

Sorry Lassie, no. No Monsterizer tonight.

Lassie, listen: you are *so* big. Epic, you are! And growing, still! I'm proud of you, but frankly, I don' t know how much more you're going to grow even without another monsterization. I've been thinking about this, and I've decided ... we need to wait, Lassie.

Oh fucking hell, Lassie. Stop doing this to me. I said no. What is sexy about the Monsterizer? The Monsterizer *hurts*, Lassie. It makes you red and itchy. You don't want that. I don't want that. I don't want ... Lassie, please ...

You know ... come to think of it ... yes, I do want it. I want it really severely and immediately. In fact, I have absolutely, positively, 100% for sure got to stick my BIG new COCK in that Monsterizer this FUCKING minute! Right now, oh yeah, oh baby, it's ON!

Rod Girder is flipping Lana Liason over on the poolside recliner, and I'm tearing through the disorganized debris on the concrete floor by my beanbag ... where is it? Shit! Where did I put it? Where's the Monsterizer? Oh shit, shit, shit ...

What's that, Lassie? Where are you pointing? Under the bean bag ... yes! The fucking MONSTERIZER! Good boy! C'mere, baby ... oh God I need to feel my Lassie in the cold hard metal jaws of that thing, yes! Its plastic pistol GRIP, oh yeah, it's a tight squeeze, OW, because we're so BIG, OW, yeah, OW, yeah, the TEETH! OW, OW, OW ... it's coming, Lassie, hang on, here it comes ... NOW!

I pull the trigger, the Monsterizer sinks its fang deep into Lassie's neck, and all at once: cuntfulls, assfulls, mouthfulls, Angelafulls of semen come screaming out of me, my testicles shuddering, my ass kicking space, Lassie spitting and spitting semen in giant arcs across the room, pink semen, all over my Lapmate, my bean-bag, my polyvinyl figurines, my Xbox, everything covered in pink semen, FUCK! Come on, Lassie! Come ON! Lassie writhes, twitches, and spits, FUCK! My spine, my feet, my mind, still coming, still pumping, yards of semen, quarts of semen, pints of red semen ... Oh! Ride it, Lassie! Squeeze it! Push it! Good boy, Lassie! Don't stop! Don't let it go! I'm spinning, I'm falling, I'm floating, I'm coming, I'm bleeding, oh God, bloody red semen, all over me, yes! I'm passing out, I'm dying, I'm dying so good ... oh, Lassie ... oh dear ... I never knew ... it could be ... so fucking good ... keep going, Lassie ... run ... get Angela ... get help ...

Mon Aug 11 06:23:40 PDT 2008:

Update: that never happened. Absolutely did not happen. I don't know what happened Friday night but it wasn't that. Something, though, something happened. While I slept all weekend long, something crawled into Retired Hardware Five and killed and ate some other thing. Racoons? Maybe ... gore on the floor, slime on the ceiling, bloody tracks leading all over the place, Jesus ... well, it was dark when I left. Maybe it's not so bad in the light. Maybe.

One of the many advantages of living in Retired Hardware Five was not needing to clean. But now ... well, this just means that it's even more urgent that Angela and I get together, that I tell her how I feel, that I show her what I've got to offer, that she see the clear logic and beauty of choosing me over that stone-headed dickweed in the black Camaro, and that we eventually find a nice apartment together.

Only ... I crept across campus at dawn and made it here to the showers without being seen, to wash away the gore and scum and whatever. But now, here I am, faced with a large and new SEXUAL PROBLEM.

Large. Vast. Containing multitudes.

It never occurred to me before, but there must be certain hardships in the glamorous porn-star life of Rod Girder. Issues of tailoring, for instance. Difficulty bending over. A light-headedness when a limited supply of blood rushes downward, away from the brain. Discomfort in chairs. And ... I don't know if Ron Girder has this particular problem, but: it just won't sit still. It won't stop jumping around, writhing like a snake. It's agitated.

Sit, Lassie. Heel!

Lassie won't sit or heel. Lassie won't stop thrashing around. He has three angry eyes and he's bigger than my forearm. It takes two hands to pin him down.

Absolutely no more Monsterizer. No more. None. This is enough. This is plenty of monster. Beyond satisfying. Lassie, I love you but you've got to start watching your weight. I'm sure that once we lay off the device for a few days, you will quit freaking out and start getting with the program. We have an important mission, Lassie. You mustn't act like this around Angela!

It's a cable management problem, really. I always carry a few spare velcro straps and some zip ties to keep unruly cables from tripping me up. The Trouble Center runs a tight ship. Lassie, I'm sorry but you're being very bad, and I need to get to work, I don't have time for this. I'll make it up to you, I promise. Please, Lassie, quit struggling!

It's Monday, so I have clean clothes. Underwear, though, is just not happening. (Ron Girder never wears underwear either. I can get used to that.) Parachute pants will have to do, and a black company tee with the ISC logo on the reverse, and on the obverse our corporate motto: Just Do It. And a struggling, squirming penis strapped tightly, painfully, to my right leg.

This can't be right. I mean, it's great —I dreamed of this, I need this, I love my Lassie, I just ... I need to talk to goldenrod13, small_paul, mosquitoboy, any of them. The elder cocksmiths, farther down the path than I. Cocksmiths.com, I need you!

Mon Aug 11 13:23:40 PDT 2008:

Good morning! Today the Trouble Center snorkles in the following biblical flood of Trouble: the East Coast and much of the Midwest now enjoy what the President refuses to call "martial law," as power stations continue to explode and everything even remotely attached to the Internet goes absolutely batshit. TV is dark, cell phones are dark, rumors are rampant. One internet-simulcasting radio station situated right on top of a hydroelectric dam on a river in upstate New York is managing to calm everybody down over there by reporting as fact the comforting rumor that an organized gang of serial killers is raping and stabbing and smashing its way from Newport to Miami. The Army and the National Guard and even the INS are busy securing the interstates and shooting people by accident and generally whipping up the panic level, setting up checkpoints from Minnesota to Texas and marching slowly eastward to figure out what, if anything, is happening. Information junkies nationwide, sick without their fix, are going through some bad cold turkey, clearly, and seeing shit that isn't real. People on the east coast do not know how to relax. It's utterly stupid.

Here in Trouble Central, we are urgently but methodically cauterizing the stumps of our network, backing up our most crucial ones and zeroes, and groping through the mudslide of spam for solid servers that respond to pings. Amazingly, a few legit packets still flow across the network and back. Sysadmins worldwide are falling back to UUCP, BBSes and pinging in morse code. (Geriatric FIDONET users, all four of them, wag their fingers at the Internet and, I assume, exchange smug notes about how right they were all along.) Mid-upper-management has given up on spring sportswear shipments, projections, tracking, accounting, given up on accomplishing any actual things at all, and wants only information. Unsuccessful probing suggests our German competition is equally bogged down in equally thick data quicksand, and mid-upper-management finds this somehow comforting. Shenzhou, when online, insists everything is fine and under control with such vehemence that we assume they are smoking opium—which we've caught them doing before.

Phil Tong thinks it's a virus. Phil Tong barges into Trouble Center with a crazed look in his eye and insists it's a virus, a virus, it's got to be a virus, demands to know if we morons have even considered the possibility that it might be a virus, and if not why not? The Chad Squad, ever vigilant, jumps on Glen Lotz and restrains him before Glen can jump on Phil Tong and strangle him by his coffee-stained tie. Phil Tong warns us not to touch him and lurches away, limping.

Users think everything is a virus. Yes, sure, that's part of it, self-replicating spam-bots are part of the Spamscape, have been for years. But they've never had this kind of traction. Somebody fucked up somewhere, some major door was left unlocked, left wide open, and in flowed the slime. Somewhere in Estonia, pimply pre-teen uberhackers are giggling and high-fiving each other. Won't somebody please shoot them?

Meanwhile: Chad D. and Chad W. are fucking heroes! The same stress that's driving Phil Tong to nervous breakdown only makes these guys work harder, think clearer, do more. No complaints, no freakouts, they just keep hacking through the tickets like spartans on the battlefield. Outside a shitstorm of mad trouble is sweeping west, but the troubles of IT are rational and we will fix them. This trouble keeps us sane.

Our firewall is under constant attack on all channels. All known weaknesses of its OS and the OS it masquerades as are probed on all protocols: IP4, IP6, ATM; BGP forgeries, timing attacks, brute force token storms, SNMP probes. The mail daemon is hammered senseless by wave upon crashing pungent wave of spam that leaves it stammering: ELHO? QUIT! ELHO? But the bulkheads are holding. The patches are watertight. The ship will not sink. And if I lash myself to the mast, I can send out signals on the open sea.

Mon Aug 11 23:23:40 PDT 2008:

It's very late. I'm in my corner cube, taking a break ... sending out an SOS to 8.231.11.22.

Ping? Ack? Knock knock? Hello? I knock 100 times on their front door ... three pings come back.

Their website is down, their mail gateway is down, but cocksmiths.com is not dead yet. I telnet to the quickchat port as I rummage through my memory for the format of this fairly stupid yet mysteriously popular chat dialect. Slow as molasses my packets march across the battlefield, arriving truncated and misaligned. Slow as glaciers, the reply advances back across the carnage. The remote qchat daemon asks:

```
001 YES?

200 USER goldenrod13 QCHAT_REQ(l=10):
its 2 big.

.... 301 BUMMER: USER NOT AVAILABLE.

200 USER small_paul QCHAT_REQ(l=28):
everythings going major nuts.

.... 301 BUMMER: USER NOT AVAILABLE.

200 USER mosquitoboy QCHAT_REQ (l=17):
wheres everybody?

.... 302 HARSH: REQUEST DENIED.
```

```
200 USER mosquitoboy QCHAT
_REQ (l=102):
hello? help me! its getting
bigger & its getting inside
my mind! How do I stop? Did
this happen to you?

.... 302 HARSH: REQUEST DE-
NIED.

200 USER mosquitoboy
QCHAT_REQ(l=28;pri=1): MB:
is it inside your mind 2?

.... 666 BOGUS: CHAT TERMI-
NATED.
```

"Hey Jack?"

Chad D. pokes his round head into my square workspace with his worry face on. He looks like caffeine death, all pale and twitchy and his meager supply of hair sticking out sideways. I can't imagine how I must look. But that's what the world looks like today.

"Jack, there's some dudes here ..."

Chad indicates behind him with his thumb, where stands a tall, grey-haired man in baggy black clothes, looking at me like I'm some kind of bug. A note-pad sticks out of the lapel pocket of his jacket. Behind him stand two cops—a bald one and a young one—and behind the two cops stands Glen Lotz, mouth opening and closing but no words coming out, and three campus security guards, dumb & zealous, ready to help with any insecurity that two cops and a police detective can't handle.

"Hi, mister, um ... Stalker? Can I call you Jack?"

I nod.

He smiles like a used-car salesman and speaks to me slowly, clearly, just in case I am retarded: "Thank you. My name's Malcolm Dean, I'm a police inspector." He extends a cautious handshake request. "I'm sorry to interrupt you, I know everybody's up to their neck in problems today ..."

"Friday."

He raises an eyebrow. "Friday?"

"Friday was my neck. Today's deeper."

"Is it?" He glances to the bald cop—a short, squinty fellow—who looks at me, smirks and issues a single muffled guffaw, as if to say: even my relatively small cop penis is larger than this jerkoff's penis. If he only knew.

"Jack," says the inspector, looking at me like I'm lunch and he's starving, "we need to talk about Friday."

Mon Aug 11 23:45:01 PDT 2008:

We talk in the Footwear History Library. Famous shoes, and digitally-antiqued photographs of the track-and-field stars who wore them to fame, shingle the walls. Shoved up against the famous footwear are commandeered desks and tables covered with hacked-together spare servers in crooked piles, some booted, some crashed, some with their guts spilling out their sides. A precarious tower of cannibalized workstation parts totters in one corner. The temperature is 81.5 degrees Fahrenheit. The whine of hard disks and cooling fans sounds like a swarm of killer bees. Data cable hangs down from the ceiling. The Inspector and I sit, facing, in ergonomic task chairs. The cops stand.

The Inspector hands me a photograph. "You know this guy?"

The guy in the photo looks like your basic mullet-headed surf-Nazi.

"Dates a friend of yours? Drives a black Camaro?"

"I think I've seen him, yeah. Once or twice."

"Thrown a beer at him, ever?"

"*Once.*"

"Well, that's it. Once is all you get. Nobody gets to throw anything at Rock Short any more." The Inspector snatches the photograph away.

"What do you mean ... is he dead?"

"*Oh,* yes. *So* dead." The Inspector places quotes around the word with his fingers. "'Dead', is the nice way to put it. 'Murdered,' is more correct, but still too nice. 'Brutally strangled and bludgeoned to death' is still actually leaving out the really nasty part of what happened to Rock Short. On Friday."

He leans close to me, leering at me with a consumed, fascinated expression, like I'm his pornography, like I'm turning him on. My head pounds ... I feel dizzy ... Lassie nudges me, taps on my knee. (Shut up, Lassie!)

"Wow," I reply. "Wow. That's really awful. Did you catch the guy?"

The Inspector leaps up out of his chair and kicks it against the wall.

"Jack! Listen! I have a theory that you are extremely smart! Maybe even smarter than me! So don't ask me stupid questions! You're connected, aren't you? In that room of yours? You've still got Internet. You know what's going on as well as anybody! It's the RFEs!"

RFEs? My mind launches a desperate bubble-sort of its three-letter-acronym cache as Lassie starts to twitch and twist. RFEs? I read lots of RFCs, used to play an RME, correspond with EFR, I'm over-exposed to RF ... I look at the two officers and even they, behind their stoic cop facades, betray just a hint of WTF? regarding RFEs.

"The ... requests for enhancement?" I weakly suggest, my right foot tapping the floor.

Inspector Dean glares meaningfully at his two cops, and they leave the room, shutting and locking it behind them.

"The RFEs. The Rampaging Fuckers of Everything. You know."

With all the things hanging in the stale hot air of this room that I'd like to not know, I am really actually excited and happy to truly, utterly not know anything at all about this one.

"RFEs. Sorry ... please, tell me. RFEs?"

"You're an Internet guy. It's an Internet thing. That's how they organize! They're trading pictures in their chat-rooms and one-upping each other. Rampaging and fucking. Raping and killing. Do you have any idea how many people have been rampaged and fucked in this country in the last week? Men and women and *children*? And *pets*? Any idea? Venture a guess?"

"I've heard some stuff, but ... rumors!"

"I've *seen* some stuff. Photos! Yeah: because I am Homicide, because I hate murder and love peace and justice, I am the lucky fucker who gets to look at, and analyze, and organize and file that particular sickening, sick *cabinet* of photos! They thought it was one guy, and then they thought it was a gang of guys, but no, it's bigger. It's a *trend!* And I'm the guy, I'm the one who has to ... has to ... *aaaah!*"

For a moment I think he's going to hit me, or cry, or throw up. He pulls his hair and squeezes his face ... but then, robot-like, he switches it all off.

"Sorry, Jack. Rough couple of days. But hey: don't just take my word for it. Wanna see some photos, Jack? Hmm?"

Lassie ... heel!

He smiles, leering. "What is it, Jack? Can't sit still? Excited? You like the photos, right? How about DVDs, Jack? You like porno, don't you? C'mon, everybody likes porno. Snuff films? The hard stuff!"

"No! Excuse me, Inspector, but you're grossing me out!"

Inspector Dean throws back his head and laughs ... while, at what might be the least erotic moment of my entire life, Lassie strains against his seven plastic leashes. Bad Lassie! Down, boy!

Smiling Inspector Dean: "Hey, okay, fine. Sorry. Forget about that, forget that. What about, you know ... what-do-they-call-em? Plastic toys. Of superheroes and stuff? Little rubber guys who fight and smash each other?"

"Collectable figurines."

"Fig-u-rines! Right! You collect 'em, don't you?"

"What's that got to do with anything? Yes!"

Lassie! Stop! That feels good, but

... stop!

"Where do you keep 'em?"

"At *home! Stop!"*

"Oh yeah? Where's home, Jack? Where do you live? 'Cause your boss doesn't know, and nobody else around here knows, and *I* sure don't know but, if I ask you where you were on Friday night and you say 'home' then, I'm like, I wanna know—Woah! Hey, you going somewhere?"

"No! My foot's asleep! *Sit!*" Inspector Dean takes several steps back as I start stamping my foot on the floor. Oh, it twitches! It itches! It burns! Lassie!

"No. *I'll* stand. *You* sit."

Oh boy. "Listen, please ... Inspector ... I haven't done anything, and I don't want to talk to you, and right now is a really shitty time anyway, and, just, I think you better leave."

"No. I'll stay. And you'll tell me whose blood we found on your bean-bag!"

I flop down in the chair, and hear the muffled pop of a zip tie snapping near my knee. Blood rushes in my ears. I'm getting light-headed. Staring at the ceiling. Oh no.

"Please, Inspector—"

"Please, *shut up!* And then, after the blood issue, and the issue of your beef with Dean Short, we'll talk about the RFEs—because I really think a computer guy, an Internet guy like you, is who I need to talk to about that."

Oh, oh, oh. Oh no. Another zip tie pops. I lean back in my chair, closing my eyes. The feeling, the pain, the pressure is exquisite. The whine of disk drives and overworked air conditioning gets louder in my ears while Lassie, oh, Lassie ... you scoundrel, Lassie!

The Inspector looms over me, sneering. I am pale and weak and tingly all over.

"But then, Jack, what I really want to know is: who else? I know you didn't do it alone. That I cannot picture. Those two badges in the hall can't picture it either, and they've seen all *kinds* of guys kill all *kinds* of guys. But you? Against Dean Short? You against *anybody*? Hah! Don't think so!"

Pop! Pop! Oh fuck. Oh no. Oh Lassie, please don't do that! Please don't make me want you to do that!

"How did you do it?" he demands. "Who helped you? What did you *use?"* Then he hears the snapping sound, looks down ... inspects my twitching pant leg, and the angry hostage struggling beneath. His eyes quiver with curiosity.

"Whatcha packing there, Jack?" Staring right into my eyes he reaches a slow hand toward the top pocket on the right thigh of my parachute pants BUT

Despite all this, despite the terrible truths in this room, despite the proximity of the sweat-stinking Inspector's hand, electrical messages of pure happiness and romantic affection and wholesome copulation begin to gather in my fingers and toes, the back of my neck, the tip of my tongue, tickling my nipples and my anus, my knees, my hips, my spine, rushing, throbbing, pounding, pushing through me, jerking me around AND

Inspector Dean freezes and stares, with utter stupid confusion mixed with revulsion and a hint of concern, at the shape in my pocket WHEN

Tue Aug 12 00:00:00 PDT 2008:

Like a whip, like a bear-trap, like a cobra striking, large, long, thick and terrifying: Lassie the Monster Cock bursts through my pant leg with a noisy slash, seizes Inspector Dean by the neck, wrapping twice around it, and throttles him with hard, white turgid clenches ... of PLEASURE!

But Lassie ... wait ... no! Slow down, Lassie! This is wrong ... I'm not into this! Please, let's try something else ... I try to pull him off but I can't even reach around him with both hands now. Oh Jesus, Lassie ... you're bigger than the both of us! The Inspector scuffles weakly at the floor with his treadless cop shoes, he claws desperately at your veiny flesh around his neck, Lassie, as you hoist him higher. You PUSH, and you SQUEEZE, and with your remaining length you smack and smash and batter the fat purple hammer of your head against his red, puffed up face, stabbing and bludgeoning over and over, demanding entrance to his ears, his nose, his eyes.

Lassie, stop! I am not comfortable with this! I don't like it, Lassie!

We fall to the floor, a tangle of desperate limbs struggling in a puddle of blood and teeth. I jam my feet against the Inspector's chest and head and pull with all the strength in my legs, as my testes start to quiver. Don't make me do this, Lassie! Don't make me feel like this while you do that!

A single muffled gurgle of defiance escapes the Inspector's throat. He pounds uselessly with his fists. I want to call for help but I'm hyperventilating, quaking, out of breath ...

Cable management! I reach my pocket and find one extra-large zip tie—the size I always carry but never seem to need! I wrap it around the root, the base, the interlink ... and I pull it tight with both of my weak hands. And you'd better believe: it hurts!

Bad Lassie! Bad penis! Not Allowed! Down! Straight to bed you go! I am cinching the strap, yanking upward as the wire-reinforced plastic zip-tie digs deep into your flesh!

The pain jabs through us like a rusty razor. You whip around to see, your three little white eyes full of dumb animal murder. With your remaining length you swat at me, but you can't quite reach all the way from my crotch to his neck, around it twice and all the way back to my face, not yet, not quite ... so you wrap yourself once more around the policeman's head. You're mad, Lassie, you are just furious, oh yes, you are thrashing, squeezing, raging, hissing and spitting! I've got the tip of the zip-tie between my teeth, I'm pulling with all my back and shoulders as I'm pushing with all my legs as you are throbbing, clenching, tightening, as Inspector Dean struggles, weakly ...

I feel like I'm ripping out my own insides ... and I think we're going to come.

Inspector Dean shudders out a last gagging puff of air, and Lassie dives deep down the dead policeman's throat! Cramming deeper as the wave begins to crest, as I begin to scream! The pain! The flesh! The body and the blood! The blood!

With a ripping, a snapping, and a wet, foetal POP ... Lassie drops our connection, unplugs, slips her leash. A massive weight and leverage falls away from me, a deep ache replaces it, and I'm alone.

Lassie slinks under a corner table with his meal, trailing the tips of vessels we once shared. I observe him keenly, watching him feed: he regurgitates a steaming pink venom, pumping it into the dead man's head and down his throat. Then: crawling deeper, squeezing earthwormlike down the bulging dead neck, exploring the entrails, sniffing and tasting. Exiting from his ass or some self-torn opening a few minutes later, and finally peeping, slick with gore and shit, from a pant leg. A small silver tongue or proboscis flits in and out of Lassie's tiny mouth, licking the blood away from his three little eyes that stare at me, innocently, questioningly.

"Oh, Lassie! You bad, bad penis! How could you?"

Lassie cowers in the dead policeman's pant leg, shy, afraid. Ashamed.

"Lassie! You can't kill policemen! You can't eat people! You're for sex, Lassie! For human pleasure!"

Lassie slithers out of the pant legs, head hung low, whimpering like a pup. Lassie is sorry.

"Look, I know you were trying to protect me. Probably. Right?"

Lassie sits up, staring at me. Blood on his chin. His ragged tail wagging. And those eyes ... my penis ... my big little Lassie ...

"Lassie ... you killed Rock too, didn't you? The surf-Nazi?"

Lassie bobs up and down, proud, excited, happy.

"Oh Lassie ... what will I do with you?"

That really excellent and pressing question—what to do, exactly, with my seven-foot-long bloodthirsty pet anaconda cock-monster, who just ripped free of my crotch and ate the policeman who thinks I murdered the abusive boyfriend of Angela Fine—and another, perhaps even more pressing question—how do I explain all this to Angela Fine, and make her understand that I did it all for her, for love, and how beautiful that is, and that the evil, morally repugnant part I didn't even do myself, not exactly, because I am so good, but at least she is now free, safe, Rock can't crush her any more, and that I love her more than love itself and will take care of her forever and make her happy in every way that doesn't specifically require me having a penis any more—these two questions overwrite each other, back and forth, on the filesystem of my head, consuming me, hanging me, crashing me ...

Because I am desperate to feel less weird, I grab a roll of duct tape from the parts pile and tape shut the crotch of my shredded parachute pants. As I do so I glimpse the empty socket, the disconnected port of flesh, the land where proud, mighty genitals once roamed ...

And then I see nothing at all, because power, finally, fails. The deafening whir of tiny high-speed spinning things spins down, slowly, to silence and a phantom ringing in my ears. The failure has finally reached us.

On the other side of the Footwear History Library door I hear an approaching scuttle of footsteps, and then an urgent pounding at the door and jingling of keys. Above me I hear a rattling of dangling data cable and a knocking aside of ceiling panels. I try to find my voice ...

"Who is it?"

It's the Chad Squad. "Jack? Are you done in there? We seriously need you in Trouble."

Tue Aug 12 00:17:40 PDT 2008:

Good morning! It's a brand new day, and already the Trouble Center is teetering on the precipice of the following gaping chasm of Trouble: the spam has sidestepped our Maginot Line, jumping the firewall in Shenzhou instead, and is pouring in through the VPN, choking us; ours is the last stable electrical grid in America; Rampaging Fuckers of Everything are apparently less rumored and more actual than initially estimated— rampaging and fucking nationwide, transcontinentally, and even in Europe, according to Netops Grunt Two, who has cleverly jury-rigged an API satellite news feed to a small barricaded zone under his desk, where he has horded food and which he refuses to leave. The Army and the National Guard and the INS are incommunicado, missing, presumed fucked. The Air Force is in midair and intends to stay there. The President is underground. Homeland Security has fled.

Also: Phil Tong has a gun, he has Glen Lotz in a half-nelson, and he wants us to "stop the Internet"—not just our small fragment of Internet but the whole world-wide shebang—for reasons that he can't articulate. Grunt One asked him to file a ticket, and is now bleeding from a hole in his neck.

And me? I cannot deal. I cannot deal at all! Impossible hell is tumbling down on me from all sides! Chad W. and Chad D. look at me with infinite reserves of tiredness in their eyes, waiting for me to finish crying.

I want my figurines! I want Angela! If I found her, if we ran away together, would it matter? Have the RFEs already gotten her? What can we do, Chad and Chad and Glen and I, about trouble on this level? Does anything in Trouble Center matter, really, compared to the last unspeakable half-hour?

I don't know what else to do, I really don't. Chad and Chad wait, needing to act, needing to fix, needing to support the IT mission. It is our purpose. It is all we know.

So I send them to yank all the

WADSLAPs, take us off-line ... and then I enter the Trouble Center.

Tue Aug 12 00:23:11 PDT 2008:

Something's wrong with Phil Tong. He's sitting upon Glen Lotz, on the institutional gray carpet floor in the center of the Trouble Center. Under the sodium vapor emergency backup lights his skin is corpse-like and blue. His breathing is shallow. Something is causing him pain—he's curled up in a ball, clutching his belly, pointing his gun at Glen, then at me. Glen, a portrait of stillness and fear, still manages in a single glance to communicate all of mid-upper-management's anxieties.

"Shut it down!" roars Phil. "Cut it off! It's got to die!"

I search deep within myself for a kind, understanding tone of voice to use with Phil Tong. "Phil, listen ... please ... there's things we can do, and things we can't."

"Don't tell me you don't know, Jack! Hah! I've been watching you."

"What have you been watching me do, Phil? Tighten the D-Links?"

Phil is momentarily confused. "No ... the treatment!" he says, leveling a finger at me. "The cure."

His eyes quiver with madness and pain. He's not, he must, he's ...

"It's hellfire! The devil's on the network! Jack ... he's uploaded me! And he's uploaded you! And he's coming out! He's coming out! Oh yes! The Internet is a vein of contagation!"

"I ... I don't disagree with you, Phil, but the verb 'to upload'—"

"Good and evil, Jack! Not ones and zeroes. *Evil!*"

"Listen, Phil, the Internet is literally millions of miles of fiber-optics and copper cable —"

"Maggots! Worms! Demons!"

"— millions of routers in millions of places, around the world, we *can't* just switch it on and off for you like a desk lamp! It's a system, with procedures! And administrators, IT professionals—

He snorts in utter, utter contempt.

"— working night and day right now to *solve* this! Things are going to get better, Phil! This is all going to pass ... in a few days ..."

Phil Tong gives me a you're-such-an-idiot expression so heartfelt it's almost touching. He looks at the back of Glen Lotz' whimpering head, looks at his gun ... and kneels on Glen's back in humble prayer, whispering the words under his hitching, shallow breath. He's blue as a vein. Bleeding.

"Okay Phil: the cure, yes. Bad. Very bad. I know that now! *I'm not stupid.*"

He's gotten to thy will be done ...

"But I don't see what that's got to do with the network!"

... he's on the daily bread ... the trespasses ...

"What do you know that I don't know, Phil? Phil?"

.. received the delivery ... entered the kingdom ...

"Phil, tell me what you know! Phil!"

... the power, the glory, forever ... Amen.

And the brains of Phil Tong rain down on us like tickets.

Tue Aug 12 00:29:23 PDT 2008:

I stagger out the back door of Trouble as cops and guards and mid-upper-management pour in the front. No more Trouble, please. I'm done. I just want some diet Fresca. I run through the emergency-lit hallways to the drink/snack/shuffleboard area, but the Fresca machine is down, so I run off towards the wiring closet to grab a spare fifty foot power cord so I can bring up the Fresca machine on redundant power, because that, I know, will work, and I need to fix something very badly right now. Passing a window I look out on the International Sportswear Campus and see a field of red and white and blue spinning lights. A rising tide of cops is licking the shoreline of International Sportswear. Searching for their fallen brother.

And I hear things in the ceiling.

I grab the cord and a few more cable ties. I take the long way back, through Information Receiving, through Marketing/Weightlifting, down the stairs, past the conference gym, up the stairs, past the padded offices of mid-upper management, around through Payroll and back to the drink/snack/shuffleboard area, and I listen:

Things are definitely in the ceiling. Big things.

I run down the hall to the nearest wiring closet and find some redundant power in the very last redundant power jack, and run it back and climb under the Fresca machine to find: a sticky, sugary mess and a total, utter failure of cable management. The minimum-wage soda techs who drive around servicing these machines are always watching the clock and just don't give a damn. I unknot and untwist and unplug all the cords from the one sticky power strip and try each of them, one at a time, in my live cable, until I see the backlit plastic close-up of the Fresca bubbles blink to life.

I fill my cup with ice and diet Fresca, and sip it, listening to the ceiling things.

Everybody has a drug. Mine is diet Fresca. And porn, too, I suppose ... but mostly diet Fresca. It keeps me steady, helps me think.

The ceiling things are restless. They're coming and going, wandering around, looking for something.

Downstairs, expensive panes of corporate glass are smashing in. Cop radios are cackling with nervous cop talk. I really don't think this is a good time for me to talk to them. I need to disappear.

Tue Aug 12 00:41:28 PDT 2008:

On my way to the Offline Backup Storage Vault, I run straight into Angela Fine!

Who sees me, and screams.

"Angela! Hey! Shhh!" Angela is panting, staring, a terrified, trapped thing. She's wearing a bathrobe and an oversized men's leather jacket, the sort of thing Rock would wear. She's clutching it tightly around her and stroking the leather lapel with the long, slender fingers of one hand. Her hair is all messy but it smells like summer, and there is nobody I could ever be more happy to see. I grab her and hold her and show her I'm friendly.

Downstairs and far away, the police announce through megaphones: WE ARE THE POLICE!

"Jack ..." Angela stands perfectly stock still, rigid and trembling, with a painful, worried smile on her beautiful round face. I step back.

"Angela ... wow! Hi! It's ... funny you're here!"

Her beautiful brown eyes stare unblinking into mine.

"Jack ... what's that on you?"

"Oh, gee ... brains I think. Phil Tong's. Sorry."

She whimpers, and stares.

Downstairs and far away, the police blare: COME OUT NOW!

"Angela ... can I get you a Fresca?"

Her voice is a quiet, desperate squeak. "Please don't kill me, Jack."

Oh no. This is completely backwards.

"Angela ... no! No way, never *ever* would I do that!"

"Okay! Sorry!" She's frozen like a deer in the headlights.

"No, *really* you have to believe me! I didn't kill that guy. Your boyfriend? Whoever. It wasn't me!"

"Okay. I believe you. Just ... don't kill me," she sobs, terrified and sad.

"I've been worried, actually, about you! With all this stuff happening ... Angela, what are you even *doing* here?"

Downstairs and far away, the police yell: WE ARE COMING IN!

"They brought me here," she says, nodding toward the loud stairwell, "they want me to talk to you. Actually ..." She breathes in a deep breath of air, shakes her beautiful head, exhales sweet perfume. "I don't really know why they brought me. I don't think they know what they're doing. They're just running all over looking for you. They're scared. They're losing. They say you raped all those people, and ..."

Downstairs and far away, the police yell: THIS IS YOUR LAST CHANCE!

"Angela, please please please don't be afraid of me. I'm a really, really nice guy. I *don't* rape people. I don't even hit people! I'm not big, and I'm not muscular, and I don't have a big ... Camaro, but ... but I'm nice! And I'm gentle! And I'm incredibly sensitive, and a keen observer! And I like you. I've always liked you."

"I like you too, Jack ... please don't kill me."

This is totally wrong, so sad and wrong and awful ... "Angela! *Hello?* Are you hearing any of this? Don't be afraid! Look, I wanted to show you ... I've been ... Oh, Angela ..."

Police: IF YOU DON'T COME OUT, WE'RE COMING IN! THIS IS YOUR FINAL CHANCE!

"Angela, I've got something really important to tell you!"

"Sure Jack! Whatever you say, just ..."

If Angela had said "just please don't kill me," I would have continued to not kill her, and to instead reassure her, and be nice to her, and maybe eventually she would have begun to believe me. And then maybe we could have moved from that topic to other, related topics: things we both like, stuff we could go do together sometime, if things were ever normal again. Or we could have just kept on talking, which would be enough for all eternity, just to talk with Angela Fine.

If Angela had said "just hold me," I would have held her tightly in my arms forever with all my strength, enveloping her in everything good that I am, and maybe she would have felt the warmth of my heart and the pure love radiating from it, and believed me.

If Angela had said "just come downstairs and talk to the policemen," I would have done that for her, sure, and who knows what might have happened next, with the world crashing, dumping core, going up in rampaging, fucking smoke all around us, but at least she would have seen that I was trying, and maybe, eventually, she would have had an opportunity to look into my heart, and believe me.

But if Angela had said "just please don't let a twenty-foot long monster cock suddenly reach down from the ceiling and scoop me up in its sick bulging skin and yank me screaming into the crawlspace ..."

Then I would have had to disappoint her.

Because it got me too.

date: command not found

It's dark, I can't breathe, I am dragged, scraped, crushed, sliced, raked through metal and wire and fiberglass and dust and heat and cold and darkness. I pass out, I wake up, I scream, I pass out again ...

I come to on a floor somewhere, a floor with scorching hot under-floor forced air that blows in my face, to crackling static and deep, angry pounding. Tongues of flame rise from the corners of the room. Smoke obscures the ceiling. Some living, writhing thing is climbing all over me! Snakes! The floor is carpeted with snakes! I scramble to my knees, but I mustn't stand up, it's a fire! A fire in Ice Station Zebra. With snakes. But where is Angela?

I hear her, she's gasping, weeping ... I

see her.

She's held face-down on the floor by writhing, squirming cables. Power cables, data cables, fiber, copper, wriggling together in a seething mass, binding her, crawling over her, plucking at her robe and jacket. Tongues of uncoiled backup tape unwind from the gaping maw of the tape backup jukebox and lick between her legs. She screams.

Beside her, in the center of the room, rises a thick, undulating tower of meat where WADSLAP Interchange 01 is supposed to be. Or rather: coiled tightly around the rack formerly known as WADSLAP Interchange 01 is an unspeakably large, long, thick and terrifying three-eyed devil penis, slamming its head against the top of the rack, over and over. My penis. My little monster.

"Lassie! What are you doing!?"

The pounding stops. The monster cock stretches toward me, nudges me playfully with a scarred, black-blue head, a head larger than my own ... it licks my cheek with its long, silver tongue and stares at me with its sad white eyes.

"Lassie ... what are you *doing?*"

Lassie unwinds himself from WADSLAP Interchange 01, and the snakes on the floor clear a path for me. I step towards the rack to inspect its status.

On the front side of the rack, I see that Chad and Chad did everything I asked them: they pulled the data, the power, the flash cards and the hot-swappable drives from every WADSLAP, severing all our Internet links four different ways. The demon cables stab and poke, jacking and unjacking the open ports of the dead units, but the non-volatile boot media is nowhere evident. These units will stay down.

On the back side of the rack, I see ... Chad and Chad, their bodies crushed and squeezed into a barely-recognizable blue-black pulp of limb, hair, blood and company t-shirt, jammed into the nine-inch slot between the WADSLAPs and the power conditioner.

Lassie taps me on the shoulder, and then ... he rubs the side of his head softly against Angela's thigh, as she screams and struggles, and the cables grip her tighter.

"What's that, Lassie? You mean ... you want me to reconnect the Internet ... and then we'll rape Angela Fine together?"

Lassie nods and wags his massive testicles enthusiastically, slapping them hard against the side of another nearby rack, knocking it sideways, shaking down charred panels from the ceiling.

I did this. I did it with my new penis. Oh God. It's me, it's my own flesh, my own cancer!

"Lassie ... oh, Lassie ... don't you want to be a good penis?"

He nods and wags, wags and nods. The cables on the floor are watching us.

"You're not a bad penis, are you?"

Lassie shakes his head, vehemently: no!

"Lassie, listen to me: raping and killing ... that's not nice. Those are bad things."

Lassie's tail stops wagging.

"Lassie, you're a good penis, but you've got to stop this. Stop raping and killing, Lassie."

Lassie shakes his head, no. All of the snakes on the floor shake their heads, no.

"Lassie?"

Lassie shoves me up against the WADSLAP rack and bangs furiously against the side.

"No, Lassie! I won't do it. It's wrong."

Lassie stares at me with its three sad eyes ... and then cudgels me in the ribs. I spit Fresca and tumble across the floor.

The serpent rises above me like a fist, as blue and pink Cat 5 cables coil seize my wrists and ankles, strapping them down. Pink saliva burbles from its head and drips down on my shin, burning me.

The giant penis coils back to strike ....

And then the charred, smoldering giant penis of Phil Tong falls out of the ceiling on top of it.

The two monster penises wrestle and strike and bite and punch one another, knocking over racks and tables. The snakes hiss and clutch and dart around. They release us and wrap around Phil Tong's unholy soot-smeared penis, which has not three eyes but four, and which is much, much, bigger than mine.

Angela and I crawl out the door as the two vast muscular coils of evil meat tumble and pound and mutilate each other, knocking apart the data center and, even now, growing larger ...

We scramble on our hands and knees past Payroll, the smoke just a foot above us, as the building shakes and windows shatter. We tumble down the stairs and scramble across the broken glass of the Hall of Sports Heroes as deep, serpentine screeching fills the air.

We run out onto the lawn. The rampaged bodies of fucked policemen litter the landscape.

Something explodes. We keep running, towards the empty cop cars in parking/basketball. Shrapnel of office equipment smashes down like comets. A spinning executive desk falls through the sky and shatters into sawdust on the ground in front of us. Angela is nearly crushed by a photocopier. A flaming shoe—worn by Jesse Owens during his heroic sweep of the track and field events at the 1939 Berlin Olympics—smacks me in the head. We keep running.

The nearest squad car is still idling with its doors open. I don't actually have a driver's license, but I'm very good with machines. We slam the doors and start moving, oh so slowly, out onto Campus and toward Victory, to the interstate, west, to the coast. To the ocean. Somewhere, there must be somewhere we can go. At least we're together now: Angela, curled up in a weeping ball in the back seat, and me, the New Me ... what's left of him.

In my rear view mirror I see them still: the two bloody monsters, larger than buildings, longer than highways, thicker than mountains, rolling and crushing and fighting and biting, rampaging and fucking over the entire earth.

Sun Jan 01 06:06:06 PDT 2013:

There really was a time before the worms. I remember.

Back in that time, almost everybody lived on land. And there were millions of people, back then. Billions of us.

And land was beautiful, and full of life. Before the worms came.

People ate all kinds of foods, and did all kinds of things, and had everything, on land.

But now there is only the sea, and the worms with their teeth, and the giant brutal holes they bore into the earth, and the ooze that pours out. And us, just the last precious few of us, the boat people, hanging on out here on the stinking brown sea. Scraping out a living on the shitting planet of the rampaging fuckers of everything.

We hunt the worms, we eat the worms ... and the worms hunt and eat us.

Call me Ishmael.

ANDERSEN PRUNTY

LOCATION:
Dayton, Ohio

STYLE OF BIZARRO:
Dark Hysteria

BOOKS BY PRUNTY:
The Overwhelming Urge
Jack and Mr. Grin
Zerostrata

DESCRIPTION: Absurd fantastical narratives. Sinister undertones. Elements of suspense and black humor with violent, horrific outbursts. Men, women and creatures sweating meaninglessness and searching for something greater.

INTERESTS: Global civilization's ridiculous decline. Anarchy. Bad haircuts. The weather. Sleep deprivation. Eclecticism. Randomness. Family. Books. Music. Film. Robots. Coffee. Spacecraft. Depression. Suicide. Addiction. Madness. Traveling. Laughing at everything (on the inside, of course).

INFLUENCES: Clive Barker, William S. Burroughs, Charles Bukowski, J.D. Salinger, Robert Anton Wilson, Barry Yourgrau, Franz Kafka, Haruki Murakami, Kobo Abe, David Lynch, Wes Anderson, Harmony Korine, John Waters, Ohio, chemical imbalances, Frank Zappa, Tom Waits, Nick Cave.

WEBSITE:
www.andersenprunty.com

THE DEVASTATED INSIDES OF HOLLOW CITY

CHAPTER ONE

In the flickering bathroom light Shell adjusts his eyepatch and runs a hand across the black scruff of his jaw before vomiting into the sink. He glances at himself in the mirror, a single cold blue eye glaring back at him, surrounded by a hundred and forty pounds of waste. He dips his fingertips into the puke, moving it around, looking for signs of infection.

He breathes a sigh of relief at the absence of the tell tale maggot- like worms. *Was* it relief? Perhaps.

He coughs and turns the tap on cold. He catches the water in his hands and splashes it on his face, trying to get the puke smell off his upper lip.

The flickering light irritates him. He reaches up to either tighten or unscrew the bulb altogether and notices that it's covered in a number of thick, sluglike worms. Adult slags. He can't bring himself to touch them.

The Rotting Man never told him this city was infested.

But Shell isn't here because of the infestation. He is here for a different reason. That reason is, as yet, unbeknownst to him.

He checks his watch. Two more hours until The Rotting Man will call. Maybe he has enough time for a nap.

CHAPTER TWO

His tiny room consists of a bed and desk. The door opens outward, banging into the far wall of the narrow hall and there it is. His bed. A single bed. No floor space. The small desk sits atop the bed. The desk has a chair but in order to lie down in the bed he has to put the chair on top of the desk before crawling beneath it. It's the worst room in the world.

He pulls all the covers from the bed, making sure there are no slags on it. He doesn't really need the covers anyway. It's nearly a hundred degrees and humid. Summer in Hollow City. He's already damp with sweat.

Lying in bed, he listens to distant sirens, trains and, closer, insects. They sound frenzied. As much a victim of the slags as humans. He falls asleep only briefly and dreams of torture and explosions. In the dream, he's another person entirely but everyone pretends to know him and, for some reason, this makes him violently angry.

He awakes to the desperate blatting of his cell phone. He looks at it. A picture of The Rotting Man, drunk, greets him. The picture was taken at last year's Christmas party. The Rotting Man had drunk way too much and kept asking people if they wanted to go out and roll winos at the train station. That was just before The Rotting Man's left ear fell off.

Good times? Doubtfully.

Shell flips his phone open.

"Yeah."

"You asleep?"

"It's like six in the evening. Why the hell would I be asleep?"

"Different strokes for different folks!"

"Is everything you say a fucking cliché?"

"Find Pearl. That's all I got for you. And that's no cliché."

"Who's Pearl?"

"Find her. Do what you do best."

Another cliché.

"I don't suppose I'll get any help with this one?"

"Help is all around you, friend..."

"Okay. Gotta go." Talking to The Rotting Man is headache inducing. There's only so much of it he can take and, because of the clichés, Shell could almost predict how he would answer his questions. So why even bother asking them?

There is an awkward pause. Shell holds the phone away from his ear to see if the call has ended. The seconds continue to roll on the tiny screen.

"Say it!" The Rotting Man blurts.

Shell takes a deep breath and says, "See you later alligator," in his customary monotone.

"After while crocodile!" The Rotting Man gleefully yells back before ending the call.

CHAPTER THREE

Shell slides out of bed, which means he's now standing in the hallway.

Help is all around you. Is that a cliché? Shell isn't sure. He thinks it sounds like a cliché. Whatever. Most of what The Rotting Man says is bullshit anyway. But he's the boss.

Shell straightens his tie and grabs his coat from the chair, pulling it on and smoothing out the wrinkles. It's what his ex-wife disdainfully calls "detective brown." He again touches his eyepatch, a weal of nausea streaking across his insides.

He walks down the short and narrow hallway until he comes to the dim living room. Miss Fitch, an older lady mostly made of bones and hair, is on her knees. Her arms are clasped around the flickering television. Her cheek is pressed against the glass and she's crying loudly. Gushing. The static has captured her hair and spread it across the television. From what Shell can tell it's just a harmless sitcom. At first he thought it might be more of the plague footage: mountains of dead, slag- gnawed children, skinny three-legged dogs wandering through it all, cities abandoned and destroyed. He stands and stares at her. Earlier, she had been sitting on the couch, her hands demurely folded in her lap while she stared catatonically at the wall.

The landlord, a fat hirsute hunchback named Mr. Blatz, had warned Shell about her. "She came with the building," he had said. "She's always been here." Then he had offered to knock ten dollars off the rent. That sounded good to Shell. He wouldn't need the apartment much more than a night, anyway.

Between the sobs Miss Fitch bellows, "Stop looking at me!" Flecks of spittle hit the screen, pixilating it. "Oh God just quit looking at me."

Shell clears his throat. "I've gotta go in the kitchen and make some calls. Do you think you can keep the crying to a minimum?" He holds the thumb and forefinger of his right hand very close together.

She is once again wracked with sobs. "Oh God now it's *talking* to me."

Who is *she* talking to?

"I'll have you know," Shell begins. "I am not an 'it'. I am a man. Living. Breathing. Human."

She pulls away from the screen to face him, her teeth bared. She snarls, "Hollow. You're all hollow!"

Shell can't take her seriously. Half her hair is still plastered to the television. He remembers what Mr. Blatz said about trying not to instigate her but he can't seem to help it.

"I'd think a resident of Hollow City wouldn't be so quick to make that judgment."

But she's turned back to the television, rubbing her cheek up and down it. On the screen, a fat man in a red bra laughs uproariously as someone sprays him with a garden hose. "Please," she whispers. "Just make him go away."

"As I said," Shell crosses the living room, making a wide berth around Miss Fitch. "I was just going into the kitchen to make some calls. I'd rather not be bothered."

But she's gone, licking the television and rubbing her nose in the saliva. Shell looks for slag movement in the saliva but doesn't see anything. He makes his way into the overly bright kitchen. A large sullen man in overalls sits at the table and stares at a plate of runny eggs.

Shell turns back to the living room to address Miss Fitch. "Say, do you know who Pearl is?"

Slowly, she pulls her glistening face from the screen and pushes a button, turning the television off and plunging the living room into darkness. Her eyes have once again gone blank. She slumps over to the couch and plops down.

"Pearl?" he asks and knows he will not get a response.

CHAPTER FOUR

Shell approaches the man sitting at the table.

"Mr. Blatz didn't say anything about you."

The man says nothing.

"That means I don't really have to let you stay. Normally, I wouldn't mind. You seem quiet and I won't be here long. But I need some privacy. I have some calls to make and that room..." he gestures toward his room, "is far too small and hot to think."

The man makes no attempt to leave. Shell picks up a handful of the eggs and shoves them into the bib of the man's overalls.

"Just take your eggs and go."

The man pats his egg- filled pouch, slides his chair back from the table and stands. "You'll be sorry," he says softly and slowly.

"Do you know who Pearl is?" Shell asks.

"I wouldn't tell you if I did. You're very rude."

Then, in a half-hearted attempt at confrontation, the man flips his plate over onto the table, the remaining eggs slathering across the surface.

"Dick," Shell says.

"Monster," the man says softly, lethargically pushing Shell's shoulder.

"I don't want to fight you."

"You'd lose anyway." The man lumbers to the door, turns back and says, "I hope you fail."

"I probably will," Shell says and thinks, *I almost always do.*

He finds the best way to thoroughly insinuate himself into a city is to use a local land line and call local people. The phone is mounted to a wall and covered in slags. He grabs the dirty plate from the table and attempts to knock the writhing slags from the phone. They fall to the floor with wettish plops. He stomps them. This is really the perfect size to combat them. Not large enough to make a giant mess but not small enough to go undetected. The baby ones could be anywhere. Even inside you. Before you know it they are all over and all hope is lost.

He picks up the phone and calls a random number.

"Hello," a male voice says.

Calling someone is like putting himself right in their house. He can hear if they are watching television. He can hear if they have a dog or children. If they're eating. This guy doesn't seem to be doing anything. It's easy to imagine him just sitting by the phone and staring out into nowhere.

"Hi," Shell says. "Um, what are you wearing?" He feels this is a good opening line. Sometimes people hang up on him but there are always plenty more numbers to call.

"Well," the man says. "I'm wearing pants and a shirt."

"What about shoes? Are you wearing shoes?"

"Yep."

"What kind?"

"Brown work boots."

"What about socks?"

"Yep."

"Ankle, crew or tube?"

"Um, well, I guess they's ankle socks."

"What kind of pants are you wearing?"

"Just jeans."

"Blue?"

"As the sky."

"What about your shirt? What kind of shirt are you wearing?"

"It's a t- shirt. And, well, I'm ashamed to say this but... it's kind of pink. It used to be red but it's faded a lot."

"Can you tell me about Pearl?"

"Pearl?"

"Yeah. Pearl."

"No. I'm afraid I can't."

"Do you know her?"

"Oh, everybody knows Pearl. She's the Queen of Town."

"The Queen of Town?"

"Well, of Hollow City anyway."

"What does she look like?"

"Do I know you?"

"Yeah, definitely. I'm Mike from down the street."

"Well, if anyone knows what Pearl looks like then I would think it should be you. Wanna do me a favor? Stop yankin my cock. Bye."

"Wait."

"Bye."

Shell doesn't hang up the phone. He waits until he knows the other person is gone. But this guy doesn't seem to hang up either.

"Are you still there, Mike?"

Shell doesn't know who the man is talking to until he remembers that he's Mike.

"Still here. Are you ready to tell me yet?"

"I just say you should know 'cause you was the last person to see her."

Suddenly, Shell feels confused, like the man is accusing him of something. He bangs the phone down in its cradle on the wall and takes a deep breath. Miss Fitch has worked her way out of the living room and is dragging herself into the kitchen by her arms, her legs trailing out behind her. Shell wonders why she does this since he just saw her walk only moments before. He has to get out of the apartment. He opens the door, slams it behind him and walks briskly out into the hallway, down the stairs and outside.

The city isn't anything like it was when he went in.

CHAPTER FIVE

When he had first arrived, the area surrounding the apartment building had been just like any other slightly rundown Main Street of a small city. Stately trees stood by the side of the road. Children played in yards. People sat on the porches of their large, old houses.

Now it is a flurry of noise and activity.

A squad of at least four helicopters, maybe news choppers, maybe police choppers, swoop low over the houses, scouring the early evening streets and alleys. It seems like everyone is outside, yelling and pointing. They parade up and down the streets, most of them looking furious and ready for a fight. The doors of many houses have been flung open, furniture and other debris flying out the door to land in porches and yards. The children have formed two large packs, now engaging in a rumble in a vacant lot at the corner. A young woman wields a chainsaw and cuts down a tree by the side of the road. The tree falls out into the road, smashing cars parked along the curb, and she ritualistically moves on to the next one. A car speeds down the road until it slams into the downed tree. Rather than driving around the tree the driver continues forward in an attempt to drive over it. The front wheels squeal over the tree in a smoky grind of burning wood and rubber until both sets of tires are suspended, spinning around and around in midair. The driver, furious, gets out of the car, slams the door and levels several vicious kicks at it until there is a very visible dent. Then he flings his arms up into the air and collapses into a screaming heap amidst the leaves fanned out on the asphalt.

Standing in the parking lot of the building Shell wonders what he will find if he ventures forward. The man in overalls stands to his right plucking scrambled eggs out of his overalls and eating them. He looks at Shell. Fear, or something, twists his facial features and he collapses to the ground on all fours. He heaves out the eggs onto the asphalt. Shell doesn't feel so well himself. He clutches his stomach and vomits next to the man. Crouching down, he once again sees that his vomit is clear of infection. The same cannot be said for the man in overalls. His puke crawls with the baby slags. Enough to make it look alive. And a smell, something Shell equates with death, wafts up and hangs around both men. The man rises and wipes the back of his hand against his mouth. Shell takes a cautious step back from him.

Apparently their vomiting together has forged some sort of solidarity.

"It's okay to laugh at me," the man says. "I know I'm dying."

Shell surveys the destruction, the fervid activity all around him, and realizes he has many questions but only one that really matters.

"I'm sorry you're dying," he says to the man. "I wish I could help you but I have to find Pearl. Do you even know who Pearl is?"

"She's the Queen of Town."

Shell watches the man's puddle of vomit as the slags disperse outwards from it, making it look like the puddle is growing.

"I've heard that. Do you know what she looks like?"

"She looks like a Queen. Only she's very small. Young. Like eight."

"An eight-year-old is your Queen?"

"Stranger things have happened. She doesn't control everything..." He takes a deep breath. "Just the stuff that matters."

Shell gestures at the chaos around him. "I would have thought she controlled everything judging by the way her absence has allowed complete and total anarchy."

"Anarchy?" The man says. "This isn't anarchy. These people are all trying to find Pearl. They want to bring her back from wherever she is. If it were anarchy then it would be like it was before Pearl and I don't... I don't even want to think of that. I'd love to stay and chat but I have to join the search. Everyone is looking for her."

"Say, you wouldn't happen to know anyone named 'Mike,' would you?"

"I know a lot of Mikes."

"Is your name Mike?"

"I have to go."

With that, the man in overalls walks out amidst the chaos.

Where to begin? Shell thinks.

CHAPTER SIX

He doesn't even have any transportation. What does The Rotting Man actually expect him to do? He sends him to a town to look for someone the whole town is already looking for. What makes The Rotting Man think he will be any luckier? This is not the standard case. The Rotting Man didn't even mention a commission and Shell, so flustered with his environment, didn't think to ask. Usually he found himself looking for people who everyone else had given up looking for. In this day of the slags and the plague it was easy for state and local authorities (those that still existed, anyway) to write people off. The common belief was that people became infected with the slags and then crawled out into the woods or the bowels of some huge city to die. For the person to be found, this could be a good or a bad thing.

Shell never knows if he is demon or angel. The Rotting Man tells him who to find. Shell sometimes finds that person and presents them to The Rotting Man. The Rotting Man gives him a certain sum, depending on the person. What happens to the person, Shell does not know. Nor does he particularly care. To borrow come clichés from The Rotting Man: A paycheck is a paycheck and business is business. Those clichés have not changed since the infestation.

According to the man on the phone the last person to be seen with Pearl was a man named Mike. Of course, if Pearl was "like eight," how old would the last person to be seen with her be? Shell doesn't think he sounds like an eight- year- old on the phone but, given other strange behaviors he's witnessed, he doesn't think he can rely too much on logic. For that matter, he can't even be sure the man on the phone was telling the truth. Shell generally assumes everyone he speaks to is a liar, whether they know it or not. Most people are living lies, Shell thinks. They live those lies until they believe them and then they take them to the grave. Maybe, if there is any justice in the cosmic universe, the truth is known in death.

Stepping onto the sidewalk, Shell approaches the woman wielding the chainsaw. She furiously saws away at a large maple tree, sawdust covering her ankle-length dress and caught up in her brown hair, a frantic look in her eyes, her jaw tense.

"Excuse me," Shell says.

She pulls the chainsaw away from the tree, not turning it off, and eyes Shell. "What do *you* want?"

"I just wanted to ask why you were sawing down all these trees."

"Isn't it obvious?"

"If it were obvious I probably wouldn't be asking."

"I'm looking for *Pearl*. You know *Pearl*, don't you?"

"I've heard of her but I don't really know that much about her." It's his common routine to act as ignorant to any given situation as he can. People usually want to inform the uninformed. "For instance, why would she be hiding in a tree?"

"Boy you really are dense, aren't you?"

"I'm not incredibly bright, no."

"Trees make excellent hiding spots."

"Like up in the tree?"

"Like *in* the tree, smartass."

Shell looks at the tree. "I still... I guess I still don't understand. How could she be *in* the tree?"

"She could hollow it out and crawl right in there. This is Hollow City. It got that name for a reason, okay? Like not everything has an inside. Some of it's just emptiness. And if I find one of the hollow trees then I can almost assure you I'll find Pearl."

"So how long has Pearl been missing?"

"Look, don't you read the paper? I don't have time to stand here and answer any more of your stupid questions."

She revs the chainsaw and begins sawing at the tree again. Shell wants to ask her how she knows she won't just cut Pearl in half if she *is* hiding in a tree but thinks better of it. One does not goad the frenzied bearers of chainsaws.

The sky grows darker. Soon it will be twilight and then evening. Shell doesn't want to think what this place is like after dark. A frumpy middle- aged woman throws open the front door of her house, charges out into the front yard, trips and falls down before raising her arms up to the heavens and shouting, "*Pearl!*"

These people are over the top, Shell thinks. Maybe he should just go home. He could just go back to the office and tell The Rotting Man that he wants out of it. That way he wouldn't have to admit defeat. He could just make it sound like it was something he didn't want to do anymore. Might as well press on for the time being. It isn't like he has a lot of alternatives.

CHAPTER SEVEN

He walks away from the tree cutter and takes a blow to the back of the head. The pain is staggering, shooting through his entire body. Everything swims in front of him before going a washed out kind of gray. His legs feel rubbery. In a city like this, in the midst of the slag plague, the last thing you want to give up is your vigilance but, unwillingly, he surrenders to unconsciousness and collapses to the ground.

He opens his eyes in a bright room. Surprisingly cool. He doesn't feel totally awake yet. A rancid smell surrounds him. He stares up at the water- stained ceiling and hears a male voice say: "He's clean. I checked him."

There's something comforting in that. By "clean," Shell assumes he means clean of slags. He has always dreaded the loss of consciousness, imagining he will wake up and find himself infested with slags, infected with the plague. The only place he really feels comfortable sleeping in is his room at home. It's in a city that has reasonably contained the slag infestation and his bedroom is guarded against that very thing—treated and secure. He wonders where he is. Maybe he's in the hospital. Maybe someone took advantage of the chaos to rob him when it was clear most people had other things on their minds. Maybe someone just attacked him because he was new and different. It certainly wouldn't have been the first time. As much as he tries not to seem like a detective, most people still figure him out. And most people confused a detective with some type of authority figure even though that couldn't be further from the truth. He is not out to find and punish any evildoers. He only looks for people. And he will do whatever is necessary to find those people because it pays reasonably well. This often means breaking the law himself. He is more of a criminal than most of the people who confuse him for a cop. He doesn't like to think of himself as a bounty hunter. People get lost. People need found. He is not the one who decides their ultimate fate.

"What'll we do with him?" A woman's voice. Shrill and old.

Shell turns his head to the right and surveys the room. It's completely wrecked. Large bookcases line the walls but all the books have been removed from the cases, strewn about the room, their pages ripped out. Furniture is overturned. Even the wallpaper hangs, ripped and shredded, from the walls. These must be more Pearl hunters. An old woman, presumably the one heard just a few moments ago, attempts to pull up the carpet. Her hair, sculpted into a tightly bound white perm, is unwavering. She wears a black bondage suit from the neck down, rendering her undoubtedly hideous body into a somewhat pleasing form.

"I guess we wake him up," the man's voice says.

Shell turns toward the voice. "I'm awake," he says, spotting the man.

Shell pulls himself up into a sitting position on the couch. The man, portly and older, dressed for leisure, uprights an orange chair and sits down in it, facing Shell. The man has a white beard and wears what seems to be a permanent smile, his head thrown back on his shoulders, his eyes little more than slits. He has a nasty cut on his forehead.

"Care for a smoke?" the man asks.

"Where am I?" Shell asks, adjusting his eyepatch and smoothing his meager amount of hair.

"I'm sorry," the old man says. "My name's Dave Happalance and this is my wife, Ingrid. You're in our home."

Shell makes to get up. "I really appreciate your hospitality and I'd really love to stay and chat but I have some business to tend to."

The man gestures for Shell to sit back down. A friendly gesture. Shell continues to stand. The man, Dave, with surprising agility, rises from his chair and pushes Shell back onto the couch. He smiles ridiculously the entire time.

"Ingrid. My pipe." The man continues to stare at Shell. Actually, with his eyes such slits, it's more like he just points his head at Shell. "I think you would find it beneficial to stay for a few minutes."

"Do I have a choice?" Shell says. "If I stand up you'll probably just push me back down."

"Probably," Dave says.

Ingrid brings Dave a pipe and a bag of something.

"You ever smoke these?" Dave asks, gesturing at the clear bag.

"I'm not sure what that is," Shell says.

Dave packs his pipe and hands the bag over to Shell.

Shell eyes the bag suspiciously. "Are those slags?"

"Indeed," Dave says. "They make a surprisingly good smoke." He flicks a match and touches it to the bowl of his pipe. Shell immediately identifies the source of the stink.

"Isn't that... bad for you?"

"Once dead there really isn't a lot of harm they can bring you. I used to have these imported from other cities but now they're all around. All I have to do is hop right out in the backyard and snag a jarful, put them in the oven for a few hours until they're all brown and toasty and... *voila*! Slagweed! Sure you don't want some?"

Dave holds the pipe out to him.

"I couldn't," Shell says. "I've been a little sick."

"I hear that's going around."

"Is that why you checked me?"

"Checked you?"

"Yeah, as I was waking up, I heard someone say, 'He's all clean.'"

Dave holds the pipe out to Ingrid who takes a long pull.

"Oh, we weren't checking you for slags. We were checking to make sure you weren't hiding Pearl."

"How could I be hiding an eight-year- old child?"

Ingrid took another pull from the pipe, bracing herself on Dave's chair.

"She's not eight. She's the Queen of Town! How could she be eight?"

"It's just something I heard."

"No. She's always been around. However, she is very very small."

"Diminutive," Ingrid says, bending down and licking Dave on the cheek.

"Diminutive?" Shell says.

Dave holds his thumb and middle finger about six inches apart.

"That small?" Shell says, amazed. "It's hard to believe she's lasted this long."

"Well, she has all kinds of powers. She's not like normal people. Not at all like you or I."

"Of course not."

"By the way," Dave says. "I'd like to apologize for clubbing you in the head back there. I guess I just got so overwrought with the reward that momentarily, at least, I would have done anything for it. You have to understand my logic. Pearl goes missing. A stranger shows up. I thought maybe you had something to do with it."

Shell wants to react strongly to the man who clubbed him in the head but knows that if he gives this man the merciless beating he deserves he won't be able to get any information from him.

"So, do either of you have any ideas where she might be?"

Dave takes a large pull from the pipe, a fresh stink blossoms in the room and his face lights up. "Oh, sure, but I wouldn't tell you. Not with the reward out there. See, I don't really care whether or not Pearl is found. I think the city was probably better off before her."

"I thought you said she'd always been the Queen."

"I think I said she'd always been here. I don't think I said she'd always been Queen. Shit, I'm so high I don't know what I'm saying."

"So who was the Queen before Pearl?"

"I think I said she's always been the Queen."

"How can she have always been the Queen if she's only eight?"

"I *never* said she was only eight. She's very old. Ancient, even. But she's never grown up. She'll always be eight. And a very *small* eight, at that."

"What does the Queen of a mid-size city do?"

"If you ask me, she doesn't—*didn't*—do a whole lot."

"No?"

"No. The whole position was trumped up and overrated. Maybe she realized how useless she really was and decided to move on."

"Wouldn't that be strange for someone who has always been here?"

"There are so many things you're not aware of. Sometimes we all have to go out and find ourselves. You ever get lost? You ever feel like your *soul* got lost? If you ask me, that's the real plague. No one knows who they are anymore. How did you lose your eye?"

"How do you know I'm not just wearing this as some sort of crazy disguise?"

"I checked. It's grisly."

"I don't talk about it."

"You're bringing me down."

"Me too," Ingrid echoes before taking another massive pull from the pipe. She woozily leans over and begins licking Dave on the neck. He giggles. The cut on his forehead cracks open and unleashes a narrow trickle of blood.

"Actually," he says. "I was going to ask if *you* had any ideas where she might be..." His giggles become louder. More uncontrolled.

"I'm just a stranger passing through town," Shell says. "And I'm sorry but I really have to be going now."

The Happalances are lost to whatever sick game they're playing. Shell shakily stands up and exits through the front door, pausing only to vomit on their porch.

CHAPTER EIGHT

He looks up to see a luminescent child on a dirt bike pointing a Glock at him. Shell throws up his arms, like that's going to stop anything, just as the kid fires. It's completely dark out now and the shot is a fireball erupting from the gun. It all happens too fast for Shell to even dive out of the way. He hears a screech to his right and looks down. Half a mature slag wriggles in Shell's puke. His first thought is that he hopes the slag didn't come from him. His second thought is that maybe Hollow City has had a slag problem longer than they care to admit. Mature slags are rare. The size of an adult male forearm with teeth. If bitten by a mature slag, the victim has fewer than three hours to live.

The slightly glowing kid on the dirt bike has quite possibly saved his life.

"Come on, patchy. Hop on. I ain't got all night."

Shell hurries for the dirt bike. The kid looks like a gang member. Red bandanna around his head. Sleeveless denim jacket over an equally sleeveless heavy metal t-shirt. Stonewashed jeans. Puffy gym shoes worn untied.

Shell hops on the dirt bike and looks back at the Happalances. Dave, now shirtless, rushes onto the porch and encloses his meaty hands around the slag. He licks his lips. There's a crazed look in his eyes, now open and round and huge. Behind him, Ingrid smacks his back with a riding crop.

Shell turns back to the kid on the bike. "Where are we going?"

"The store, fuckmunch. I gotta get some supplies. And booze. It's not a good night to be out. Can you handle a weapon?"

"Sure," Shell says.

The kid hands the Glock back to him. Shell holds it in his right hand. He's always been rather fond of the Glock, its angular Austrian lethality. It was designed to stop people. The owner of a Glock is not fucking around.

The kid pops the clutch and they speed down Main Street, zooming past a SWAT team unloading from a truck.

"Everything's coming to an end, douche," the kid says.

"What do you mean?"

"Hollow City. It's falling."

"That sounds pretty outdated. I don't even think that can happen anymore."

"What do you know, gramps?"

"Do you think you could stop calling me names?"

"I have to. It's what I'm all about. I don't kiss no one's ass. 'Sides, I could just throw you off my fuckin bike."

"I'm not asking you to kiss my ass. I just think the name calling is uncalled for."

"Clever, asswipe."

"I am holding the gun."

"Don't you fuckin threaten me!" the kid shouts. A mist of spittle covers Shell's face. "I'll fuckin slit your throat and leave you in a goddamn ditch! You don't know what's goin on."

"Maybe you could tell me."

"I'm not tellin you shit."

"Fine."

They ride for a while, the only sound the high-pitched whine of the dirt bike. They leave the city proper and enter a series of back roads, corn and soybeans growing all around them.

Shell works with what he has. He is here to find Pearl. She is, or used to be, the Queen of Town. She's small. She might be eight. She might be ancient. She might be ancient but mildly retarded. Everyone is looking for her either because they love her as their queen or because there is a sizable reward for finding her. Allegedly, the last person to see her was someone named Mike. Why would The Rotting Man send him to find her? And when he finds her, he is supposed to take her back to The Rotting Man. Or is he? The Rotting Man never really said. He's usually more specific about these things. He'll have to call The Rotting Man if he finds her. The prospects of Shell's finding her, he thinks, are amazingly small. He only finds about half the people he searches for and, most of the time, it's not like this. This feels like a race. With everyone looking for her, he'll have to be the *first* to find her. And he doesn't know this town nearly as well as people who have lived here their entire lives. Which could be to his advantage...

The dirt bike plows into a pothole and Shell's concentration is shattered as it wobbles violently back and forth. The boy expertly straightens out and they are once again cruising smoothly along.

"What's your name?" Shell asks.

"Used to be Mike but I changed it to Kid Rider."

Shell suppresses a laugh. That's an awful name. But his previous name... that could be something.

"Why the change?"

"I escaped from the House of Mikes. And don't fuckin condensate to me."

"The House of Mikes?" This is the most promising thing Shell has heard all evening. It even takes his mind off Kid Rider's atrocious use of words.

"That's what I said, buttmunch. See, Hollow City had too many Mikes so they put em all in a house on the outside of town. They was all given a number and a chance to live around themselves. It was supposed to help us establish an identity but it was terrible. The lower numbers pulled rank because they were there first. I was Mike 31. A hardluck fuckin number. Thirteen backwards. Like ass rape. I'll show you the tattoo when we get to the store. I definitely didn't get no breaks. That place was a fuckin prison."

"Did you know Pearl?"

"Shit no, man. She wouldn't have nothin to do with me, dicklips. She started hangin around the House but she was only interested in the lower numbers like maybe 1 through 4. Why? You lookin for her too?"

"Are you?"

"In my own way, I guess."

"Why are you looking for her?"

"Without her, Hollow City ain't for

shit. Without her, people just run around doin whatever they wanna do and then it gets to be just like the House. And it ain't just the people either. You see that slag I capped back there? That wouldn'ta been around if the Queen was here..."

"Why not?"

"I don't know, man. You ask too many questions. She had like powers or something." Happalance had mentioned something to that effect, as well. Shell adds it to his mental list. Magical powers.

"You talk about her like she's dead."

"Well she ain't *here*, is she? Best to assume the worst."

They are on a narrow country road. A corona of light floats in the distance. "Is that the store?"

"Sure is."

"Do you drive this thing when you're all boozed up?"

"Totally fuckin crocked, man!" Kid Rider laughs. Shell spares him the lecture.

"You know what you remind me of, man?"

"A walking asshole?" Shell guesses.

"No! A fuckin pirate! With that eyepatch and shit!"

"Gee. I've never heard that one before."

"Arrgh. Shiver me timbers, matey!"

For laughs, Shell places the tip of the gun against the back of Kid Rider's head.

"Knock it off," Shell says.

"Okay. Okay. I was just kiddin. You shouldn't aim a gun at someone unless you plan on using it."

"You want me to?"

"Fuck off, Long John."

Kid Rider veers sharply to the right and into the parking lot of the store. A lonely gas pump adorns the deserted parking lot.

CHAPTER NINE

They dismount the bike and walk into the bright fluorescence of the store, Shell tucking the gun into the back of his pants. Even in this day of the slags, it's not a good idea to walk into a store with a drawn weapon. It doesn't seem to have any kind of name. Kid Rider comes up to Shell's nipples. He holds his arms away from his body and puffs up his chest like he's well- muscled, vigilantly turning his head from side to side. He heads to the back, to the booze, and Shell decides to question the young black- haired cashier. She wears a lot of makeup and looks kind of skanky. Her shirt is black and says, in bright pink letters: SUMMA THIS. It is stretched tightly across her small breasts.

"Hi," she says.

"Hi. Do you know how I could get to the House of Mikes?"

"Why?" She chuckles. "Your name Mike?"

"No. But all my friends are named Mike."

"You just continue on out this road here until you see a big house. I mean really big. That's it. They have to fit a lot of Mikes in there. If you reach Fugueland you've gone too far."

"Fugueland?"

"Don't ask."

"I see. Do you sell the paper?"

She gestures to a small wire container below the front of the counter. "Only a couple left."

Shell picks one up. It's about six pages covered in crayon drawings and letters and stapled on the left hand side. It looks like it was done by a child. The letters are all very large and crooked. Most of the words are misspelled. Shell doesn't imagine it'll be very informative and places it back in the container. The cashier snaps her gum and waits for Kid Rider to bring his fifth of whiskey and bucket of slag repellant to the counter.

"Who's paying?" the cashier asks.

"He is," Kid Rider gestures toward Shell. "I'm not nearly old enough to buy whiskey."

"Okay. Get back here," the cashier says.

"Excuse me?" Shell asks.

"Come on. You have to fuck me. That's the payment."

"That's the payment," Kid Rider echoes. "I'll leave you two alone." He exits the store. Shell watches him to make sure he doesn't drive off.

"Come on. It'll be quick," she says.

"I'm not even hard," Shell says. "And I don't feel very well."

"Just get back here."

Shell walks around the counter until he's standing behind it. He's never been behind the counter of a convenient store before. He finds it kind of exciting. The girl wears a short black skirt, fishnet stockings and combat boots, which he also finds kind of exciting. She leans against the counter, her back to him, and lifts her skirt up over red underwear. She slides those down and rubs her ass.

"I'll need a condom," Shell says, suddenly hard.

"There's plenty right back there." She throws a hand over her shoulder.

He opens the box, takes the gun from the back of his pants, places it on the counter behind him, unbuttons and unzips his pants, slides them down, tears the condom from its foil wrapper and unrolls it onto his cock, the sterile smell of latex and spermicide hitting his nostrils. He probes her sex with a finger, making sure she's wet. She is.

"I'm always wet," she says.

"Um... good?" Shell says.

"Better for everyone."

He slides into her slowly and comes almost immediately. It feels like the walls of her vagina are quivering, pulsing around his spurting penis.

"Told you it wouldn't take long."

He pulls out and hears a sickeningly familiar plop. Three slags are writhing on the floor between the cashier's boots.

"Oh God," he says. He loses it. Vomits on the back of the cashier.

"What the fuck?!" she says. She reaches down and pulls a slag from her inner thigh. "Oh shit," she says, vomiting onto the floor.

"I gotta go." Shell hitches up his pants, grabs the gun and heads out into the parking lot.

Kid Rider stands in front of the open bucket of repellant, covering himself in the powder. This, apparently, is what makes him luminescent.

"Want some before I close it up?" he asks.

"Why not," Shell says, still shaken. He covers himself with the glowing powder, dropping a little down his pants for good measure.

Then he faces Kid Rider and says, "You're not gonna like this."

"What?" Kid Rider is slightly shocked, expecting the worst.

Shell levels the gun at him. "I'm taking this." He holds the gun up. "And I'm taking the bike."

"You fuckin cranksucker. I saved your fuckin life."

"I know. And I do apologize. I just can't be held responsible for a minor. If I ever see you again, I'll give it all back."

CHAPTER TEN

He slams the Glock down the back of his pants and mounts the bike. He wants to look cool driving away but he's almost too large to control it and tips it over, skidding across the parking lot. He hears Kid Rider running for it and pulls the gun back out. "Stay away!" he shouts. "I'm okay." Kid Rider freezes. Shell puts the gun back, uprights the bike, mounts it and speeds away into the night. Smoother this time.

He isn't on the road for long until he reaches what has to be the House of Mikes. He checks his watch. It's nearly two o'clock in the morning. The whole night has been a blur and he doesn't think he's any closer to finding Pearl than when he first started. Behind the House of Mikes are a couple banks of floodlights. Shell dismounts and hears cheering and shouting coming from back there. He wonders if he should pull the gun out and keep it in his hand. Are the Mikes dangerous? Well, if they are, he figures it's probably best not to put them immediately on guard.

He walks around the large house and sees a circle of people gathered around something. A few of the Mikes are walking from the house, probably to watch whatever spectacle is being played out. They all seem to be slightly different, which means they are also slightly the same. Short hair. A little meat on their bones. All shirtless and wearing khaki trousers. Each of them has a large number tattooed on his chest. Shell guesses the number is permanent. Once a 25, always a 25. So says the tattoo.

He imagines, perhaps from what Kid Rider said, the Mikes to be a closed society but he is welcomed immediately.

"Hey!" Mike 16 shouts. "You gotta come and watch this! We're practicing Mike control."

Shell wanders over to the circle of men. They surround a pit. In the pit is a boy with the number 38 on his torso. Also in the pit are three mature slags. They snap at the boy as he frantically tries to climb the dirt wall. Shell doesn't want to watch this but, at the same time, he needs to find a Mike who can supply him with information about Pearl. Most likely Mikes 1 through 4.

Watching the boy frantically try to get away from the slags, Shell has a revelation.

He no longer cares about finding Pearl. What is one girl's life, even if she is a queen, in exchange for someone else's? There are enough people looking for Pearl. There is a sizable reward for finding her. But what about this boy who is trying so desperately to get away from the slags? Born into Mikedom. Handed over by his Mike brothers, turned into some form of perverse entertainment.

Of course, he never really cared about finding Pearl in the first place. He cared about the money. He still cares about the money but fears he may have to end up writing it off.

Nevertheless, he can't stand around and watch this kid get devoured by slags.

Shell pulls the Glock out and fires down into the pit.

The Mike in the pit drops to his knees and covers his ears as the first slag explodes. Shell aims again and fires. The second slag explodes. The third slag, now desperate and alone, makes a lunge for the boy. Shell fires again and catches it in mid- flight, its toothy head disintegrating.

"Aw, man," Mike 12 says. "We was just havin fun."

"That is not the way to have fun," Shell says.

"Who the fuck are you? Your name ain't Mike," Mike 6 says.

Shell holds the gun out in front of him, suddenly feeling very threatened.

"I need to speak with Mike 1, 2, 3 or 4. And one of you needs to help that kid out of the hole."

"Well, Mike 2's dead," Mike 18 says. "He's been dead for years. As for the other Mikes, they're fulfilling their civic duty by searching for the Queen."

"What can you tell me about the Queen? I heard she used to come here a lot."

"I wouldn't say a lot."

"But you've met her?"

"Sure I've met her."

"Have any ideas where she might be?"

"If I had any ideas where she might be then I'd be the one out there looking for her instead of the other Mikes."

"Do you know anyone who would want to kidnap her or hurt her?"

"No, man, everybody loved the Queen."

"Is this true?" he asks the rest of the Mikes.

They all nod their melon- sized heads.

"What wasn't to like? She was just a little old lady who didn't have any real power anyway."

"A little old lady?"

"Shit. I don't know. I always thought she was old. I never got too close to her. All I know is she's real small. Most queens are old, I thought."

"How do you feel now that she's gone?"

"Well, I feel like hell. She was the life of this city. I don't know how to explain it exactly. It was just... just good to have her around, you know?"

"What will I find if I go to Fugueland?"

"You don't want to go there."

"Why not?"

"Nobody goes there. It's dangerous."

"Dangerous how?"

"It's why they call this place Hollow City. Fugueland empties people out. I don't know how it does but... people who go there, they ain't the same when they come back. But, like I said, no one goes there anymore."

"Thanks," Shell says, turning to leave. "You've all been a big help."

"Mister?" Mike 18 says. "You ain't goin there, are ya?"

"I think I have to," Shell says, turning his back on the Mikes and heading for his bike.

Interlude: Fugueland

Birth

The bike long discarded he comes upon Fugueland. No. There are no blinding lights. No carnival signs. Just a swirling mass like a fogbank and standing there looking at it he feels life catch up with him. His body aches. His empty socket throbs beneath the patch. Nausea continues to gnaw at his stomach and head. Shell. He finally feels like his name. Takes a deep breath. Puts the gun down. Sheds his clothes and steps into something very much like pure consciousness. Each droplet clings to his skin and he feels it and he likes the way it feels and even though his eye is open it might as well be closed because he can't see anything. The gray darkens but he doesn't see it. He feels it. Darkens all the way to black. Deep space black. And he's floating through this space and is suddenly aware that it is not space at all but the womb and the womb smells like the earth. All the dark rich fertile loam of things long dead and things coming back to life and when he reaches out he clasps two handfuls of dirt and pulls away at them. Rending the womb. Opening the womb to the outside world and he pours out screaming.

Life

And comes to a plateau of sorts. Flat smooth earth and he's at the top of something maybe the top of everything and this is all new to him and this feeling of newness feels good. He's all emptied out and this lack of insides makes him less aware of his outsides. But awareness builds. He feels his bones coming up from nothing. Massing around themselves. And he feels his muscles and his nerves take shape and strengthen and then his skin. Blood chugs through everything and he takes his first deep breaths and fills his lungs with this unsullied air. Aware of his solidity in this space. He approaches the edge of the plateau and looks out onto a world not yet built. He knows what is to come. It hits him in a single blinding flash of knowledge. The people will come. The buildings will come. The cultures will come and with them will come all of those dangerous human emotions. With them will come everything that can gnaw a person away from the inside. And he is also aware of the inescapability of that. He becomes aware of life's grim march. Onward. Forever onward. Meeting whatever cruel fate awaits but it is through this cruel fate and face of humanity that true beauty can shine. No death is a good death but all death is inevitable. He turns to meet it. Casting out his insides to the blank world around. Hollow. Full. And now hollow again. Approaching through the fog is a pack of wolves. Except for their heads. Their heads are the tapered toothrimmed heads of mature slags. He lies down on the cool earth. Feels the air swirl around him and drop down onto his face and kiss his lips as the first of the slag wolves bites into his flesh.

A Kind of Death

It's a mangled form emerging from Fugueland. Whole on the outside. Slagwolf gnawed on the inside. The human body is an ever expanding collection of things some of which have to be trimmed away. Sometimes death is necessary. It gives us something to bury far beneath the ground so more light can shine on the life that is left. Some people are here. Some people have always been here. Some people deserve to live. Some people deserve to die. He is only the messenger. Only the envelope. Only the shell. He could break and crumble at any minute.

CHAPTER ELEVEN

Shell dons his clothes, mounts the dirt bike and heads back into town. He isn't sure what just happened to him. The taste of vomit lingers on his tongue but he feels a renewed sense of purpose. He will look for Pearl in one last place and, if she isn't there, he's decided to go back home and quit the agency. And if he decides he can't live without the agency, can't live without a job, then he'll take a gun and put it in his mouth or perhaps his hollow eye and pull the trigger. Maybe the Mikes were right about Fugueland but Shell doesn't know if being a different person is a good thing or a bad thing. The world certainly doesn't need *more* people like him.

The final shreds of darkness are still all around him and he can feel the immense weight of the day breathing a sunny whisper on the other side of the curtains.

CHAPTER TWELVE

It's dawn by the time he gets back to the apartment. He's tried to shut everything else out of his mind and concentrate only on finding Pearl. Everything else will have to wait. Fuck everything else. Whether he finds her or not, he's decided this is his last hurrah. He might as well go out with a bang.

He thinks about Mr. Happalance saying Pearl has always been here. He thinks about Mr. Blatz saying Miss Fitch has always been here. He thinks about the man in overalls saying everyone was looking for Pearl. Shell knows someone who is not looking for Pearl. He knows someone so wrapped up in psychotic insanity she has to drag herself from the living room. Hollow City. Okay. So some people are hollow. Some people make good vessels. Maybe Pearl is in the apartment. Maybe Pearl is in Miss Fitch. Maybe her psychosis is the act of a diminutive Queen trying to fight her way out. Maybe Pearl has chosen to hide in the one place where she will go undetected. The insides of every other house are devastated, torn apart by people, the occupants, searching for Pearl.

Shell figures it's time to do some devastation of his own.

He pulls up in front of the building. Main Street at dawn is only slightly buzzing. Trash and the insides of people's homes, often one in the same, line the street. The sound of the chainsaw continues to rip through the air. He makes sure the Glock is still tucked into the back of his pants.

He opens the door to his apartment and crosses the kitchen. Miss Fitch lies face down in the living room. She is covered in slags. Shell kicks some from her hand, grabs it and drags her into the kitchen. He then goes about ripping the apartment apart. Cabinet doors torn from hinges and then the cabinets themselves from the walls. Cushions and beds ripped apart. Carpet up. Drywall smashed. Nothing. Nothing. And more nothing.

Panting, sweaty and out of breath, Shell maneuvers into the kitchen and picks a butcher knife up from the covered floor. He rolls Miss Fitch over and doesn't even bother to feel for a pulse. Briefly, he feels a sense of contradiction. How could he save that kid at the Mikes at the possible expense of Pearl and then open up this woman to find her? The feeling passes. He wills it to. If Miss Fitch isn't dead yet with all those slags writhing on her, she will be soon. Miss Fitch isn't doing anyone any good. The good people of Hollow City *need* Pearl, Shell convinces himself. Because convincing himself of that is better than believing he wants the money or wants to go out on a memorable note. It seems too perfect. The only thing that could make it more perfect would be if Miss Fitch were named Miss Oyster. Open the oyster, find the Pearl.

Shell slashes her from the hollow of her throat down through her rotten sex. Gullet to groin.

And there's nothing inside. She's filled with slags. Absolutely packed with them. Shell hopes his repellant is still active. He stands, takes a deep breath and lets the knife drop to the floor. He wanders outside to vomit and just keeps wandering home.

CHAPTER THIRTEEN

The Rotting Man sits behind his desk, plump, gray and stinking. A small pile of cash sits on the left hand side of the desk. His once white dress shirt is stained yellow at the shoulder and plastered to his skin. Shell sits facing him.

"I failed," he says.

"You gave it your best. We can't all be winners."

Cliché after cliché after cliché.

Even though he spouts words of encouragement, The Rotting Man looks unusually depressed. He pushes his glasses up his fleshy nose with his right hand, turned a purplish gray with the rot. "I am sorry to say, however, that you will not be receiving any of this." He pushes the pile of cash off the desk with his left hand. It hits the floor and scatters only slightly in a puddle of fetid fluid.

"I think I'm giving it up anyway," Shell says.

"Quitting the agency?"

"Yep."

"But you're the best detective we have... In fact, you're the only detective we have..."

"And a failure."

"Come on now. You're too hard on yourself. Tell me: when you were out there in Hollow City... they ever tell you how *small* Pearl was?"

"Pretty small. Diminutive."

"That's a pretty fancy word. You pick that up there?"

"Yeah. Well, I kind of knew what it meant. That was probably the first time I'd ever heard it in conversation. This was an interesting case. I know you have confidentiality clauses with your clients but, seeing as this is my last one, I was wondering if you could tell me who was offering to pay you for looking for Pearl and what exactly they wanted with her."

The Rotting Man looks down at his

desk and shakes his head. "You're right," he says. "This was a strange case because there was no client. Actually, I guess there was. The client was Hollow City. It was an open reward. To the first person who finds her."

"I knew that."

"I was going to give you this amount," he gestures to the sopping money on the floor. "And take Pearl back to Hollow City, claiming to have found her myself. Their reward was roughly double what I offered you."

"Actually, you didn't offer me anything. I just assumed it was the standard amount."

"Which it was."

"Which is probably why you never went into specifics."

"Could be. I needed someone who could bring her back here without anyone ever knowing it. Or else they would have pounced on you, restored Pearl and given the reward to you."

"You really are a greedy shit."

"I know. That's what this business is all about. Pure greed. Anyway, it'll be tough to see you go."

"It's not just the failing. I haven't been feeling well lately. Nauseous all the time..."

"Maybe you have a parasite or something."

The Rotting Man holds his middle finger and thumb about six inches apart. Shell notices he has lost a pinky since the last time they met in person. "They say she was about that big? Say anything about her 'magical powers'?"

Shell nods.

"Maybe more like this?" The Rotting Man decreases the size considerably. "Do me a favor before you go—just to satisfy my morbid curiosity—let me see what's under the eyepatch. You never have told me how you lost it."

"My ex- wife plucked it out during our last great battle. It's kind of gross- looking."

Shell slides his chair back from the desk and stands up.

"You visit Fugueland while you were there?" The Rotting Man asks.

"I don't know what you're talking about." Shell leans over the desk. He's kind of nervous. He's never voluntarily shown anyone what was under the patch before.

"That's where I caught the rot," The Rotting Man says, standing up to meet Shell over the desk. "Yep. Many years ago. I used to live there. In Hollow City."

"I never knew that." Shell puts his fingers on the patch and lifts it up, seeing his reflection in The Rotting Man's glasses.

He sees The Rotting Man tense up and, in the reflection, he sees why.

A brown eye stares back at him. He moves his fingers up to poke at it. How did that get there?

"You have her," The Rotting Man says. "That's her eye."

Shell takes a step back.

The Rotting Man unleashes a noxious stink.

"So what if I do?" Shell asks.

"She's mine."

"Actually, she's the people of Hollow City's. If anyone's."

"She's in you. I need her powers. They're the only thing that can stop the rot."

"And now we come to the truth. I think I'll take her back myself. Maybe I'll take the reward."

"You won't." The Rotting Man throws open a drawer and removes a huge, antique revolver. Shell immediately regrets leaving the Glock at home.

"If you shoot me then she'll die too."

"I only need a little bit of her power. And then you'll be free. Both of you will be free."

Suddenly, Shell feels a whole other system of thoughts move in his brain. It takes control of his brain, his processes, and he feels himself recede to the back of his skull.

"I've never been free," the Queen

says loudly, with Shell's voice, with Shell's mouth. "So you want to keep me here as a cure for your sick condition or take me back and throw me to a pack of sycophants. I don't see how I can win."

The Rotting Man thumbs a button under his desk. The lock in his door clicks closed.

"Heal me," The Rotting Man says through rotting lips.

"Let me go," the Queen says.

"Just touch me in the rotting parts. Please."

Pearl moves Shell's arm across the desk, within an inch of The Rotting Man's torso, hovering just in front of it, before driving the fist forward, into the feverish insides of The Rotting Man's body. The Rotting Man chokes on his insides, aims his gun and fires for Shell's heart but hits his shoulder instead. Shell is thrown back into the door and, looking at The Rotting Man standing there with the gun in his hand, doomed but bent on destruction anyway, he feels a giant force build inside. It starts at the base of his spine, works its way up through the back of his throat and erupts from his mouth.

The Rotting Man is driven against the back wall by this invisible force. He continues to gargle and spew and now he is rotting at an alarming rate, the stench of putrefaction filling the room as his insides explode from puffy, rotted flesh to land on the dingy tiled floor. The gun falls to the ground and it isn't long before The Rotting Man is a pile of dried meat and bones.

The Queen directs Shell's body outside into the gray summer afternoon.

CHAPTER FOURTEEN

An unlikely pair, Pearl and Shell drift as one into a dim, narrow alley. The conscienceless Shell and the consciousness of a whole town. Shell's insides feel swollen. He drops to his knees, bracing himself against the grimy brick wall. He feels his skin stretch to bursting and then further. Ripping. He can hear it rip and he wants to scream, wants to cry out but doesn't want to attract attention and, besides, Pearl controls his mouth. And she, apparently, doesn't feel like screaming at all.

Shell collapses onto his back and watches Pearl rise from his split flesh. She is not diminutive in the least. She is a beautiful young woman who looks lovingly down at him. She places her index finger over her lips, "Shhh," and reaches down toward Shell. She takes a fragment of bone from his rib and a long strand of her hair. The bone becomes a needle and she feeds the hair through its eye.

Within a few minutes he is all stitched up but strangely flat. She leans toward him and at first he thinks she's going to kiss him. Instead, she lifts up his eyepatch, encloses her generous lips around the socket and exhales. Shell watches his body inflate and feels her breath move through his insides. He coughs, dragging himself up into a sitting position. He doesn't feel so sick anymore. In fact, he feels kind of great.

"Why?" he asks. "Why all this?"

"To get away," her actual voice is soft yet authoritative.

"Away from what?"

"Hollow City. I don't know. Everyone."

"Being adored must be difficult."

"It is if that's not what you want. Or maybe it's because it's the only thing you've ever known."

"So you get to just walk away?"

"It looks like it. But think about it. You get to be a human again."

"I've always been a human."

"You call what you used to do for a living being human?"

Shell shrugs and says, "It put food on the table," and feels like The Rotting Man.

"I guess you'll justify it however you see fit."

"Since you're so pious, how do you justify leaving your city in ruins?"

"I'm sure I'll be back to pick up the pieces. Eventually. They need a little self-sufficiency. Besides, they're not really in ruins. They're just crazy because they've always had me to look after them. Maybe they'll grow up."

"Speaking of growing up—I thought you were, you know, diminutive."

"I was. Now I'm not."

"It was Happalance, wasn't it?"

"I shall not tell."

"Yeah, Happalance put you in my eye socket and..."

"You can sit here speculating all you want to but I've gotta go. There's a whole world out there to see."

She walks down the alley, toward the city street and Shell feels a brief pang of regret. Regret and pity. He fears for her insides and wonders how long it will take them to become devastated and smashed. He hopes they won't. He hopes the world she wants to see is still here a little bit longer. He stands up, coughs, adjusts his eyepatch and heads home. He has to find a new job.

ECKHARD GERDES

LOCATION:
Chicago area

STYLE OF BIZARRO:
Subterficial Fiction

BOOKS BY GERDES:
Projections
Truly Fine Citizen
Ring in a River
Cistern Tawdry
Przewalski's Horse
The Million-Year Centipede
The Unwelcome Guest
Nin and Nan
My Landlady the Lobotomist
Aasvogel

DESCRIPTION: A trailblazer in dark psychedelia and experimental lit, Gerdes uses hundreds of different techniques, some common, some secret, to create fictions that at turns are as inscrutable as a Jackson Pollock painting and in the straightaways read like Peter Brueghel coming into the home stretch.

INTERESTS: Hanging out with my sons, music, disc golf, Bundesliga, tennis, cooking, drinking, getting drunk, falling down, forgetting what I was going to say, wondering where was I going with this?

INFLUENCES: Firesign Theatre, Kenneth Patchen, Frank Zappa, Captain Beefheart, Richard Brautigan, John Barth, Donald Barthelme, James Joyce, Samuel Beckett, Alain Robbe-Grillet, Arno Schmidt, Italo Calvino, Eugene Ionesco, Raymond Federman, Harold Jaffe, Yuriy Tarnawsky, Kathy Acker, William Burroughs, Jack Kerouac, Pere Ubu, Kraan, Guru Guru, Can, Epitaph, Scorpions' Lonesome Crow, Neu, Gong, Steve Hillage, Federico Fellini, Karlheinz Stockhausen.

WEBSITE:

www.myspace.com/egerdes

NIN AND NAN

CHAPTER ONE
THE SIGN

Nin and Nan sat at the top of the hill together and observed the goings-on below. Nin's mind was sufficiently empty. Nan's was insufficiently so. The future was never not far enough away. Enough that neither of them would never know.

Nin liked straw. Nan liked Styrofoam. The hill obviously disliked the straw because the hill did all it could to free itself of the itchy stuff: it begged the winds to come and blow it away, it enraged the fireflies and it shook itself fiercely. It didn't mind Styrofoam, which was just fluff, but everyone else did, especially the bugs who came to rest on the hill, and because the bugs were such terrible whiners, the hill decided not to tolerate Styrofoam either.

Nin said to Nan that one fateful morning, "Look—beans are encroaching upon our hill."

Nan looked around. True—the beanfields seemed much closer than they had just a few months earlier.

"No, not those beans," said Nin, pointing to the beanfields. "*Those* beans." Nin pointed at a newly constructed billboard alongside the not-too-distant highway.

Nan at first did not see it and imagined a different billboard: "Coca Beans—put some toot in your toot!" But Nan quickly dismissed the idea as too silly to even mention to Nin, and by then Nan saw the offending blot on the landscape, a billboard so enormous and gaudy that why Nan hadn't previously noticed it was worthy of some psychological investigation perhaps. But that would have to wait for another time, for at the time the only item being investigated was the billboard: a fifty-foot wide by twenty-foot tall luminescent green-and-pink lettered atrocity featuring a photo of a smiling, dancing string bean in top hat, tails, can and spats. The bean was ascending a spiral staircase. The advertisement text read, "Dance up a stair to good health with Rogers' brand beans."

"Oh, that has to come down, Nin," said Nan.

"Exactly, Nan," replied Nin.

Nan rolled down the hill, across the highway and along the shoulder up to the billboard. Fortunately, it was cheaply constructed of soft pine. That gave Nan an idea for the moral justification for the destruction of the sign.

Back up the hill, Nan said, "Nin, they've killed the trees that went into the manufacture of that sign."

"True, Nan."

"And they've drained the trees of their life energy."

"True again, Nan."

"Would it be wrong . . .wouldn't it indeed be a holy thing for us to restore to the trees their energy?"

"Yes, indeed."

"And what are the spirits of pine called?"

"Why, turpentine, Nan. We have some at home."

"Yes, we should get it."

"Yes, and then we'll soak the sign in the spirits of pine and restore the life energy."

"Yes."

"But Nan?"

"Yes, Nin?"

"That may not be enough. For this to be a *holy* transformation we need more. Do you remember the holy transformation of Christ's disciples?"

"Of course, Nin. The Pentecost."

"Wasn't the spiritual transformation described as taking place in tongues of fire? Hasn't it been depicted so by artists for centuries?"

"Ah, yes! So after we douse the sign, we must ignite it with the spirit of the Lord."

"Yes, Nan. You get the turpentine. I'll get the matches."

When Nin lit the fire, Nan was reminded of Abednego's surviving the flames of Nebuchadnezzar's furnace in Babylon. From the German *abend*, or "evening"; the English "a-bed," meaning "to take oneself to bed"; the Hebrew *neg*—, meaning "south" [to the Hebrews, of course, the black races lived south]; and the Latin *nec*, meaning "not," a statement of contrast. Abednego's surviving the flames contrasted the darkness of night yet also upheld it. That it was both things contradictory simultaneously was inherent. All things confirm their opposites. The atheist is as dependent upon the concept of God for hir (i.e. "his or her") self-definition as the theist is. By standing in opposition to theism, the atheist acknowledges the existence of theism. Indeed, the atheist *needs* the existence of theism in order to exist hirself.

Of course, unlike Abednego, the billboard did not emerge from the fire unscathed. Coca the dancing string bean shriveled and writhed as the bill separated from the board. The wood was freed to dance according to its grain, and as Nin and Nan watched, it danced itself away completely. The billboard turned dark as it was consumed by fire, and then, in turn, fire gave way to the darkness of night. The spiritual transformation of the wood was complete. Nin and Nan watched the last embers give way before returning to the home inside the hill.

CHAPTER TWO
THE ROAD

Days passed, and Nin and Nan enjoyed the return of the landscape to the state it had been in before it had the sign: the purples, yellows, reds and blues of the wildflowers on the heath, punctuated by thickets of gnarled black oaks, weeping willows, scarlet buckeyes, and Eastern cottonwoods, and connected by a two-lane road that reticulated through the countryside like an unwelcome python. The hiss and smoke from the occasional automotive parasites crawling along its skin was repulsive. Both host and parasites had to go.

"We should do something about those pesky cars," said Nin, pointing again.

Nan expected to see a billboard advertising automobiles. A celebrity, perhaps, someone like Imogene Cocabean, holding open the driver's side door to the newest Studebaker, the Studebaker Hawk, and welcoming the viewer into the seat. And something lewd to connect image and purpose—a double entendre: "Come inside," perhaps.

"Where?" Nan asked Nin. No new signage had been put up to replace the obliterated one. The liberated one, that is.

In the distance, a dark Lincoln Continental was approaching. Even at a distance it seemed to be moving quickly.

"I don't think we'll be able to catch it, Nin. It's moving too fast."

"True, Nan. And to be fair, they wouldn't even be coming along here if there were no road for them to travel on."

"I agree. But we can't get rid of the entire road, can we? It's not as easy as a billboard."

"You are correct that it won't be easy, but I know we have to do it."

They sat quietly, gathering their thoughts.

"Nin?"

"What, Nan?"

"I know why we have to do this."

"Why, Nan?"

"Because the road is a false god, and we must tear down all false idols."

"Exactly!"

"Jesus said, 'I am the way,' but the road pretends *it* is the way."

"*Via* in Latin can mean 'road' or 'path' or 'way,' so you are correct, Nan."

"But how can we remove a road without being noticed?"

"Like Hadrian said: 'One brick at a time,' Nan. We must determine the vanishing points on either horizon and begin there, gradually removing a narrow strip of pavement from alongside the shoulder and then, eventually, from the road. This way, gradually, the road will become narrower and narrower until it just ceases to exist."

"But, Nin, do we have a maul?"

"Yes, we do."

"Do we have a spade?"

"Yes."

"Do we have a wheelbarrow?"

"Yes."

"Okay, so let's go find the road's horizons."

On one end, the road came over a hill and was lined by huge willows on both sides. At the other, the road vanished into a valley between two hills dotted with enormous granite boulders. The road's sacrilegious alpha and omega had been easier to define than Nin had anticipated. Very good, thought Nin.

They began mauling and shoveling the road into the wheelbarrow. Load after load they carted off over the horizon and buried in a field. Many days, weeks and months were spent by Nin and Nan in this pursuit. They were vigilant and successfully avoided detection by all occasionally passing cars.

Nan figured they had moved enough wheelbarrow loads and carried them far enough that, if the moved material were laid lengthwise in a one-inch wide strip, it could from where they were reach Point Barrow, Alaska.

Nin said, one day, "Every time we finish a strip, the road seems just as wide as before."

Nan replied, "Remember St. Cyril of Jerusalem's famous Parable of the Holy Trinity."

Nin asked, "No—what was that?"

Nan said, "In the 4th century, St. Cyril wrote that St. Augustine was walking along the beach one day and met a child who had dug a hole in the sand and who kept carrying water from the ocean to the hole, only to see the water disappear. When Augustine asked the child what he was doing, the child said he was trying to put the entire ocean into the little hole. Augustine said to the child that it was impossible to fit the ocean into that little hole. The child replied that he'd be able to fit the ocean into the hole before St. Augustine would be able to explain the mystery of the Holy Trinity."

Other days saw Nin encouraging Nan not to despair. By bucking each other up, they finally saw the day come when they could see their progress. It was a day of joy, and that night they celebrated. They feasted and drank wine. The road was certainly more narrow than it had been!

They ordered a couple of "Road Narrows" signs for the horizons and placed them just beyond where they could see. This would avert the passing drivers' suspicions. Even the occasional trooper would suspect little more than an incompetent DMV. These signs would suffice until the road became too narrow for two-lane traffic. At that point, the "Road Narrows" signs were replaced with "One Lane Road Ahead" signs. When the road had narrowed to within that proportion, the signs were replaced with signs stating, "Road Closed for Repair," and a week later, with railings and "Road Ends" signs. Exhausted but satisfied, Nin and Nan collapsed into their hill and slept for the better part of a week.

CHAPTER THREE
A VISITOR

Nin's and Nan's surprise was not altogether unsuspected when one day they saw a Range Rover churning up dust along the former road.

"What do you think he's up to, Nan?"

"I don't know, but we just finished seeding the ground. That meanie is undoing our work."

"Do you think it might be a revenuer?"

"Oh. You mean like Daddy used to shoot?"

"Yes."

"What do you think he wants?"

"Only two things the government ever wants, Nan: money or land."

"Heck, we don't have any money, Nin."

"Then I guess he's coming for our land."

"But this isn't even our land. It's God's land."

"I think he'd say that the domain is *eminent*."

"What's that mean?"

"That means no one's allowed to own any land except the government."

"Even God?"

"Especially God."

"But God made all this."

"Sure, but the government wants what's God's."

"Aren't we supposed to render unto Caesar what is Caesar's and unto God what is God's?"

"Yes."

"So we've got to stop this revenuer, Nin."

"Yes, we do. Let's go out and meet him by the road."

"The garden, you mean."

"Of course. Sorry. The garden."

"Okay, Nin."

Nan felt angry that this revenuer was destroying the newly planted beds of melon, squash carrots, cabbage, lettuce, and radishes. Nin and Nan had worked hard on these after recovering from removing the road.

Nan jumped out in front of the Range Rover, which turned sharply to avoid Nan and rolled onto its side. A furious bear of a man with a cut on his nose that was bleeding a river clambered out. He was wearing a ranger uniform.

Nan yelled at him: "You idiot! You're going through my vegetable garden! What are you doing?"

The ranger didn't seem to understand. He held up a finger as if to make a point and fell over dead. His brain had hemorrhaged.

Nin and Nan righted the Range Rover, pulled the ranger in, and then drove over the horizon. They jumped out just as the Range Rover and its occupant drove off a promontory point into the lake below.

They hurried back and wiped away the Range Rover's tracks. Nan spent the next two days re-seeding the dirt and swearing. Nin left Nan alone when Nan was like that. Nothing could have consoled Nan just then. The working of the dirt with fingers and replanting of seeds was therapy enough. And, for good measure, Nan also planted mustard seeds.

What worried Nin was that when one lone-wolf revenuer appeared, others were sure to follow close behind. They always worked in packs. The lone wolf was sent like the right eye, and having offended, it was plucked out. But now the rest of the *corpus lupi* had to be dealt with.

Nin and Nan dug pits in which they stood up logs with sharpened ends. They covered these pits with sod. The next Range Rovers would be skewered before they knew what had hit them. The fact that the dirt had turned to sod and that enormous piles of dirt stood alongside the road and wouldn't even be noticed by the revenuers, who were notoriously stupid, was fascinating.

Actually, seventeen revenuers came by to inquire, but all met mysterious disappearances, all obviously incapable of learning from the vanishings of their predecessors.

Eventually the revenuers stopped coming. Nin and Nan relaxed, confident, celebrated.

CHAPTER FOUR
A PIED PIPER ARRIVES

Uncle Sam pulls them along in a sling towed by giant razor-toothed clams. Or so went the song.

Nin and Nan listened to American music. They liked America. They just couldn't suffer her misrepresentatives' intrusions.

Musicians showed them a way to hear music as tastefully touching as they had sniffed it out to be.

Fanfare could have announced the approach of music but did not. Its arrival was sudden and surprising.

"Hullooo?" boomed a musical voice from outside of the hill one morning.

Waking up, Nin looked at Nan, and Nan looked at Nin.

"What in the realm of rowdy ratchets was that?" asked Nan.

"A visitor?"

"Not another revenuer, I hope."

"I don't think so. We haven't seen a revenuer in nearly a year. This must be something else."

"Like a gypsy?"

"Or a salesman. Or an evangelist for a mistaken cult."

"Why mistaken?"

"No true believer would ever be so hostile as to use direct confrontation at someone's home as an evangelistic tool. True evangelism cannot occur in a hostile climate. That's the whole principle behind the Rogerian Strategy."

"The what?"

"Carl Rogers's conflict resolution model for argument and persuasion. Rogers said that to reduce the sense of threat that prohibits people from considering your ideology, you must demonstrate that you have carefully considered and respect theirs. Only then might you get someone to agree to reciprocate by listening to you. That's why confrontational proselytizing always fails. Forced conversions are false conversions."

"Hmm..."

"I remember going to the grocery store once. I was standing in the cereal aisle, trying to find a breakfast cereal without BHA or BHT, which are carcinogens, when I felt holes being bored into the side of my face by some stranger's stare from down the aisle. I turned and looked to see a bug-eyed fellow coming toward me. I knew he was either a religious zealot or a drug addict. In either case, I did not want to talk to him. But then, sure enough, he confronted me. Without so much as a 'by your leave,' he asked me if I'd accepted the Lord Jesus Christ as my personal savior."

"Did you tell him about your beliefs?"

"No! He wasn't interested in my beliefs! All he wanted was to force his own XYZ Brand of Christianity on me. You know what I said?"

"No."

"I said, 'Excuse me. Would you accompany me to the customer service desk so that I can have you thrown out of the store for harassing a customer?' Then he said, 'I'm not harassing you,' so I replied, 'Then shut up!' He had no chance in hell of converting me to XYZ Brand that way. If he'd been smart, he'd have asked me about the cereal boxes. He'd have talked to me for five hours about cereal boxes if I wanted before ever saying anything about XYZ Brand."

"That's like what I read about W. Clement Stone, who wrote that Success through a Positive Mental Attitude book. He was an insurance salesman, and when he went on his rounds, he'd stop in at folks' houses and just talk to them about their families and such. You know—you have kids? You ever envision them going to college? Oh, really? Where? Mind if I ask you what you do for a living? And so on, never revealing once anything about himself. When his supervisors made follow-up phone calls to those folks later, you know—our man Stone was out there last week and we were wondering what your impression of him was—to a person these folks all said, 'Oh, Mr. Stone? He was delightful! What an interesting person!' But as I said, he never said anything about himself. What these folks found interesting, apparently, was themselves! They loved talking about themselves. Stone knew this and used this to entice them into wanting to reciprocate, which they could, of course, by buying a little piece of mind from him."

"Hullooo?" came the voice again.

"Should we let him in?" asked Nan.

"Yes, but be careful. Be on your toes. Don't tell him anything. He may work for the revenuers. They're everywhere, I tell you, and are just waiting for a chance to destroy us."

"Okay. We'll be very careful. No cult evangelist is going to fool us."

"Let him in, Nan."

"Certainly, Nin."

The man at the door was weird and had silver stars in his long white beard. His shirt had white stars on a blue background, as did his duffel bag, and his loose pantaloons were pied red and white. His stovepipe hat swirled all four colors together. But he was barefoot.

Slung back over his shoulder was a folk guitar on a white silk strap. The strap had the initials "SRV" embroidered into it in silver thread.

"Couldn't stand the weather?" asked Nan, assuming the visitor to be a Stevie Ray Vaughn fan.

"Hulloo? Oh—the strap. My brother found it in an alley in Austin, Texas. It was a night when Jimmy Vaughn was playing with his brother's old band. Everyone said they could sense Stevie's presence that night, and then my brother, who tended bar there at Antone's, went outside for a smoke and spotted the strap. He brought it in and one of the guys in the band went pale and asked him where he'd gotten it. He said the alley. The band guy said that was spooky because it was Stevie's old strap."

Nan looked at Nin, "No Rogerian Strategy here, eh?"

Nin laughed. "Apparently not." He turned his attention to Uncle Sam. "What can we do for you?"

Nan's attention began to wander.

You know, at some point I stopped writing, and I started talking. Is this the epiphany I, as a Joycean, had set myself up for? Or am I delusional?

"..., so I'd be happy to play a song." Nan had missed the first half of the sentence, the cause in the causal connection. Without that, for all Nan knew, Nin and Nan could be facing a *post hoc ergo propter hoc* argument or a deceptive enthymeme or a nonsequitur. Unless the premise is true, the conclusion is invalid.

Nin was distracted by the strange look on Nan's face, and responded for them both: "Depends on the song."

Nin ushered Uncle Sam in, and Nan went to the fridge to get some Jesus' Own Brand cheap wine with a smiling half-crocked Jesus on the label, halo and all. In the famous TV commercial, Jesus would sing, "You gotta have J.O.B. if you wanna be with me."

"Halooo?" pointed out Uncle Sam, touching the label like God touching Adam's outstretched finger. To his credit, he shook his head and said, "No, don't drink."

Nan responded with, "Don't mind if I do," and poured two glasses. Nan handed one to Nin.

They clinked, and Nan said, "To the song! What song have you brought us, oh Elliptical One?"

"Elliptical One?"

"That's good, isn't it?"

"You just make that up?"

"Yep."

"Okay. Good. Keep going."

"Oh, Bringer of the Tune, we'd like to hear you soon."

Uncle Sam snapped to attention as if he'd forgotten he was part of the conversation and had been playing at being Strictly Silent Observer Man. I don't think he has a superhero complex.

"Okay," said Uncle Sam. "Here goes." He flipped his guitar around, pulled a pick out his pick pocket, and prestidigitated, but no sound came out for the longest time until a slight bell could be heard way far away, like a church in a blizzard, just barely audible. It began to shape itself around a letter, a note.

<u>Z. Buzz. By Uncle Sam</u>

Z. Buzz. Z. Buzz. Z. Buzz.
Zeboombadoom!
Z. Buzz. Z. Buzz. Z. Buzz.
Zeboombadoom!

We send our bombs hailing down on you,
those of you in Sector Blue,
you who've been so gravel-blind (as to)
take Granny Smith for Gravenstein.

A. Smash! A. Smash! A. Smash!
Krackaragnarok!
A. Smash! A. Smash! A. Smash!
Krackaragnarok!

We saw the signs come down in flames
and the erasure of our agents' names.
We saw the road get taken down (by)
a modern James Gang, as they say in town.

Clickety snap! Clickety snap!
Cuff 'em! Read 'em their rights!
Then string 'em up from the highest tree!
We'll have peace in town tonight!

There'll be no deviation from our prescription.
The road will have to be rebuilt.
Kill the wrecking crew before they kill you.
Can't you see their guilt?

Snap swing swing swing! Snap swing!
Zeboombadoom!!
No one can stop us now
or tell us what to sing!

Death to our friends, our enemies!
Death to all we see!
Death to the infidel and to the god-fearing!
See them in that tree!

Z. Buzz. Z. Buzz. Z. Buzz.
Zeboombadoom!
Z. Buzz. Z. Buzz. Z. Buzz.
Zeboombadoom!

Uncle Sam had been singing since 11:55 a.m. By noon, nonconformists Nan and Nin knuckled under and announced that they could stand no more of his music.

"What kind of music was that?" asked Nin.

"I call it 'political satire,'" said Uncle Sam.

"No—it sounds more like propaganda," said Nan. "Redneck propaganda."

"Truly," said Nin, "you suck. Those were the lamest lyrics. What were all the goofy sounds? Did you want them to be onomatopoeia? Or is this a song for silly little children?"

"And the nitwits."

Uncle Sam looked offended. "Then which are you? Children or nitwits?"

"Neither."

"Did you even *listen* to the lyrics? They're a warning."

"I heard enough to hear that they blow," said Nin.

"No no no—you need to *study* the lyrics!" replied Uncle Sam.

"No no *no*," said Nan, mockingly. "*You* need to go!"

"No, here. Here's a copy of my CD," and Uncle Sam opened his duffel bag. The odor of dirty laundry quickly filled the room. Nin saw dozens of CDs inside the bag besides the stinky clothing. Uncle Sam pulled out a peach-colored CD case with black lettering announcing its title: *CD for Nin and Nan*.

Nin realized that Uncle Sam's visit could not have been accidental.

"Why would we want your stinkin' CD?" asked Nan. Nin picked up the CD and showed the title to Nan.

"Hey, Brother Sam did this just for us."

"Oh, he just has a different cover for each copy he brings to each house."

"No, interjects Uncle Sam. "That's the actual title. I've sold dozens of them. Look," and he pulled dozen more of the same CD out of his bag.

"How much are you selling them for?"

"Only ten bucks."

"All right—give us one." Nin pulled a ten-spot out. "Here, Brother Sam. For your CD and your rap."

"Should I sign it?"

"Please. Sign it, but don't inscribe it," said Nin (whispering to Nan, "resale value!").

"A lyric sheet's inside," said Uncle Sam.

"Enough with the lyrics already," said Nan. "It's time to leave."

"Read the lyrics," Uncle Sam said, closing his duffel bag, flipping the guitar back over his shoulder and then picking up the duffel bag. "Thanks for the beer."

"You're welcome, Brother Sam," said Nin, guiding the "intruder" out the door.

"What an ass!" said Nan as soon as the door closed behind Uncle Sam. "Do you believe that song? Snickety-snack? Wasn't that a line from Lewis Carroll?"

"I think so. 'The Jabberwocky.'"

"And you! Why were you being so nice to him?"

"What do you mean, Nan?"

"Calling him 'Brother Sam'! My gosh!"

"Well, I figured if Uncle Sam is the U.S., then Brother Sam is the—"

"Oh, that *is* funny. But why did you buy the CD?"

"To get rid of him. Told you he'd be a salesman. That's all he wanted. So, ten bucks and now he's gone. That was simple, and relatively cheap. Imagine if he'd been a Bible Salesman ? We'd have spent ten times that."

"Yeah, because we like the Bible."

"Well, we'll give this a listen. Maybe it'll sound better all produced and slicked up."

"I hope so, because it reeked live."

"Okay, I'll put it on."

"Not *now*. We just survived it once. Let's regain our strength first," implored Nan.

"Oh, no. Then you'll never get around to it. I know you. Now or never."

"Later. You can't catch me with a false dilemma."

"And you won't catch me with Big-Legged Emma."

"Zappa! That's right. Your Brother Sam doesn't seem to know Zappa."

"*My* brother? Fine. I don't care if we ever listen to the CD. Even if it *is* about *us*."

"Just *to* us, I think," said Nan.

"How do you know? What does 'skooby skippy' mean, or whatever he said? It could be an insult in his own personal secret language."

"Like *Magma*? What was their language? Kobaian?"

"I think so. That sounds right. But that's not what it was."

"You don't think so?"

"No—I'm pretty sure it was just scat."

"Scat? It *was* B.S.!"

"Ha! No," said Nin, laughing. "*Scat*! As in Scatman Crothers. Zippy de zow eye! He had a version of 'Be-Bop-A-Lula' that rocked! But he was big with scat singing!"

"Big scat? B.S."

"Oh, back to your Zappa with your potty humor, you!"

"Anyway, that crap of your Brother Sam's was no language. Heck, that fool didn't even speak his *own* language well," and then he added with a sarcastic snort, "Kobaian."

"Didn't Nirvana sing in Kobaian also?"

"No—that was Cobainian."

"Well, in both cases, the bands didn't care if anyone could understand the lyrics. So why do we have to?"

CHAPTER FIVE
THE CD

Two weeks later, they still hadn't heard the CD. They were sitting around bored one afternoon when Nin asked, "What do you want to do?"

Nan absently replied, "Nothing particular. Anything you want is okay."

Nin leapt up and grabbed the CD case. "Ah, ha! In that case, we are *now* listening to this."

"No! I didn't mean I'd agree to *anything*."

"Yes, that's precisely what you *did* say, and I'm holding you to it right now."

"Well, let's at least smoke some satistiva first."

"Okay. We can do that."

Nan rolled up a cigarette, and they shared it down to the end before Nin stood up and grabbed the CD case again. Nan was too stoned to object.

The CD player gave Nin a little trouble at first, but in a few seconds the sound of a faint church bell tolling could be heard. Nin sat next to Nan on the couch and folded the lyric sheet open for them to read.

That's rather cliché, thought Nan. *He stole that from AC/DC*. And then the buzzsaw lyrics began. Bombs dropping. Okay. Got that. Sector Blue? The blue part of the election map? The Democrats?

Gravel-blind? And two types of apple? This makes no sense. Smashing? Ragnarok? The end of time?

What? The signs come down in flames? Like the pea sign or bean sign or whatever it was? Erasure of agents' names? The buried? The road get taken down? Shit—he is singing about us? "He can't do that," said Nan out loud.

"We're no James Gang," said Nin.

"Listen—what the fuck? He's trying to incite people against us! He wants a lynching!"

"Death to us? Wait—which one's the infidel? Which is god-fearing?"

"Oh, jeez. What are we going to do?"

"Ignore it."

"*Ignore* it? He's going to spread this song around until even the police like it."

"Oh—I remember reading an interview with Mark Mothersbaugh of *Devo*, and he said the scariest thing was that, when Devo was arrested for obscenity, the cops in the jailhouse started a conga line and removed their belts and snapped them in a dance circle to the CD of 'Whip It.' And they sang along, knowing all the words!"

"Maybe that's why he quit Devo and began writing music for *Rugrats* and other cartoons."

"Maybe," said Nin. "I still don't know if I get it all, even with the lyrics right here. The gibberish is beginning to sound like the Beatles' fake Italian in 'Sun King.'"

"Fake Italian or Kobaian?"

"Oh, shut up. Let me think."

"Okay."

They fell silent and went to opposite corners of the room and looked out the nearest window, as if in meditation. The truth was that they both had the dickens scared out of them. Of course, I'm scared of Dickens, too. Horribly out-of-date social satire aimed at targets long since dead. And with Dickens' being paid by the word, by the installment, one could smell something afoul in the air.

"*Snap swing* is definitely a lynching. We've got to stop him."

"Oh, that's easy," said Nan. "Where did he go?"

"Well, I'd say he went on down the road, but—"

"There isn't any road! We tore it up, remember?"

"Okay, so we just follow his direction."

"Did you see the direction he left in?"

"No. We were busy arguing over petty shit."

"Well, I didn't either. And we have no idea the direction he came from."

"I'd guess from the urban sprawl."

"Well, that would make sense. So, he's heading into the wilderness? That makes no sense, because he has to spread his song."

"He could do that on-line. He could have his own internet radio station dedicated to hating us. They could be building an army against us!"

"Calm down! They can't do any of that until Brother Sam gets here. We have to figure out where he went. Or where he came from."

"Wait! We're assuming that he came from a place other than where he is going. What if this was not a stopover? What if it was the destination? He was reconnaissance."

"No. I don't think so. That guy was a leader of nothing. Even his bullshit was fake. That's it! A guy who bought dozens of novelty gag gifts to spring on his friends EVERY DAY! But that's a different subject. What were we talking about?"

"I don't know."

"How to catch him. How to corner him and collect him."

"Come now—he is human, after all," said Nin.

"*Is* he?"

"You're not back on your Kobaian thing again, are you?"

"No. No. No. Sorry," replied Nan.

Nin returned to the center of the room. "If you're right, then Brother Sam might just have come from the nearest city over the hill and returned there!"

"I think that must be, Nin."

"Well, Nin, let's go"

"Should we bring umbrellas?"

CHAPTER SIX
FINDING BROTHER SAM

As soon as they saw a road, Nan broke down. Going on was inconceivable, so they stopped at the closest motel, the Stampeded Antelope.

"Your foot it needs reinflation," said Nin. They'd been arguing about whether to walk or use the golf cart.

"Yeah, but I rolled," replied Nan, as if that were the answer. Well. Maybe it *is* the answer. What do I know?

Nan rowed while Nin looked at a map.

"What's up there?" asked Nan, pointing to a spot on the map.

"North," replied Nin.

Up the side of a rocky cliff, alongside mountain goats and big horn sheep, stood the Stampeded Antelope.

Naturally, therefore, the motel was decorated with a pirate motif. Rudders, nets, crabs, steering wheels and harpoons festooned the walls.

A coat of arms featured an oar at the fess point of an escutcheon.

Paintings of large vessels were hung in each room. Nin and Nan's room featured a frigate incongruously named *The Estancia.* One assumed she had transported cattle.

"Arrrr...," said Nan, in the best possible pirate accent that could be mustered. "They must have been pirate cattle. Arrrr…."

Why pirates? Who knew. The nearest navigable body of water was the Big River, some 200 miles away. As far as Nin knew, pirates had never broached it.

The lobby sported another incongruity—a loaded and ready freewheeling trebuchet, pointed at the front door in case of a Viking incursion, perhaps.

The motel restaurant was called Captain Snagglebeard's, and Nin and Nan ordered "all-u-can-eat" clam strips from the limited menu.

Nan asked the one-eyed waiter if the restaurant carried HoJo cola, but the waiter stared back blankly and shook his head.

"Ow!" said Nan. "Stop shaking my head!"

"Arrr…," said the waiter, "then don't ask impertinent questions, if ye know what's good for ya."

After the waiter left. Nan asked Nin, "Who are Ye and Ya? Are they cousins of ours?"

"Shut up, will you? Drink your grog."

The atmosphere of the restaurant began changing later in the evening, and the waiters began leading the dining patrons in a sea chanty sing-along and, as Nan called it, Okefenokee Karaoke.

"Our ship, it sails at morning tide—
I signed aboard to leave my bride.
I'd met her when the night was young

and so was she, but not for long.
I went to bed aged 24
but woke up with a toothless whore.
Ten thousand pints can't wash away
what happened to me on that day.
Ten thousand knots I now must sail
Before I forget that harpooned whale...."

And so forth. Very uncomfortably sexist. Mindless. Of course. He could never mind his manners.

He starts the lawnmower. Now, briefly, he is alone. Then he turns, and you see him. You turn also.

He exceeds the posted speed limit for Buckhorn. 99¢ a 6-pack. And that's just the fine. Old way is different from : than the new way.

Older is newer.

Only squares get around.

"Our names? Oh, sorry. We are, as you know, Late Night Traditions."

"What the hell are you talking about?"

"Oh—I was just talking."

"No. You were dreaming," said Nin, propping up Nan.

"'I Have a Dream,'" laughed the collapsible one.

"Okay, over here. Just lie down in bed. Sleep it off." Nin unceremoniously stepped away from being Nan's crutch, and Nan crumpled onto the bed and was out cold. *Good thing's Nan's not face down*, thought Nin. *Nan can't die like Hendrix.*

Nin turned on the TV with the remote. The only TV in the room. Obviously.... No.

Fellini's *Clowns* was on. Ah, the unbearable sadness of the clowns who used to be in the late great European circuses! They'd all been out of work for thirty years and still were sad. What a film!

Nin pulled a beer out of the microfridge and nuked some popcorn and began watching just in time to see the closing credits being interrupted by a station promo for a new sitcom featuring an unsuccessful gas attendant who smokes around the pumps. It's not a question of *if* he'll kill himself, but *when*. Following Monday Night Football. Then a commercial for vaginal cream. I wonder why the station wants us to link those two messages. Then an Army recruitment ad. What's the LCD? "Have a ball"?

Nin switched channels and got sucked into the episode of *Monk* that consisted mostly of flashbacks to middle school, when Adrian was stuffed into his locker by a bully.

A cognac from Nin's suitcase and a copy of Kenneth Patchen's *Sleepers Awake* were all Nin needed to begin taking repose.

Nin lay down and started in on his durante. He caught a big one but was too lazy to get up, so he buried it in his shirt.

Nan was snoring in the other bed. Nin realized that Nan was now face-up. Rolling Nan over again was hell—but Hendrix....

Nan needed a diet. Now!

Nan stopped snoring. Nin remembered a story on NPR about how each year hundreds of college students at party schools choke to death on their own vomit.

Nin personally had clung to toilet bowls and "let his face slide down the cool, smooth tile" like Jim Morrison.

They'd been unable to find out anything at Captain Snagglebeard's.

In the morning, Nan stumbled to the toilet, hung over, and threw up. Nin quickly exited to the hall and almost collided with a man wearing a pink bandana. He turned around and had a pink beard.

"Arrr.... I'm Pinkbeard the Pirate" does not instill fear. Nin laughed and walked on. This hotel spares no gag.

"Hurry," said Pinkbeard. "You'll miss him!"

"Who?"

"He's speaking in the conference room!"

"Who?"

"It's the first time he's ever been here!"

"*Who*?"

"Who? Why, Emperor Pinocchibush, of course!"

"That guy with the big donkey ears? Why's he here?"

"Where have you been? This is all newly annexed territory, you landlubber. You are inside the empire."

"Oh, jeez."

Nin stopped and let Pinkbeard hurry on. Oh, no—Nin and Nan were not just criminals—they were criminals inside Pinocchibush's empire. Pinocchibush the Ruthless. Pinocchibush the Patsy. Pinocchibush the Wooden Headed. Pinocchibush the Liar. He had a thousand faces and a thousand names.

The hotel bar was open, so Nin popped in for a shot and beer before facing the Oily One. A greased pig.

Into the crowd let's be herded.

Politicians all herd their constituents.

There he is, straw hat, barefoot, chewing on dried grass. "Yew people of the heartland are the heart of the Empire Pinocchibush," he was saying. Nin could have sworn Pinocchibush's nose had just grown.

"We have liberated you from yourselves. Now you will fashion yourselves in our image."

Sounds like the royal "we," thought Nin.

"Bull crap!" comes a yell from a few feet back in the crowd. "You liberated us from our oil! You eat while we starve!"

The outburst was quickly subdued by the Emperor's Secret Service, the notorious ESS.

"That young man is an example of the sort of dissent a free culture cannot tolerate," said the Emperor. "His lies—" at this point his nose grew again— "are anathema to an athematic society." What?

"Your Highness?" yelled a reporter from the front rows. "Would you tell us about your new nose?"

"What nose?" He looked cross-eyed at his nose, but stopped abruptly and said, "My nose is as it always is. Are you mocking your Emperor?" And the reporter was removed by ESS.

People began whispering. His nose! It grows when he lies, like that Italian puppeteer's little masterpiece. Ah, but he can't see it! The Emperor's New Nose!

The joke spread like free beer, and soon everyone was laughing at the Emperor. He got red as a Texas chili pepper and exploded. No—that wasn't him—that was a gunshot!

Nan woke up again later. Nin? Where was Nin? Obviously there'd been a struggle—furniture was overturned, and the bathroom smelled like the scene of a crime [Nan, of course, did not remember tripping over the furniture in the mad rush to the toilet].

Nan came to the inexorable conclusion that Nin had been forcibly removed. The lack of blood suggested kidnapping.

Nan took the Mauser from the suitcase. Loaded it. Put it in a shoulder holster, strapped the shoulder holster on, put a windbreaker over it—the windbreaker was blue and cotton-lined and had a red C in a blue circle, signifying the Chicago Cubs.

When Nan found Nin carrying on in the company of the enemy, thoughts of betrayal took over.

No—the room was not overturned in a struggle! Nin had arranged it to look that way. Nin was selling them out for thirty pieces of silver. To save Nin's own ass, Nin had betrayed them. Nin would get off easy for collaborating. Nan would fry. Oh, that's how it's going to be, is it? No way. I can't permit that.

Nan rushed towards Nin, pulled out the Mauser, pointed it at Nin and fired just as he tripped over some idiot's stupid feet.

The bullet lodged itself in the Emperor's ample behind. Before Nan could think, an insanely motivated Nin leapt up from the orchestra seats and landed at Nan's side, spun Nan around and pushed Nan through an exit into a waiting cab at a speed too fast for even to ESS to react to.

"For the border," said Nin. The cabbie turned around. For a second Nin thought the cabbie was Brother Sam—from behind the hair was similar. Thank goodness it wasn't. Or, rather, curses that it hadn't been!

Nan said, "This is great, just great! Now they're probably after us for attempted ass—"

"Shh!" Nin said, clapping a hand over Nan's mouth. "Taximeter cabriolets have auditory capabilities."

"And you! You were about to betray us!"

"No—not in a million years."

"But you were up there."

"Just an innocent spectator. I was carried there by the throng of the crowd."

"I thought—I was going to—"

"Shoot me? Ha ha! You've never been able to hit the side of a farm."

"A barn."

"That, too," laughs Nin. "You'd never have hurt me. It was all an accident."

"But—"

"It was all an *accident*. Now, drop it. We have to find Brother Uncle Sam."

"Excuse me!" the cabbie interjected. "You're lookin' for Uncle Sam the musician?"

"Yep."

"You're in luck. Look over there." The marquee at the Dune Beetle Lounge announced "One Night Only—In His Last Officially Permitted Concert—Uncle Sam Slammassasoit!" Apparently the Emperor was not going to tolerate American propaganda.

"Quick!" yelled Nin, throwing a couple of bills at the cabbie. "Here we are!"

The thick, putrid aroma of thick, putrid people came pummeling all who approached, compounded by a pounding that could loosen fire hydrants from their moorings.

On stage, Uncle Sam, solo acoustic again, was caterwauling some inhuman sex song. The audience was grunting in unison.

Nan didn't want another explosion, but Nin pushed. When the god-awful noise ended, Nin rushed up to Sam, pulled his hair down towards his shoulders for attention, and said in his ear, "You will not play that song."

"What? What song?"

"Don't give me that. *The Nin and Nan Song*, you perv."

"No—not a perv. Just an opportunist. But Pinocchibush is shutting me down anyway."

"Have you done the song?"

Nan came up, too. "Yeah, have you done the song yet?"

"Sure—a couple of places before I visited you."

"Here?"

"No."

"You're lucky."

"Hey, I hate that pig Pinocchibush as much as you do. I'll tell you what—I'll lose that song forever if you can help me get artists' rights reestablished in this country. The media's been bought out by the Emperor, and the artists dominating all the charts are plants."

"What?" asked Nan. "Venus Flytraps?"

"No, goofball," said Nin. "Like government spies."

"Like revenuers?"

"Exactly like revenuers."

"Then Old Brother Sam here isn't a revenuer?"

Sam started laughing. "Me? A revenuer? That'd be the day. I spit on revenuers."

Nan looked confused. "But the song…."

"A tribute, man," replied Sam. "I heard about what you two were doing from some old sheep herder, and I thought it was cool. So I wrote the song. It's sarcastic."

That shook Nan's head. "Oh, boy," was all Nan could say.

"Cabbie!" yelled Nin once they were outside, pointing at one.

"Don't do that—I have a van. Here—help me load my equipment and I'll drive."

"Drive where?" asked Nan.

"I'm assuming you want me to help you find the shepherd."

"Excellent. Let's go, Brother!" said Nin.

CHAPTER SEVEN
THE WAY OF THE SHEPHERD

Shall not the way of the shepherd be but a tree in the ocean? A lone shepherd, flock before him, stands on a hillside and sees something interesting.

Who's he going to tell? The sheep? His dog?

Oh, I see—a well-placed rocket grenade and even his dog won't be able to tell anyone anything.

Maybe he can be reasoned with. Unlikely, but I should never overlook that possibility.

They stopped at a diner for dinner.

Sam lifted his knife from his Salisbury steak and gestured with it. "The shepherd could be anywhere in a twenty-mile radius, I figure," he said.

"Oh, spare me," said Nin at the same instant that Sam's grand gesture signifying a twenty-mile square led his hand into contact with Nan's nose. The knife scratched Nan's cheek.

"Ow!" said Nan. "I said, 'spare me,' not 'spear me,' you clod!"

"Well, at least you get my point," said Sam."

"Let me look at that," said Nin, examining the cut. "Oh, that's not even deep enough to rub salt into for a good fencing scar. Now, come one. Listen to Brother Sam."

"Well, when I met him," said Sam, "he said he'd just come from the eastern edge of his sheep's run, where the large pond over by you is."

"It's a small lake," said Nin, "and it only touches on the edge of our area."

"Whatever. That's where he saw you. And he's old, so he's not going to graze his sheep over an endless expanse."

"Okay."

"And everyone knows that shepherds graze the sheep between a water hole at one end and a salt lick at the other—"

"So all we have to do," interrupted Nin, "is find where the nearest salt lick is, and we can define the grazing grounds!"

"I think that's how that works."

"I hope you're right," said Nan.

"Oh, ye of little faith," said Nin. "Trust me. We'll find him."

Nan looked out the window at the parking lot. A salmon Stingray was at one end and a white Pathfinder at the other. The street signs identified the restaurant as located on Morton Street between Pickles and Lam. A blue Barracuda was cruising the lot. Abruptly, the driver switched the Barracuda into reverse and backed into a stall without ever looking behind. Unfortunately a refried-bean-colored Pinto was already in that stall and exploded when the Barracuda slammed into its infamous and exposed rear-mounted gas tank. Refried-bean-colored crap blew all over the place. Someone with overalls and firefighter boots showed up with a shovel to clean up the mess.

"Nan!" Nan became conscious of the fact that Nin had been saying 'Nan!' for a few minutes. Seconds?

"What?" snapped Nan, not wanting to lose the reverie.

"Nothing. The waiter wants to know if you want another beer. Duh."

Nan looked up. Sure enough the waiter was standing there expectantly.

"Bring me a Colt 45," snarled Nan, remembering a movie title: *They Shoot Horses, Don't They?* When the 24-ounce can arrived at the table, Nan asked to borrow the waiter's pen.

Nan turned the beer upside down and slammed the pen tip through the bottom of the can, puncturing a neat round hole in it. Nan began sucking the beer out of the hole while turning the can rightside up and popping the top. The entire contents of the 24-ounce beer flew down Nan's gullet so fast that a bunch of it came out through Nan's nose. Nan's eyes watered, but, shaking it off, Nan snorted and said, "Now, what were you saying, Nin?"

"Sam was saying that the old shepherd's a crook," said Nin, which was enough for Nan, whose instant guffaw brought all the beer back up over the table.

Nin got up and got some bar rags and threw them at Nan. "Here, pig. Clean up your mess." And Nin and Sam changed tables.

The Emperor came on the television and began to speak:

"I'd like to respond to the recent outbursts that occurred at my appearance at the Stampeded Antelope resort. Those responsible will be brought to justice and, I swear, will not be misapprehended. Those who resort thus are declared enemies of the state, and their deeds will not go unattended. They will be tried, true, and convicted upon sentencing to corporal punishment of the worst kind when we find them. Let this be a lesson to those who would defrock their Emperor! Thus have I spaken!"

"Holy crap. Did he just declare tourist resorts illegal?" asked Sam. Nan wiped up the beer at the next table.

"I don't know what the hell he said," replied Nin, shaking his head. "Does *he* even know?"

"No—he just tried to read those cue cards."

"Well, I hope he gives his son some acting lessons. We can't have an Emperor acting like this."

"No," chuckled Sam. "We can't. Maybe, after we find the shepherd, we could do something to help." He winked at Nin.

"Yeah. Maybe."

While wiping the next table, Nin noticed a fellow at the table on the other side of Nin and Sam paying undue attention to the conversation. "Nin. Sam. Shh! Taximeter cabriolets have auditory capabilities," Nan said.

Sam and Nin turned and looked at the man, who immediately hid behind a menu.

"All I know," said Sam, "is that anyone eavesdropping will be sorry."

"That's for sure," rejoindered Nin. The man buried himself even deeper in the menu. "An eavesdropper is like a peeping Tom. And you know what happens to them."

"The Emperor's dungeon, if he's lucky. But I heard they're usually beaten to death on the way." The waiter went to the man's table.

"They're stoned by the crowd lining the streets to the dungeon." The man asked if the restaurant served squab.

"Unless they're maimed for life by those they've wronged, who, of course, get the first shot." The waiter shook his head. The man, feigning indignation, stood up, turned and hurried out of the restaurant.

"I guess the restaurant doesn't serve stool pigeons," said Sam, laughing.

"Or any other kind," said Nin, laughing along. Nan, finished with the wiping, tossed the rag onto the table and rejoined the two.

"Now, that wasn't necessary," said Nan, grinning.

"*Au contraire*," said Nin. "*Au contraire*."

"Well, we'd better move along," said Sam, "in case that was someone." They dropped a tip onto the table and went out into the parking lot just in time to see their neighbor speed off in a cream-colored Dodge Ram.

"After him?" asked Nan.

"No. We don't have the time," said Nin.

"Guys," said Sam. "I just remembered where I'd seen that guy. He seemed so familiar. And younger. But I'm pretty sure, without his wild white hair and long beard, that was our shepherd. He's gone incognito. He knows we're onto him! Quick! Into the Batmobile!"

"I thought it was a three-quarter ton Bonventure."

"Okay. The Samobile!"

"Yeah."

By the time they were all settled into their seatbelts, the Ram was long gone.

"Nin?"

"Yes, Nan?"

"Did you see the direction he left in?"

"No. We were busy buckling up."

"No problem, gang," said Sam. "It's all one-ways from here. He could have only gone one way." Nin noticed the construction detour signs ahead.

"Too bad we don't have something that corners," said Nan.

"Hold on," said Sam, flooring the accelerator. The afterburners kicked in as the van switched to turbo. It lifted up onto its two hind wheels and took off.

"If he's hungry, he's going to be stopping at a restaurant soon," said Nan. "Did he stop to eat, or to spy on us?" asked Nin.

"I think that must have been a coincidence," said Sam. "And when he saw me with you, he must have assumed that the song was my using him for a chump."

"So he's figuring you gave him the song to distract him while you collected us for the bounty," said Nan.

"Otherwise he would have known the bounty is on all our heads and would have tried to collect us himself," said Sam.

"He's too little to get all three of us," said Sam.

"Not if he had his pals Smith and Wesson with him," replied Sam.

"So we can assume he's not out to collect us," said Nin.

"True," replied Sam. But he might sell us out to the highest bidder."

"Crud! How did we get into this in the first place? Nin, it's all your fault. Opening doors to strangers. What were you thinking?"

"Actually, I did us a favor. The shepherd had already seen us, remember? He could have gone to turn us in and we'd never have known until the ATF showed up."

"True."

"You can kiss my feet now in gratitude."

"Not until you've been defeated," said Nan.

"Then you're going to have a long wait," replied Nin, "because we're not going to lose."

"Up here is another restaurant. Cruise the parking lot. Look for the Ram," ordered Sam.

They came upon the Crow Bar cautiously. The parking lot and an automobile wrecker stood side-by-side with a barbed-wire fence separating them, and one couldn't tell the cars belonging to one from those belonging to the other. Sam thought he spotted a Ram inside the wrecker's yard and said the wrecker might be in cahoots with the shepherd.

When they walked into the place, the entire joint was watching the TV and singing along the "My Beloved Emperor," the song preceding all ball games and Emperor's Addresses.

The patrons looked like mostly employees from next door: automotive coveralls were *de rigueur*. Some of them had to dry their eyes after declaring their fealty. A royalist crowd, to say the least.

The speech began:

"My citizens," began the Emperor, nose neat and trimmed short. "I stand before you because we cannot stand for any terrorist activity in our land."

"Yeah, and because you can't sit," laughed Nin.

"The terrorists need to resort their priorities and should only uphold the sort that is not traitorous."

"Huh? Oh, make him stop already, Nin."

"Shh!" Sam whispered. "Royalists! Sit here!" He sat down and abruptly pulled Nin and Nan down into a booth facing the giant screen face of Pinocchibush. "Copy their movements!"

When the patrons dropped to their knees, so did Nin, Nan and Sam. When the patrons swooned, so did Nin, Nan and Sam. When the patrons cheered, so did Nin, Nan and Sam. Well, maybe not Nan, who instinctively suspected any synchronized activity. But, even without being fully convinced, even Nan played along.

The speech droned on. "And so henceforth we shall seek death for all international terriers that try to get in our way!"

A couple of dog owners got up and hurried out of the place.

"Only terriers?" asked a reporter.

"Them and all those beasts that support them."

A few more pet owners got up, and among them was the shepherd. He hadn't noticed Nin, Nan and Sam.

What was really unfortunate was that this was the very weekend the World Terrier Championships were being held in the city. Dogs all over the place started acting strange. The terriers were being hunted. Sometimes packs of mongrels would turn them in.

The Emperor's popularity ebbed, especially in the new territory, but one would never have known that in the Crow Bar. Heck that crappy Bruce Springsteen song "Born in the USA" was even playing on the jukebox.

"The Way of US or the Way of None!" read a biker's bottomrocker.

"Um, Nin?"

"Yes, Nan?"

"Did you see the direction he left in?"

"Don't worry. If he's hungry, he's going to be stopping at a restaurant soon," said Nin.

"That's right!" said Nan, relieved.

CHAPTER EIGHT
THE 3RD RESTAURANT, THE 3RD TV

"The Third Eye. I've been visited by something that doesn't want me to succeed."

"That's ridiculous, Nan," said Nin. "Superstitious hogwash."

"Like you'd know."

"Stop it, you two," intervened Sam. "It's bad when I have to be the mature one here. I'm a musician, damn it!"

"Wait! There's a flaw in the ointment!" interjected Nan.

"Meaning a fly?" interpreted Nin.

"Cut it out, you two," intercepted Sam. "I mean it. Or I'll have to intra-duce you two to my two dukes," he said, holding up a suspiciously-not-so-frail-looking pair of fists.

At this rate, by the time dinner's over, we'll have been to a dozen restaurants and Sam will be as large as

a bounty hunter? thought Nan.

or worse, thought Nin.

What's worse?

A stooge for the machine.

"And what evidence have ye?"

"Empirical, of course."

"Hey, guys," said Sam. "I know her," pointing to a corner table inside the Third Eye.

"That's a table, Sam."

"No—the woman who was sitting there a minute ago."

"Who?"

"You didn't notice her?"

"Not really, Sam. I'm not here to score with the Chicks of the System. We're here to get that shepherd."

"Don't worry. We got him. This time I got his distributor cap."

"If you had the right car."

"Of course I had the right car! Who do you take me for? A Pinocchibushy?"

"Okay. So he's here somewhere. This is a huge place."

"Well, duh. It's a casino."

They walked past an old patron at a slot machine who was so heavy into her addiction that she'd forgotten herself and had soiled herself. Badly. One employee walked over to help, but a manager stopped him. "Not until she's finished betting, son. Then you can go get a mop and bucket since you want to be so 'helpful.' And thank her for coming to Pinocchibushoil Casino, where every handshake is greezy!"

They walked over a roulette wheel looking for shoeblack.

The crap tables stank. Madam Comnist walked over to Sam, whispered in his ear, and took off.

"What was that?" asked Nan.

"Nothing. I couldn't even understand her. Nin, do you have a pen?"

"We're staying?"

"Let me just say I think I got us a room."

"Sam, you're okay," said Nin.

"We'll see," said Nan. Muttering.

"What?"

"Nothing. Sounds great." For you. I'll be left without a friend.

"Beth, here, will be your friend tonight, Nan."

"Cool. Hey, Beth. What's your favorite rock and roll band."

"Ew. Maybe, oh, the Beatles!"

"Good answer. Okay. Now we've got something to talk about!"

Nin and Nan went up to the room, 369, just as they had said they would. And the room was open just as Beth had said. Unfortunately, Beth wasn't in it. That was sarcastic. Beth had to score some crank. But she had a room. And room service! Neither champagne nor caviar was too good for Beth!

"Get the Dom Perignon and make sure that's 100% Caspian Sea black sturgeon caviar."

"You got it! Thanks, Beth! Wherever you are! Hey, aren't we supposed to be looking for the shepherd?"

"No. That's Sam's job. We're just supposed to get drunk and pass out."

"Oh," and they did. The TV woke them. It came on automatically at 3:30 a.m. to share an urgent message from His Highness.

"But first a word from our sponsor, Makil Health Care. Now that Asian Bird Flu has been found in poultry in Turkey, protect yourself with a Makil flu shot. Payable in easy monthly installments of $29.95!"

"How did the poultry get eaten by turkeys?" asked Nan. "Are turkeys cannibalistic?"

"I don't know. Shh! Our illustrious leader is about to speak."

"Nothing up my sleeve. Presto!"

"Shush!"

"Maybe it's just the sick ones. Like those mad cows that were going around eating sheep."

"Don't tell that to the shepherd until we've caught him."

"Maybe we should disguise ourselves as a mad cow!"

"Oh, hush. Listen."

"And now! Live from the Empire City, His Highness!" Canned applause.

"Good evening, My Subjects. I have been told by my advisors that some of you have tried and failed and have deconstrued incorrectly what my earlier states meant, er, statements, er, meant. If you have assumed I have leveled a permanent ban on resorts and terriers, you have misapprehended me incorrectly. Though we need to guard against terriers' activities in our resorts, I of course am not suggesting we close our hostilitality industries. But let me not allay your fears one more second—every dog has his day.

"Now is not the time to take the streets in protest—"

Nin and Nan exchanged a glance. *We* took a street.

"Now is the time to reclaim the streets in the name of the Empire. Streetwashers, stop washing. Streetwalkers, stop walking. Give back what has always belonged to the people. The streets, sidewalks, and the gutter.

"Thus have I spaken!"

Man, thought Nin. He just condemned the commoner to the gutter. If *that* doesn't stir them up, what will?

And the station broadcast the Makil Health Care advertisement again. People walking down the street, albatrosses on their backs, turn into the Makil Health Care Center, then come out a revolving door, sans albatross. Wait! One of those people! It's the shepherd. He goes in, but he never comes out. He didn't have an albatross on his back. Almost as if he'd just coincidentally decided to enter the building there just then. Of course, accidents don't exist, chaos doesn't exist. William Burroughs said that if you ever think chaos exists, look to see if anyone's profiting by it. Sure enough, someone will be, and you'll realize that chaos does not really exist. Nan was lost in thought.

"Did you see that?" asked Sam.

"That was the shepherd?"

"I think so."

"Nan? Did you see it?"

"Huh? What?"

"The shepherd going into that building."

"What? Oh, the shepherd. Where?"

"That was the Makil Health Care Center."

"Graceless," said Nan.

"Gracious," corrected Nin. Nan scowled.

"Graceless," repeated Nan, with emphasis.

"That's the first target, kids," said Sam.

"We're short, not young," replied Nan indignantly.

"It's designed as a huge cross, each wing dedicated to one speciality: hysterectomy, tonsillectomy, circumcision, and cosmetic surgery."

"How do you know that?"

"TV commercials, Holmes. Like everyone else."

"Which one do you think our shepherd would be involved with, do you suppose?"

"I suppose stockings. I don't know. What does he prefer: playing with his mouth, playing with his pud, playing with his neighbor's toys, or conceptualizing bodily perfection?"

Tough question. I don't even know if I could tell you for myself, even less for someone else.

Yes, that's me! "Even Less For Someone Else." Nin looked at Nan, who was falling asleep. I hope Beth has a sense of humor. Better order some more Dommy P. before she gets back. She's not likely to order it herself. Oh, well. She thought Nan was cute and I was clever. Madam Comnist knew them. From years ago. We don't talk about it. It's over and done with. It's in the pond in the park, and ducks down to use it.

Ducks drown to use it.

CHAPTER NINE
THE MAKIL HEALTH CARE CENTER

"Of or pertaining to the uterus" is the definition of "hysteria." Thus, to cure women [note: *only* women exhibit hysteria, by definition] of their hysteria, doctors rip out their uteruses.

Whenever a typical doctor treats a woman and cannot figure out what is truly wrong with her, that doctor dismisses it as "hysteria" and cuts out her uterus.

Of course, the doctors caught on to the fact that the jig was up about the word "hysteria" and changed their prognosis to "premenstrual syndrome" and came up with expensive placebos to cure the imaginary ailment, or rather the single ailment that included thousands of unrelated symptoms.

Take these pills, Alice. They'll cure you. How dare you stand there and bleed all over the place?

I remember my insurance paperwork once stating, "Pregnancy will be treated like any other illness," i.e. as a disease only doctors know how to cure. Before doctors, women could not be cured of their pregnancies.

A man was arguing with a nurse at a nurse's station. His gestures were violent, his pointing finger a dagger in the air.

"My wife loved me before she came in here for this completely unnecessary operation, and now she won't have anything to do with me," he was saying. "And it's *your* fault."

"Sir, I wasn't even on duty that day."

"Not *you*. All of you. You greedy slimebags who'd rip out a woman's innards in exchange for memberships at the exclusive 'no-women, no-Blacks, no-Jews' country clubs. You hate women so much you can't even stand to have their innard-less bodies on your links. That's it, isn't it?"

"Sir, I wasn't there. And I don't golf."

"Of course not. They don't allow you to."

"Who?"

"The doctors. The greedy scum who cut out my wife's love for me."

"Sir, I'll get you a supervisor. Just a minute."

Nin watched her mouth the word "security" into the phone. Nin walked up to the man.

"Hey, man. I agree with you, but you'd better get the hell out of here. She just called security, and the rentacops will be here to rough you up in just a minute."

"They cut up my wife—"

"I know. And they'll cut you up, too. I think they're still conducting Mengele's phosphorous experiments on the behavior ward patients."

"What?"

"No joke, man. Go!"

"Thanks," and he ran. Nin saw him wave from his car in the parking lot just as the rentacops showed up.

"A friend of yours?" asked one of the steroidal rentacops.

"No—not at all. I was only telling him what the time was. I'm here to see a friend. A shepherd friend of mine who until recently had a beard checked in, and I want to visit him. Where's his room?"

"How should I know?" asked the rentacop.

True, thought Nin. Steroids have rotted your brain. You are way too stupid to be qualified for anything other than being a rentacop or a politician. At least two regions had, within, recent memory, "elected" (such a term could only be used lightly inside the Empire) steroid-befuddled former pseudo-athletes as their governors. Several others had hired empty-shelled actors to play the parts of their representatives. The worst, though, were incapable of discerning between ministers and "ministers of state," so they gave over their governance to whatever religious organizations had their boys by the balls.

Sam derailed this train of thought. "Excuse me, my good man," he said to the friggin' rentacop. It was embarrassing, conciliatory, submissive. A sort of Stepin' Fetchit routine. "I also am a friend of the shepherd. Whom may I make my inquiry of regarding his room location?"

The rentacop's head spun around three times and then exploded.

Another rentacop came over. "Model J42 just exploded. We need a replacement." Presumably he was communicating with someone.

The nurse said, "I just looked up our admissions. He's not here. Of course, this is mostly a women's ward. Have you tried Circumcisions?"

"Why?" asked Nan. "Aren't there women admitted there?"

"No! Female circumcision? How barbaric!" said the nurse, seeming shocked.

"But male circumcision?"

"That's for good hygiene."

"Oh. You know, toes have more infections and hygiene problems than penises do. Why don't you just lop off everyone's toes?"

"They might over in cosmetic surgery. I'm not sure. You'd have to check over there."

"Okay. Come on, Nan. Sam, come on. We've got to go to the circumcision ward."

"Why would our shepherd want a circumcision?" asked Nan.

"Who knows? Maybe he heard the voice of God," said Nin.

"And so he wants to cut off the head of God?" asked Nan.

"I have an idea," said Sam. "But we're going to need to find the hub of this place."

"Hub?"

"Yeah, you know. The physical plant. The communications center. The hub of the nexus."

"Here's the next ward. Ask the nurse."

"Excuse me. Where's your physical plant?"

"Mnnnbrngrnrbrngr…."

"What?" Nin and Nan exchanged confused glances.

"Oh," said Nin. "This is the tonsillectomy ward. They're pulling *everyone*'s tonsils out, apparently. Even the nurses'."

"We'd better keep going. I need my tonsils. They protect me against infection," said Sam.

"Look—a poster for a bargain. Today only—they're doing free appendectomies with every tonsillectomy sold," said Nan, feigning excitement.

"As I said, we'd better keep going. I'm led to believe that stepping onto the hospital grounds is implied consent for experimental treatment."

"Here's a sign that says, 'no admittance.' This must be it," said Nin. "Here we go." Nin and Nan followed Sam into the communications center. He whispered something to the operator, who scurried away like a cockroach. Sam picked up the hospital's P.A. system microphone and switched the "all on" button.

"Attention, all hospital patrons. This is God. And I'm looking for the shepherd whose beard was recently shaven."

Sam covered the microphone with his hands. "You go out to the entrances and catch him if he tries to leave," said Sam. Nin and Nan hurried out. "I am your God, and I want you to prepare a sacrifice. Bring your son to the altar and sacrifice him to me." Sam was betting the shepherd had a son whom he had left in charge of the flock. "Should you so much as question my demand, and I shall smite all your descendents throughout all of eternity."

The shepherd, looking up at the loudspeaker, understood. However, he had no son. That he remembered. He sped out of the hospital, sheath intact, and hurried into the arms of Nin and Nan.

"Wait a minute, shepherd," said Nin. "Where are you hurrying off to?"

"I have to find my son."

"Oh, and where is your son?"

"I don't know." Just then Sam joined them. "Hey, you, singer—I know you."

"Hello, old shepherd. Where are you off to?"

"To find my son, but I don't know where to find him."

Nan began to say, "Leave him alone and he'll come home," but Nin elbowed Nan's ribs hard. "Ow!"

Sam winked at Nan and Nin. "Hey, we were just talking about how we needed an adventure. How about my friends and I help you find him?"

"Really? I'd be grateful."

"Of course." Sam whispered into Nan's ear, "We'll be able to keep a close eye on him now, at least."

Nin was thinking they'd take a long walk down a short beer.Chapter Ten: The Happy Hunting Grounds

"I had a wallet made of foreskins. Whenever I rubbed it, it turned into a briefcase," said Sam.

"That joke is as old as the heels," said Nin.

"So's that metaphor," said Nin.

"Do not mock the Lord," said the shepherd.

"Man, you sound like Nan," said Nin.

"What's your name?" asked Nan.

"Said," said Said, the shepherd.

"Said?" asked Sam.

"Said," said Said.

"Said?"

"Said said, 'Said.'"

"Said said, 'Said'?"

"Said said, 'Said said, "Said,"'" said Sam chuckling.

Said said, "Said" again, for emphasis.

"That's your name?" asked Sam.

"Man, you sound like Nan," said Nin.

"Do not mock the Lord," said Said.

"And *that* saying predates the meteor that killed the dinosaurs," said Sam. "Want me to turn on the radio?"

"No," said Said, so Nan did. A woman was singing a song about society. Nan immediately was captivated by the timbre of her voice and the sloppy arhythmic drumming behind her.

"That drummer's as sloppy as Keith Moon," said Nan.

"So turn it off, then," said Nin.

"No. I love Keef Spoon."

"Nin, you should appreciate all kinds of music," said Sam.

"Sheesh," said Nin and Said simultaneously.

"*Parescum paribus facillime congregantur*," said Sam.

"What?" asked Nan.

"Birds of a feather flake their feathers," said Sam.

"Oh," and the jingle announcing a speech by the Emperor came on.

"Not again."

Nin turned the radio off.

"No, leave it on," said Nan.

"Oh, god, it's awful."

"You gotta know what he's saying." Nan turned it on.

"The trade imbalance is impaired by terriers and bailiffs," said the Emperor.

Nin turned the radio off. "Be real. He doesn't make any sense anyway."

"Leave it on," said Nan, switching it on again.

"For the most part, the peoples stink the way I do," said the Emperor.

Then a well-timed ad for deodorant soap came on. Even Nin couldn't take it, as when even strengthening accord.

As when even strengthening accord, evening was more than we could afford. Through the telephone was broadcast the voice of irate Beth: ripped me off, Dom Perignon? You didn't even leave me a glassful. My Big Brother knows you're there.

"Sam, you idiot. You gave her your number?"

"It seemed like a good idea at the time."

"Famous last words. You've got to ditch that phone. They have global positioning systems in them. Now that you called in for messages, they can find us."

"Do not fear her big brother," said the shepherd, flinging the phone out the window. "Only the Lord can see where we are and where we are going."

"I guess in the larger, philosophical sense, that's true," said Nan.

As when even strengthening accord, Nin kicked Ninself in the butt. They needed some of the rest of the saints. That'd recover their divanity. And even a cute angel has angles. A dowager turned to a dowitcher and said, "Fly me away over the firewater and set my keester on the kieselguhr." Nin turned awee.

"Stop that!" said Nan. "Your spinning's making me dizzy."

"Don't tell me. Tell Jenny."

"Beth," said Sam.

"Oh, play us a song on the spinneret," said Nin. "I'll see you all later." And Nin left.

"What's gotten into Nin?" asked Sam.

"Nin's not big on the radio," answered Nan.

"Bad ratings?" asked the shepherd.

"No. Not like that. Even God has bad ratings. Nin just doesn't like much popular music or talk radio."

"What does Nin like?"

"Old radio shows. *The Green Hornet. The Shadow. Inner Sanctum.* That kind of stuff."

"Politics today are the greatest radio play of all," said Sam.

"I don't think Nin thinks so," said Nan.

"Sure he does. This is part of Nin's act in it."

"I do not think that Nan does not think that Nin thinks so," said Said. "For if Nan did, the Lord would think, So what? But he has not revealed that to me."

"The Lord would think? So what? What are you saying, man?" challenged Sam.

"We must be in a moon void-of-course."

"'We must be in a moon void, of course'?"

"Never mind."

"Nevermind? What? In Bloom?"

"Is that Joyce?"

"You mean Beth?"

Will you all just shut up? My house

has just been invaded by ladybugs and box elder bugs—there go those elders chasing the young ladies again—and I can barely walk without crunching something. Even the harmless can be annoying. Unless annoyance is their harm.

They attack the paper I am writing on. They distract me from the table. Now I have nothing to Chase Manhattans down with the fascist regime! What am I hunting for, again? Meaning? Or just the next word? Or do I want the last word? Omega. Which ends in an alpha, which begins the whole stinkin' process all over again.

Similarly, the consonant alphabet ends on a vowel. What? Only one vowel ends on a consonant. I tell you, English ain't fair. Ignore that linguist behind the curtain. He's not really the Great Linguini!

"Poseur!" I want to hear you yell.

Help that shy manicotti come out of his shell, would ya?

Recording the events as they occurred is difficult when all the voices come at once.

"Nan? Wake up!" The writer crashed the cymbals like Mick Fleetwood in the *Blues Jam in Chicago*.

"He's no fun—he fell right over," said Sam, quoting Firesign Theatre.

And pop goes the weasel.

Ping! The arrow was loosed, and the weasel was killed, teeth locked on the eagle's jugular. And eagle-weasel stew fed them at the campsite that night.

Eager-Weasel Stu came upon them from the freight yard and asked if they would share their libation.

"If you mean this god-awful stew," said Sam, "be our guest."

"Do not blaspheme!" said Said.

"No, I mean what he's drinking when you're not looking," said Stu, pointing to Said's jacket pocket.

Sam reached in and pulled out a pint of rotgut. "Aha! Don't talk to me of blasphemy, old man. For all you know, this could be your son."

Said squinted at Stu, sized up his features, and said, "Are you of the covenant?"

"Huh?"

"Are you of the covenant?"

"What do you mean?"

"He means," explained Nan, "have you had a chunk of your penis lopped off by illiterate believers who don't understand what Paul meant in Galatians when he said the ritual had been 'abrogated.'"

"What Nan means," explained Sam, "is are you circumcised?"

"What a rude question," answered Stu. "I only wanted a snort."

"My son was circumcised."

"Well, not that it's any of your business, but so was I."

"Aha!" said Said. "Tie Isaac to that rock. I must prepare the sacrifice."

"No, Said. Don't you have to take him to the top of the mountain first?" pointed out Sam, gesturing towards the top of the hill.

"Oh, yes. Well, Son. Well met. You will accompany us. You will be well fed and made ready for the Lord."

"Can I have a snort of that bottle?"

"Sure. Have it all. We'll get you more tomorrow."

"Thanks, Father."

Sam said as an aside to Nan, "I think we can assume Said believes in the God of the Old Testament, not the New."

"And you think they are different?" asked Nan.

"Well, at the very least, the Old Testament God was far more immature than the New Testament one."

"Ah, you've read Alfred North Whitehead."

"Who?"

"Forget it."

"Alfred Lord Penishead?"

"I said forget it. You're as bad as Nin."

"Speaking of whom," said Sam, raising his voice to include Said and Stu, "I wonder where the hell—"

Said raised his eyebrows.

"—where the heck Nin is. Then Sam reboarded his previous train:

"Alfred White Skinhead?"

"Hush."

"Alfred Popped Blackheads?"

"Be quiet."

"Didn't he write *The Idiots of the King*?"

"*Idylls*, and that was Alfred Lord Tennisball, as Python said. Now please be quiet. You're giving me a migraine."

"I pain, you pain, we all pain for migraine."

"What a reet. No wonder your music career is shit."

"Hey!"

"Wait, young Nan," said Said. "You are unfair. Sam here has a brilliant ballad he once shared with me. I don't remember the words, but it was called 'Busy Buzzy' or something."

Nan rolled the eyes at Sam. "He doesn't remember the song?"

At the top of the hill, Said said again, "Now tie Isaac to the rock!"

Nan looked around. "What rock, Said?"

"Do not call me Said. My name of the covenant is Abraham."

Nan laughed. "I can't believe I'm up here with you three stooges.

Said tied up Stu with twine, pushed him down onto the ground, and then pulled out a long, serrated chef's knife. He lifted the knife and was about to bring it down. Then an 8000-watt amplified voice boomed across the hillside: "Abraham!" The voice was so loud, Nan's ears rang.

It repeated: "Abraham!"

"Yes, Lord!" said Said, trembling.

"Put down that knife!"

"Stupid knife! Ugly knife! Knife of the guttersnipe!" said Nan, laughing.

Sam slapped Nan's arm.

"What? The Lord said to put it down."

"Ha ha."

Said backed away from Stu and dropped the knife. "Lord?"

"I want you to leave here and get a job at a 7-11 and never say anything about this to anyone ever again!"

"Yes, Lord."

"And I want you to forget Sam's song."

"I don't remember it anyway."

"Oh, shit," said the Lord.

"The Lord just cussed," said Nan, elbowing Sam in the ribs. "Come on. Let's get out of here."

"What about Said and Stu?"

"Forget about them. It's over."

Down the hill, Sam and Nan got in the car, and Nin ran up and joined them.

"They really fell for that, didn't they?" said Nin, tossing a microphone and a small Pignose amp into the back of the van.

"Hey, you took my Pignose?"

"Borrowed. Not took."

"That was good. That was really good," said Nan.

"That should do it," agreed Sam.

"For Said and Stu. We still have Pinocchibush to worry about, though," said Nin. "But for now, let's get a few drinks."

CHAPTER ELEVEN
FINDING THE NEEDLE IN A HAYSEED

"No, the Emperor is many people. The true Emperor never appears in public. He has a series of doppelgängers appear for him, pretending to be him," said the bartender to Nin.

"The problem must be finding doppelgängers stupid enough," said Nan.

"Actually, that's not difficult. The plastic surgery required to duplicate them must be the most complicated part of the procedure," said Sam.

"Where's all this plastic surgery done, do you think?" asked Nin.

Nan and Sam looked at each other and answered simultaneously, "the Makil

Health Care Center!"

"Yes. We need to go back there."

"To the cosmetic surgery wing?"

"Of course."

The receptionist looked at them as they approached the hospital's cosmetic surgery registration desk.

"May I help?" she asked with suspicion in her voice. Her gray hair was long, like a little girl's, but her face had given up childhood decades earlier. Her voice was raspy, like a lifelong, boozin', smokin' cabaret singer's. Sam half-expected her to burst into Brecht and Weill's "Alabama Song."

"What procedure are you here for?"

"Do you guys do toe-lop-off-to-me's?" asked Nan. "The penis mutilators said you might."

"No. If you're here to cause trouble, I'll just call security now," she said, reaching for the phone.

"No!" yelled Nin. "Excuse us. Nan here sometimes loses site of our objectives. Actually, we would like to speak to someone in cloning."

"That's a restricted ward, sir. Not just anyone can come and clone himself or herself."

"Of course not. Ridiculous. Clones of *us*? Good god, that'd be horrible. We're here to ask on behalf of Vice Admiral Dickless (by the way, your circumcision ward did fine work on the removal of his genitalia!) whether or not you can clone a heterosexual daughter for him. The press, as you know, has been merciless to his poor lesbian daughter."

"Poor?" screeched Nan. "Do you know how much money that family has? Enough to build a whole new ward for the hospital and a recreation center for the staff. That *is* what the Vice Admiral was talking about, wasn't he?"

"Yes, but that's not to be discussed!" scolded Sam, trying to come across as the boss. "We just need a quick tour of the facilities."

"Well, we don't have any guides…."

"Not to worry. We'll just discreetly show ourselves around. We won't get in the way. We'll only be a half-hour or so."

"Did you say a recreation center for staff?"

"No, we didn't. Sh!" said Sam, winking.

"Okay, then, but a half hour only. After that I have to call security. We're not supposed to allow any unauthorized visitors."

"Oh, we're authorized. The Vice Admiral is in such a hurry, though, that we had to forego the traditional red tape this time. He couldn't spare the extra two weeks."

"I know what you mean. Okay, go ahead then," she said, and she returned to her registration files.

"Quick! Come on," said Nin.

"Right behind you," said Nan.

They went in through the out door of a sealed-off area when an orderly left. They entered a hallway filled with display cases of clone models, and each model was the Emperor. They saw Bulked-up Muscleman Emperor, Super-Tall Basketball Emperor, Darth Emperor, Sumo Emperor, Super-Sized Cranium Emperor, and, for the kids, Fashion Designer Emperor, Army Guy Emperor, Horse Groomer Emperor, Movie Star Emperor. And dozens more. Collect them and trade them with your friends! An entire culture of clones coming soon!

"Any deviation from the Pinocchibush agenda is damned unpatriotic," read a sign on the wall. "You either agree with Pinocchibush, or you are a heathen member of the axis of evil."

Another sign read: "One world, one culture, one mind: Pinocchibush's!"

They read the signs and were appropriately dumbfounded. The room was as quiet as a Cistercian blog.

"This is worse than the ward of toe-stirs," said Nan, finally breaking the silence.

"Or a jar of mixed penis," replied Sam, with a single chuckle.

"Assaulted jar," added Nin, nervously. They located the control center of the room, to which was attached a presumably-cloned brain of the Emperor.

"Okay—there's the brain. Nan, hand me the plastique."

"What if that's the *real* brain," said Sam, "and the rest are clones?"

"I think there'd be better security."

"You're probably right."

"I don't know," said Nan. "It looks like some of the emperors are male, others female, and still others androgynous or even hermaphroditic. Maybe this is the sort of advancement needed by society."

"What? You idiot!" answered Nin, placing the plastique at the brainstem. "A fascism of androgyny is still fascism. Approving of dictatorship just because your side would benefit is unconscionable. Remember how the Emperor solidified his power: by staging a mock terrorist attack on the cultural center of the empire. This way he could simultaneously silence dissident artists while setting the table for an imperialist expansionist war." Click!

"Okay," said Nan.

"Come on," said Nin. "We have ten minutes to get out of here."

From across the field beyond the parking lot, the explosion was beautiful, its plume reaching to heaven for purification and justification, which it received in its dissipation.

Fusty, lis pendens took my breath away. Would I get it back? That was hard to say.

Breathing had been made illegal in 2004. And canned Pinnochibush air smelled like a killing floor. Polyphemus Pinocchibush staring at a mirror at its own Gorgonish hair, the most evil emperor gormandizing there.

Millennium alimentary elementary aluminum laminates the luminous elimination of mellifluous lepidopterists who malign my line of neo-Malthusian malediction while claiming "butterfly" means "flutter by" rather than "butter excrement."

The banana moon fills the cold with emptiness. Driving west, I, my destruction left, behind, find myself unfindable, I'll never understand myself, so my reason is gone.

I thought, by throwing myself into politics like Lennon I could stave it off a little. Even he only staved it off briefly.

I thought by focusing outward, my innards would heal themselves. However, what I've found is that, as polluted as I am, the outside is polluted more.

There are the realities of life. Learn them now and decide if you want to continue:

No one will ever really love you. They all have angles and games and needs and desires that pollute the purity of real love.

No one will ever really like you. Only when they have to seem like they do to further themselves in others' eyes will they bother to pretend.

No one will ever really tolerate you. Even your parents and spouse will wish you dead over continuing to have to deal with you. They'll love criminals and charlatans over you. Actually, they'll ascribe criminality and charlatanism to you while praising the integrity of the criminals and charlatans.

Pay them no mind. They want to destroy you, or, as I have said elsewhere, they want to *destory* you.

Here is their message: Hatehatehatehatehate....

I hope you are not overwhelmed by its complexity. They cloak it like Joseph, but it's still hatehatehatehatehate.

"Nan!" A voice. Nin's. "Come on, snap out of it!" And then, apparently to Sam, Nin said, "Nan's lost in reverie again."

"Oh, yeah?" Nan snatched a bugle out of a passer-by's hand and played about twenty notes of a boisterous call and then stopped.

"What are you doing?" asked Nin.

"There! Now I'm lost in 'Reveille'!"

"Isn't that a ghost town along the extraterrestrial highway near Area 51?" asked Sam.

"Nan's been lost there for years," laughed Nin, climbing up into the truck.

"Here," said Sam, "throw this in the CD player."

"What's this?"

"A book-on-CD about Area 51."

"Who roaded down?" asked Nan.

"I don't know. I snagged it in the hospital as we were walking through."

Nan opened the box, but the Area 51 CD was not inside. Instead, Nan found a CD entitled *Preventive Hysterectomy for Troublesome Female Toddlers*.

The CD argued that early hysterectomy, especially infant hysterectomy, prevented not only potential hygiene problems and infections—the same argument used for circumcision—but also prevented undesirable sexual behavior problems, including emotional upheaval due to hormonal imbalance. Of course, circumcision and excision, or female circumcision, are both prescribed as methods of preventing randiness and nymphomania and other sexual maladies. Thus, argued the CD, preventive hysterectomy was the best way to assure parents of having well-mannered and cooperative daughters.

"Hey," said Sam, after ten minutes. "What's that got to do with Area 51?"

"Maybe the aliens swapped the CDs," answered Nin.

"Maybe we should go back and blow up the rest of the hospital, too," said Nan.

"Are you kidding? We disabled it as much as we can. We now need to put some good distance between us and it," said Sam.

"And then on to the capitol!" said Nin.

"Yes!" agreed Sam.

CHAPTER TWELVE
AND BETH AGAIN

"Why not?"

"Oh, come on, Nan. She's probably still pissed about the Dom Perignon on her hotel tab."

"I bet she didn't remember not drinking it herself."

"Maybe, but we need her."

"No, Sam. *You* might need her. I don't."

"Well, just apologize."

"No. I'm going down to the bar to find Nin. You let us know when you're done."

Nan left the hotel room at the casino, amazed that they were back there again. But they'd agreed. They'd hoped Beth could be persuaded to worm her way into Pinocchibush's inner circle. There she could keep an eye on things.

"I'm none the better for the wear and tear on my own old clothes, so ye'd better be keeping to the center lane," said Beth to Sam. And so they talked about her role in an elaborate play designed to humiliate and disgrace Pinocchibush, forcing him at the least to abdicate his throne as had his father, Pinocchiclinton, whose nose grew out of his pants. At least his father had not been an imperialist expansionist working in cahoots with oil companies.

In Beth's hotel room, following her tirade and the ensuing reconciliation with Sam, the television came on, and Pinocchibush's ubiquitous face appeared. Nin and Nan returned.

"The broodish attack on the Makil Health Care Center this afternoon has resorted in one nambatory response on behalf of this excathedra: we have discovered oil in the hill country and must begin drilling immediately to finance our counter-insurrectsurgence effects, er, efforts. We expect our neighbors to lower all braid terriers—"

The Emperor turned his head to the side to hear something shouted to him by someone off-camera—

—"er, trade barriers and open their arms to the flow of our oil…."

"Yuck. What an image," said Sam.

"So he's using the attack as an excuse to mine public lands," said Beth.

"Yeah—*our* public lands," said Nin. "We've got to stop that madman!"

"Shh!" said Nan. "Taximeter cabriolets!"

"To thine taximeter cabriolets?" asked Beth, not understanding. She's braided her hair like a terrier, thought Nin. We've got to change her hair before she enters the capitol.

Crossing the river to the capitol they were robbed by crook trout. One seemed familiar to Nan. "Wasn't he in *Star Wars*? The country-and-western bad guy, Darth Brooks?"

Nin, not listening, shrugged. All Nin wanted was for all this to be over, to be home again, in the hill, watching satellite TV until boredom brought sleep.

Sam was rehearsing Beth in how to be a sleazy girl. Nan didn't think she needed much coaching.

Nin went over strategy with Sam and Beth—how to enter the capitol, where its weaknesses were, where to penetrate it, and what to do when inside. Nan helped her with her mental sharpening—they played go and chess and skat, worked crosswords and acrostics, and listened to Mozart.

Seduction wouldn't be enough to guarantee a scandal—Beth would have to "bobbitize" the Emperor, after a fashion. Sam began working with her on musical scales and jaw-strengthening exercises. Like a clarinetist, he wanted to fortify her bite.

"No hands!" he'd yell at her. "Hold that note in your teeth! No hands!"

Beth was happy to do her bit for the plan. Her family had been prominent before Pinocchibush had himself coronated Emperor. In the old kingdom, Beth's family had been haberdashers to the king's family. Beth's family's outspokenness against the king's imperialistic plans to annex the poorer nations surrounding the kingdom met with the ire of the king and a dismissal from all official business in the new empire. Beth's maternal side of the family had included three members of parliament, so the Emperor's dissolution of parliament had similarly left that side of the family disenfranchised.

Thus Beth had stacks of money and an enormous chip on her shoulder. She had been but five years old when her family was kicked out of the inner circle, and she had grown up fixating on her hatred of Pinocchibush.

The Emperor's wrath was growing. He kept appearing on TV, interrupting Nan's favorite TV show, *Daphne the Diabetic Duck-billed Dinosaur*, for sillier and sillier reasons.

"We have decided to curfew instead of many" was announced one day.

"You may be aware that we are not seeing you" was heard as "Naziing you."

Airplanes were being inspected for their "fusel" age.

Public mental health funding was no longer going to be awarded to oxymorons.

Former wards of the court would be rewarded.

The psalter was peppered with profound profanation.

Anachronistic anarchists would be executed by hangfire.

All watchmakers were to be arrested under suspicion of aiding and abetting on escaped cockfights.

"No clone could ever be that stupid," said Nin. "He's got to be the real one. I know we can get to him at the TV studio."

CHAPTERTHIRTEEN
TV

The key grip was wagering with the gaffer when our heroes waltzed into Western Sitcom Town.

Jingle jangle. "Howdy, strangers. What brings you to Western Sitcom Town?" asked a sheriff.

Sam put on a Sam Spade accent and said, "We've got you dead to rights, law man. Where are you keeping the talking heads?"

"Oh. You want the talk show and news sets. Studio 13."

"Don't say a word about this to anyone, go it? Or you'll be sleepin' with the fish and chips. Got it?" Then Sam patted the sheriff's paunch and walked off, the others following.

"Why antagonize him? We could have blown it!" demanded Nan outside.

"No. He's used to making his will subservient to that of a superior. All we had to do was show him *we* were superior and he caved. It's easy. It's basic personality disruption."

"It's messing with people. Remember—you're not supposed to mess with people or you'll get hurt."

"Thanks, Televangelist."

"At least I have no guilt," said Nan.

"Oh, yeah? Where's the money, then?"

"Back up in the hills with the Indians," said Nan.

"Very funny. Anyway, that was no regular sheriff. It was just an android."

"He could be saying the same thing about you."

"Sam, I think that was an authentic actor," said Beth.

"There's no such thing, babe. They're all androids."

"Oh, so you were saying *actors* make themselves subservient?"

Sam shrugged.

"Sheriffs?"

Sam shrugged again. "Both. Most people, as far as I can tell, are androids. That's how Pinocchibush took over so easily. They are easily duped."

"And we nuts bolted," said Nan.

"Beth, the Emperor is due to arrive in a half-hour. You go ahead, and we'll wait in the commissary."

Beth went ahead to Studio 13. Her fake ID stated that she was an intern.

Surprisingly, the Emperor's dressing room had been left unguarded. It took little effort for her to change into the guise of a chambermaid—they had heard that the Emperor favored them—and hide inside the wardrobe, waiting for his arrival.

Finally, after an eternity of nervous breathing, Beth relaxed, and the wardrobe opened.

The Emperor, as expected, was alone, and he took the bait. He was an odd man in intimacy, Beth discovered, and he wanted her upside down and astride his nose atop the divan. With a bite and a twirl, the Emperor's lower appendage was severed and his mouth duck-taped shut. She taped him to the divan and, with a second, unplanned bite, she bit off the other offending appendage in the middle of his face.

Both of these she took up and quickly flushed down the toilet. She washed her face, changed her clothes, climbed onto the veranda, reentered the building through another window and, before anything was noticed, she, Sam, Nin and Nan were leaving the commissary and walking towards their waiting vehicle. Beth was enjoying an egg salad sandwich that she had purchased from a vending machine in the commissary. The mustard washed the taste of Pinocchibush out of her mouth.

It was not the loss of the lower appendage that eventually proved Pinocchibush's undoing. Of course, rumors of the deed spread rapidly throughout the Empire, and the "Emperor without a Staff" became a pet joke in international diplomatic circles.

Actually, it was the loss of the other appendage that undid the Empire.

The people of the Empire had been able to tolerate their jackass of an emperor so long as they could easily tell when he was lying or if he was being truthful (and, to be fair, there had been a handful of occasions of the latter). What, however, they found intolerable, was not knowing. And without his growing appendage, his word became suspect, which was worse than being ridiculed for lying. One can deal with a liar. One cannot deal with a person who is unpredictable. Within a few weeks, members of the inner circle, now completely paranoid because they could no longer read the Emperor, conspired against him and had him poisoned in his bed. So many claims to leadership ensued that the Empire fell apart into its natural divisions, and life as it had been before once again resumed.

Nin and Nan returned to their hill, alarmed to see the road rebuilt and a new billboard being erected. For the moment, however, they decided not to do anything about it at all.

BRADLEY SANDS

LOCATION:
Northampton, MA

STYLE OF BIZARRO:
Absurdist Humor

BOOKS BY SANDS:
It Came from Below the Belt
Disappointing Sophomoric Effort
My Heart Said No, But the Camera
Crew Said Yes!

DESCRIPTION: Bradley Sands writes about bizarre worlds. If the Earth became one giant carnival sideshow overnight, it would resemble the worlds of Sands' fiction. His books and stories are transgressive, zany, and crazy as hell. He is also the editor of the journal *Bust Down the Door and Eat All the Chickens*.

INTERESTS: Finger monsters, comic books, hiding out in his room, knock knock jokes, making fun of life's calamities, all-night diners, and loud music.

INFLUENCES: Steve Aylett, Grant Morrison, Mark Leyner, Raymond Chandler, Robert Anton Wilson, Banksy, Woody Allen, Airplane, British comedies on TV, Strangers with Candy, The Adventures of Pete and Pete, and Danger Mouse.

WEBSITE:
www.bradleysands.com

CHEESEQUAKE SMASH-UP

CHAPTER ONE THE DERBY

The Golden Arch was covered in blood and the Egg McMuffins were being sold at fifty percent off for a limited time only.

A Burger King smashed into its competitor, shattering its window to a chorus of cheers that were soon drowned out by screams. Fast food connoisseurs poured out of the McDonald's like vermin: crying, bleeding, clutching severed body parts to their chests. Some city denizens stopped to watch with ghoulish delight, while others knew when to get the hell out of the way.

The Home of the Big Mac levitated up and away from its attacker, heading towards the Wal-Mart parking lot down the street. Reaching its destination, it stopped and revved its engine. Then it drove back to Burger King at full speed—plowing down the faithful customers who weren't able to pick themselves off the pavement after the first attack—and crashed through the front of the building.

Nearby, hundreds of buildings lifted off the ground and smashed into each other, turning downtown into a giant mosh pit. The skyscrapers and restaurants slam danced to the sound of their own destruction.

***

"Welcome to Cheesequake City, home of the fast food industry's first and last demolition derby. You're in for a special treat, folks. We've replaced the run-of-the-mill cars that you're used to seeing in this sort of competition with mobile buildings. And where else would you see such an incredible competition than in Cheesequake, the only city where buildings come equipped with levitating technologies.

"But this game isn't being played exclusively for your entertainment. Our government has decided to put a stop to the competition between all the fast food companies by forcing them to compete in a no-holds-barred battle royal. Winner takes all: a monopoly over the entire fast food industry.

"Each corporate headquarters will be competing in conjunction with the franchises that call Cheesequake City home. Some familiar names may be missing from the roster, and I'm saddened to tell you that those companies have been recently destroyed by the terrorist acts that the fast food barons have perpetrated against themselves. You can expect to see some eye-gouging action from the following companies:

Subway (with 301 franchises)
McDonald's (275 franchises)
Burger King (254 franchises)
Taco Bell (216 franchises)
Wendy's (201 franchises)
KFC (176 franchises)
Hardee's (144 franchises)
Arby's (112 franchises)
Carl's Jr. (99 franchises)
Popeyes (78 franchises)
White Castle (52 franchises)
Jack in the Box (42 franchises)
Whataburger (28 franchises)
Hot Dog City (12 hot dog stands)
NGA Corp (1 building)

"Wait! What are the NGA Corporation doing here? They don't own a chain of fast food restaurants! Umm…what is it that they do?"

CHAPTER TWO
NGA BUILDING

The hot dog stand was just aching to be my bitch. I watched on my computer monitor as it sashayed from side-to-side. I wondered if he was trying to intimidate me? The giant weiner on his roof made a heck of a target, so I pointed my mouse towards it and slammed down on my spacebar.

Huh…this thing was moving really slowly. Even slower than an old man trying to cross the street in a broken wheelchair. The building crawled forward like a stagecoach pulled by hamsters.

I looked around the call center to make sure that no one was on to me. My co-workers had no idea that our building was competing in the demolition derby, and none of them ever would if the building managed to stay below the speed of a paraplegic. But hopefully I would be able to pick up the pace, or else I would need to come up with another super-awesome plan to win the derby. My current one where I harass the little hot dog stands, run away from all the other buildings that attack me, and wait until they annihilated each other just wouldn't cut it.

No one seemed to notice that the building was in motion. Customer service reps were busy with their callers. Stuart, who worked to my left, was telling a caller to shut up so he could listen to rap music. Gordon was stationed over at the office supply closet, pulling out one of the few remaining hairs on his head as he chastised a co-worker for exceeding the daily amount of paperclips. Babs was busy adjusting her cleavage in the next cubicle over. Mr. Tomfoolery, our CEO, was going through rigor mortis in his office. The employees who worked on the other floors were at home, sleeping. They didn't have to go to work because their floors were under construction. I couldn't have picked a better day to get smashed-up.

Maybe the building's levitation technologies were malfunctioning? I looked out my window to get a better view. It was the only window in the room. The other employees despised me for having it. But since I'm a heck of a likable guy, they only held a grudge during the summertime since Mr. Tomfoolery was too cheap to pay for air conditioning.

I stared down at the street below. No, the levitation engine was working fine.

"I wonder if gramps will get across the street before I die of old age," I grumbled.

"Monty, stop harassing the elderly," Babs said, giving me an eyeful of her thong as she bent down to pick up a pen.

The old gal was sensitive about things like that because she was close to death herself. She was also very touchy-feely and I had to be constantly on guard so that she wouldn't rub my funny spot. "My taste in men may have been extraordinarily picky during my first eighty years," she would say, trying to grab a handful of my boy-berries, "but now I'm making up for lost time."

Fifteen minutes had gone by and I still wasn't even close to running over the hot dog cart. Frustrated, I bashed my head on the desk, hitting my stapler on the way down. Then there was a ding, the NGA building picked up speed, and the cart made a little crunching noise as we drove over it.

Aaaaah! How do you stop this thing?

While my building fender-bendered everything in its path, I frantically searched for the brake, pushing every button on my keyboard-twice.

Someone tapped me on the shoulder.

I shot up out of my seat to block off the window.

"I'm embarrassed for you, Monty."

Oh, phooey! It was Gordon.

"Leaving your phone off the hook when you should be working, aye?" he said, recording my transgression in his notebook. "I'll make sure Mr. Tomfoolery finds out about this at my earliest convenience, which happens to be right now."

He turned, but the sound that a four wheeler makes after a building crashes into it at one ninety-eight miles an hour caused him to reconsider. "Whu…what was that?"

"The construction workers are getting rowdy."

"I'm writing up a report on those goons," he said, attacking his notebook with a Bic. "That kind of noise isn't appropriate for a work environment." He glanced at me as I tried to cover up the window with my body. "Did you know that you've stretched six times in the last five minutes, exceeding the company limit of five stretches a day?"

Gordon wasn't always such an anal-retentive prick. He used to be just a really boring guy who everybody hated to eat lunch with. But ever since the vice president of the water refilling department died, he's been brown-nosing the heck out of Mr. Tomfoolery, hoping to get chosen to fill the position.

I had no faith in Gordon's methods. Mr. Tomfoolery was too smart to promote the office's new rat. The instant he made the announcement, Gordon would get a shiv in his back.

It made more sense to work really hard like the other employees.

But not Babs. She had a different strategy for promotion: seducing Mr. Tomfoolery with her prehistoric boobies.

As for Stuart, he keeps reminding me that he doesn't want the promotion, practically making daily announcements at the top of each hour that "vice presidents don't get to make whoopie around all day." Actually, he used another word; a dirty, dirty word that he can't force me to say.

But everybody except for Mr. Potty Mouth is in for a disappointment. The promotion was as good as mine.

I didn't think I had a chance, until I squeegeed my computer monitor a few days ago. I guess it hadn't been cleaned in like forever because removing the squeegee from its Velcro pouch made the building RRRRHUUUMMM like a monster truck. This was when I discovered that my computer was the building's control panel and my monitor squeegee its ignition.

Soon after, I found out about today's demolition derby. Knowing that meat was Mr. Tomfoolery's favorite food, I entered us into the competition. And when I win, the NGA Corporation will branch out of telecommunications and gain control over the entire fast food industry.

Mr. Tomfoolery will have no choice but to give me the promotion.

I cannot lose!

Well, I might have a hard time winning if the NGA building doesn't stop accelerating until it falls into the ocean.

Wait…what the heck was I doing? How could I have possibly thought that I could win? I don't even know where the brakes are located. I wish someone would teach me how to drive this gosh-darn thing.

I've had it! I'm going to swap my computer with Stuart's when he goes on his next bathroom break. Let him deal with the derby while my life goes back to normal.

I really need this job. I have too many child support payments to make. I can't be fired for demolishing our office building. Stuart can take the blame. He lives with his mom. He doesn't pay rent. He spends all of his paycheck on beer and novelty toys.

But…oh poop.

I forged the documents to register the NGA building for the derby. I accidentally smeared my fingerprints all over the entry form in chocolate. I wrote my own name in the signature line by mistake. I don't own a bottle of White-Out. I thought that crossing out my name and writing Mr. Tomfoolery's in its place would be good enough.

I am totally whoopied. Mr. Tomfoolery is going to find out it was me for sure.

There's no way out.

I cannot lose.

CHAPTER THREE
CRAPVIEW APARTMENTS

Scabies crane-kicked down the door, revealing an apartment filled with a thousand cans of hairspray that were stacked up to the ceiling. And with a swing of his black velvet cape, he lunged into the room, gun ready for anyone that he might find inside.

"All clear, Bubbles," he said, his smile-shaped mustache glistening with perspiration. Then he took a bite out of a Big Mac.

Scabies' platonic lifemate pogoed into the room, moving with the intensity of a bouncy ball. He wore a fish bowl over his head. It was the only way that he could exist in the world of humanity.

He was a giant goldfish.

A giant goldfish with severe pyromaniac tendencies. A giant goldfish who had just lit a butane lighter in a room full of flammable hair care products.

"Will you put that out?" Scabies said, looking like he was about to shit his pants.

Bubbles stared into the flame and grinned with delight.

"Hey, you!" Scabies said, snapping his fingers next to his lifemate's ear. "Bubbles!"

The goldfish stopped pogoeing and grinned.

Frantic, Scabies removed his top hat and fanned out the flame.

"What's your problem?" asked Bubbles.

"You almost cremated us again," said Scabies, on the verge of hyperventilating. He was so sweaty that his wifebeater looked like it was made out of Saran Wrap, exposing a svelte figure.

Bubbles opened his eyes wide, as if seeing the room for the first time. "What's with all the fucking hairspray?"

Scabies looked like he was about to lose his patience. "I don't know what the cans of hairspray are all about," he said, taking French fries out of the sack that he wore around his shoulder, then he swallowed ten of them in one gulp. "I didn't know the first time you asked me that question and I haven't been able to figure it out during the last sixty-five times. I don't know why the majority of the rooms that we've broken into are filled with cans of hairspray instead of loving families. I didn't know that we'd be hijacking a hairspray warehouse. The police aren't going to back off if we start shooting cans of Aquanet..."

Bubbles made an attempt to be helpful. "Well, maybe we'll get chased by the fashion police and they'll cater to our every whim until each can is returned unharmed."

"Cut the sarcasm. This is serious. How am I ever going to put McDonald's out of business when I'm working with nimrods like you?" he said, and took a sip of a medium Coke.

Bubbles puffed out his cheeks. "I resent being called a nimrod."

Scabies looked at the fish's empty rocket belt and sneered. "And why in Steven Seagal's name are you wearing that thing? You don't even have a rocket launcher, let alone any rockets."

"It's a fish thing. You wouldn't understand."

"I should have just applied for a job at every McDonald's in the country instead of hiring you nimrods. I could have concealed rodents in their hamburgers and poured hot coffee on the crotches of old ladies when they'd least expect it. And when I was through with him, The Clown's legal bills would have been so astronomical that he would have had to file for bankruptcy and close all of his restaurants. That's what I should have done instead of relying on others to take down The Clown. I hate McDonald's so much," he said, biting into an apple pie, "that I can taste it. I hope we have enough hostages. Maybe we can use mirrors and make the seven of them look like seventy."

"Don't worry, Scabies," Bubbles said, holding his lighter beneath a can of hairspray. Then he sprayed it into the air and set the mist on fire. "Cans of hairspray are more flammable than hostages."

CHAPTER FOUR
NGA BUILDING

The NGA traveled over crowds of demolition derby enthusiasts, porcupine petting zoos, and city fountains that sprayed Tang. The building was out of control and there was nothing that I could do to stop it. Panicking, I tried various techniques: I slammed the side of the computer screen, sweated all over the keyboard, whimpered like a hungry puppy, kicked my desk, and prayed—but I still couldn't locate the brake.

Frustrated, I picked up my wastebasket and emptied its contents out onto the floor.

Then the building stopped.

I was so happy that I didn't even care that Gordon was standing besides me, writing me up for excessive perspiration, inappropriate outbursts of emotion, defying the separation of church and the workplace, abusing office property, and littering. I was absolutely thrilled about knowing how to stop this thing, not even Gordon could take this moment away from me. Not even when he was marching towards Mr. Tomfoolery's office, impersonating an Imperial stormtrooper.

I picked up the phone, waited for the light to blink, and said, "Thank you for calling the NGA Corporation. My name is Monty Catsin. How may I help you today?"

"Hello," said a throaty whisper. "My six-year-old swallowed my dildo and the instructions said I should call this number."

I never knew what was going to happen after I said my greeting. I could end up talking to someone who praised my computer know-how after I asked them whether or not they had turned on their computer. An old crone like Babs could be on the other end of the line, telling me that "she's fallen and can't get up"—calls like that always stumped me. It could be someone who was a beginner tampon user and needed me to clear up her perplexity. Once a lonely old man called and told me that he was willing to pay ten ninety-nine a minute to find out what I was wearing, then demanded that I take it off. And since Mr. Tomfoolery just threw me to the sharks without training me, I had no idea if fulfilling my callers' every desire was part of my job description.

For the ten years that I've worked for the NGA Corporation, I've been winging it and making everything up as I went along. The calls must come from a variety of 800 numbers that rarely seem to repeat themselves. And I'm starting to think that they might not have anything to do with NGA and get forwarded to my phone by mistake, but no one around here ever gives me a straight answer. "Is your six-year-old still breathing?" I asked.

A Subway franchise smacked into the front of the building.

Compared to the black monolith of the NGA building, the thing was tiny. So tiny that it caused me to rethink my super-awesome plan to win the derby: I would now attack the little guys who were one-tenth my size. At least it would give me something fun to do while I was bored silly on the phones.

I put a hole in the side of the Subway, and the unfit mother on the phone said, "I don't know, but he has a giant erection. I think it's his first. I wish I had a camera..."

"Ok," I said, "what you're going to have to do is hang up, redial this number, and speak to someone who actually knows what to do in the event of choking. Can you do this for me?"

"I don't know," she said, and forced a fake laugh. "But I sure can try."

While I waited for the woman to hang up her phone so I could take my next caller, the Subway franchise did a 180 and tried to destroy me with one of its remaining walls.

Stuart yelled, "Cool video game!" into my ear. "Can I play?"

Terrified that he would discover my secret, I showered my casual business attire in a nervous sweat.

Gordon sprung into action. "Stuart, I'm writing you up for being out of your seat for more than fifteen seconds."

Stuart turned towards him and I sighed in relief.

"Gordon, I'm writing you up for writing people up without having the authority to do so."

"And I'm writing you up for not recognizing my right to make a citizen's write-up."

"And I'm writing you up for being a gianormous whoopietard," Stuart said at the exact second that the Subway franchise caused our building to experience a 3.0 on the Richter scale.

Mr. Tomfoolery popped his head into my cubicle, and his rotting nose fell off and landed in my lap.

CHAPTER FIVE
CRAPVIEW APARTMENTS

The Syphilitic Kidz flickered on the TV, and Scabies was not a happy hijacker. During the recruitment process, he placed special emphasis on the job seekers who listed "loyalty" as one of their special skills.

Loyalty was not watching cartoons instead of the road. Loyalty was not laughing at dumb jokes instead of destroying as many McDonald's franchises as possible.

Felix watched the television from the couch, oblivious to the string of saliva that was hanging down from his eyeglasses. He was a talented driver, but Scabies hadn't hired him for his ability to drool in reverse.

Loyalty was not singing a lullaby instead of making sure the police didn't arrest them for competing in the demolition derby illegally.

Paulie the Sloth sat beside Felix, rocking a cradle containing an AK 47. His body looked as if it were shaped like a home entertainment center. But he was just your everyday overweight Mafioso. The arsenal of guns that covered every square inch beneath his suit was what made him resemble Super Saver Electronics' bestselling item. He liked to tell people that they made him bulletproof.

Scabies and Bubbles had entered the apartment during the scene where the syphilitic kidz were trading their kidneys for video equipment. Scabies had been feeling calm as they made their way towards the living room, but catching his driver goofing off had now made him a candidate for heart disease. He opened his mouth so wide that he could have swallowed a basketball.

Noise boomed through the wall, disturbing Felix's program. He banged back with his fist, yelling, "Can you be quiet in there? I can't hear the television over all the noise you're making."

Scabies gave him a wedgie, grabbed the TV remote, and turned the channel. The screen showed a Wendy's franchise, plowing into their apartment building.

"Why are you watching cartoons when we're under attack?" Scabies asked, hands wrapped around Felix's neck.

Tired of waiting for a response, he let go and popped a Chicken McNugget into his mouth.

"My brain will explode if I don't turn on a television program once every few minutes," Felix said. "I thought I told you that during the job interview."

"You did tell me, and I called you a moron. Brains don't explode from not watching TV. It's a scientific impossibility. And I don't really care if some obscure medical journal documented your unique, make-believe affliction. If your brains explode, just keep driving. No more changing the channel. You grok me?" he asked, handing him back the remote.

Felix nodded. Then, anxious to control the building through the TV, he aimed the remote at the Wendy's on the screen and pressed a few buttons to strike.

Scabies gave him another wedgie. "Save your strength. I don't want to see you attacking anyone but McDonald's. Lose the Wendy's and find them. Seek and destroy, my wage slave of calamity, seek and destroy."

Picking his underwear out of his anal crevice, Felix tried to outrun the Wendy's, but they kept coming, sticking to the side of the building like rubber cement.

Bubbles squinted his eyes at the franchise. "I know a way to get rid of that fuck," he said, pogoeing out into the hall.

A symphony of police sirens pierced their ears.

"Pull over and show me your license and registration!" megaphoned a cop from down below.

"Paulie," Scabies said, "get your ass to the back of the building and make those cops bleed with your bullets."

"No prob," Paulie said, trying to pick himself off the couch, but the weight of his guns made this difficult.

After ten minutes of watching his man moan, sweat, and make a face as if he were trying to squeeze out a dry turd that was as big as his head, Scabies expressed his frustration by giving Paulie a headache.

Paulie bent over and guns poured onto the floor like he was a slot machine in a casino owned by a survivalist.

He managed to get on his feet and dragged them slowly across the room.

Scabies forced himself to wait patiently.

CHAPTER SIX
MCDONALD'S

"Would you like to supersize your salad?" Jo-Jo asked, her eyes bursting with excitement.

"No," the customer said, trying to stare at her tits, but they were barely noticeable underneath her baggy uniform.

"I'm a vegetarian too. It's REALLY nice to have you here. We don't get many veggie lovers around these parts."

Jo-Jo wasn't against eating animals. She didn't let ethics dictate her dietary habits. But the taste of meat reminded her of earwax. "Listen, you hippie," said the customer, "I'm no lettuce muncher. Why would a vegetarian even buy a salad at a McDonald's?"

"Well I do, because I get a discount," she said, trying to remain civil.

"I was just ordering a salad to be kooky and ironic. And I've changed my mind. I'd like you to slaughter a baby calf in front of me and use its blood for salad dressing."

There was an earsplitting crash.

"What was that?" asked the customer.

"Our building is competing in the demolition derby. I'm super excited about it!"

"You're full of shit."

"No, look outside," Jo-Jo said, pointing to the Burger King that was engaging them in combat.

The customer refused to look. "I didn't see anything going on when I came inside, you stupid bitch. Why don't you go fuck a piece of tofu?"

Jo-Jo jumped over the counter, yelled an "AYEEEE!" and dropkicked him in the face. The force of her rage sent him through the restaurant's front window.

The Burger King picked up the customer with a giant spatula and smashed him against Jo-Jo's building. It did it again. And again, not satisfied until his face resembled a Chicken Tender. Then it pummeled him to the ground.

Jo-Jo went out through the front door and gave the dying customer a look of disgust. "Tofu tastes like urinal cakes," she spat.

CHAPTER SEVEN
NGA BUILDING

Mr. Tomfoolery opened his mouth, releasing a family of maggots. "What's this I hear about your phone being off the hook, Mr. Catsin?"

"I don't know what you're talking about," I said, casually pressing the buttons on my keyboard in an attempt to get away from the Subway franchise that just didn't know when to quit.

"Mr. Liddy tells me you've been using this tactic all day to avoid calls."

"Gordon must have taken it off the hook so he could drive up the number of write-ups that he's written today."

"Is this true, Mr. Liddy?"

Gordon scowled at me. "I would make Monty choke on his lie if it wasn't against company policy."

I wondered if Mr. Tomfoolery realized that his decayed nose had rotted off his face and had been perched on my thigh for the past ten minutes. "Would you like your nose back?" I asked.

He snatched it out of my hands and reattached it with a thumbtack. A layer of skin peeled off his face "It's your word against Mr. Catsin's, Gordon, but since I dislike his nasally voice, I will see that he's disciplined accordingly. Hmm, what shall I do to him?"

While he smirked with delight, trying to determine my fate, something fell out of his pocket. It looked like a crown that had been constructed out of yellow sticky notes.

"What is that?" I asked, pointing to the object.

"Something that's none of your concern," he said, picking it up. He staggered into the direction of his office, shouting "I'll think of your punishment later, Mr. Catsin."

I had never seen him wobble so quickly. He didn't even bother to stretch out his arms in front of his body like he usually did.

The Subway launched another attack, creating a loud bang. Slamming his office door, Mr. Tomfoolery yelled, "Whoopieing construction!"

I decided to make a slight adjustment to my super-awesome plan to win the derby: I would now run away from little guys who were one-tenth my size if they happened to be better than me at driving.

Gordon pointed at me, gritted his teeth, ran a very intimidating pencil eraser across his neck as if it were a knife, and walked away, scrawling into his notebook furiously.

I went back to the derby, trying out my newest super-awesome plan. And the Subway never saw it coming. I swerved, turning the building quickly onto a side street, and the franchise crashed into the back of a truck that was hauling manure, causing an avalanche of stinkiness.

Stuart peeked back into my cubicle. "What video game are you playing again?"

I had to tell him something. "It's called Cheesequake Smash-Up."

"You know," he said, stopping mid-sentence to blow air into a whoopee cushion, "you probably shouldn't take your phone off the hook while you're playing. I'm sure you can do perfectly fine while you're talking on the phone."

He put his whoopee cushion on the top of his chair and sat on it, making it sound like he was on the toilet after winning a seven layer burrito eating contest. My co-workers looked up, slightly less amused than I was.

He stood on top of his chair and shouted, "Excuse me." Then he came back down and said, "Listen, guy, I know that you have a hard-on for Mr. Moribund's old job, but you'll never get the promotion if you keep getting in trouble. Not that I understand why you would even want it. Vice presidents have too much responsibility. I mean, you won't even have enough time to play any video games."

"I could really use the money. My entire paycheck goes to child support and I'm living in a bathroom stall at the gas station down the street."

Stuart's mouth opened wide in disbelief. "Child support? What the heck are you talking about? Didn't you tell me you're a virgin?"

"Oh, I am. But I used to bottle my sperm during high school and store my collection in the refrigerator. After I moved away, my mother sold every last drop to a black market sperm bank. And I didn't find that out until after I started getting letters from paternity lawyers. It turned out that there was an accident with my sperm. It had gotten mixed with the sperm bank's brand of vaginal lipstick and a gazillion women had gotten pregnant from it."

"Happens to the best of them, guy," Stuart said. "With a complexion like yours, you're just lucky that you're not the last of the

Catsin family bloodline."

The light on my phone lit up. "I have to take this." I picked up the phone and rattled off a greeting.

"Yeah, hi," said a voice that was oozing in sadness. "Can you tell me if I'm supposed to cut down or across when I'm slitting my wrist? I always forget that."

Oh sugarballs. It was from the suicide hotline. How come I never get those callers anymore who ask me to tell them a joke?

Babs walked to her cubicle and sat down. Her suit was so skimpy that I wouldn't be surprised if it were from an era when fabric was a costly luxury. "Tomfoolery totally wants me," she said. "He just showed me around his office, and let me tell you, he's decorated it to look like he's about to have a Roman orgy. And it's not like the man's interested in anyone else besides me. He's probably commissioned six dozen Real Dolls to bear my image. He'll be fondling all of my mannequin titties while I'm whoopieing and sucking him…"

"Hold on, you want me to whoopie and suck my wrist?" said the gloomy gus on the phone. "What does that have to do with my permanent solution to what my therapist tells me is a temporary problem?"

A Chihuahua in a sombrero lit up on my screen, glowing an alarming shade of red. Uh oh, Taco Bell wanted a piece of me and I still needed to finish the call.

"…and he poured a cup of water over his head and purred like a kitten," Babs said, whispering into my ear lasciviously while she licked my lobe.

A creepy-crawly feeling dripped down my spine and the Taco Bell pounced on me while I was busy being incredibly grossed out.

Trying to relive the joy of getting a jokeline call, I asked my caller, "What do cats like to listen to after a hard day's work?"

The Taco Bell tried to drive through our lobby. They may have been unsuccessful, but the impact still shattered my nerves.

"I don't care what cats listen to! Tell me if I should cut up and down or side to side. Up and down or side to side!"

"Give up? Cats listen to meow-sic. Get it? It's like music, but it's a little different. It's meow-sic!" I burst out in laughter. "Now doesn't that cheer you up? Haven't you lost interest in this silly up and down or side to side business?"

"…Tomfoolery took off his shirt," Babs said. "His nipples hung down with twenty-five pound barbells."

"That's it! I don't need to use a razor. I'm getting in my bathtub and using a microwave for a rubber ducky."

The Taco Bell continued its assault, getting closer and closer to turning the NGA building into pulp.

CHAPTER EIGHT
CRAPVIEW APARTMENTS

"Why is there a bong on your head?" Scabies asked the gorilla as they stood in the room that had been designated for the hostages.

The simian ooked a response.

To avoid possible embarrassment, Scabies pretended to understand what she grunted. "Have the hostages given you any trouble?"

The gorilla nodded her head, charged at the group of hostages, and bellowed, unleashing a stench that could exterminate a colony of ants. The hostages cowered back.

Scabies pinched his nose. "Kill anyone that moves."

"HOOCK HOOCK HOOCK."

Scabies' cell phone rang.

"Hello, Scabies' crime scene cleanup service. This is Scabies…No, officer. I don't know how fast I was going…No, I'm not going to pull over. I don't have to pull over. I'm hauling a gaggle of hostages. And that means that your commanding voice has no authority over me. I don't want to hurt anyone, but I'll start executing one hostage every twenty minutes if you and your cronies don't stop tailgating me."

One of the hostages sneezed. The man next to her moved to dodge her snot projectile.

The gorilla smashed both of their heads together, creating a pair of Siamese twins that shared the same gore-dripping head. Then she threw them out the window.

Their bodies crashed through the windshield of a police car.

Scabies turned towards the gorilla and growled.

"I'm so sooory," he whined into the phone. "That wasn't supposed to happen this soon. If there's anything…"

He reconsidered his words. "Scratch everything that I just said, pig. That was to show that we're serious." Then, munching on a Bacon Double Cheeseburger, he hung up.

Scabies put on a mean face for the gorilla. "We need to have a talk about what should be considered 'moving' and 'not moving.' 'Moving' should be punished by death, while if they're 'not moving,' you shouldn't do a damned thing." He took a deep breath. "Sneezing and leaning back to avoid getting drenched in the mucus. NOT MOVING. Reaching for my gun and shooting me in the armpit. MOVING. Blinking. NOT MOVING. Fondling your hairy tatas. MOVING. Chest going up and down while breathing heavily. NOT MOVING. Trying to escape. MOVING. Grok it?"

Before the gorilla could respond, a fireball shot through the sky.

CHAPTER NINE
MCDONALD'S

The morticians wore black hockey jerseys. As Jo-Jo watched them cart off her rude customer in a dump truck that was designed to resemble a hearse, she wondered if they played in the NHL and subsidized their incomes by working in the death industry during the off-season. She imagined a hockey game where a still-beating heart was used instead of a puck.

Her daydreams were interrupted when the Burger King franchise's giant spatula lunged towards her.

She slipped back inside to avoid capture.

El Jefe, her manager, had been waiting for her. "Why did you escort a paying customer off the premises?" he asked, sharpening his immense beard with a hedge clipper.

Jo-Jo tore out a few of her hairs as she tried to concoct an excuse that would get her off the hook. "Umm…he ordered an extra value meal, the number three, and demanded mustard on his burger instead of ketchup."

Satisfied, he let her pass. El Jefe ruled over the menu like a dictator and would not tolerate any alterations to its contents. Patting her on the back, he praised the actions that she took to defend his menu and asked if she wanted to drive the restaurant for a little while.

"Boy, do I ever!" she said. "Thanks so much for this wonderful opportunity, Mr. Jefe. I hope to make Ronald McDonald proud."

"James! Take over for Jo-Jo at the counter," he called.

James stumbled out of the kitchen, reading a copy of *The Conspiracy Times* and smelling like a wet fart. "Hey, El Jefe, hey," he said, trying to get the big man to look at a newspaper article. Before his boss had a chance to refuse, he started to read, "Know WHY the beef supply is in DECLINE? Well, the INFORMATION that we're about to present to you is WELL KNOWN to THE MAINSTREAM MEDIA who have chosen to SUPPRESS it: SECRET Malaysian government UFOs have been roaming the countryside, MUTILATING cattle after FORCING them to compete in EXTREME tetherball competitions."

El Jefe flaunted his might. "Stop yelling arbitrary words or I'll toss you out on the street. There's a simple solution to the beef shortage," he said, licking his lips, "and all will be revealed in a delicious new menu item."

CHAPTER TEN
NGA BUILDING

The brutality of the Taco Bell's attack shook the ceiling, sending a rain of plaster down on our heads.

Babs brushed it off like it was only dandruff and continued with her gross story, "He made me put on a tail and chased me around the room, calling for his mommy."

"Ok, I'm getting into the water now," said the sadsack on the phone. "I'm blaming you if the microwave cooks me a TV dinner instead of ending my pathetic life."

I realized that I couldn't do my job and win the derby at the same time. I would have to choose one or the other, so I chose the derby since getting a promotion was infinitely more important than helping people. This time, I would have to be more discreet. No more leaving the phone off the hook. From here on out, I would pretend that I was working, occasionally taking calls but being less than helpful. And I would have to do something about this Babs situation.

"I'm not even going to ask why there's a TV dinner in your microwave," I spoke into the phone, "but it should still be able to do the trick. Get to it."

"It's going to take me a while to work up the nerve."

"That's no problem, sir. I'm willing to wait until you see things through. But put the telephone receiver down while you're blubbering. It's not my job to listen to your drivel." I turned towards Babs and said, "Stop bothering me with your porny grandma fantasies so I can get some work done. You've already killed one man and I don't want to be added to your kill count."

This was the official cause of death on Mr. Moribund's death certificate: "Flashed by geriatric while changing water bottle at cooler. Too terrified of fossilized breasts to notice water spilling on floor. Slipped in puddle. Fell down, losing his grip on bottle. Bottle landed in mouth, face-up. Drowned in ten gallons of Poland Springs."

Now that I had taken care of my distractions, I was free to triumph against the Taco Bell by running away as quickly as possible. But I still wouldn't know true freedom until I was in the clear—because man, I *really* needed to pee. That would have to wait until I got rid of this pigheaded franchise.

Ogar, the janitor, entered the room, carrying a broom. While he swept the plaster off the floor, he used his brute strength to try to get people to sign a petition to make him the vice president of water refilling.

I was about to use a school bus as a shield when Ogar punched me in the small of my back and grunted, "Sign. Petition. Now."

Fingering the keys to ensure that a kindergarten class would be the ones who were facing extinction rather than my co-workers, I told him that I refused to sign his petition because I wanted the job for myself.

Angered, he gave me a bloody nose, knocked me out of my chair, and threatened to shove his broomstick in my hiney.

Since his argument was very persuasive and I didn't think the petition would convince Mr. Tomfoolery, I gave him what he wanted. But I still signed it as Osama bin Laden to be on the safe side. And he went away to bother Stuart—who pledged his allegiance to the janitor's cause—leaving me to show the Taco Bell what happens when they mess with a desperate man.

After a few fancy maneuvers, I left them in a state of total bewilderment. Those taco scarfing ninnies probably thought I had escaped into the sewers.

I couldn't take it anymore. My bladder felt like it was going to explode. I got off my seat and power-walked to the bathroom, hoping that no buildings would attack while I was away from my desk. But Mr. Tomfoolery stopped me on the way while I was crushing my peepee between my fingers in hopes that it wouldn't erupt without my permission. "Mr. Catsin," he said, "get your butt in my office. I've thought of an appropriate punishment."

I tried to tell him that I was about to

wet my pants, but he just stared at me with his scary, dangling eyes. The fear that they would escape from his sockets at night and look down at me with disapproval while I slept gave me no choice but to obey.

Mr. Tomfoolery's office was decorated to look like a Roman coliseum. Banners covered the walls, made up of pieces of copy machine paper that had been scotch-taped together. There was a throne at the top of his desk that someone had constructed with thousands of paper clips, wrapped around one another. A giant tank of water sat in the center of the room, shaped like a fighting arena.

My boss hid behind his desk for a moment and came back wearing a familiar looking crown of sticky notes and a toga that must have been a window curtain in a former life.

"Welcome, Mr. Catsin. Welcome to the NGA Corporation's first annual Gladiator Games. Please take a seat beside me," he said, motioning to a pile of boxes.

I did as he asked, crossing my legs to get a little relief from my full-bladdered affliction.

"Try not to think of this as a punishment, but a feast for your senses," he said, and blew into a trombone. "I, Tiberius Tomfoolery Caesar, proclaim that the games have begun."

I waited for something to happen. After a few minutes, he turned a shade of red, stared at the tank of water intently, and snarled, "Men, pick up your weapons and fight!"

I did not see any men, weapons, or fighting. I thought that Mr. Tomfoolery might have been a little funny in the head. Maybe his brains were finally melting down his neck?

Mr. Tomfoolery began speaking very loudly as if he were a sports commentator on the radio. "And Falco Pilatesclass cuts off Titus Aquatis' head with his sword. Oh, what an upset! I thought Titus would last until the end. But, what's this? Euripides Pertinax has just hit Falco over the head with his morningstar. Ouch! That's gotta smart."

Totally befuddled, I said, "Sir, is something actually happening or have your brains melted into soup?"

"When's the last time you had an eye exam? The gladiators are sea monkeys, you imbecile!"

I squinted my eyes and I thought I saw little dots swimming in the water, but my urgent need to pee could have been playing tricks with my head.

"Did you see that, Mr. Catsin? Cronus Caltavious just knocked Euripides unconscious with a bowling ball."

And before I was able to say, "No…I did not see that, Mr. Tomfoolery," he stood up from his throne, thrust out a fist, and gave the 'thumbs down' sign as if he were a scorned movie critic.

I don't know what happened next, but Mr. Tomfoolery announced that Cronus was the winner, awarded the prize of allowing him to live for another day, and told me to get the heck out of his office and stop taking my phone off the hook.

I sprinted to the bathroom and slammed my body through a stall door. As I pulled my zinger out of my underwear, there was a loud crash and I found my feet slipping out from under me. Without any hands free to brace myself for the fall, I slammed face-first onto the hard, sticky floor.

Something had just smashed into the NGA building, and worse yet, I had also pissed my pants.

CHAPTER ELEVEN
CRAPVIEW APARTMENTS

Surrounded by cans of hairspray, Bubbles chanted, "Pretty flame! Pretty flame! Pretty flame!" trying to set the universe on fire. He pogoed next to an open window, spraying four cans simultaneously into a funnel that had a ring of fire around the end of it. A stream of flame poured out, heading for the Wendy's franchise.

But the attack was overkill. The restaurant was already a raging inferno. Employees and customers were fire-dancing in front of it, trying to remember how to stop, drop, and roll. Then the fish pointed his device towards a fleet of police cars who had driven up to the side of the building.

Scabies was so pissed off that he almost choked on his milkshake. Huffing and puffing, he blew the ring of fire out, letting the hairspray spring forth unmolested.

The stream of styling liquid sprayed into the police cars, giving them all stylish new hairdos. This forced the officers to pull over so they could admire their new looks in police-regulation hand mirrors.

Bubbles turned towards Scabies, looking as if he were about to cry.

"For the last time," Scabies said, stopping to relieve his frustration with a Quarter Pounder, "it's not safe to expose a room full of flammable chemicals to an open flame. The concept is pretty simple. You've already demonstrated it with that ridiculous weapon..." Then he vomited up twenty-five Happy Meals.

CHAPTERTWELVE
MCDONALD'S

"I hate you, Jo-Jo," Harold said, sprinkling onions on top of a burger patty. "I hate your silly bangs and your dopey smile. I never had to deal with nitwits like you back when I was an aerospace engineer."

Jo-Jo smiled, lost in the excitement of battle. She was maneuvering the fry station's console, controlling the building with the tips of her fingers. "What's an arrowspace engineer?"

"It's pronounced aerospace engineer, you idiot. And I used to build rockets."

"Wow, you were a rocket scientist! That's so cool! When I was younger, I would shoot those little things up in the air. But I was never able to launch them into outer space. They always came down, and sometimes the parachute didn't work and they came down really hard."

Harold had lost his patience. He threw a Filet-O-Fish against the wall, almost hitting the retarded dishwasher, Big John, in the back of the head. The Tarter Sauce dripped down, making the wall look like it was the thigh of a teenager who had just woken up from a wet dream.

"I worked on real rockets, not that kid stuff. But the job market in that field is so competitive because NASA only blastoffs one rocket every couple of years. And I should be driving this thing, not you."

"I don't know..." Jo-Jo said, levitating the McDonald's down onto the Burger King in an attempt to crush it, "I'm preeetty good at it."

"You're delusional," Harold said. "That roof is made of reinforced steel. You're barely denting it."

Disappointed, she gave up and floated back to the ground.

Jo-Jo noticed a shiny red button. This excited her. She pressed the button and a cybernetic monkey's claw shot out the side of her building.

She aimed for her enemies' drive-thru window and pushed the button again, sending the claw through the window, where it snatched up the building's driver and gave him a horrifying ride towards Jo-Jo's McDonald's.

The Burger King spun out of control and crashed into the statue of a very constipated man on a horse, totaling the franchise beyond repair.

The monkey's claw popped into the McDonald's kitchen and dropped the Burger King driver into the top of an industrial-sized meat grinding machine. Jo-Jo was too busy stomping on the heads of the Burger King survivors to notice the screams.

Two dozen burger patties tumbled out of a panel, landed on the conveyer belt, passed through the oven, and rolled out in front of Harold.

But before he could put the first burger in a wrapper, El Jefe swiped it out of his hands, took a bite, and proclaimed its deliciousness.

He spat out a finger-sized bone.

Jo-Jo stared down at it. "Isn't that a health code violation?"

"The health code is my party whore," El Jefe said, "and bends to my every desire. She is as flexible as a sexy contortionist." He guided Jo-Jo's hand, causing the monkey's claw to once again visit the helpless franchise. "You like my secret weapon, yes? Make Ronald McDonald happy and attack anyone who comes out of that Burger King, kay?"

Jo-Jo nodded. Over the next few minutes, hundreds of bodies uttered their final screams while they were being carried towards her.

And the beef never stopped flying down from the ceiling. Frantically, Harold tried to trap as many patties as possible into buns while a never-ending supply of customers burst through the front door, demanding to sample the franchise's newest taste sensation.

El Jefe scrutinized the chaos and declared that the McDonner Burger was a success.

CHAPTER THIRTEEN
NGA BUILDING

"Pow! Pow! Pow! Ratatatatat!"

Stuart was sitting behind my desk when I got back, pounding on my keyboard with his elbows. Three franchises were taking turns abusing our building. Stuart was even worse at driving than I was, and he didn't know he only had one life.

"Oh hey, guy. This is the best time I've had at work since mom gave me pot brownies with my lunch. Why do you smell like a urinal?"

I pushed him away from the keyboard and whispered in his ear, "It isn't me. Babs has a bladder control problem."

Stuart took an unhealthy interest in my window while I got us to safety. "Holy worm penis! You're moving this thing!"

"No, I'm not," I said, shoving my computer monitor in front of the window. This was the best chance I had to confuse him. I crossed my fingers, hoping that Stuart was the sort of guy who would mix up a window with a monitor.

He pushed the monitor out of the way and commandeered my keyboard. "We're in the burger derby, aren't we? I thought I was going to miss it because I had to work. This is the single greatest moment in my life," he said, crashing through a shopping mall.

I grabbed the keyboard back and drove out of the mall by way of JCPenney. "You can't tell anyone about it."

"Why would I want to tell anyone? It'll just end up getting back to the big kahuna and he'll send a company-wide memo banning fun in the office. I've always wanted to drive through a mall. I have an endless supply of things that I've always wanted to do that you can help me accomplish." He pointed to a spot on the screen. It was a CD store near the mall. "Let's destroy that place. They caught me shoplifting on my eighteenth birthday. Do it!" Then he crushed my fingers until we were headed in that direction.

Before I was able to get us back on track, we smashed through the store's front window display, decapitating a life-sized cardboard cut-out of R. Kelly.

"Wow, guy. That sure makes a lot of noise. How come none of the retards who work here have caught on yet?"

"The building's been under construction for a while, so nobody suspects a thing."

"That excuse won't work for long. Those noises are too intense to be construction worker-related. We'll have to do something else to cover it up. Hey, we should hire a marching band to walk up and down the halls playing Pomp and Circumstance. I *really* like that song."

"I can't afford a marching band."

"Oh right, that whole impregnating the entire universe thing. How about this idea?

I can go down to the floor underneath us and bang on the ceiling with a hammer or something. I can cover up the sounds of extreme building battle with actual fake construction sounds. C'mon, tell me I'm absolutely brilliant."

I told him what he wanted to hear to get him out of my way. And before long, clanging noises were coming from downstairs. Problem was, no buildings were assaulting me.

I cursed Stuart's name, wishing him a lifetime of flatulence.

Then the corporate headquarters of Carl's Jr. attacked.

I couldn't believe that my favorite fast food restaurant was trying to kill me. I thought about their delicious Six Dollar Burger with 100% Angus Beef and how they brought your food to your table instead of making you pick it up at the counter. I imagined the lips of that cute cashier who was nice to me that one time. I imagined those lips as they wrapped around my cheek.

For a brief moment, I was glad I lacked the skill to destroy them.

"You should flatten the doorman. I hate those guys."

Stuart stood behind me, waving a sledge hammer is if it were a flag.

"What the heck are you doing here? You should be downstairs making noise."

"I got bored."

"Well, can you go back there and make some noise? I'm trying to get rid of an angry skyscraper here."

A huge hole exploded into the side of the wall, sending a handful of NGA employees towards their messy deaths.

They were all still talking on their phones as they fell, desperate to finish their calls before their shifts ended.

CHAPTER FOURTEEN
CRAPVIEW APARTMENTS

Scabies' barf pitter-pattered into toilet bowl water. Bubbles was beside him, holding his hair out of the puke's way. The fish's rocket belt was finally serving a purpose: he could now carry cans of hairspray wherever he went. His homemade flamethrower was resting on the floor besides Scabies' top hat.

Stomach now empty, Scabies pulled his head out of the toilet and scarfed down a McRib. "I'm really uncomfortable with you seeing me this way," he told his fishy pal.

"Yeah, it's pretty fucking gross."

"I've never told this to anyone before, but I can't stop eating McDonald's."

"What a humongous fucking surprise," Bubbles said.

"No, I REALLY can't stop. I'm addicted to it. If I go a short time without it, then the withdrawal symptoms set in: headaches, sleeplessness, a stomach that feels like its home to a crocodile, heart palpitations, and beginning every word that I say with 'Mc.' Every time I try to quit, I'm in so much agony that I run to the nearest Mickey D's and kill my pain with an Extra Value Meal. The damn things are on every city block. The only way I'll ever make it through withdrawal is if McDonald's goes out of business and that's why I need to destroy their franchises and corporate headquarters. If I ever see that Clown, I'll gouge out his eyes so fast that he'll be bleeding special sauce."

The Golden Arch whizzed past the window and Scabies nearly knocked the bathroom door off its hinges.

CHAPTER FIFTEEN
NGA BUILDING

If I were to choose between having Stuart for a sidekick or a fussy parrot who sat around and ate crackers all day while he insulted my fashion sense, I would have to go with the bird because it would be less annoying. But Stuart wasn't totally useless. For instance, he was really good at covering up the huge hole in the wall with furniture. Now anybody who looks at it will think that some crazy guy has been stacking furniture, not that we've been pulverized in an attack.

"Hey, guy," Stuart said, pushing the copy machine along the floor. "Can I drive for a little bit?"

"Keep your voice down. And of course not." I wasn't going to let Stuart goof off behind the wheel while we were still being chased by Carl's Jr. "Maybe later," I added.

Gordon blocked Stuart's path and said, "I'm writing you up for the misuse of office furniture.

Stuart didn't stop pushing, and knocked Gordon off his feet. Even a nasty fall couldn't separate him from his notebook.

"How about now? Can I do that thing that we talked about. You know, *that thing*?"

"Not right now!" I shouted, trying to get away from the Carl's Jr.

Mr. Tomfoolery came out of his office and glanced at the wall of furniture. "Why is there a hole in the wall?" he asked, clenching his jaw with such anger that his chin broke off and fell to the floor. "And why is Mr. Sutcliffe moving furniture in front of it?" He bent down to reattach his fallen appendage.

"The construction workers dynamited the wall to make room for your new, private swimming pool. I'm covering it up because it was supposed to be a surprise. And now everything's ruined!"

Our boss put on a grumpy face, lurched back to his office, and slammed the door.

"Can I do it now? Can I can I can I?"

Worn down by Stuart's onslaughts and comfortable in the knowledge that the corporate headquarters had gotten tired of my gutlessness and gone off to fight someone else, I gave in.

"Don't worry, guy," Stuart said, abusing the buttons on my keyboard. "None of the other building will even know that I exist. I just want to drive around and frighten pigeons."

I tried to sit down, but I almost fell on my face. Stuart had used all the empty chairs to conceal the hole. So I leaned up against the wall.

I glanced at my computer monitor. It was filled with a crapload of little squares. Looking through the window, I saw hundreds of buildings in front of us, smacking into each other as if they were bumper cars.

This probably wasn't the best time to let Stuart drive.

CHAPTER SIXTEEN
CRAPVIEW APARTMENTS

The Vain and the Vacant was on the TV when Scabies thundered through the door, screaming for Felix to destroy the McDonald' franchise. Within seconds, Felix found his tighty-whities pulled up over his head.

"If you blow this for me, Felix," Scabies said, channel surfing until his hated enemy filled the screen, "I'll split your head open like a pomegranate." He forced the remote back into his driver's hands.

The McDonald's had glided farther away from the apartment building since Scabies first caught sight of it, and Felix tried to catch up by increasing the speed.

The NGA building came out of nowhere and slammed into their apartment.

Scabies looked up at Felix's head, visualizing it as a pomegranate.

CHAPTER SEVENTEEN
NGA BUILDING

I wished I hadn't worn my teeny weeny purple polka dotted bikini briefs today. This was the thought that was racing through my mind as I fell to my death. Not "Golly, I wish I hadn't let Stuart drive!" or "Why was I standing next to the hole in the wall when I knew that I was in danger of being knocked out of it?" No, I was worried that the demolition derby's official morticians would point at my dead body and laugh at my ill-conceived choice of underwear.

CHAPTER EIGHTEEN
MCDONALD'S

The manager now wore a giant, novelty cowboy hat for the purpose of shouting out the window. "Come down to El Jefe's McDonald's and try our newest sensation, the McDonner Burger," he hollered, as if the hundreds of crashing buildings outside were television viewers at home. "They're taste-tastic!" He shoveled one into his mouth and moaned.

Jo-Jo liked the word "taste-tastic" so much that she considered sampling the new product, but lost her appetite after smelling earwax on her fingers.

Finished with his advertisement, El Jefe approached her as she steered the building away from a corporate headquarters. "That's right, my little chickadee. Defensive driving is the name of the game and your name is the young lady who preys on the weak, the half-destroyed, the easy pickings. You're gonna monkey-claw all the survivors and fill our customer's tummies with essential nutrients."

Jo-Jo did as he commanded, weaving in and out of buildings as they engaged each other in physical combat, scavenging the survivors. She was very good at her job, and the meat piled up to the ceiling.

"Woo-hee!" El Jefe howled, cradling a phone beneath his ear. "The corporate office is proud of you, my dear. And they're gonna back us up from here on out," he said, pointing to the enormous corporate skyscraper as it collided with an Arby's that had gotten a little too close to them. "They'll take care of any pesky critters who try to take us down."

"Don-ner Burger! Don-ner Burger!" The chant was coming from the front of the building.

Thousands of customers were crammed together in the room, human bricks in a wall of flesh. They continued chanting, pumping their fists in synchronicity as if they were at a Nazi rally.

El Jefe beamed at the crowd, exhilarated and trembling a little. "We need more meat," he said, grinning at the dishwasher. He grabbed Big John by the ear and led him over to the microwave. The retarded man clapped his hands, thinking they were playing a really fun game.

El Jefe shoved his victim's head into the microwave, smashed him with the door until he yelped, programmed the timer to cook his brains for the next five minutes, and pressed start.

The microwave turned on, giving off a high-pitched buzz. It wasn't equipped with the safety feature that prevented it from being used while its door was open.

Big John's head exploded, spraying gore over the faces of the kitchen crew. They stared at El Jefe, aghast, as he picked up the dishwasher's headless body and carried him over to the drive-thru window. Waiting until his monkey claw was nearby, he threw Big John into its warm embrace.

Man-meat rained down from the heavens.

And Jo-Jo finally realized what McDonner Burgers were made out of.

CHAPTER NINETEEN
CRAPVIEW APARTMENTS

A roof broke my fall and a mound of bird poop stopped me from breaking every bone in my body. I watched as the three hundred and thirteen floors of the NGA building drifted to the other side of the battlefield and pouted. Normally, the stench of evil that wafted off its pitch black paint job made me want to run home to my bathroom stall and hide beneath the covers. But this time, I only felt a desire to pole vault back to it so I could resume the demolition derby.

I was cleaning the bird droppings off my casual business attire when the building lunged forward to avoid four White Castles, knocking me back into the poop headfirst. While accidentally swallowing a mouthful of the gross stuff, I realized that this building was also competing in the derby. I wondered if its driver would be nice enough to drop me off at the NGA building. *Of course he would*, I thought as I went inside through a door on the roof.

I strolled down a hallway, trying to forget about the taste in my mouth by pretending to eat a hot fudge sundae. A series of grunts interrupted my dessert, and I looked up to see a gorilla lumbering towards me.

I did a double-take.

What the heck was a gorilla doing here? Was this building some sort of zoo? Would I find an elephant painting abstract art around the corner? And why were animals roaming the halls instead of goofing off inside cages?

Wow, the gorilla was really big. I mean, *really* big.

It stomped up to me, sniffed at my clothes, and looked disgusted.

I held out my hand. "Shake?" I asked, nervously.

It looked down at my palm and itched its back.

"Yes, Mr. Monkey. Let's shake hands and be friends."

The gorilla put out its paw, took my hand, and accepted my offer.

I couldn't believe how well-trained my new hairy friend was.

"WOOK WOOK WOOK," it said, continuing to shake my hand with vigor.

"Ok, you can stop now."

"WOOK WOOK WOOK."

It started to crush my fingers. "You really need to give me my hand back," I said.

The gorilla opened its mouth as if it were about to eat my face off and growled.

Before it could pop my pimples with his sharp teeth, I unleashed a high-pitched yodel.

The gorilla froze, clutching its ears.

I escaped through a door and slammed it shut.

What a weird room. It was filled with cans of hairspray. I wondered if the zookeeper styled his animals' hair each morning.

"Stoopid monkey doesn't know how to use a doorknob, huh?" I yelled, giving my hairdo a touch-up.

The horrifying creature charged into the door, leaving behind a gorilla-sized indentation.

I went out the window quicker than you can say, "Hello, police? Yes, I'd like to report an incident with a killer gorilla."

Now outside, I tried to enjoy the big battle, but I couldn't see very much from where I was hanging.

Gosh-darn it! It was a really crappy view.

The McDonald's corporate headquarters plowed into the building. It nearly killed me, but I was able to grab onto another windowsill and pull myself away before it turned me into a casualty of war.

While the skyscraper mauled the side of the building, I swung to the other side where I was safe from its attack.

I was so exhausted from my workout that I collapsed on top of the windowsill.

I peeked through the broken window and saw a guy in glasses playing a video game. Neato! It was Cheesequake Smashup.

Oh wait…

"Felix, get the whoopee out of the way and let me realize my destiny," said a sinister man in a top hat whose voice resembled a wild hyena's. I wondered if he was an amateur magician because he wore a velvet cape. Or maybe he was the building's zookeeper.

Four Eyes handed him a remote control.

"McDonald's is going down like a midget on a tricycle who's just peddled into my lane of traffic," said the top hat man, working the buttons on the remote.

Then every building in the corporate headquarters' vicinity turned on it, launching a synchronized attack.

The gorilla scurried over to Mr. Tophat and started to play charades. I covered my mouth to stop myself from squealing.

It put its furry fingers together, creating the shape of a deformed face.

Tophat pushed the beast out of the way and kept fighting the McDonald's. The gorilla twitched its nose, smelling something.

Golly! The buildings were beating the ever living heck out of the McDonald's! It was almost on its last column.

The gorilla came over to the window and smelled some more.

The fast food buildings continued to work out their frustration on the McDonald's, with a Burger King and a White Castle sacrificing their lives to ensure its destruction.

The gorilla smashed its head through the window and glared at me with murderous rage.

CHAPTER TWENTY
MCDONALD'S

"Honey, sweetheart, light of my life," El Jefe said. "Can you do me an itsy bitsy favor and turn the monkey claw on our faithful customers. We're almost out of meat."

Jo-Jo's job passed before her eyes. She didn't want all those people to die, but she really couldn't risk being fired. No one wanted to hire a fast food employee who had gotten herself canned. But she had already killed today. Could a few thousand more deaths be any worse?

Sensing her hesitation, El Jefe placed his hand over hers and forced her to bring the claw indoors, where it made fast work of the McDonald's customers, turning the front of the store into a ghost town.

He walked over to the cooking station. "Everybody must taste the new McDonner Burger," he said, plucking the burgers one by one out of Harold's hands before he had the chance to wrap them, "EVERYBODY!"

So zombified by all of the repetitive work, Harold hadn't looked up once to see what was happening.

El Jefe pushed a button that was hidden beneath the ketchup dispenser, and a portion of the wall lifted up to reveal a wall of cannons. Half of them were marked "naughty" and the others were marked "nice." He filled each of them with a McDonner Burger, lit their fuses, took a step back, and yelled, "Fire!"

The hamburgers soared through the sky, with the naughty burgers damaging buildings and killing people while the nice ones flew into the mouths of the hungry, who devoured them with zest.

"Hey, Jo-Jo," El Jefe said, "be sure and give those lucky, lucky people who are enjoying my burger the claw. It'll taste twice as good when it's made from the meat of someone who has experienced its yumminess."

Not being morally opposed to murdering customers and employees from *other* fast food establishments, she made all of his dreams come true.

CHAPTER TWENTY-ONE
CRAPVIEW APARTMENTS

The gorilla was not happy with me. Its angry howl reverberated over the graveyard of demolished buildings that now surrounded the McDonald's corporate headquarters.

I leapt over to the next windowsill to avoid its wrath.

The zoo building bashed into the headquarters. The gorilla was the first one to feel the impact. Its legs had been severed from the rest of its body. I got off easy—the crash had only torn my shirt sleeve.

"That's what happens when you try to scare me," I said, watching the gorilla take its last breath as the corporate office collapsed under the strain of the attack.

Laughing manically, Mr. Tophat did a spastic happy dance to celebrate his victory. "The clown is dead!" he yelled. "The clown is dead!"

CHAPTER TWENTY-TWO
MCDONALD'S

El Jefe gawked in complete shock at the wreckage of the once great McDonald's Corporate Headquarters. Tears wiggled out of his eyes as he blew his nose into his beard. Then his sadness turned to rage. He jumped onto the counter, tore off his clothes, and proceeded to give what may have been the angriest tap dancing recital in the history of mankind, singing:

Attack!
Attack!
Attack that apartment building
Attack!
It eradicated our patron
Winning my hatred
And now, Jo-Jo, it must be destroyed

Jo-Jo tried to hide her eyes from his naked body. It was covered in body hair. The hairs had been dyed green, making it look like he'd poured the contents of a Chia Pet's seed packet all over his body.

Knowing she probably wouldn't have a job for much longer since the corporate headquarters no longer existed on this plane of reality, Jo-Jo climbed up on the control station, pulled down her pants, squatted, and urinated all over the French fries.

"*You* do it," she told her boss, wiping herself dry with her McDonald's visor.

CHAPTER TWENTY-THREE
CRAPVIEW APARTMENTS

I watched the NGA building hover in the distance, its dark shadow passing over hundreds of wrecked buildings. No one followed. Except for a nearby McDonald's franchise, the battlefield was quiet, still.

The derby was nearing its end. Three competitors were all that remained.

I tried to get Stuart's attention by waving my arms, sticking out my tongue, showing him my tushie. But he was too far away to notice me.

I would have to take matters into my own hands and destroy the building from within. I would have to reach into my dark heart and kill everyone inside so that no one would be around to walk down to the winners' circle and I could claim victory for the NGA Corporation. This is how badly I wanted to be the vice president of the water refilling department. I was willing to engage in hand-to-hand combat for the first time in my life. And it was going to be a cinch. I've learned from the best: Kung Fu Stu on TV had shown me how easy it was to kill a guy.

Then the McDonald's franchise rammed into the zoo building, and I crawled back inside through the window for my own personal safety.

The room was full of people. They all sat on the floor and were staring at the walls.

Approaching them, I asked how they were enjoying their day at the zoo.

They didn't respond. Instead, they flinched away and looked frightened.

I wondered if they were all mimes. Maybe today was Mime Day at the zoo and they had all gotten a discount on the admission cost? I threw a few quarters on the floor and requested the "Help! I'm Trapped in an Imaginary Box!" routine.

They just sat there and did nothing. If they were mimes, then they were the worst ones that I had ever seen. Maybe they were beginners and hadn't learned the box routine yet?

"Are any of you competing in the demolition derby?"

They remained silent.

Since I had a soft spot for mimes, I decided to let them live. Bored out of my mind, I tried to leave through the door. Locked.

"Does anyone know where the key is?" I asked.

They didn't move an inch.

Unsatisfied with their performance, I bent down to get my change back and left through the window.

Choosing another one, I stumbled into a second room that was filled with hairspray and walked out into the hall.

Mr. Tophat was coming from the other direction. Flexing my hand into the Deadly Kung Fu Claw of Deadly Death, I waited to make the kill.

At least until I saw the monstrosity who was bouncing next to him: a giant goldfish, wearing a spooky fish bowl mask, carrying a funnel of fire.

I ran back into the room o' hairspray, muffling my EEK! with a closed door. After counting to one hundred Mississippi, I went back out into the hall to discover that it was now a giant goldfish-free zone.

I roamed the halls, listening for the sounds of my enemies.

I heard a BAM BAM BAM coming from inside a room. So I went in, positive that it would be a good place to try out some Kung Fu moves.

A man in a suit was juggling four guns and pumping bullets out of the window each time he caught one. The artillery didn't make any noise, so his vocal chords were providing the sound effects for them. He would have looked like Joe Pesci had the actor grown a couple of feet overnight and eaten a Winnebago.

I came up to him from behind and tried to chop his head in half like Kung Fu Stu would do with a stack of bricks. But my Kung Fu was weak. He remained in one piece and didn't even notice that I was in the room. So I put my hands around his throat and squeezed.

Mr. Wheaties gasped, flopping his hands around. Bullets sprayed all over the room.

I tried to grab one of his weapons. He refused to part with it. Noticing his affection for it, I decided to give him what he wanted and let go.

He seized the gun with such force that he lost his grip on it and it fell out the window. "Oh my god!" he screamed. "My baby!" Then he jumped out after it.

CHAPTER TWENTY-FOUR
MCDONALD'S

Jo-Jo gave Harold a wet willy, hoping to knock him out of his work-induced stupor.

Color crept back into his cheeks and his lips curled into a look of disgust. He looked down to the burger that he was holding, perplexed. "Why does this beef patty smell like B.O.?"

"Oh, that's the new McDonner Burger," Jo-Jo said. "It's made from human flesh."

"It's made from *what*?"

James strolled into the kitchen, leaving a trail of blood as he carried his own severed arm. The bloody hand was clutching the newest copy of *The Conspiracy Times*. El Jefe was on the cover. Below his picture, it said, "CANNIBALISTIC AGENT FOR THE SECRET MALAYSIAN GOVERNMENT?" James turned to the first page and began to read. "Know why El Jefe has TURNED his customers into CANNIBALS? Well, the INFORMATION that we're about to present to you is WELL KNOWN to THE MAINSTREAM MEDIA who have chosen to SUPPRESS it: He's a SLEEPER agent for the SECRET Malaysian government. They've MIND CONTROLLED him into BELIEVING that he's a MCDONALD'S manager. Earlier today, a GREY ALIEN who has been working in CONJUNC-

TION with the Malaysians came into El Jefe's establishment to give him the PASSCODE PHRASE that ACTIVATED his mission. The word was "McGriddle."

A stream of flame shot through the wall, setting the kitchen on fire.

Harold picked up a fire extinguisher. "I don't want to work here anymore if we're going to serve human flesh," he said, spraying the room with foam. "But I'm afraid to quit. Who's going to hire an aerospace engineer with a stint as a fast food cook on his record?"

"We'll probably lose our jobs at the end of the derby anyways," said Jo-Jo. "Our corporate headquarters has been destroyed."

Harold choked on his spittle.

"But even if our building wins," she said, "I don't think I want to work for El Jefe anymore. I don't know what I'm going to do. I *really* need this job."

James read from his newspaper, looking light-headed and confused from all the blood loss. "Don't know what to do about El Jefe? Well, the INFORMATION that we're about to present to you is WELL KNOWN to THE MAINSTREAM MEDIA who have chosen to SUPPRESS it: Jo-Jo should murder El Jefe, cut off his SKIN, and take over his IDENTITY by WEARING it. Then she can BE your BOSS and the SURVIVORS from CORPORATE won't ever KNOW the DIFFERENCE."

Jo-Jo grabbed the newspaper out of his hands and looked at it. "James, you're hallucinating. It doesn't say that."

"I can hear you, you know!" El Jefe shouted from the fry station as he fought Crapview Apartments to a standstill.

CHAPTER TWENTY-FIVE
CRAPVIEW APARTMENTS

I kung fu hustled into the room to find Mr. Foureyes battling a McDonald's with a TV remote. Guns decorated the floor, and even though Kung Fu Stu always frowned while in the presence of firearms, I reached for one, gung ho about blowing my enemy's brains all over the television screen.

While I struggled to lift a gun off the floor, Mr. Foureyes interrupted me with a variety of questions and comments including "Who the heck are you?" and "You're not supposed to be in here," and "Why do you smell like my suicidal parrot after he tries to drown himself in the toilet?"

I stopped trying to lift the gun, went to snatch the remote control from Mr. Foureyes, knocked it out of his hands, threw him off the couch, and put him in a figure four leg lock like the one that Kung Fu Stu did during the episode where he joined a pro wrestling league to kill a bad guy.

Face twisted in a mask of pain, Mr. Foureyes reached for the TV remote, but it was too far away.

He started to shriek. "Must…watch TV…or brain will…explode."

I snickered at the silliest excuse that had ever been used to break out of a figure four leg lock.

Mr. Foureyes pounded on the floor with his fists, pleaded for mercy, and offered me his life savings.

His head popped like a frozen burrito in a thermonuclear chamber.

I loosened my wrestling hold, feeling really bad about not believing him. I looked over at his headless torso and started to freak out. It wasn't cool looking like in a horror movie. Instead, it was really upsetting. I couldn't understand why a dead thing was more terrifying than a monstrous gorilla who wanted to kill me.

An image of the gorilla's death popped into my head, and I freaked out even more.

Hyperventilating, I pushed the couch on top of Mr. Foureyes' corpse to hide his hideousness.

After calming myself down, I decided to take control of the navigational system, so I plucked the remote control off the floor and aimed for the NGA building. The McDonald's franchise was still hot on my tail.

Mr. Tophat exploded through the door, yip-yapping, "Felix, why in Steven Seagal's name are you running away from the McDonald's? We can destroy them without even breaking a sweat."

He noticed Mr. Foureye's corpse, looked at me, and glared.

I gave him my best poop-eating grin.

He called out into the hall, "Bubbles, sic this vermin."

The giant goldfish put down its funnel of fire and leapt into the room, looking ravenous for fish food.

I panicked and tried to crawl through the window. But before I could escape, it thrust itself towards me.

I went into defense mode-putting my hands over my eyes.

Something cold and hard hit my elbow, and I heard the sound of shattering glass. Opening my eyes, I saw the fish's bowl lying on the floor in a zillion pieces. And next to the broken bowl, the fish lay, doing the flippity-floppity dance.

After half a minute of solid gold dancing, the fish was still, his tongue hanging out of his mouth.

"You've killed my platonic lifemate," Mr. Tophat cried.

The last thing that I saw was the NGA building's front door and the tips of Mr. Tophat's pinkies as they poked me in the eyes.

CHAPTER TWENTY-SIX MCDONALD'S

El Jefe celebrated his triumph over Crapview Apartments by swallowing a bunch of McDonner Burgers whole like they were pills. Eyeballing the final resting place of the apartment building's ruins—a hole in the front of the NGA building—he dreamt of a McDonner Burger in every household. Once he realized his life's ambition, the burger would make all other foods obsolete, conquering the three meals of the day.

Desperate to keep her job, Jo-Jo interrupted his reveries with a "I won't quit if you stop with all the cannibal ickyness. Let's forget today ever happened."

"I have a better idea," El Jefe said. "The McDonner Burger will now be the only item on our menu, and if you want to continue working for McDonald's, you'll have to do a few...umm...favors for me." He waved his penis around as if it were a conductor's baton. "Quid pro quo, Miss Jo-Jo, quid pro quo." He gobbled down another burger, clutched his throat, and sputtered, "I ... think ... I'm ... choking."

Jo-Jo watched her boss as he turned blue. She didn't know the Heimlich maneuver, but even if she had, she wouldn't have used it to save his life.

El Jefe let out his final belch.

CHAPTER TWENTY-SEVEN NGA BUILDING

I woke up with my arms wrapped around last night's sexual conquest. I lay in the warm, erotic glow, trying to reconstruct the events of our encounter. She must have headbutted me a whole lot of times because I didn't remember a thing. But maybe it was better this way. This was the first time that I ever dipped my zinger into a vavavoom. No doubt it had been an awkward, slimy experience. Now I could choose how I wanted to remember it. And let me tell you, I was absolutely sensational.

Trying not to wake up my honeypot, I nuzzled her arm as gently as possible and ended up getting her body hair stuck in my teeth. How peculiar.

I noticed she was still wearing a hat and that it happened to be a top hat. Curiouser and curiouser.

Then her crotch caught my eye. I contemplated her unsightly bulge and memories of the demolition derby and Mr. Tophat flooded into my head.

Now that I was fully awake, I looked around the room. It had been totally destroyed.

I heard the trickle of urine coming from outside. Through the window, I saw the fountain from the NGA building's lobby, topped with a statue of Mr. Tomfoolery's father as he passed a kidney stone. I crawled forward to get a closer look.

"Don't make another whoopieing move," a voice said.

I turned to give the speaker a piece of my mind about his dirty mouth and screamed.

The giant goldfish was hopping up and down beside me.

"Aaaaah! Begone, zombie goldfish!"

"I was just pretending to be dead, you whoopieing moron," he said, then his teeth crunched down on my ear.

The pain shot straight through to my tear ducts. I whipped my head around, trying to knock the fish off my ear, but he didn't budge. I was surprised how light he was for such an enormous monster of the sea.

I jumped through the window to test the fish's tolerance for broken glass and landed in the fountain. The water must have made him stronger because he bit down even harder.

I gave the lobby the once-over. The zoo building was lying inside the room, totally destroyed. It had been smooshed together, reduced to one-hundredth of its size and now resembled a very large accordion. The thrill of victory rushed through my body, almost overpowering the agony in my ear. I only hoped that the NGA building was still operational and that pesky McDonald's franchise hadn't won the derby.

I raced towards the elevator, longing to find out the status of things and to see if Stuart had any tips on getting the goldfish off my ear. Once inside, I pressed the button for the ninety-seventh floor, which was where I worked.

"Hold the elevator, please!" shouted Mr. Tophat. For some reason, maybe because of my ingrained politeness habit, I did as he asked. Once I realized what I was doing, I started banging my head on the wall and tapping intensely on the door-close button. But it was already too late. Huffing and puffing, he had made it inside the elevator.

A hairy paw grabbed him by the nape of his neck and pulled him back into the lobby.

"Sign. Petition. Now."

I waved to Ogar the janitor as the elevator doors closed. He elbowed Mr. Tophat in the face and a spurt of his victim's blood shot out through the crack in the door and dripped down my shirt.

As the elevator went up, I punched the fish, repeatedly, in the nose. His counterattack was to scratch my face with his fins, which was actually somewhat pleasant since it made me forget about the pain in my ear for a little while.

But it didn't last. The pain soon shot back, full blast.

Sick and tired of the torment, I tried to get the fish off of me by yanking as hard as I could.

It worked, but I suddenly found myself in tremendous agony.

I watched the fish as he flopped to the ground. Blood poured out the side of my head, showering him in red.

My ear was still in his mouth.

CHAPTER TWENTY-EIGHT
MCDONALD'S

"I don't think I'll ever get used to this beard," Jo-Jo said, now wearing El Jefe's skin.

"You'll have to," Harold said, smoothing down a wrinkle in her new forehead. "El Jefe treated it like a head of lettuce that he was going to enter in the state fair. You'll never convince the board of trustees if you shave it. Not only will you lose your job, but you'll also buy yourself a murder charge. But do whatever you like. I don't care who's ordering me around as long as I don't have to cook McDonner Burgers."

Jo-Jo tied a scrunchy around her new beard. It made it look like the shape of a fist. "Do you think Corporate will suspect if I keep it like this?" she asked.

"You're pushing it," he said. "How does it feel under there by the way? All gooey?"

"It's like I'm swimming in a vat of liquefied gummy worms. I hate it. Not only do I feel totally nasty, but this thing is really creeping me out. I can't believe I'm actually going through with one of James' ideas. Next, I'll be looking over my shoulder for agents of the SECRET Malaysian government. Well, back to the fry station," she said and returned to her post, eager to put the NGA Corporation out of business.

CHAPTER TWENTY-NINE
NGA BUILDING

The elevator door opened as I threatened to bite off the goldfish's ear for payback.

Gordon was there to greet me. "I hope you enjoyed your extra-long lunch break, Monty. It'll be the last one you'll ever take after I report it to Mr. Tomfoolery. What's that smell? All employees must wash themselves properly before visiting the office. And what's this? You've dared to enter the office without an ear? Company policy mandates that all employees must be in possession of both ears while on the call center floor. And now you're littering again? All droplets of blood must be disposed of in a proper trash receptacle instead of on the floor. Failure to do so-"

He was interrupted when a mechanical claw wrapped its fingers around his body and pulled him out of the building through the hole in the wall. He remained calm as he flew through the air and started to write in his notebook. He was probably writing up the claw for interfering with his work.

I rushed to my cubicle, followed by the goldfish. He was moving very slowly, wheezing like an asthmatic.

Stuart was sitting in my chair, pressing buttons with his tongue. He saw me and took a breather. "Hey there, guy. Cool wound! Guess what? I've discovered that my tongue is a much better driver than I am."

I motioned over to my pursuer. "Do you have any suggestions for dealing with that fish? I think he wants to tear off all my body parts."

"You should buy him a fake, decorative castle to play in. It would make him a very happy fish and he'll forget all about his sadomasochistic tendencies."

My monitor flashed red to indicate danger. The McDonald's franchise was climbing up the side of our building with its claw and shooting burgers at the walls.

Stuart tried to shake them off with his tongue.

Mr. Tomfoolery staggered by, glanced at Stuart, and stopped dead in his tracks. "Why are you tasting the keyboard, Mr. Sutcliffe?" he said, getting angrier with each breath. "And where is Mr. Liddy? Why is there blood all over the floor?" His face was flushed red and he was shaking. "What is climbing up the side of my building?" His skin had turned the color of burnt toast and sizzled like a frying pan. "Why does the call center look like it's been hit by a comet?" He turned towards me. "Why…"

Then a burger smashed through the window and landed in his mouth.

Mr. Tomfoolery bit down, with hesitancy.

Satisfied, he hungrily devoured it, teeth grinding like a buzz saw. "That was the most scrumptious meal I've *ever* tasted, he said, plopping himself down onto the floor to have a food-induced orgasm.

I smelled the stink of fish. He had finally caught up with me.

"I'm gonna chew out your whoopieing intestines," the goldfish hissed menacingly.

I squealed and ran away.

I watched as the fish flopped towards me from across the room. I felt relieved. At the speed he was traveling, it would take him a week to catch up with me.

But then he hijacked the office's mail cart by threatening to commit a federal offense: opening mail that didn't belong to him. Taking the fish's threat very seriously, the mailroom guy did as he was told and gave the fish a big push into my direction.

Anxious to get out of the cart's way, I ducked into Mr. Tomfoolery's office.

I heard a crash.

The goldfish came into the office, riding the mail cart like a skateboard.

He hopped out of the cart and lunged towards my healthy ear.

I dodged his attack and he belly-flopped into the gladiator tank.

The fish let out an underwater shriek as tiny puncture marks appeared on his face, and the water filled with his blood. Within seconds, the sea monkeys had stripped him of flesh and his skeleton floated up to the surface.

Overjoyed about his death, I went back to my seat. Stuart was giving his armpits a chance to drive.

"What the heck are you doing? That McDonald's is about to crush us into a pancake!"

I reached for the keyboard, and stopped when the elevator door opened and Mr. Tophat strolled out of it, covered in bruises. Our eyes met.

He charged.

The door to the staircase crashed open and oodles of police officers with stylish hairdos swarmed onto the floor. "Stop where you are, Scabies Awful-Awful, or we'll brutalize the criminality out of you."

Bab's blocked the officers' path. "Hey, cuties," she said. "How would you like to satisfy all of my erotic needs?"

The cops took off their pants and lined up in front of her. The first man on the scene said, "Ma'am, let's make this quick. We have urgent police business to attend to."

She complied and the officer inspected her antique vavavoom with his fleshstick.

I felt cold metal on my chin.

"Tell me where Bubbles is or I'll make you bleed with my bullets," Mr. Tophat said.

I shrugged. "Who's Bubbles?"

He poked me harder with his gun. "My platonic lifemate. He's a giant goldfish."

"*Oh*," I said. "Sorry, but he was just killed by a bunch of sea monkeys."

"No, *really*, where is he?"

I pointed to Mr. Tomfoolery's office.

He walked away.

After hearing Babs slurp and moan for the next few minutes, Mr. Tophat came out of the office, carrying the goldfish's skeleton. Weeping, he lifted his former platonic lifemate up into the air and shouted, "No!"

Taking advantage of his grief, I knocked the gun out of his pants.

The weapon slid across the room and left the building through a hole in the wall.

Mr. Tophat crouched into fighting stance and punched me in the arm. His attack was accompanied by a "boomshakalaka" battle cry.

Shrugging off the pain, I grabbed a handful of his velvet cape and swung him around the room, smashing his body into a variety of office furniture. But before I could dish out the appropriate amount of punishment for making my arm hurt really bad, the cape ripped and we both toppled to the ground.

Mr. Tophat's hat slipped off his head as he fell down, revealing a set of pigtails.

I crawled over and put him in a bear hug. We tumbled around the room, screaming, biting, and pulling each other's hair. He scratched my chest, leaving marks, raw and sore. I tried to give him a taste of his own wussyness, but my attack was useless because I had clipped my nails last night.

"I could really use a Big Mac right now," he said, sweating like a tourist on a tropical island, and he puked all over my shoes. Then he tried to disfigure me with a stapler.

I tried to get him to stop by stabbing him with a handful of thumbtacks.

But he didn't seem to notice. He kept pounding the staples into my flesh and grinning maniacally.

Fed up and on the verge of passing out from the agony, I unleashed my secret weapon—my spot-on impression of a shark—and nibbled on the lower half of his body.

He yelped. "Did you just bite my dick?"

I swished the saliva around my mouth, tasting its flavor. "Yeah, I think so," I said, shocked by my behavior and ashamed of myself.

Enraged and foaming at the mouth, Mr. Tophat tried to knock my teeth out.

The mechanical claw hovered nearby as he pummeled my head. While he brought the pain, I tried to direct the claw towards him like an air traffic controller, but it didn't follow my instructions.

"Stop hitting me!" I pleaded. But he continued with his assault, so I kung fu kicked him with both of my feet. It knocked him towards the claw, which scooped him up and lifted him away as he wailed.

I noticed that Stuart wasn't in my seat. The McDonald's franchise was still attached to the side of our building, and there was nobody behind the wheel.

I searched the room for Stuart, but he was nowhere in sight. Except for Babs and her male companions, the room was so empty that it was starting to feel like a Sunday. I wondered if the claw had escorted Stuart off the premises along with my other co-workers.

Then Stuart waved to me through the window. He was standing inside the McDonald's franchise, ordering food.

Flabbergasted by his betrayal, I hurried to my cubicle and grabbed the controls. The McDonald's might have been aggressive, but I had the advantage of being a hundred times bigger than it. All it took to end Ronald McDonald's reign of terror over the digestive systems of the American people was one little maneuver: I tilted the side of the NGA building towards the ground and brought it crashing down on top of the franchise.

CHAPTER THIRTY
MCDONALD'S

Jo-Jo leaned against the counter. It was the only thing stopping her from being hurled into the call center below. The McDonald's was now pointing down as if it were a slide and its entrance had been replaced by a row of cubicles.

Stuart stood on the other side, propping himself up on the condiments rack as he ate from a container of fries. His clothes were ripped and blood dripped from his nose, bathing the fries in his plasma. This didn't seem to bother him as he crammed twenty bloody French fries into his mouth.

"Why is there a McDonald's in the building?" said Mr. Tomfoolery from down below, looking as if he was about to go on a killing spree.

Stuart dipped a fry in barbecue sauce. "This is our new snack bar. And all of us at the NGA Corporation just want to thank you for the tasty grub."

Mr. Tomfoolery exploded in rage. "Do you think I'm stupid, you imbecile?"

Stuart nodded his head, caught himself, and switched to shaking it.

"This isn't a snack bar. I didn't order the construction of a snack bar. Why has a goddamn McDonald's crashed into the side of my building?" His eyes widened in understanding. "Who's responsible for using my building to compete in today's demolition derby?"

CHAPTER THIRTY-ONE
NGA BUILDING

"I am," I shouted, feeling like the happiest telecommunications employee in Cheesequake.

CHAPTER THIRTY-TWO
MCDONALD'S

"I'm going to scoop out your brains and use your skull as a urinal in my private bathroom," Mr. Tomfoolery snarled.

He noticed a McDonner Burger by his foot, which caused him to release a gallon of drool. His pupils rolled to the back of his head.

"You there with the marvelous beard," he said, addressing Jo-Jo. "I would like to purchase this burger."

"I'm sorry, sir," she said, "but we're no longer selling that item. Can I interest you in a Big N' Tasty?"

"I'm prepared to offer you one million dollars for this hamburger," he said, taking out his checkbook.

Her eyes looked like they were about to leap out of her sockets. "In that case, you can have all the McDonner Burgers in the restaurant, but I still can't sell you that particular one. It would be a health code violation. There seems to be a man attached to it."

Mr. Tomfoolery noticed that the burger consisted of one half patty and one half Scabies. Again, he salivated.

"Our meat grinding machine malfunctioned when your building destroyed ours," she said.

"This looks like a perfectly good burger to me and I would love to sink my teeth into it. I can make the health code inspector a very wealthy man," he said, fanning himself with his checkbook.

Scabies let out a whimper and scurried between Mr. Tomfoolery's feet, escaping into the call center.

The CEO sighed and wrote Jo-Jo a check. "I don't have the time to hunt for my own food. I am a very busy man." He folded a check into a paper airplane, threw it at her head, picked up the nearest McDonner Burger, and gobbled it down.

A man in a plastic toupee scaled down the wall in suction cup shoes and said, "Congratulations, Tom Tomfoolery, for winning Cheesequake City's demolition derby. Donna, show Mr. Tomfoolery the prize that he's won today."

A voluptuous blonde dropped through the ceiling in a parachute and waved a board game from side to side.

"It's an iron-clad monopoly over the entire fast food industry," the man said.

Reaching for seconds, Mr. Tomfoolery grinned so wide that his lips rolled down his chin.

CHAPTER THIRTY-THREE
DONNER BURGER

I stood inside the first Donner Burger franchise, filling up the drinks dispenser with water. This was my first official act as the vice president of the NGA Corporation's water refilling department and boy was I excited!

I gave Mr. Tomfoolery the thumbs up, but he didn't notice. He was too busy trying to hold up the weight of a giant pair of scissors. A crowd of fast food enthusiasts surrounded him on all sides. They were here for the franchise's grand opening, and I had never seen anyone as fascinated as they were about a giant ribbon.

I smiled and gave Mr. Tomfoolery another thumbs up. Again, he didn't notice me. I didn't blame him. He was now focused on cutting the ribbon with his scissors. You can say a lot of things about Mr. Tomfoolery, but you can't say he isn't a heck of a nice guy. Not only did he promote me, but he also changed his mind about using my skull as a urinal. Plus he gave me a new ear and an advance on my paycheck so I could move out of my bathroom stall and live with Stuart in his mother's house.

Outside, Mr. Tomfoolery succeeded at cutting the ribbon and the crowd let out a cheer. I gave him the thumbs up again, and I didn't care about not getting a response. I was just so proud of him.

"Monty, can you grab some empty cups from the kitchen?" El Jefe asked in his funny girl voice.

And I slipped into the back before the customers stampeded through the door, although I did catch a glimpse of Stuart cutting to the front of the line.

James was in the kitchen, revealing the truth about the SECRET Malaysian government to a homeless man as he bashed his brains in with a hammer. "Oh, hi, Monty," he said. James was a friendly guy.

I gave him a thumbs up and smiled.

He frowned and looked down at the stump where his arm used to be.

Harold was standing next to Mr. Tophat, putting the finishing touches on his design. Half of the demolition derby's bronze medallist was surgically attached to the fry station, filling containers of fries for the customers, while his other half was lounging around in the cesspool beneath the Tomfoolery mansion's front yard.

He tried to eat a French fry. But before he was able to put it in his mouth, the mechanical claw grabbed it out of his hand and disappeared into the wall. Mr. Tophat made a pouty face.

Since I don't hold grudges, I had forgiven him for trying to beat me up. Attempting to lift his spirits, I gave him a thumbs up, but he was too busy frowning to notice.

Refusing to admit defeat, I gave him another one and held it until Harold tasered him into thumb-upping me back.

I loved my new job.

STEVE AYLETT

BOOKS BY AYLETT:
The Crime Studio
Bigot Hall
Slaughtermatic
The Inflatable Volunteer
Toxicology
Atom
Shamanspace
Only an Alligator
Dummyland
The Velocity Gospel
Karloff's Circus
Lint
Fain the Sorcerer
And Your Point Is?

LOCATION:
Kent, England

STYLE OF BIZARRO:
Satire

DESCRIPTION: His writing is a multigeneric tapestry of science fiction, horror, fantasy and detective fiction. "Not only conceptually brilliant and satirically walloping, but stylistically innovative ..." —Paul DiFilippo, Asimov's

INTERESTS: Blaming, staring, lurching, disappearing, shuddering, sleeping, rays & other sea animals, pale bigmouthed girls, Gamera the turtle, non-sea animals, hibernation, resentment, codeine, tea.

INFLUENCES: Voltaire, Ken McMullen, CH Hinton, Jeff Lint, Scorces, Delacorta, Cardiacs, Brautigan, Brothers Quay, Tarkovsky, Greg Egan, Monique Ortiz, My Bloody Valentine, Ladytron, David Lynch, Marina de Van, Kerouac, Caterer comic, Spalding Gray, Cocteau Twins, Max Ernst, Louise Lecavalier, Bingo Violaine, Vance.

WEBSITE:
www.steveaylett.com

SHAMANSPACE

Caught by mortals in old age,
an angel scattered itself like leaves

SIG

To those who know that the inhabitants of heaven and hell are political prisoners, that the law is as preventative as next year's weather, that the post-human's too predictable, South London has always been a playground.

'Don't think so hard—he'll hear you, if he's bothered.'

Young and deathblown, two edgemen walked past stripe walls, blending and there were walls, nobody. The pavement didn't recognise them, drawing no colour. The younger, the boy, tipped his head back in a bone-flavour rain, seeing air rich in nocturnal swirls.

'What about you?'

'He won't know I'm here,' the French girl told him. 'He never knows.'

'You must be good,' said the boy—if she could screen from Alix. They said Alix could enter the face of a guitar without making a sound. Melody had once seen his body splitting open as he bleached out behind geysers of infra-red, lightning in the blot of his mouth and angel blowback gusting stuff off the breakfast table. And as he reversed out of the human bandwidth he pulled depths into the house, furniture exploding into blurdust and splinters. He could lose it across to otherspace as soon as think about it. He stared and it was hell that blinked. Back at the Keep Alix featured in heavy books, his icon head in colours kitsch as Indian firework art.

She said they were near but the boy couldn't feel anything strange in the trafficjam of structures. He ran his hand along a pedestrian subway's paracetamol walls as they ascended into an angled wasteland where a traffic light hung like an earring. Melody was now a more stripped-down version of herself, invisible to anyone but the best edgemen—Sig saw a flicker of her wrapped in protein mapping. They said he had the gift but no brains. Bad steering.

Mood rang across the slamming street, abandoned. They stopped at a metal door covered in rust like coffee grains. Alix's door and still no energy signature. They valved through, and the boy found himself clattering up the dodgy stairs alone. Glancing back, he saw the girl had sat down sadly to wait.

Sig pushed carefully into the dim room. It was as cold as stone and became slowly a distinct space of callused books and abraxia. Everywhere softening, withered and dead flowers were arrayed in the gloom. Seated near the hollow fire of this dry worry shrine was Alix in clowntorn rags faded to a pupal grey. How old was he meant to be? Twenty-seven? But his hair was white, his face empty. Not cloaked—just not giving out any energy to start with. Was it a new, deeper sort of disguise? Living right down in the detail?

His eyes were turns of liquid gold, glistening and unseeing.

'What's this,' said the living legend without looking up, his voice that of an old man. 'A little novice godstopper, ripped to the tits on righteous fury.'

'I like to think so, sir.'

The eye-gold shifted, meaningless. 'Well answered. I had a dream just now. Bomb season rushed in, flinging back loose particles of the house, blew bodies into me like leaves. Then you swanned in. You and your neurotrash friends getting on alright? Teaching you to field-strip and reassemble yourself like a gun? Watch yourself. You think being permitted is the same as being free? You're allowed to siddown.'

Sig pulled a wooden chair over and sat down, staring in silence past Alix at a bug which jotted across the wall.

'D'you like stories? They say our enemy likes stories and that's why we're here. Well we haven't provided it with anything interesting lately have we.'

'I've heard a lot of stories about you, Alix.'

'So you drop by to sip my ghost. Like I've plenty to spare, the hero. Expected a couple hundredweight of angels entertaining me? Established to heroic glory in a Sistene scene, right?'

'I don't know what I expected.'

'You're lying. Or the next thing over. Lying still reveals stuff because it's directly connected, they haven't taught you that? I used to be that way—all of six years ago. Thought truth was the stone in the snowball. Truth was really the whole shebang.'

'Tell me.'

'It's a secret no matter how much it's told. Our enemy hides in plain sight. I believe you already know that.'

'But you found its heart.'

'I got the coordinates, in the shabbiest way. And I went there. Jabbing a dagger at the sky. You think it's cool, making me remember? Good for your rep out there? We're white minutes, disposable ghosts, many per hand. We're nothing.'

Sudden pockets of failure went geomantic, flashed into expression, twisting the moment through the room. He had abruptly opened his pain. Sig saw Alix journeying in the big huge, an electron speck on electric white.

'Yeah, it's a little bit triggery,' Alix said. 'I mean it. Into every word I weave thorns.'

1
CHAOS PAD

Darkness turns on a dime

The girl was surgeon and singing bird, deadly queen of sharps. Resentments at the ready, we met in a nerve storm club. I went in as an untextured nobody, walls showing through me. Scar incarnate, third generation cool and moral omitted, washing one drug down with another as the world toxified around us. Sad shadows in her hair, a slow ballet of cigarette smoke, cold bottle touch going warm as outcome diagrams watched our way. The streets, treasure lights bobbing underneath the real. Her rough ferrous oxide tongue as we went up in a cage elevator somewhere. Her hair hides the phone.

After that I lost track of time for a while. Someone's flat. I was looking at a strange box of bone parts, all hoaxed up with operation wire—an october switch, it was called. I had one of those, it was an activan machine. A what? My head frazzled through a series of pulls, releases and dissolves. The body is King on Earth, I remembered, a vital lie.

A lightbulb was swinging like a hanged ghost as I drew a thin blade through the smudged centre of the entry stamp on my wrist. The wound pulled open, stretching gluey blood. It looked like a mainline station in there, parallel tracks converging and splitting in a soak of red light. Who was I?

The elemental flutter of etheric draw flickered in the soda blackness to my right, barely visible through brain spuff. Outside influence, drawing like silver stage ropes.

I was in such a bad way. Deep cover - I'd lost myself in it again. I was Alix the ultravivid hero or something like it. I stood up, pushing through thick space, and pull patterns shrivelled like cobwebs around me. The girl was a loft baby, rigged up in a back room, the leather cocoon of her flightbag the centre of a massive kirlian web.

Transformation adjustments mashed in the dark, heroine wear backing up, discovered and obliged to die. I had to do a techie before the end. Etheric strands were still trailing into me - all the better.

I used the blade to split the suspension bag - lengths of gelatinous activan stretched from her pale face, she didn't stir. Laying on hands.

An armchair was already dwindling into the corner as electrovistas opened up in front, the stream of cells blowing past. Bloodshot intervals of subterranean transport and the racket of magic.

Her head was a lovely little number. Creation-fresh, her spirit entering a litter of fallen winter, momentary people reproached her angrily for delicious visions and she died a notch or two. Together the years conspired, denying eachother. Fame admiration trapped the family, their lives in dry dock. Children were plucked like pillows and shoved into formation. Surgeons hand over a mistake, culture paints leaves green which were green, complete and repeated, sickening, and mother birds drop coins into the waiting mouths of chicks. She learnt to keep her eyes closed when crying, tears flowing under the skin and over the skull. Early dreams collapsed like empires. At least there was little chance of her rage dying among the lies. Truthful and ousted, she saw structures in events, sat in crowds watching the armatures of human need and fantasy anglepoising between the people, linking them in a jagged scaffold, and later learnt that others couldn't see this. Bloodshot canyons of wounds, ward screeches, remote money, a cell padded with snow, a white girl curled round a white soul.

And the Prevail picked her out of the chorus. New fathers taught her to use a sigil gun and walk with street-sensitive claws. Something of herself was left, a miniscule mischief which rifled a secret and took it away. Sacred telemetry. And this rushed into me the instant before her head jumped apart like a balloon filled with water.

The left side of my body was on fire and I was shaking with sobs, several layers of skin gone. She'd been achingly, corrosively beautiful under the make-up. People who've had a lot of good luck deny that luck exists - those who've had a lot of bad know it does.

2
THE SWEET HALFWAY

Inconsistencies are shown to be limbs on the same creature

The Internecine pulled me in immediately, my headshout summoning a unit before the Prevail swung by in response to the girl's phonecall. I was ghostburnt, in mourning and voiding lumps of the cover personality. After a few days in my cell at the Keep, I went to see Lockhart in his study, a room tumoured with statuary and patched with a lot of detail. Chairs of red leather polished like cherry skin, floors of heart pine, fruit hugged in a bowl and a fire the colour of drugs. Here we sat and talked in the utter sadness and treasuring of golden mischief which came of knowing it was all for nothing. The Keepworks rendered everything ironic instantly; and all the while we meant it. 'You know this bit of barefaced enlightenment could have smashed the neighbourhood?' Lockhart said, his face full of the vitality of old wisdom. Misery glows better with fibres of experience.

'I got sloppy, then lucked out - that's all.' I was healthier. Matter felt right. 'Where's Melody?'

'Paris, sidebanding the Prevail motherhouse. She sends her congratulations. She was interested to hear the Prevail have located the heart of god and this assassin girl of theirs happened to know about it. So you're to do the job.'

'Looks that way, doesn't it? Slingshot into the monster's eye. Why shouldn't it be me. A crack in the furnace may be fiercer than the mouth.'

'Quite. But I've been wondering, if the Prevail have the location, why haven't they carried out the hit?'

'They're limousine rebels. Riddles retreat, if they're weak. This one keeps staring until they look away.'

'We don't. You don't. You're getting faster. If anything you're over-confident. We bleed outside the history books, Alix. However tempting to scorn through victory and leave it wrapped in whispers. Don't become so attached to your rep that you delay the final act forever. Allow for etheric wind-sheer—and that of cowardice.'

'What the hell does that mean?'

Lockhart's face congested with concern. 'People, unlike our target, can give way to pity. I believe the Prevail feel something like that. Individual versus society, or versus god. Either way it's the resistance to absorption. Independence of spirit. Pause any country and you'll spot subliminal torture in the frame. The sky of culture looks downward, obstructive and unambitious. The edgemen are a circus of parallel citizenry. So we sometimes forget the pain that drove us here in the first place.'

'God, camouflaged by sheer familiarity, different to nothing, essence of agony.' This was re-examined rote, out of an old but good edgemen book called *The Ultimate Midnight*.

'The debate is: Destroy the universe entire? Or cut god out like a cancer? We in the Internecine believe that in destroying god, we'll bring everything to an end—that it runs through all matter. Because the Prevail believe the universe will continue after god's destruction, their considerations are entirely different from ours. When men assume they'll continue, responsibility is postponed.'

'Listen, what if it made no difference, neither ended it all nor made it better—why do the hit?'

'At the simplest level? Revenge, and honour satisfied.'

'Then death wouldn't be punishment enough, would it?'

Lockhart twitched a small smile. 'You and old Quinas have a lot to talk about.'

I didn't like the sound of this—Quinas was a charred moon dropped from the sky, yesterday's hero gone to margin remnants and remains. 'I've met shamanic burnouts. Some shivering leftover with weird eyes? I haven't got the patience to hear about some gold-rimmed yesterday.'

'He's rather younger than I am,' Lockhart muttered tersely, and I felt like the idiot I was. I loved this kindly gentleman who had been born in the days before our enemy's existence had even been verified. 'In any case it's important you meet him before the big push. And be surprised by nothing you see or hear. He's ... on the night side of right.'

I decided I needed a little more recovery time. I'd stripped my gears being something deliberately counterclockwise with my idea of myself—someone out of control. Hip discord wasted my time. But I was the great age for edgework - faced with truth, the young merely fizzed with its acid clarity. They weren't crippled—they were connoisseurs of the delicate tension between alive and nonalive, the sweet halfway.

In my cell I watched the alkaloidal motion in the wall, and asked for stories. I knew books could see people around them, they ground their tiny teeth, tried to rattle like windows, stories to tell. Here were stored Arabian secrets uncynical and sensate, books tattooed in pain-ink, buds turning open, suburb flagstones, broken down gardens, a tin barrow red hot in the sun, insects in the dusk-fluctuating wind flying against shallow water, a mind where river floor scenes flutter unseen, all in the worming walls of the Keep. I treasured the safety here. Dead entrances withstood storms and there were aimless stains of music on the air. Outer platitude galaxies tapped ineffectual at the door. Kneeling to see along two thousand miles of architectonics I found the accumulated density of civilisation, the food chain binding scraps of posterity. Society flowed along the vibration, unchallenged and unchallenging. What kind of world was that for a growing lad?

3
PAINLESS BLOOD, A SECRET

Originality irritates so obscurely that people may have to evolve to scratch it

I went through the ivied gate to the locked quarters, a guard allowing entry. Quinas was meant to be batshit crazy and acquitted himself well. He sat at the centre of his cell like an albino frog, working at some obscure cabalistic grid, probably a malice puzzle. Proceeding around him was a polychrome exchange, the walls trancing with sickly refractions. His head was sprouted with white death-hairs, and when he turned my way I saw his eyes were liquid mercury, the surfaces flowing like oily water. 'My,' he said, 'people come and go so quickly here. Alix—I've heard of you. Dark harlequin, toxic clown or something, yes? Ridiculous that even among our kind we need our little superstars. Sit down. I wonder what they expect me to tell you? Maybe I'm just a warning of what can go wrong, like a mad uncle, eh? Last little initiation.'

'Whatever you like.'

'An open mind? I feel privileged.' He seemed to consider, his seemingly sightless eyes blank. 'Perhaps you need to know what's gone before. The winning side writes the history books, the losers adjust in translation, thus all is homogenised. The Sequel Coming, one messiah eaten by the next. The Internecine Order began with Tagore Ros, who over there in the asphalt world is mainly known for the saying "Say which exists and which doesn't—the gallows, harmony, yourself." He knew that genuine power doesn't have to enforce it by example. Assumed power, on the other hand, requires folks' belief—it depends upon the victim's industry. Without that, it ... just sits in a room, referring to itself as authority.'

'I know all that,' I told him. A lot of edgemen contracted that turn of the head that got them talking weird—past and future helixed together.

'But do you see that even genuine power may have something to hide? Too inquisitive and it pulls rank. Always that in the end. It seems that whenever god has a fight with us it's never over what he's really angry about.'

'He?'

'You're right, that's more of a girl thing. But we're living amid its moulted material, including the hothouse cultivated hell some call civilisation. Democracy, for want of a better word, denies the song every day with a din of affairs, our opinions yelled above the sound of hope scratching in the dust, all in faith eyes and alarm. Though hysterical, folk are proud—and it's hard for people to stampede when they're strutting. Genocide, a million jet-trail outcries, easily ignored. Unconcerned we are not awakened - are we perfect, or imperfect? Public fountains haven't answered us in years. And all the while a thin film of identity separates you and oblivion.'

By now bored and languid, I hadn't the patience for this crumb-cupboard past. The twists of tacking convention are pretty to some, not me. 'This is a lot of damp news.'

'Yes—I apologise. You need to know about the Internecine's failed attempts, these things our own people bet their shirts on. Let's see then. Did you know they tried a sort of MK Ultra programmed agent scheme? But of course it could sense something—everything, in fact. They decided the only hope was to operate in a way about which it didn't care. We knew there's a vast percentage of events about which it doesn't especially care, and those involving human suffering seemed a safe bet—so we raised an agent from scratch. Lived in a monastery and so on, and died unaware he was a virus—to sneak him into heaven. He'd then be activated and do the hit. But they found the heart of the creature wasn't there—this "heaven" was just a place to get people squared away, one of countless infinite bandwidths for etheric soul material.'

This story was brand new to me. I couldn't quite believe it, but Quinas was transparent. I should have known a blaze of honesty is a fine decoy.

'I used to be the bigshot like yourself, but I believed a quick hit wasn't enough, I thought the creator should be tortured beforehand. I loaded our pain—guided crawling to the only choice, deference to the lucky, extorted worship, full-body entropy, incinerative powerlessness, the medicinal smell of lies—in to a million etheric traps throughout subspace. If one was tripped they'd all tip at once in to god's mind. But like a clumsy poacher, I managed to trip it myself.'

'If you survived, god certainly would have.'

'But it would have suffered more—with it being the source, the experience would have been a feedback loop. Torture was the point. Anyway, I realised it had delayed me from the inside. The sheer bravura of that, the regard the project would get me. Yes, I should have just gone for the hit. You see, we're part of our enemy. It hides by walking in its own footprints. It's everything. Luckily this means anywhere's an entrance to it, in fact we're already there. The question is, how to reach a vital organ.'

'Well I've found that, and you're wasting my time. All I want to do is say goodbye to a few people, let them know it's about to end, and do the job.'

'The stars of reason corrupt your sky, Alix. You're too coolheaded. You'll need anger that would turn sand to glass. God depends on our becoming distracted—as you have, with your style, as the Prevail have, with their politics. It knows you're coming.'

'We take precautions—we're hidden here.'

'The Keep's made of anglematter—antimatter reversed through its own dimensions to make a near-neutral greyspace. Tied off sidelong to society with false entrances of whole years. Normally the body eats space equal to its size. Not here. The Keep's not camouflaged. In fact it stands out like a scar that won't tan.'

'If it knows, why doesn't it stop us?'

Quinas smiled winterly. Geometrics whirled through the albescent walls. He was a fine one to accuse me of a lack of passion. The man had been ghostburnt to ice.

'Without consciousness there's no cruelty—only objects without pain. God made us conscious for a reason. It knew that when its cells became self-aware, they'd experience a pitch of pain that'd send them for revenge. We're nano-assassins. It just takes one of us little viruses to get to the right place. In our capacity as god's suicidal impulse the idea's always been to work covert, like a drink habit—god's cowardly, it doesn't want to know or take responsibility for what it's doing. That's why it delegated in the first place, yes? A part of it knows what we're doing, because we *are* that part of it. Just don't make too much noise. It'll *let* us sneak up. A telescope is god looking at itself. We are god cursing at itself. When we kill it, we'll be god killing itself.'

Behind him was the image of a nerve in earth growing a grassblade thin and already dying.

'Well,' I said, 'it's been good, Mr Quinas.' I stood, feeling headachy. Not good.

'You like books—let me give you a going-away gift,' he said, standing as an opalescent shelf extruded from the wall. Amid the junk I noticed curse needles and a very rare spinelight camera. He took down a book of mirrors, flipping through it in an absorbed sort of way—I thought he'd forgotten me. Then he handed it over, his dead silver eyes knowing exactly where I stood. 'Acqueville's *Flightless Land Without Clouds*. It's said this book learned the ultimate secret, lain in sun on the tiles for a million years - the pages extracting a store of the mystery, closing. Truth revealed, the sky one big X-ray.'

'Thank you, Mr Quinas. Goodbye.'

I passed through the security sweetwall and glanced back. Quinas was flickering, his body fading to a tintype image. His voice rasped right against my ear. 'Maybe you didn't hear me. You expect the stars to know you? We're nothing, snuff-zeroes in a vacuum.'

I knew it—he was creating a diversion. An etheric exertion was throbbing in the air. 'What's this,' I said, stupid. Quinas was a red electric outline scrambling from the mirror book—I dropped it as he formed up with a sort of dazed laugh and sprang toward a fast clearing in the outer sweetwall. He hung aside from the crackling gap, behind him a city glittering distant as beads. Phenomenal effects banged past him—he winked his eye and let go, vanishing. The wall closed.

So it was to be human drama and delay after all.

4
ETHERIC SPEEDWAY

The threat of ending has been taken as a promise

Quinas valved down in Paris and this suggested he had some business with the Prevail. I should have known when he called the world god's 'moulted material'—Prevail philosophy. Lockhart was saying I should regenerate and keep my powder dry, whatever the hell that meant. But there was a chance I could stop Quinas from blowing the surprise. I joined Melody in a safe house in the rue Fromentin, loving her but weirding on the city—my nerves sang sickly with the left-handed landscapes and cathedrals brittle as candy. The style layer was so thick it put a two minute delay on the registration of actual flesh. Melody tried to distract me in a skirt made of brain skin. 'What's this?' she asked, holding the mirror book.

'Quinas gave it to me.' The only words were an inscription etched on the cover. *Mirrors are roots—buried here with us. What they feed is elsewhere. We are a mirror to show god its cruelty.* Did Quinas give me this thing to root me deeper into the world? If so it wouldn't make it. I asked Melody for directions to the Prevail motherhouse and she pointed in the ninth direction. I took that very deliberate half-turning step which tilted an edge in the air, showing me a dense cross-section of several etheric miles. A bright band of rich rubine red was immediately noticeable, not far away. I raised an arm toward it, the funhouse-mirror limb stretching to infinity, and let it draw the rest of me into subspace like an elastic band. The room started to funnel and I gained a sense or two, then blurred through a wedding-arch of cobalt flame. Vision wedges cut in, passing. Ahead was an audio hole surrounded by warp, liquid voices stretching. Subfrequencies coalesced and sharpened.

'... A society will manufacture an image of progress and locate it in the direction it wishes to take us.'

'Enough smalltalk.'

It was a typical motherhouse, all mystery windows and trees in the attic. And here was an arcane basement - broad steps and a massive wall into which was set an impressive geomantic gateway. Moving through solid air, my angle cut the visible bodies into edges—aligning a little, they swelled from blood buttons to focused form. Drifting unseen and insulated, outside the colour, I peered in.

Here was Casolaro, head of the Prevail, gravitational decades telling on his body and no humour to shore him up. 'You're here under heavy manners, Quinas.'

'It's a fragile conquest that bad manners can undo.'

'Amusing, such language.'

Quinas, his head like a birdcage and

one song, made a fluttering gesture of dismissal. 'I'm a sixty-two year old edgeman, Casolaro. I've spent life watching the truth going in and out of focus. I'm no longer holding out for happiness, just a better turn of phrase.'

This continued a negotiation in the spirit of sinking hoods and strange smiles, all that elite malarky. Everyone here was shielded, all but Moon, a blond kid about my age. I could see sideways in him like a sandwich man. He pretended he was already what he planned to be, a display fragile as a scale model. Casolaro's partner Wireless hung back. He wore a uniform that looked like a done puzzle, joins worming in the surface. The pattern continued in tattoo across his sleek bald head.

'I'm aware you're a burnout—I see it in your eyes. As it were. You've run with the ashers a long time—why trap you behind the planets if you weren't dangerous?'

'They think I'm insane.'

'What does that mean, in this context? Your bargaining position consists precisely and entirely of your being insane and capable of anything.'

'Very flattering, I'm sure.'

'Your bullethead—Alix—he's not a mere technical instrument, no? Individuality's not the problem?'

'No, to go all out for differences, that's us. He's the etheric surfer boy in the summer of his stardom. Playing a swiss army harp. Getting high on what's meant to kill him. A certain style, that's all—the bud's brittle and dry, it'll never open.'

'The funeral's still young. And the Bluetooth's in ready dock. You're right that a valve journey's too great an escape risk. What's your strategy up front?'

'Forgetting, with all the comforts and drawbacks of addiction.'

'The girl we sent, he got what was in her head?'

'I told you he was a brain bandit, Casolaro. Of course, he's curious as to why you haven't initiated the hit.'

'And Lockhart?'

The young guy Moon stepped toward my view with a jugular gun, his face curious. He was better than I thought—he was sensing me. And the other two stopped, darkness between them. A secret had been taught.

Moon started crossing over, leaving his outline. I recoiled through the etheric, allowed him to dwindle in the middle distance, a nearly-nothing pinned on the air. He was tracing me even as I entered my body in the safe house, a sticky settling of form. 'Get a hotel,' I told Melody, 'we're rumbled.'

We made the street and split up, falling in with shadows. Streets and acres of slick rain, the night black with astral smoke. A six-gun-signature body fell in behind me, Moon treading the length of silence. You can tell an edgeman—his shadow's strongest furthest away from him. He was smiling already, ahead of himself.

Passing the mouth of an alley, I folded down to a single element and streamed sideways into the architecture—what a clever evening this was turning out to be. Moon sifted in also and we were fleshtones flushing through the walls on either side of the alley—branching up into rooves and undoing bundles of air before dipping into masonry again. I was rushing through a distinct room of carpet and woodwork, then skeins of bloodlace and a realm of flurrying protoplasmic urgency. I'd merged with a stranger, a librarian unkissed and professional, her accomplishments trim in misery, prayer-pecking and mean. Feathery snowbursts took me out and an armchair went on forever. Before realising I left the end of the block and slid through a parked car, which baulked sideways into the road in an explosion of glass. Moon was right behind me as I blurred through a car park, a whole row of vehicles shattering with etheric drag. Then I slammed to a stop inside a car, slipped upward through the roof and apported, jumping down to the tarmac. Moon materialised too fast, merging with a Volvo—

the windows were instantly painted red from the inside and then shattered as metal warped out. Elbowed armatures punched out of the chassis and gut lava tumbled out the headlamps. The scene settled down.

I was stood in an alarm-hooting hypermarket car park like a failed angel, wearing a simplistic memory approximation of my clothes. I don't know anything about fashion.

5
VAMPIRES OF PARIS

The world began as an insurrection - but later joined the vacuum

It's said that all societies contain only a finite number of persona—those left over merely have fun and good ideas. But our little heads suck in questions like air. I lay in Melody's hotel room, half my insides phantomburnt by the scrap with Moon. I'd been stupid caning it at a time like this—I should hibernate, heal, say goodbye, do it, whether god knew I was coming or not. A pretty poor virus. The running dematerialisation and rebuild had healed my arm, at least. What a strange and total vocation, blotting the sky.

Distance in the windows.

'Don't turn a corner in the air and go all angel on me Alix.' The way she said it, with honey somewhere behind the word.

'Just outside. Books.'

She made a face.

The delicate old city was beyond price - birds immediately felt faster, fish like flitting gems, waters opened the flowers, students my age and older, platinum skies, the stale subway sound of ghosts coming on like cigarette fog. This was the tying of emotional loose ends, saying goodbye before the push - if the Internecine were right, everything and everyone would vapourize moments after the hit.

I took the mirror book into an antique bookshop on the rue de la Bûcherie, a place to all appearances the victory of habit and knee-jerk illumination. Yet here and there were books produced by cabinetmakers, passwords under the blurb. Lies flowed into their diaries and they died pure, leaving behind cure documents white as cream. Spreading the mirror pages to those of the old books, reflections showed the snail trail left by the author's bile, invisible behind print. 'Our secret broken law', a law so irretrievably broken its existence had to be retroactively denied. 'Medicine is the slightest species of magic', the true title of a treatise on the Napoleonic wars. 'The Dictionary of Endless Independence.' 'Perhaps theology is dwelling in hell,' began another. Tasting hidden chapter names behind the visible.

I felt like I was returning to my own vomit. This was old, frustrating stuff. God, I was itching to go on.

It was like a dream, that day. I was picking up history like coloured flavours. Railway furnaces, chestnut ancience, pistol cloaks, hooded horses in a dark tunnel, a symphony of something through long corridors of wide avenues, a slow viscous sky. A white drunkenness in tails and waving coats, galleries murmur and sermon in a scene ceremonious and moving, infinite standing landscapes waltzing under olive trees, open-air festivity walking away. A seat by the shore of these things, chairflap beaches of afternoons. Pierview figures stroll at the rail, children at a distance change, yellowing, momentariness. The streets speeding over land. My eyes felt innocent.

The hotel was a practical hard station, I needed it. Melody, her coal eyes far away, told me about a boy using some kind of reverse philtre. 'When more of his body was drug than human, the drug became hungry for humanity and went out night after night, addicted. This is how vampires are born, when a drug ventures out in the shell of a man or woman, trying to re-establish the biological balance. But he fed on a girl who was like him, a drug, and left all humanity behind. The girl lay in piss and blood staring up at the night against which he was shrinking like breath on a mirror. It was the first time she'd met one like herself, and in seconds he was nothing more than a ghost fading from her eye.'

Melody drew tears into a syringe. Pure among edgemen, it was an intimate act to taste one-another's protest. Minutes cancered, infrared lightning running up our arms. Pinlights were scrambling over the furniture. Space rushed like the scorched air of a man's damnation gathering speed, and then the neon dust thrown slowed and stopped. Grief had ploughed us into a seventh heaven where penny wishes rusted. Bloodtime passed in satellite colours and secret deeps, seeing radio species like grain electrons. Little burdens like kisses. Marble holes in the clouds, the journey finishing in other colours, blurring and clamorous, a waterfall of tears.

A hate girl, sunken pain, a climb through the thirst world, every compromise. A blood father in work glasses. A million miserable mirrors and all was worn. Scarred sighs. Gathering a hole among sheets, dying in a hug. She was so beautiful.

By windowlight snowstyle bodies entangled ... hissgravel cars ... boiling parks ... big flapping days of lawns ... slow shifts ... breasts flatten to a young stretch ... yawns falling among moments ... brushing all things an hour away ...

'Alix.'

'Yes.'

'Wait till I'm asleep. Do it when I'm asleep.'

'Yes.'

Soon she was sleeping, her jet black hair fallen over her face, and I went quietly on to the balcony to drink tea, say goodbye to the sky and obliterate the creator. There were coppery clouds out there, a sunset the colour of ale. I apologised to my victims, expecting no forgiveness. Moon, the hot wind bending his scream. The Prevail's London assassin. *And we won't be long in getting to heaven from here,* whispered the girl with the white skin and thin blade. Two signposts had led through the girl's head. Anything in life can serve as a doorway to understanding. Dimensionally, a sure way of being everywhere is to exist in time. I finish my tea. The view is done. Like hell I'm not alone.

The buildings drained out as I braced for takeoff, the horizon flashing into negative. Pain rained through my head and new silence poured over me.

6
STITCH THIS

Gold can't answer, it wonders why the fuss

An edit can contain infinities. I was aware of a sleek void. I could sense little more than gravity hurtling the world, and a smaller nausea of motion. I was in an enclosed space about the size of a coffin and restrained by an etheric body buckle. I'd been knocked out from behind at the hotel, the Prevail's unsubtle handiwork.

They wouldn't kill me—that would be like driving me to the launchpad with songs and champagne. But the ghost belt and shielded casket limited me to re-runs, math and anger—the pulpy gut in the head. They'd locked the door to the etheric.

Edgemen recover by accepting our cages over and over. Muscles shut. In blackness I observed the faint geometrical directions of my own thoughts - all I was allowed. Back at the Prevail motherhouse, Casolaro had mentioned their sub, the Bluetooth. I laid bets I was aboard. Serves me right for getting ambitious.

I used the time to sort the sawdust from the glass. Why do this if they believed they were right? Were they doubting now that the time was nigh, was that why they hadn't used the information themselves? We were gunning for the same enemy—a creature which did nothing but explode continually in every direction. Hell, I could do that. In an infinite universe, virtue was bound to happen—accidentally unearthed and resembling intestines and veins. And so we became inevitably better than our creator—or a better limb of it than had existed before.

I didn't think it was possible for burnouts to recover. They were terminal, chained to the centreweight which draws down, taking walls chairs books people like a hole in the floor under sagging carpet—step on the sag and disappear, sucking everything with you. It was the exhaustion of pretending we weren't in a universe which had curdled immediately. Quinas was too well shielded to tell. He seemed involved in the mere spectacle of darkness but burnouts haven't even the energy for that. And he'd sided with Casolaro, a bloated aesthete with as much sense of humour as a cat. Lockhart at least was like a father - one who was good but not weak, wise but alive.

Retinal darkshapes blooming into absence, I passed days or hours watching scenes from this one-horse planet and listening to head music. Chewing the trance slow. Peekaboos of clarity like mint. I passed through the sea watching mental recordings of black lava beds, forests which lapped and rushed in gales, close-ups of aged, scarred wood. Willing castles into urgent detail. Symphonies from start to finish. Walking through cities. And I began drowsing, losing my conclusions. That all of us are the subconscious thought impulses of a shabby god. That many of us want to die. These were the truth-halves of one picture. I was dreaming of purple pastures and captivity kept me warm. I'd diminished to a mere mood. I could hear techies talking outside—clamour sounds like a factory. The vessel had docked. I rushed to get alert. Etheric fuses were banging open, arm restraints slapping automatically aside, but I was still locked down at the chest and legs. The sarcophagus lid cracked and opened - I thumped up with both arms, connecting with Wireless's puzzle-suited chest, and valved into him. His body flew to pieces around me, leaving me stood in blood on the jetty. England, it had to be.

Techies were staring like cod on the slab. The sub was nestled into a roofed dock, a giant gasometer in a dirty swimming pool. I ran down a disused abduction tunnel, new pants winding up my legs like a graphics restart. The exit lintel still bore the dialist inscription 'Euphoric corpses look to no savior.'

The clamber tunnel opened on to a sinkland paved with grey hardpan. Song in the wind hit me like a bottle. Right in front of my face a blown candy wrapper rattled against a vent. Half a ferris wheel was buried in the horizon. Hydraulic London was occupied.

The stars hurt like needles as I walked to the Internecine motherhouse. Rains varnished the street and raised dirt in acid walls. Resurrection is an encore uncalled-for, and as mortifying. To be young and full of poison in streets raining strychnine, moving through tilted shadows past all-night chemists and locked launderettes. Even the creator could do nothing more than adequate with this red liquid. Here a small dark door from the street, fizzing with rain. Valving through, a short walk up a path and into a grey textureless house like a church.

Lockhart wasn't in his study but I could feel a token energy signature through my exhaustion. I had a look at the stuff on the shelves—a tobacco-coloured photo of a young Lockhart at the base of a jungle temple; a small ikon of St Isidore hunched under popular forgiveness, wanting out; a Turkish shrike lamp as dusty as a railroad radio; sigil ammunition. I trusted Lockhart more than anyone. Certainly since he'd learnt to manage his mysteries some action had dimmed in him, died. But as mentors went he was impeccable. I threw myself into a leather swivel chair and half-dozed. The downpour was like heavy static on the window. I opened my eyes as

Lockhart sauntered into the room and halted. He was clearly less than impressed with my dulled condition, and seemed strangely uncomfortable. I began spilling my Prevail theory before I forgot it or fell asleep again. 'They think we're out to stage-manage the death of the universe whether it ensues naturally from god's death or not. Why they call us ashers isn't it? Flattering that they think we're capable of it. But you see what the effect is? Even though both groups are out to assassinate the same target, it still has us arguing and delaying each other. The last little uncertainty's manifesting—does the creator want to obliterate completely, or does it want to leave its works and deeds intact, in testament?'

A cold twist of air came in as the other door opened behind me. I read the vibe before turning—an almost-flatness swerved out of true. It was Casolaro.

And looking to Lockhart in simple surprise, I saw something in his eyes. An impossible flicker of retreat.

7
SUICIDE CELLS

Let my heart loose on the authorities - distant laughter

Suppressed practicality will out. 'Careful, gentlemen. I've watched him play hopscotch on the ceiling.'

I was a bit punchy but I could still talk bollocks as they forced me down the short flight of steps to the basement. 'Your etheric stylings are not welcome here, Casolaro.'

If I'd been healthy I'd branch into a wall, ghost up a structure and exit via the guttering, merge with a stranger and split out later without making a huge fuss about it. We've all done that, watched a room thrown into bright constellations as the washing machine changed cycles. But then it was too late—they were fastening me to an upright auraracik at the far end of the chamber. The motherhouse basement was an etheric runway. The old ascension containment cross had been dragged out of storage and stood on the cocoon platform between amplifier housings. The cross was an ancient but effective trip preventer which worked in part by keeping the subject spread and unable to focus inward—like trying to sing low with your head high. An electrostatic discharge closed the etheric airlocks and threw me back against the main spar. It was Saturday morning.

I was looking at a large room coated in dust, rust and groundwater. Three figures stood against the darkness of the generator—Lockhart, Casolaro and Dreva, a young Prevail techy and strongarm. I was about to say something clever when Quinas ducked under an oppressive stone lintel, stepping into the light. He looked smart and healthy in a white leather coat, his death-hair slicked back to the skull.

It seemed they'd agreed it would be braver to sacrifice their principles than their present circumstances. I was positively relieved I was alone—that I wasn't quitting anything of value after all. I was sneering with bitter mirth. 'So the gang's all here. You're all cowards after all? Even you, Lockhart. I admired you like a boy should love a father—is this it?'

Lockhart was staring at the floor. People forget how powerful he was, the grand old man. He seemed as harmlessly proud as a library lion but he could pour iceflame from his mind and freeze a moment for inspection, the air ghostly as cathode light. He'd been the first to give me a demonstration of etheric cocooning, enamel shine flowing over him in ectoplasmic encapsulation. Freaking me into hope. He looked terribly abashed now.

'You know what he thinks, your iron-haired mentor?' Quinas asked—ofcourse, the albino could read me. 'He thinks of great years, dust justice in oxblood rooms. Ageing and drumming the clock like he's okay with it. Night growing in his mouth.'

Lockhart glanced up and muttered gruffly, 'Sorry if they hurt you.'

'They can't hurt me.'

'Fetters are not toys,' said Quinas, and the boy Dreva smiled behind him. 'Your St Sebastian fantasy's getting real and Casolaro's getting a hard-on.'

'Let's get on with this,' rumbled Casolaro, not one for wit or theatrics.

'I was careless enough to be born in England,' I said. 'I'm not about to compound the error by dying here at your hands.' And I began wondering why they hadn't just plastered me with sigils; why they hadn't killed me by remote inside the containment coffin, dropped it in a sinkhole.

Casolaro stepped forward, looking grim. Never having had an original idea, he'd never gotten a taste for them. 'You killed three of my people without a second thought.'

'Oh yes as slaughter goes I'm the blue ribbon winner round here. For the sheer eloquence of the thing. And I don't need a trip cocoon like your little girl assassin, Casolaro. Flightbags are for fucking amateurs who can't believe anything's an entry point.' I was letting them know I could take off from anywhere without preparation, boasting as if things weren't bad enough. 'First thing I learnt. *Honesty is the voice that is acceptable in every matter.*'

Quinas sniggered. 'The universal assassin quoting edgeman writ from the cross - this is priceless.'

What they had duct-taped to this cross was a body bleached with ghostburns and dissolve scars. It was my ghost which pulled to lose it across to a hyperdimensional location triangulated upon by the input of hundreds of edgemen. To face an enemy covering so much ground the beginning of its definiton differed from the end. We'd been hung out to dry by our leaders. 'He misses nothing, this one,' chuckled Quinas, picking up my thoughts easier than dropped change. 'You think it's coincidental that at precisely the time the greatest number of people feel indignant at god's works, the fewest ever people believe in it? It's ducking for cover, denying its own existence. If its works *are* seperate from it—if it is not everywhere and everything—then our desire for its death is not its desire.'

'So you're bone scared, plain and simple. Afraid you'll make the big enemy mad. You want it to like you?'

Quinas quoted sarcastically. '*Hate adds only to hate. Cross through the angel of death and you give it extra wings.*'

I was catching featherweight visions, apple green skies, a pink and black chessboard. Yes, I could remain here a mummified potential. That tranced laziness was in me. So the plan would be buried and they'd all begin to live happily ever after? 'I expect status will go with everything else, eh? You're terrified of our little one-step peace process aren't you?'

Casolaro was indignant. 'You've an eye to status yourself, ultimately - won't your memory be regarded with awe by everyone?'

'Only if you're right.'

But this was all ridiculous.

'We're talking here like a fucking debating school. Denounce the sky like it gives a fuck. D'you realise this isn't theory?' My mind twisted useless at the restraint—I saw myself kicking my legs to crash it off. 'You realise you take these ghost locks off me, I go and do it? For real? You're late for this? We're cornered, bracketed in comparisons. Let's cut the crap, shall we? The Prevail are withered, diminished, and you took the Internecine with you. We're reduced to stupid intrigues, hitting each other round the head in hotel rooms—the First Mystic Renegades would be ashamed.' The edgemen were mystic rebels from worm one, building observatory cathedrals and arcana grenades covered in spines like the black hands of a clock. All that righteous dying, for what—sacrifice swings the spotlight onto absence.

'Diminished,' said Casolaro sourly. The man was little more than a sack stuffed with chains. 'No, reconciled to our level. And you. Resigned to your mind, stuck to a face, and called finally to the solo, there you hang. Your vanilla calculations, these naiveties - they can't serve you. What you do in your head, you do in your head. You're weak.'

'Yeah, as water.'

'And the Prevail didn't hit you in the hotel - it was your girl Melody.'

Melody appeared at that moment, framed in the door like a thought of escape. She'd trailed in with one of my old books and seen me, nailed to their cross-purposes. And I'd thought I'd been alone before. I thought of the hotel: Melody whumps her hot face into the pillow and grinces her expression. People think there are limits to betrayal because they see it all black and white, onion layers - the skin, the skull, the brain, the thought. Cliches.

Quinas was delighted. 'Agonising isn't it, the terror of the expected?'

8
SMILE

When do you know finally that a secret's successful?

She stood frozen, eyes ticking across the scene. And I thought, I'm a better man than her by far. 'You all report to the specimen above as surely as churchmen.'

Casolaro looked grim. 'You're alone, Alix. Nobody knows you're here.'

'Then I can do whatever I want to you.'

Quinas gave a contemptuous snort and shook his big, crafty head. 'Always the next trip, eh? Which of us here withholds the most power through prevarication? Louder concerns are not necessarily deeper. You're still part of a population that's been craving more vacuum and less content every hour - sanity its madness, song its science, fashion some right-hand nothing. Tedious repetition is exalted and boredom is a sign of sweetness. For brains I fear this is more than an interlude.' How could eyes of dead silver be so full of humour?

Within this device I couldn't project an etheric image of my view and so had to use the arcane code of words. What was I doing here anyway? Tuning up for silence?

'I feel awkward watching while you sort the pottery shards of your justification. If you're the spokesmen for god's niggling doubts, I think I can deduce that it's ready and waiting.'

'It probably is. If it created our nature to rebel against force, our nature not to submit, will it be surprised? Can it be, on any score? Heaven and hell - both offer immortality, which ultimately doesn't get us very far. All is one, as they say. So why not be at peace, Alix, with what you have. It won't go unrecognised.'

'What, smart job on the train? Neon headstone? The only real peace is a defeat you cowards intend never to concede - an admission of reality. The refusal to help it pretend we've every reason to be grateful. Through inventing justice we've earned the knowledge that we hate the constancy of our suffering. Crimes against humanity.' Yes, the revenge was self-destructive, nuclear. The only act of dignity left to us. All great events close as many doors as they open. Open as many doors as they close. Fear the less-than-great. Does Spring smash Winter? 'I can't help you feel anything better. Fuck you old men, it's the golden mischief - this if nothing else. I complied with myself. Do better, if you can.'

I even suspected it was a dare, a set-up. Sainthood, you could feel it coming up like dust. *Escape.*

Casolaro stepped up with a hypodermic. 'Death in etheric containment,' he said coldly. 'Very nasty.'

'Sometimes the needle hurts most when they pull it out,' Quinas called, enjoying himself.

Casolaro looked me in the face. 'It's not personal.'

'Everything's personal.'

Technology masked the old blade.

Melody had handed Quinas the bound book. 'I found this in his hotel room.'

Quinas looked at it vaguely, lump-fanned it open—Melody had put the mirror book into an old cover. A scream tore in half as Quinas was drawn eyes-first into the object, a cloud of blood sizzling across the floor and ceiling, drenching the onlookers. Casolaro looked back as Melody whacked down the generator switch, breaking the current to the rack.

Ah! Melody.

'I've lost all feeling in my gob, gentlemen. Time to go.' A shiver of static trailed away from me and everyone stepped back in panic—like they'd no idea I could be this far into the countdown. My teeth powdered in my mouth as I slipped the lifeline.

Sparks of nervous system rushed shooting past my release.

I felt like a white maggot as I pulled out of my skin. Neat as the meat from a lobster.

9
IT'S PRETTY BUT IT'S VERY VERY HEAVY

Chains live without air

I left the body on the ground like an old cracked shoe.

The onlookers' faces were turning to porcelain, then to thin paper masks on the surface of flowing film—still shielded, then irrelevant as I swept behind the pasteboard stage of architecture and on into the airwaves. The end—every tiny hero, remember their story. The end - every history. The end—every youth in the adventure street. The end —every lover. If you won't do it, then I will.

Men's fields were old rags of land, the setting sun was enraptured, a huge edge and wheel, fire descending a sky covered in bruises. Intersecting dimensional sightlines tangled the continents, a mountain was a green city of things, stone depths.

A little air high in the sky singing as the universe flew into my eyes. I was a single monochrome cell accelerating through kidstuff and clashing superstorms. A squall of ultraviolet geometrics and other junk intended to distract. Red gold elements and shifting clarity.

Another forgotten firmament rolled into view, dark pulses teeming with stings of light, waves of a billion perishing cells. Gigantic flavour tides in high definition, space overdoing it and washed by fizzing toxicity.

The sawtooth strobing of side-viewed dimensional edits ended in the seething, chaotic mass of quantum foam. Hypergrey depths rumbling with the accumulating density of what was ahead. It was letting me approach. It hadn't flattened the steps yet. Bringing its own poison to its lips.

But when the thing drew near, it precipitated from all directions in a vastness of intricate, nonrepeating evil. A slow spectacle of dark vanes and complex underside, a titanic black insect floundered on its back at the centre of an infinite nerve net, fiddling a million legs amid the ferocious stench of vomit and scorching wires.

Its mouth rimmed with lashes like an eye, biting in space at an end, it was eternally frantic in its convulsions, evils tangling and stretching about its mindless ratchetting. Shackled by its own influence. Seeping cold corrosion in a night of oceanic tragedy. No cure ever, a constantly breaking heart.

And before this thing I felt the blossoming of total exposure. All resolve atomised by horror. One particle of poison in a sea of poison. No guts in a zero. No hero. On the cross, my eyes turned gold.

SIG

Daylight air gnawed off the curtains. Each molten tear frazzled down Alix's face like a fuse. 'Truth crosses the blood/brain barrier intact, boy.'

The boy leaned forward. 'But you *are* sort of a hero. You found the heart despite everything, everyone. They all talk about you back there, the ashers.'

Alix rasped, old and faded as a photograph. 'You don't get it. Quinas's escape, the abduction, the final act in the basement, it was stage-managed. The whole deal had been to send me off with passion. My friends. To save me from being a mere dry ironaut, easily turned. Quinas knew he'd get it in the neck—he welcomed it as a burnout. But he had more mischief in him at the end than a lot of us start out with. He parlayed the coalition. I thought I'd seen everything. I was surprised, just as you'd be.'

'They talk about the forgiveness of god—I could never forgive it before, maybe now.'

'You've missed the point—Lockhart urged me not to feel pity because Quinas had got a sense of what the enemy was, during his failed try. It's the reason I failed too. Remember the cause of it all, and what is the enemy. There's a furrow through fortune - it's not irrigated with mercy. You know the one thing I can say that'll help you live a life? We're shit, but we're better than It.'

'And part of it?'

'The better part maybe—by a small margin. Now get out of here. You're too young.'

The boy stood as tiny pin-minutes sprang over silence. The room was aching. The living legend had gone dismal in the skull, lording it over dead flowers and dead books. Inside the ink, night alone was prophecied like black confetti.

Alix's metallic eyes seemed to move. 'Someone else is here. I can hear her smile.'

Melody was in the doorway. 'I'm not smiling.'

He didn't turn. 'Nor am I. Heaven sickness. Too many exits drown the soul. I've talked to your rookie - honour's satisfied.'

'Thank you, Alix.'

'I really got a big rep out there? I remember me—stars in my pocket. Young rebel gun. Remember? I can see you and me in the street, believing it. I don't even scare myself now. I'm dust.'

'You're a star.'

'I know it's you brings the flowers.'

'Yeah.'

Melody and the boy left him in the small room, victory ghosts in his hung head.

They reached the street through a fence, stepping over broken tarmac pieces with the scent of oil.

'That was intense, Miss Melody. I didn't know he'd be like that.'

She stepped in front of the streets, stood watching rain on asphalt, tears hidden in the downpour. 'Let him alone. Let him figure in a cloud, not in history.'

'So why bring me here? I've read the books. What do I do now?'

She looked back at him. 'You could wait for a surprise, that the fruit won't always correspond with its seed. That's evolution, after all.'

'You think I'll back down because of this? You think I'm a re-run head just because I'm not so bright?'

She didn't answer. Maybe he'd think she hadn't heard him above the rain.

'Wait a minute—this is a setup, right? Like what you did to him. And he's in on it, yeah? I knew he couldn't be a burnout. You want me to fight forward, push against you. I'll do that. I'll go for the big trip. The enemy's up on blocks? So bring it on. I'm ready.'

She watched the rain sussurating in the street, clouds fighting over the sky, and the bandaged windows of the edgeman's house behind them, in which there was no living human energy whatever.

'He was right,' she said. 'You're young.' She saw Alix and herself in the streets he had described, the psycho heroes, coats full of death-welcome and belief. Nothing can be reclaimed.

She began striding back across town, the boy hurrying after her. And turning corners only they could see, they lost themselves between the rainfall.

APPENDIX 1:
A Brief History of the Internecine

"Any triumph is merely initial," stated Isabelle Feedi, and so through its history the Internecine has hoped that its single success would take place in the very last instant of the universe.

In the four thousand year old Yezidi belief system, there is no false introduction of another force that can exist against god - no satan. Slavers cross-fertilized Yezidism with toxic wicca during the Roman conquests, resulting in angry faces all round. Of the fifty or so gospels excised from the trad Bible, the most influential on the early Internecine were *Thunder, Perfect Mind* and the *Complete Archontics*, which now reside only in the Keep's etheric library. Peter the Assassin's insistence that authorities on Earth exist merely to confuse the aim of those who would "loose an arrow at the true sacred heart" was recorded in the true *Archontics* by the man himself: "Impertinence merely confirms authority's greatest fear." *The Reality of the Rulers* also touches upon this, using higher dimensional symbolism (in the dimensional one-jump manner of *Flatland*—the gods higher than god and shielded by god, as a symbol to portray the god higher than Earth authority and shielded by Earth authority). This truth was interesting enough for the priesthood of the time to frantically parse his statements into Christian quibbling (soft gnosticism)—recording him as Peter the Gnostic in the physical fragment which now poses as a piece of the *Archontic Gospel* (but which was written by St Epiphanius of Salamis, the same overweight gentleman who claimed there was a holy statuette gestating in his belly).

The third early text was *The Distractions (According to the Persian Prince)* which related the travels of an invisible Prince who slips through the rooms and palaces of this world and those adjacent, "making of deception a continuous window," to conclude that: "The world went from vast to artistic, a bad choice." The text was used by Hasan Sabbah and the 'hashishins', an early manifestation of the assassinator Internecine, used to discipline its soldiers in the matter of focus, intent and the irrelevance of surviving the task. Their initiation ritual (trancing with hashish potion, after which the initiate would awake into a beautiful garden and a servicing by a dozen teenage girls) has continued to this day in the Cryers' Climax and the occasional orgy at the Portugal house.

One of the guises under which the so-called edgemen operated was that of the alchemical brotherhood, whose 'transmutations' often masked the construction of massive 'sky guns' whose medieval payloads of propellant explosives were ahead of their time. The age of sky guns gave way to more sensible initiatives. (For an idea of the levels of sophistication reached, see Basil Valentine's ironically codified text *The Triumphal Chariot*, in which cypher generates the request "Just kill me" more often than the number of words in the manuscript.) It is recorded in *Disciples of the Discarded* that Elizabethan alchemist Doctor John Dee witnessed the scarab star of god blooming with a creak from the surface of the wooden table at Clerkenwell—a vision immediately waylaid by the arrival of unwitting holy agent Edward Kelley, who wasted years of Dee's time with useless signs and wonders. At the instant of death, Dee tried to remember the shape of god, while to onlookers it spread across his chest like a set of dark alien ribs and only black blood poured from the mystic's mouth. Yet even upon recognition of the universal facts within such visions, we remain utterly powerless - the number of false walls for us to pierce are truly infinite.

In the mid 17th century, the salvaged table itself was to be double-apported to its supposed former shape by our very own Sebastian Cockayne (entailing the destruction of parts of London) and the inaccurate depiction obtained was used for a symbolic target in an etheric misfire which resulted merely in Cockayne being reversed into himself in the most messy way. Similar 'dartboard' projects were carried out by the late hashishin splinter group known as the Unforgiving, a group more about cloak-and-dagger glamour than effectiveness. But it was from this group that Ralph/Chaim Foxcroft emerged, bringing to the Greek pre-Internecine the craft of the geomantic portal and the notion of projecting a missile into etheric sidespace (at a time when the mundane was still perceived as being separate from the all, and god a separate creature—the term Internecine was not yet used). These creations of Persian and Dialist architectonics can still be found embedded in several pieces of Internecine real estate. Finally the notion of a physical weapon was abandoned for good, but not before the geomantics were sealed against the espionage of the emerging Prevail.

For some time the Internecine initiative was codexed through history by those known to us as the Whispers of the Road (such as Villon) and the later Strychnine Scholars (such as Voltaire, Trepannier and the over-casual Bierce), as well as by what some have called 'Akashic resentment', a wish for revenge passed down through generations at the atomic level. It was this consideration that led the late-Victorian fourth-dimensioner CH Hinton (who by the use of 'casting out' was teaching edgemen to see four-dimensionally with a visionary result similar to sonar) to consider that we are the self-destructive impulse of god. In presenting this and other information to the main council, he led Tagore Ros to reconfigure the assassin programme to that of pure etheric manouevres, with the conclusion that the assassination of god would lead to the certain obliteration of everything—a small price to pay. The first purely etheric hit attempt was performed in 1903 by Ros, who was an instant burnout. An amplifier accident in Siberia in 1908 set back the technical side for some time and lost a talented man in the Russian Persikov. The use of Sauniere etheric amplifiers finally put edgemen into what was termed the 'body of god', but none were ever so foolish as to claim to have reached the heart—though many returned as babbling madmen or the walking dead. The splinter group known as the Prevail—formed by those who considered that god was a thing separate from its works, and that the universe would persist after god's assassination—began a series of spoiler skirmishes against the Internecine (or, as they began to call us, the 'ashers') which soon became a full cult war or, as the Invisible Prince might have put it, "an Almighty delaying tactic." The Prevail have speculated: "The space where god was, it will perhaps seem bigger than it is—like the feel of a missing tooth."

In 1942, Kosmon Lavant, on the rim of death, placed himself within a circle of twelve amplifiers and, witnessed by edgemen of all ranks, died, leaving his nerve rig to run for a full hour on automatic. Cleared of philosophical interpretation, the shell ran through a well-practiced etheric journey, according to all coordinates gathered thus far. The unfiltered vision accomplished is recorded in the locked section of the Keep files, but proof of the enemy's existence had finally been obtained.

In the second half of the last century, Internecine affairs have been complicated by intrigue—the matters of the Paris '68 Decoy, the googolplex-agent Alfred M Hubbard, and the so-called Russian 'scanner battles'. Yet there have been concerted pushes—that of Salii, a burnout, Quinas, a brilliant burnout, and the recent push by Alix, which has spawned the so-called 'Cult of Alix' about which we have such debate—another inventive distraction from our purpose (spawning the first open tell-all to be published by the straight press). The edgemen coalition broke down almost as soon as it began. A thousand times more powerful than 'the man on the street', we are universally ineffectual. Did we expect anything else? As Trepannier stated, "Emptiness tilted is yet emptiness."

APPENDIX 2: Internecine Bibliography

'Thunder, Perfect Mind' - describes the All: 'It is I who am the voice whose sounds are so numerous/ And the discourse whose images are so numerous.'

The Complete Archontics (Tales of the First Mystic Renegades) - the edgeman classic residing in complete form in the Keep - a series of interlocking parables leading to the conclusion that 'It gets boring to be terminal for eternity. Invite the end with disregard.'

The Reality of the Rulers - gnostic cypher laid to the phrase 'Infinity is infinitely divisible.'

'The Distractions (according to the Persian Prince)' - 'Invest a grapefruit with authority - what do you expect?'

The Priceless Moat of Disinterest - early assassin manual which started the fad for embroidering into sword blades the phrase: 'Actually the hapless celebrate.'

Flightless Land Without Clouds, Charles d'Acqueville - a thermaturgical fuel cell built from absorptive surfaces, this device worked on the false principle that an undefined sense of loss is better than nothing.

The Triumphal Chariot, Basil Valentine - interesting mainly for the lengths to which edgemen have gone to codify their dissent.

Disciples of the Discarded, which dwells upon the Q Gospel or 'that which is forever and meticulously evaded'.

The Ultimate Midnight, Robert Livingstone - an early deicide text detailing many (mainly symbolic) edge practices including a technique to float a razor on the sky.

Sacrifice Excludes, Stoll Trepannier - this man of mischief spoke straightfaced about 'the feeling of patriotic respect I feel when looking at heaps of dust.'

'The Dictionary of Endless Independence', Isabelle Feedi - shuffling her texts into other people's books like a cardsharp, Feedi asks 'How do you hurt poison?' and replies, 'By living oblivious.'

The Scientific Romances by Charles Howard Hinton - Vol 1 includes 'Casting Out the Self' and 'A Picture of Our Universe'; Vol 2 includes the reverse-coded allegory 'An Unfinished Communication'.

Pigs on the Stage, Harold J Shepstone - this title speaks for itself.

Tenaglia, Ambrose Bierce - in the first book after his 'disappearance', Bierce begins by stating that 'The grayness of a thousand miles begins with a single disappointment', concluding finally that 'A dissolving corpse is an honest finale.'

Stations of Loss, Tagore Ros - 'Our children cut god, unawares in play. Noticing blood hours later, they wonder at the source.' A great doomster, Ros loved ripping the piss. 'When a culture which is flat out on the floor insists on looking down as though from a progressive height, its perceptions are reduced almost to zero. Have a nice day.'

'Nursing, cursing, hearsing and a bill', Ben Gallic - Gallic plays at mundanity, commending god its achievements - 'Another dog invented, future made bright' - and arguments in favour - 'A manmade bird would look like a dusty grape in a dress.' Good point.

CHRISTIAN TEBORDO

LOCATION:
Philadelphia, PA

STYLE OF BIZARRO:
Dada Street Life

BOOKS BY TEBORDO:
Better Ways of Being Dead
We Go Liquid
The Conviction and Subsequent Life of Savior Neck

DESCRIPTION: Christian has written books about gas huffers, panda and polar bears, and an adolescent boy who gets spam from his dead mother's email account. Often accused of meanness, more concerned with comedy and pretty sentences.

INTERESTS: Well-written books, loud rock, mid-90s hip hop, warehouse parties with tons of dancing, experimental theatre, sitting on my stoop.

INFLUENCES: This particular piece owes a debt to Jorge Luis Borges and Robert Coover. In general: Vladimir Nabokov, Harry Mathews, Ben Marcus, Brian Evenson, The Coen Brothers, The Knife, Mogwai, TV on the Radio.

WEBSITE:
www.myspace.com/saviorneck

THE ORDER OF OPERATIONS

Staring at himself in the mirror. It seems certain that this time it's all going to end.
"This one's healing nicely."

He fingers a wound on his belly, a deep red circle, stitches in the center and a bruise surrounding it corona-like, fading outward from blue-black to yellow-green. His hand covers other, older wounds, also circles, in different pales of pink—scars—no bruises. His eyes travel from the reflection of his wound to the reflection of his eyes.

"You have a face like a moon," he says. "Moonface."

You could say he has a face like a moon, a full moon. Not like a moon. Like the way you see the moon in the sky—glowing pale, broad, flat—deep-set eyes like too-symmetrical craters, reflecting light, but poorly. His fingers follow his eyes from wounds to face, feeling its broadness, its flatness, its eyes. It touches like it looks. It touches like a moon-face.

"So what," he says.

He goes back to the wound, fingers followed by eyes, eyes on the reflection, straining toward the wound itself, back to the reflection. It's hard to tell from the face what the brain is thinking. Probably something like it seems certain that this time it's all going to end, because, eyes and fingers still on the wounds, he says: "Too nicely."

He peels a square of sterile gauze from the stack on the shelf beside the mirror. He takes the tape from beside the stack. He tapes the gauze over the wound. He reaches into the wardrobe on the other side of the mirror, pulls a shirt from a hanger one-handed, puts the shirt on, buttons it. He's looking at his moon-face again.

"This time I'm pretty certain," he says.

He grabs a sweater from the shelf, tugs it over his head, adjusts the dark hair like space curved around his face, tugs the collar of the shirt through the neck of the sweater, adjusts.

"Too nicely," he says.

On the way to church, he stops to think about whether he should call her.
There are no payphones around here.

He stops to call her.
There's a payphone on the corner a few blocks up, next to a community garden turned sandlot. He pulls up across the street from it, puts the car in park, leaves it running, jogs over, inserts a quarter, dials the number. The phone rings four times and her answering machine answers. He hangs up quickly but gently.

She could be in the shower. He checks his watch. Not too long until church, but she doesn't live far from church. She could have gone to church already, for prayer—would she intercede for him? he'd like to think so. He hopes so—or a last minute choir practice. But she could be in the shower. He inserts another quarter, dials again.

"You gonna be a while?"

He turns around. A car—a newish station wagon—has pulled up beside him facing traffic. It'd be facing into traffic if there were any traffic. The driver is leaning his mostly-bald head out the window in expectation of an answer.

"You've reached such and such a number," says the machine. "Please leave a message after the beep."

It isn't her voice. He knows it's her voice, but the machine does something to it, something worse than similar machines do to other voices, similar and otherwise. There are no voices similar to hers.

"Just a minute," he says.

He holds up an index finger. Beep, goes the machine.

"You mean you're just gonna be a minute," says the man in the car, "or in a minute you'll tell me how long you're gonna be?"

"I mean just a fucking minute," he says.

"That's uncalled for," says the man in the car.

Not angrily. He sounds almost sorry. That's uncalled for as in why'd you have to say it.

Beep, goes the machine.

"Sorry," he says, "sorry."

"Okay," says the man in the car.

"Not you," he says.

"What?" says the man in the car.

The machine goes: click.

"Shit," he says.

Dial-tone, payphone.

"What?" says the man in the car.

"Shit," he says. "Now I'm gonna be a while."

He turns back toward the phone, inserts a quarter, dials again. The man in the car opens the door, steps out, walks over, stops behind him.

"How long is a while?"

The phone rings four times. The machine answers.

"You've reached such and such a number…/two minutes?/ beep/however long it takes/how long does it take?/just shut the fuck up/uncalled for/beep/sorry/okay/not you/dial-tone."

He reaches into his pocket for another quarter, but comes up with lint. He checks his other pockets half-heartedly and finds nothing with as little heart or less. He looks at his feet, at the sand and gravel at his feet. He slips a finger into the coin return chute at the base of the phone, still staring at the ground.

"You got a quarter?" he says.

The man is silent but for heavy and frequent exhalations from his nose. He turns around and looks up at the man. Up, he's tall. He's got a broad face, too, but you wouldn't call it a moon-face. It's much too busy. His complexion is reddish, a combination of burn-scars and acne. His head is mostly bald, but there is no method to his baldness—a wisp here, a feather there—mange and skin-grafts. And the nose on him, the nostrils on him, the nose is just nostrils, big holes in his face that he calls attention to by exhaling so loudly.

He looks back down at his feet to keep from staring.

"You got a quarter?" he says.

The man pulls a quarter from the pocket of his blue running suit, reaches past him—he flinches—and inserts the coin into the payphone. He turns back to the phone, dials the number, says thanks over his shoulder.

The phone rings four times. The machine picks up.

"So you gonna be a while?"

"What the fuck," he says.

He turns around again. The man is pointing a gun at him, a .22.

"I'm doing this for your own good," the man says.

But it just feels like they're going through the motions. The man fires the gun into his belly. He falls backward to the ground, still holding the receiver, ripping it from the coiled-metal wire that connects it to the payphone.

"You broke it," says the man.

A man with a fucked-up face doesn't really want to use the payphone.

He pulls his car—a newish station wagon—up to the corner, facing traffic if there were any traffic. There's a payphone on the corner, next to the sandlot. He leans his mostly-bald head out the window, doesn't see anyone using the payphone, and decides that the man who should be using the payphone is going to be a while.

Which isn't to say that he has any reason to decide this.

The man who should be using the payphone has never been a while before. That is, he never shows up late. He's always either there or not there. Nor is there any should be about it. The should be is all in the man with the fucked-up face's fucked-up head. Should be. As in, why isn't he? As in, if the man who should be using the payphone isn't using the payphone, if he doesn't use the payphone, then someone else will have to use the payphone instead. Notably the man with the fucked-up face.

It's worse than it sounds.

But he isn't listening anyway. For now he'd rather think in terms of should be. For now he'd rather pretend that things aren't so either/or. For now he's going to sit there in his car and imagine himself sitting there in his car waiting for the man who should be using the payphone to come along and use the payphone.

Church passes uneventfully.

Because he isn't using the payphone when he should or shouldn't be, his perfect pew is waiting on the left side of the center aisle, seven rows from the back, thirteen from the front. Not so far back that the choir loft is directly above him, not so far up that he has to strain to see her. All he has to do is turn his head and look upward, and there she is, in her dark-blue robe, floating above him like a dark-blue saint.

Or standing, in this case, above him like a woman in dark-blue.

Even the best have their off-weeks, and this week her singing, the sound of her voice, isn't quite what it sometimes is. Not that it isn't good. Not that it isn't better than the sound of any other voice he's ever heard. It is. It's better. He decides to tell her, on the way to lunch, or at lunch, when he can look her in the eyes, that her voice is better than any he's ever heard, that her voice is the best voice even on an off-week.

The congregation seems to agree. It was an off-week. As the service ends, they begin to file out, eyeing him as they pass, as though it were his fault. He vacillates between eyeing them back defiantly and turning away, until the last of them have left and he looks up toward the choir loft, where she's just finished hanging up her robe.

She looks less grandiose without the robe. A pleated, ankle-length skirt and a button-up blouse that almost makes him want to cancel lunch. But they always go to lunch after church.

He yells up: "Ready for lunch?"

She stops with her back to him. She stands up straight. He knows she's heard him, but she doesn't turn around. She's still upset.

"You're still upset?" he says.

She turns around, but doesn't respond.

"But we always get lunch after church," he says.

She steps over to the staircase and disappears. He jogs to the narthex and cuts her off, or meets her, at the bottom of the staircase. She gives him a resigned look and says: "Take off your shirt."

He takes off his shirt and reveals his hairless chest and belly, covered with circular wounds, most in different pales of pink, though there's a bandage covering one of them, a little spot of deep red on the bandage indicating the freshest wound.

"The bandage," she says.

He removes the bandage from the bottom upward, slowly, and with both hands. She moves in close and fingers the deep red circle, the stitches in the center, the bruise surrounding it corona-like, fading outward from blue-black to yellow-green.

"This one's healing nicely," she says.

"Too nicely," he says.

Lying on the ground, a bullet in his belly, he makes two mental notes in case it doesn't end this time.

1. Call the telephone company, and inform

them that the payphone is broken. Don't tell them that you broke it, even though you did so inadvertently. Tell them that you went to use it and found it broken, and

2. Find that man, and fuck his face up even worse.

He continues with his plans, assuming that it will end this time. He checks his watch. He's late for church.

A little boy tries to heal a man's fucked-up face with Jesus' blood.

He hasn't given up on waiting for the man who should be using the payphone to show up and use the payphone, but even with the window open the air is stuffy and his long legs are stiff.

He opens the door, gets out, and stands up—up, he's tall—making sure to stay by the open door so that, in case the man who should be using the payphone should turn the corner or appear over the horizon, he can jump back in, close the door, and be unobtrusive for a few minutes before being obtrusive.

He still hasn't given up on that scenario. Which is why he's still standing there between the car and the door when a little boy appears as if out of nowhere.

One moment he's making another quick glance over at the payphone, to make sure the man who should have been using it hadn't been there using it all along, the next, there's a little boy standing in front of him.

A dirty little boy. He looks like he hasn't bathed in at least a week. He looks like he's spent that week outdoors, sleeping under the stars on park benches and scavenging for his food. And there's blood on his hands.

"It's Jesus blood," he says.

"What is," says the man.

"The blood on my hands," says the little boy. "Jesus blood."

The man looks over at the payphone, the corner, the horizon.

"Go away kid," he says.

But the kid doesn't go away. He stands there quietly for a few seconds. Then he says: "You got a fucked-up face."

Rude, yes, but it isn't like the kid means to insult him. He says it in that matter-of-fact way so common to kids. He could just as easily have been giving the man the time, or informing him that his fly's unzipped, or that Jesus' blood can heal his fucked-up face.

"Your fly's unzipped," says the boy.

The man looks down, but his blue running suit doesn't have a fly. Elastic waist.

"Tricked you," says the boy. And: "Jesus blood can heal your fucked-up face."

It sounds as ridiculous to him as it would to anyone else, but anyone else doesn't have his payphone problems. The odds are slim-to-none that Jesus blood is Jesus' blood, and even if it is, the man has his doubts about whether it would help. Still, he can't see how it could hurt to try.

He grabs the little boy by the wrists of his outstretched arms, just above the palms where the crusted-blood is thickest, lifts him up—up, he's tall—and places the little boy's hands on his face.

It does hurt to try. Jesus blood burns.

A man with a fucked-up face uses a payphone even though he doesn't want to.

There comes a point at which even he has to admit it. No one is coming to use the payphone. This point comes a good while after the little boy has run away, afraid of the power in his hands. The power on his hands.

The smell of burning flesh still lingers around his evermore fucked-up face. He lifts the receiver to his fucked-up ear, inserts a quarter, and dials a number. The cellphone in the pocket of his blue running suit rings four times in stereo with the earpiece, and his own voice, slightly altered, answers.

"You've reached such and such a number," says his slightly-altered voice. "Please leave a message after the beep."

Beep.

"Two things," he says into the mouthpiece. "1. You're going to need more salve than usual, and 2. Remember to lock the door."

They get lunch after church.
"So what's wrong with this one?" he says.

She tactfully ignores his tactless question.

"He's a mason/He's a newspaper reporter/He plays the lead guitar in a wedding band/He's a lawyer/He's an interior decorator/He runs a soup kitchen/He teaches middle school history/He's a carpenter/He just got back from inoculating refugees in Algeria/ Nicaragua/Michigan/He's an investment banker/He's a farmer/He's independently wealthy/He runs guns/He's a doctor/He's a database administrator/He's a college professor/He hasn't said/He's been on social security but he's hoping to get into nanotech/ He's a migrant fruit-picker/He's middle-management/Mafia. Mafioso/He's a real estate agent/He's a novelist/He won't say/He's a cabdriver/He's a city councilman/He's a process engineer/He's a nurse. A male nurse/He made his fortune in moonshine and retired young/He's a stuffed shirt/He's a genius/He's a catalog model/He's a philanthropist/He's between jobs/He's a librarian/He's a gardener/He can't say/He writes an advice column for a women's magazine/He's in plastics/Government something/He's having a hard time finding anything steady because of his record. He's anything but... what is it you do?"

It's not a great restaurant. A diner, really. They go there every week after church because it's only about a mile away. Everything is stainless steel and formica. There are televisions in each of the four corners.

"No, I mean what's wrong with him?" he says. "Club foot? Lazy eye? Harelip? Distended..."

"Can we talk about something else?" she says.

They sit in the same booth every week. He sits on the same side of the booth, and every week the television in the corner opposite him seems to be resting atop her head. Bad eyesight or something.

"I'm done," he says.

Church has started without him.
The congregation is standing as he enters, singing the first hymn. He hasn't missed anything. No one notices him stumbling up the aisle. He heads toward the perfect pew, where all he has to do is turn his head and look upward to see her floating above him like a dark-blue saint, but it isn't empty.

There's an old woman, a Sunday-school teacher—she was his Sunday-school teacher however many years ago—an eternal Sunday-school teacher sitting in his pew. She's engrossed by the hymn, singing her old heart out, a voice like a lamb trying to squawk like a crow, though she looks more like a chicken, her gizzard jiggling with each croaking bleat.

He taps her on the shoulder. She's startled, all the air she's inhaled for the next line released in one sudden wheeze. She turns her head to try to make him out from behind three or four cataracts, but her face shows no signs of recognition.

"Mind if I join you?" he says.

She can't hear him. She doesn't hear well, and with the entire congregation singing the final verse, she doesn't hear anything but the final verse. He assumes she doesn't mind. He slips into a pew and begins to hum along with the rest of them, a familiar tune, but he doesn't know the words, and by the time he could go through the bulletin, find the page number, open the hymnal, and find his place, the hymn would be over.

He doesn't have the strength anyway.

The woman turns her head back toward the front. She doesn't sing or hum.

She checks her messages.

"You have four new messages," says her machine. "Message 1: Click. Message 2: You mean you're just gonna be a minute, or in a minute you'll tell me how long you're gonna be?/I mean just a fucking minute/that's uncalled for/click. Message 3: However long it takes/how long does it take?/just shut the fuck up/uncalled for/click. Message 4: So you gonna be a while?/what the fuck/I'm doing this for your own good/BANG/click."

There was a time when this sequence of messages would have terrified her. Now, even the act of erasing them feels like going through the motions.

A little boy is not coming in this house with Jesus' blood on his hands.

"You're not coming in this house unless you wash your hands," says his mother.

"But mom," says the little boy.

It's taken him over an hour to walk home from church. Not that he took the most direct route. His mother has never allowed him to walk such a long distance alone before. He usually has to get her permission just to ride his bicycle around the block, so he took advantage of this new permissiveness, or the strictness that supercedes her usual strictness, and took the time to explore some streets and alleyways in greater detail than he's been able to through the window of her car.

"Go around back and use the hose," she says.

"It's Jesus blood," he says.

She wasn't there. She drops him off and picks him up, but doesn't attend herself. She can't understand why he does. She doesn't make him. It isn't as though having him out of the house for a few hours on Sunday morning makes up for having to wake up so early on her day off. He just came home from school one afternoon saying something about his teacher singing in the choir.

She's pretty sure there are some Constitutional issues there, or legal, but she's always tried to encourage him. Now she's questioning the wisdom of her encouragement. Not all of it, but this particular case. She's questioning the sanity of that church. She knows it isn't Jesus' blood, but she wonders how he got it into his head that it was, not to mention how he got it onto his hands in the first place.

Right now though, her main concern is getting it off.

"I don't care if it's...," this one makes her stop and think. "I don't care whose blood it is. It's not coming in this house."

"I'm not washing it off," says the boy.

"Then you're not coming in the house either."

He remembers to buy salve.

It would be hard not to remember with the smell of burnt flesh following him around. It follows him all the way to the store, all the way to aisle thirteen, the one with the sign that reads skincare hanging euphemistically, from his perspective, above it.

He doesn't have to read the sign. He knows the way to aisle thirteen, and he knows where in aisle thirteen to find his brand of salve.

Which is why he's surprised not to find it where it ought to be—roughly three-quarters down the left-side of the aisle, third shelf from the bottom. The rest of the shelf is well-stocked, but there's an empty space where he's used to finding what he's looking for.

He looks around. The whole aisle is something of a blur, a spectrum of labels on glossy boxes, everything shining yellowish beneath the fluorescents overhead. He's on the verge of panicking when the stockboy, who's been working the section long enough to know what the man with the fucked-up face is looking for, notices the man with the fucked-up face from the other end of the aisle, drops the basket of bottles, tubes and boxes he was in the process of shelving, and jogs over to him with an intensity that might not be called for.

By the time he reaches him, he's breathing heavily and sweat is breaking out on his brow. The stockboy puts up a finger to indicate that he needs a moment, and hunches over, palms on knees, until his breathing steadies.

"Don't worry," he says. "I'm in the middle of restocking. We got more in the back."

He runs off before the man with the fucked-up face has the chance to tell him he'll be needing more than usual.

Meanwhile, twenty-eight aisles over, a woman holding several bottles of stain remover catches the unmistakable smell of burnt flesh. She has a nose for these things, and without quite deciding to do so, she begins to use that nose to follow the smell to its source.

The stockboy returns to the source of the smell—wheezing and completely soaked in his own sweat—carrying a single jar of salve, which he offers to the man one-handed while hunching over and resting the other on his knee.

"Thanks," says the man, "but I needed two this time."

The stockboy looks up at him, loses his balance, and falls to the floor.

"I'll come back later," says the man.

But the stockboy won't hear of it. He puts up a finger, again indicating that he needs a moment, props himself up into a crouching position, and half-runs-half-crawls back toward the stockroom as the woman with the stain remover turns the corner at the other end of the aisle.

He can barely make her out in the distance. Just a beige blouse and a dark blue skirt, but if he can't see enough to attract him to her, he can see her attraction to him. As far apart as they are, though getting closer with each step she takes, he senses something of her sense.

She pauses halfway up the aisle. She's still a few yards away, but close enough to see what she's been smelling the whole time. She bursts into sobs and closes the gap between them, diving at his feet, washing his sneakers with her tears, and drying them with her long chestnut hair.

The stockboy returns at a crawl, clammy-looking and blue around the lips and eyes, and collapses nearby, an arm outstretched, the hand at the end of the arm offering a jar of salve. The man reaches down and picks up the second jar of salve with the hand already holding the first. With the other, he gently pulls the woman from his shoes, and then to her feet, looks into her bleary eyes and asks her: "Why are you crying?"

He calls the telephone company to inform them that the payphone is broken.

"I'm calling to report a broken payphone," he says.

"Location?" says the operator.

"I don't remember the cross-streets," he says, "but it's on a corner, next to a sandlot that used to be a community garden."

"Could you describe the damage, sir," says the operator.

"The receiver's been ripped from the wire that connects it to the phone," he says. "It's still lying there on the ground, the receiver, next to a pool of blood."

"One moment sir," says the operator.

He hears the operator's muffled voice say: "It's that guy who breaks the payphone," and another voice responds: "Put in a repair order, but get him off the line before he gets crazy."

"What are you talking about getting crazy," he says.

There's a pause at the other end of the line, the operator kicking herself in the proverbial for assuming that a hand over the mouthpiece could mute her conversation.

"What about getting crazy," he says.

"Sir, I didn't say anything about getting crazy," says the operator.

"Someone did," he says.

"I don't know what you're talking about, sir," says the operator.

"I don't get crazy," he says, "and I don't break the payphone. I didn't break the payphone. I'm just a concerned citizen who went to use a payphone and found it broken. I'm calling you for the first time. I've never called this number in my life."

"Calm down, sir."

"What's calm got to do with it. You people can't even keep your phones in working order. I just tried to use it. I didn't even break it. If I was shot while trying to use a payphone and it was broken in the course of the shooting, would it be my fault? It isn't even my fault. If you want to talk about faults, if you want to talk about getting crazy you should talk to the guy who shot me."

"Sir, if you don't calm down, I'll hang up."

"Hang up! See if I care. You think I don't have anything better to do than report a broken payphone I didn't even break. I got better things to do. Fucked-up faces to fuck-up worse…"

Click.

During the service, the preacher says:
"Beloved, these are the last days."

Loss of blood or lack of concentration.

He hears: This is the last day.

"Amen," he says.

And what of the beloved.

Jesus' blood.
At first Jesus' blood is dry and crusted, but bloody enough that the average onlooker would recognize it for blood. The color is somewhere between scarlet and brown. In this stage of its development, it has been known to burn any skin that it comes into contact with.

Next, Jesus' blood has been worn away by the elements—winds and possibly some rain—and by friction, hands shoved into pockets to protect Jesus' blood from wind and certainly from rain. It would take a forensic scientist to tell that the tan streaks on your hand were anything but common dirt. At this point it is probably safe to allow Jesus' blood into the car if not the house, but be wary of it if you don't wish to be healed. It will surely close your finest wounds.

Finally Jesus' blood is proper blood, dripping and smearing from your hands in all the reds of a Renaissance palette. When Jesus' blood is flowing good, no upholstery, no fabric at all is safe.

She receives a call from the mother of a little boy.
"Hello?" she says.

And the little boy's mother gets right down to it.

"We have this thing called the separation of church and state," she says.

"Who's calling?" says the teacher.

"I wasn't going to say anything about it," says the little boy's mother. "I believe in encouraging my son."

"I'm not sure who your son is," says her son's teacher. "I'm not sure who you are either."

The stand the phone rests on is beside a mirror. She's looking at herself in the mirror.

"But today he came home from church with blood all over his hands."

Now she knows who her son is, and by extension, who she is. She notices a patch of blood on the beige blouse in the mirror. It'll be hard to clean, and she's run out of stain remover.

"I told him to get away."

She can hear the mother's surprise, as though she'd expected some sort of denial, like he couldn't have gotten it in church. Now the mother probably thinks the church is some sort of cult, practicing blood sacrifice on Sunday morning between the pancake breakfast and the coffee hour, but her mind isn't on blood sacrifice, or the blood on the little boy's hands, it's on the blood on her blouse, though they're all the same depending on your perspective.

"You knew about it?" says the mother.

She unbuttons the blouse and slips out of it. She holds it up before herself as though holding it up before herself could help her to estimate how much stain remover she'll need. She makes a mental note to buy extra, knowing she'll need it soon enough.

"He thinks it's Jesus' blood," says the mother.

She laughs—a weary laugh full of unwanted phone calls and wardrobe worries—and drops the blouse to the floor.

"You think this is funny?"

"No," she says.

She's looking at herself in the mirror. She reaches back with her right hand and unclasps her bra, letting it fall to the floor atop her blouse as her breasts fall to her ribs.

There is silence on the other end of the line. The silence of the boy's mother not knowing where to go from here. She finally finds something to say: "Do you think it's Jesus' blood?"

Another laugh, though this one is full of nothing, an empty laugh.

"No," she says. "Regular blood," she says. "Blood of a man who got shot."

She runs a hand across her chest, her belly. She lifts her hand, pulls it away, and stares at it, back and front. No blood.

"He's in the hospital," she says.

She drops the phone to the pile that has formed on the floor and looks back to the mirror. She can hear the mother still talking, asking questions—who? which hospital? what's his name?—but she's imagining her chest and belly covered with circular wounds in different pales of pink, and one, the one that would have been covered by the spot of blood on her blouse, a deep-red circle, stitches in the center, and a bruise surrounding it corona-like, fading outward from blue-black to yellow-green.

A little boy is allowed in the car with Jesus' blood on his hands just this once.

His mother stands on the porch hollering his name, before she gives up and goes around to the backyard, expecting to find him curled up in his treehouse, asleep, exhausted by his explorations, and hunger.

On her way, she glances at the spigot on the side of the house, at the patch of dirt beneath the spigot where the grass never grows, and notices that the patch of dirt remains a patch of dirt rather than the muddy puddle that would indicate he'd finally come around to her way of seeing things and rinsed Jesus' blood from his hands.

Reaching the tree, she looks up at the house, more of a large wooden crate really, surrounded by leaves in their seasonal yellows, oranges, browns and deep-reds. She hollers his name once, but gets no response.

She places a hand on one of the planks nailed into the trunk, then a foot on another, lower plank, and cautiously climbs her way up, occasionally grabbing a nearby branch, because she has some inkling of the difference in weight between her son and herself, and has had visions, while watching him climb, of snapped planks, broken limbs, broken limbs. Nevertheless, she makes it to the last plank without incident. She reaches up, pushes open the trap door, and sticks her head into the roofless room.

It's empty.

She hollers his name again, several times, but he isn't any more likely to hear her hollering from his empty treehouse than from beneath the treehouse or on the porch.

She is still hollering his name when she reaches the car, jumps in, and starts it. Still hollering as she pulls out of the driveway and accelerates down the street. She's still hollering when she finally gets around to rolling down the window.

She hollers his name all over town, from one end to the other and back, and as she turns to begin another circuit, day turns to dusk and adrenaline turns to shock and she begins to despair of ever finding him, over what has happened to him, what could happen to him, and her voice begins to hoarsen and fade, and she finally stops yelling altogether.

She spots a payphone on a corner next to a sandlot, and pulls up next to it facing into traffic if there were any traffic, puts the car in park, leaves it running, jogs over, inserts a quarter, and just as she's about to put the receiver to her ear, notices something on the receiver. Something a little bit liquid and a little bit solid. It looks vaguely organic, and smells like a burnt steak.

Despair is despair, but there have got to be other payphones on other corners in the city. She jumps back into her car and goes looking for one.

She doesn't get more than a block or two before she sees her son, strolling casually down the sidewalk. She slows down and hollers hoarsely. He stops, turns his head, and strolls toward her window just as casually as he had down the sidewalk.

"Get in the car," says his mother.

He seems to have that same steak smell about him.

"Get in the car," she says.

"But I thought I wasn't allowed in unless I washed the Jesus blood off."

"Just this once," she says.

A love-struck man with a fucked-up face.
He skips out of the store with a number in his pocket and a song in his heart. On the way home, he turns on AM radio and sings along, enjambing every line with his own trills and flourishes.

One look at him, you can tell he's been hit smack in the face by cupid's arrow. A flaming arrow. He does a little dance between his car and his apartment.

It shouldn't come as any surprise that he forgets to lock the door.

A late night rendezvous.
The door is locked. There's nothing he can do about it right now but leave a note saying he'll try again later.

"I'll try again later," says the note slid under the locked door.

He'll try again later.

When she sings:
It is the ecstasy of Saint Theresa composed by Salieri and danced by Saint Vitus, and it sends him to the floor in an ecstasy of his own.

He awakens in a hospital bed.
The doctor's face hovers above his own. It's a young face—younger than his—though it has that ageless look, chiseled, like a soap-opera surgeon.

He doesn't like this one with his sculpted face and sculpted hair, his confidence or over-confidence—he can't decide which—his jibber-jabbering.

"Jibber jabber," says the doctor.

He's groggy and can't find his voice. He tries to speak but his throat is too dry. His mouth tastes like pure oxygen. He tries to swallow. He coughs. That's about all he can get out.

"Jib?" says the doctor. "Jib jab?"

"Water," he wheezes.

The doctor looks around. He finds a small plastic pitcher on the stand beside the bed, pours some water into a plastic cup about the size of a shot glass, places a bendy straw into the cup, and positions the straw at his lips. He sips. He says: "Thanks."

His voice is still weak. It sounds like something between a scrape and a whisper.

"Jibbety," says the doctor. "Jibber jibber jabber."

"English, doc," he says.

"Jibber? Jabber jabber jibber?"

"Eng. Glish," he says.

"Gibberish gibberish gibberish…"

"Quack."

"Jib?"

"You're a fucking quack."

"I'm all there is," says the doctor.

A diagram of the wounds, with accompanying exegesis:

O
O O
O O O
O O O O
O O O O O
O O O O O O
O O O O O O O
O O O O O O O O
O O O O O O O O O

At this particular moment, this particular wound is the freshest. If only this was anywhere close to over.

A denial of responsibility for what.

She's still standing there, shirtless before the mirror, but it's been long enough that who knows what she's thinking about by now.

The chatter from the phone atop the clothes atop the floor has since stopped, replaced by the drone of the dial-tone, and eventually the signal meant to snap her from her stupor and remind her that her phone is not where it was meant to be.

The signal snaps her from her stupor. She sees herself standing topless before the mirror, registers the incessant sound emanating from the receiver, looks around, then down at the receiver, there on the floor where she left it. She bends down and grabs the whole pile from the bottom up—shirt, bra, phone—and replaces them from the top down.

As she finishes tucking her beige blouse into the waistband of her dark-blue skirt, the phone rings, and she answers automatically.

"Hello," she says.

"It wasn't me," says the voice on the line.

"What wasn't who?" she says.

"Your phone's been busy," says the voice. "I've been trying to reach you."

She isn't even thinking about it. She doesn't even notice until she's got the top three buttons undone, and she's running her fingertips across her chest, her ribs, her belly, the imaginary wounds.

"Don't you have call waiting?" he says.

"It was off the hook," she says. "What do you want."

She can see it all in the mirror—blood, guts, scars—the whole neverending order of operations. She wonders if it will ever end. She wonders how much it would cost to get a new phone jack installed, somewhere out of sight of the mirror. Or one of those cordless ones.

"Why was it off the hook?" he says.

"What do you want," she says.

"I just wanted you to know it wasn't me."

"What?"

"Nothing," he says. "That's what I mean."

He awakens in a hospital bed.

There's a face hovering above his. A woman's face, but he doesn't recognize it. His eyes are still full of sleep, and his brain is floating in the ether, but even if these weren't the case he wouldn't know if or where he'd seen it, that is, her, before.

"This is unconstitutional," she says. "I don't care how you feel."

His throat is dry and his mouth tastes like pure oxygen. When he speaks, his voice is lost somewhere between a whisper and a scrape.

"Do I know you?" he scrapes.

"No," she says, "but you know

him."

She reaches down and lifts the little boy onto the bed, onto him, his freshest wound. He groans in pain, and pushes the little boy away. The little boy tumbles to the floor, but doesn't make a sound.

"No I don't," he says.

The little boy stands upright. He can barely see over the mattress. He grips one of the bed's metal siderails with both hands, places a foot on the other, and climbs back up onto the bed.

There's a face hovering above his. A little boy's face, but he doesn't recognize it, even though his eyes have cleared enough to watch as the face is replaced by two dirty little waving hands.

"Jesus blood can heal you," says a voice behind the hands.

"Who says I want to be healed," he says.

But the little boy doesn't seem to care. He's got both palms on his chest, and his chest is feeling better, if that's the word to describe it. The most recent wound is going from painful and red with stitches and a blue-black bruise, to numbish and scar-pink with a green yellow no-bruise-at-all beneath a now-redundant bandage beneath a pair of dirty little healing hands. He pushes the little boy away.

The little boy tumbles to the floor, but doesn't make a sound. The man sits up straight and rips the bandage from his chest. The wound underneath is almost no wound at all. The scar itself is less pink and textured than even some of the other, older scars. The little boy stands up and begins to climb back onto the bed.

"Keep him away," he says.

He pushes and shoves and kicks the boy away.

"What are you doing?"

The mother takes her little boy by a Jesus'-blooded hand, and leads him toward the door.

"This is what happens when you don't separate church and state," she says, though not necessarily to him.

They get dinner.

He isn't talking very much. She tells herself he's probably just the quiet type, shy, that he'll warm up if she can break the ice.

"So you're an insurance salesman," she says.

It's a pretty nice restaurant, a far cry from the diner she always seems to be eating at, the one across the street. Everything here is hard wood and real silver and lace, cloth napkins, not a television in sight. The food's good, too. At least hers is. He doesn't seem to be very hungry.

"You don't seem to be very hungry," she says.

He takes a sip from his water glass. It's the kind of restaurant where they give you a glass of water before you get the chance to ask for one. He crunches some ice between his teeth.

Break the ice. He smells like he's burning up. He smells like he smelled in the store where they met. When they met. He looks like he's burning up, too, sweat dripping from his temples, not to mention the patchwork of burns and burn scars covering his whole face. It could just be the light from the candles. It's the kind of restaurant with candles on the tables.

"I'm not very hungry," he says.

His eyeballs roll backward into the fire of his face and he swoons. His head slides through space—backward, forward, side-to-side—finally coming to rest against the lace curtain against the window that looks out onto the empty street.

He is unconscious. She isn't surprised.

A later night rendezvous.

This time they knock. This time it's a they.

They hear a series of clunks that might pass for walking. Or they hear a rolling. Or a hopping. The deadbolt sliding the door unlocked. The door opening inward and away from them to reveal a man perfect in every way but one—a clubbed-foot or a harelip or a lazy eye.

And to him—a moon-faced man with a spot of blood on his shirt, and a burn-faced man still surrounded by a cloud of smoke.

The lights are on in the apartment. They can see the clothes left scattered across the sofa, the armchair, the floor. Half-full and empty takeout cartons on the coffee table and the kitchen counters. They can't smell the rotten food, or the medicinal smell if that applies, over the burning smell emanating from the burn-faced man.

There is a silence, and then the moon-faced man points to the burn-faced man and breaks that silence: "This man's face was not always covered in burns," he says.

"I already gave at the office," says the man in the doorway, trying to close the door.

The moon-faced man takes the burn man's hand, and shoves it into the doorway just as it is about to shut and kicks the door open. The man behind it falls backward onto his ass. The burn-faced man looks like he's screaming—there's a gaping blackness in the middle of his burns—but he doesn't make a sound. The moon-faced man drags him into the apartment until they're standing over the man on the ground.

"We don't want your money and we don't want to hurt you," says the moon-faced man.

"What do you want?" says the man on the ground.

"We, that is, I, want you to cancel an appointment."

The congregation has gathered around him.

A circle radiating from his body, radiating outward from and bending down toward his body, the ones nearest him kneeling, those farther out standing on pews. His eyes are twitching. He's starting to come to, feels hands, one on either side of his head. He opens his eyes, sees the old woman—her face just above his—and gazes into her compassionate cataracts.

"There's something on my chest," he says. "It's heavy."

"It's the spirit," she says.

But he can't hear her. Her hands are covering his ears.

"The spirit's convicted him of something," she says.

The congregation confirms his conviction with amens and nods.

"I have a word," someone says.

Some of them turn toward her. On the outskirts. An enormous middle-aged woman in a formless dress, standing on a pew that wasn't built for her to stand on. She's rocking from one leg to the other in her excitement over the word, and you can hear the bench creaking with each shift of her weight.

"She's always got a word," under someone's breath.

"What's the word?" says a man who looks as though he's just stepped out of a thirty-year-old photograph, not just his clothing but the color of his clothing, of his skin, everything a bit more sepia than real life.

"The word," says the fat woman, "is that the Lord has given him a word."

"What's the word?" someone says.

"What's the word?" others say.

He can't hear them. The old woman's hands are still covering his ears, pointing his face into her face, and she isn't one of the others who say what's the word, so he doesn't even know that something is being said, that they want a word, that he has a word.

"Jesus Christ!" says someone in the balcony, looking, in her dark-blue robe like a dark-blue saint.

"Amen," someone says.

"What's the word?" someone says.

"Jesus-fucking-Christ!" she says, squeezing her own head between her hands.

"Amen?" someone says.

"Is she discerning?" someone says.

"Are you discerning his word?"

"Is the word Jesus-something-Christ?"

"Are you interpreting his word?"

She disappears from the balcony. The sound of stomping, of sneakered feet stomping down the stairs as the crowd around him amens and prays and speaks in tongues, beseeching God for an interpretation, for a word, for a word other than Jesus, which is a word they already know.

The old woman is speaking now. Though he still can't hear her, he sees her, speaking, praying, mouthing something important, something necessary, something sincere, something that he can't make out. And he doesn't want to make it out. He wouldn't tell her the word if he knew she wanted the word, if he had the word, if he had a word, because he wants that look forever.

But the old woman turns away, distracted by the stomp of sneakers—not as loud against the carpet of the aisle, but more menacing—and the swish of a robe.

"Idiots!" says the woman in the robe.

The side of the circle she's running toward parts a path for her as though idiots is a command. She commands them: Idiots! Make a path.

She commands, she runs, she swishes, she trips. She trips over her flowing, dark-blue robe, sailing gracelessly through the air, onto the old woman, and over. They tumble over each other into the crowd on the other side of him.

"Fuck!" she says.

He can hear now. The old woman's hands are several feet away, tangled up in the crowd, in her robe, in her.

"She's possessed," under someone's breath.

"Get behind me."

She's untangling herself. They're trying to lay hands on her.

"He's been shot," she says.

"I resist you in the name of…"

"He's bleeding," she says.

"Jesus blood," says a little boy.

"Blood of the lamb."

She's gotten untangled, gotten away from the laying on of hands. She hurls herself over to him, hunches over him. His skin is pale, damp like cheese left out under plastic wrap. His breathing is shallow, and he looks confused.

"No," she says. "Blood of him," she says. "Blood of he got shot."

She runs a hand across his chest, his belly. She lifts her hand, pulls it away from him covered in the blood of him, unredeeming, unredeemable blood of he got shot. She shows her palm to the congregation, and there are shrieks and gasps. The little boy runs toward them, and she pushes him away with her bloody palm.

"Call an ambulance," she says.

He shrieks. He gasps. He says: "No."

He's stirring, grunting. He's trying to stand up.

"I'm fine," he says.

"Call an ambulance," she says.

"No," he says.

He props himself up on his elbows, turns himself over, supports himself with his palms. He pulls himself onto all-fours, one knee at a time, onto his feet one leg at a time. He stands up wobbling, supporting himself against the pew, like a child about to take its first steps.

"A miracle," says the little boy, staring at the blood on his own hands.

"An ambulance," she says.

"No," he says. "Lunch."

"Lay back down," she says.

"But we always get lunch after church," he says.

A late night rendezvous.

The door is unlocked. He lets himself in, and shuts the door behind him quietly.

All of the lights are off, but there's a window open, and he can see the messy apartment by the light of the silvery moon. Clothes left scattered across the sofa, the armchair, the floor. Half-full and empty take-out cartons on the coffee table and the kitchen counters.

Nothing unusual about any of that. Nothing unusual about the smell, either—rotten food and salve.

He walks over to the kitchen area, opens a drawer, finds it empty, save for a book of matches and a small, plastic bottle of lighter fluid lying there beside each other as though they'd been left there for him. He takes them from the drawer one-handed, leaving it empty and open. He leaves the kitchen area, the room itself.

He walks down the short, narrow hallway into the other room, the bedroom. The moon only makes it halfway down the same hallway, and he lifts his empty hand to the wall, uses it to guide himself down the hall—as short and as straight as it is—until it comes to a dead end.

He looks over his shoulder in the direction he just came from. He can just about make out the shapes that make up the room and its furnishings.

He looks back. Nothing but black.

The door is on the left. He uses his free hand to feel for it. It's closed. He uses his free hand to feel for the knob. It isn't locked.

He opens the door so quietly he surprises even himself, letting the knob slip from his free hand as the door swings to a rest without so much as a whisper from the hinges.

The bedroom is darker than the hallway. There are no windows, and once inside, none of the light from the other room reaches this far, even if he looks over his shoulder.

With a little bit of fumbling—how to pull a match from the matchbook, how to strike the match, once pulled, against the matchbook, in the darkness, with a bottle of lighter fluid in his hands—he manages to ignite one of the matches in the book, and the fire creates its own little orange hemisphere.

There's a man with a fucked-up face lying in bed on the northeastern cusp of that hemisphere. The man with the match moves northeast, bringing the man with the fucked-up face into his little world, until the match goes out, leaving darkness upon the face of the deep, and a smell of sulfur.

He flips open the plastic bottle of lighter fluid, turns it upside down, and pisses it all over the space where the man's fucked-up face used to be. He closes the bottle, drops it, and in a quick and graceful series of motions, pulls a match from the matchbook, strikes it against the matchbook, and tosses it in the direction of the lighter fluid.

The fucked-up face returns, a ball of flame at the center of its own little orange hemisphere.

The man awakens, startled, and sits straight up in bed. The man with the matches laughs: "I told you I'd be back."

The man with the fireball face reaches for the glass of water on his bedside table.

"Are we done now?" he says.

"Not yet," says the man with the matches.

The man on fire dumps the glass of water over his head, extinguishing the flames, leaving them in darkness again. Yet somehow the man with the matches can see the smoke rising pale to the ceiling.

He awakens in a hospital bed.

Her face hovers above his. He recognizes her face, despite the fact that his eyes are full of sleep and his brain is floating in the ether, because her face is the idea of her face, and her halo is a florescent light.

"You're up," she says.

His eyes still haven't adjusted to the light, to being awake. His eyes won't adjust. He lies there in the cloud that is him, enjoying the blur that is her, and the down of her face catches her halo just so, refracts it.

"I brought someone," she says.

She glides away, and another face limps into her place, if this is applicable. He doesn't recognize it. There's nothing to recognize—just another face off the dissembly-line, except for the pox scars, the missing eye or tooth or teeth, if any of these are applicable.

He tries to ask whose face it is, but his throat is dry and his mouth tastes like pure oxygen, and his voice is lost somewhere between a scrape and a whisper. He tries to gather some saliva in his mouth, but the glands don't seem to be working, the oxygen sealing them off. He coughs. That's all he can get out.

The face looks around, finds a small plastic pitcher on the stand beside the bed, pours some water into a plastic cup about the size of a shot glass, places a bendy straw into the cup, and positions the straw at his lips.

He sips. He looks over at her. His eyes are starting to clear and her face is her face. He clears his throat. He says: "Why'd you have to bring him?"

She walks over to the face and puts a hand on its shoulder.

"Maybe it would be better if you stepped out," she says.

The face bows its head, turns, walks out.

"Maybe it would be better if you stepped out, too," he says.

Staring at her self in the mirror, it seems certain that it will never begin.
It seems like she's always imagining her chest and belly covered with circular wounds in different pales of pink, and one, the one that would have been covered by the spot of blood on her blouse, a deep-red circle, stitches in the center, and a bruise surrounding it corona-like, fading outward from blue-black to yellow-green, but no matter how hard she looks, there's nothing there but breasts and belly and pale, downy skin.

For this.
The phone rings again as soon as she's got the receiver back in its cradle, before she's even had the chance to button the top three buttons of her blouse and get away from that phone, that mirror.

She picks up the receiver. She says: "Hello."

Silence on the other end, then a click, then a dial-tone.

"Hello?" she says again, as though the dial-tone could explain itself.

But it can't, and she knows it, and she puts the receiver back in its cradle.

Her absent-minded hands move toward her blouse, whether to button or unbutton further she doesn't know, because the phone rings before they even reach it. Her hands reach for the phone. She says: "Hello."

Silence on the other end, then some breath, some breathing, and what sounds like a sob.

"Hello?" she says again, and the sob answers her: "You don't know what I saw."

"And how do you know what I do and don't know," she says.

"I don't," he says.

She says: "I know," and then it's his turn for the click and the dial-tone.

A little boy tells his mother it's Jesus blood.
She's picking him up. It seems like as soon as she drops him off she's picking him up again. Maybe if church were an all day affair, like in the olden days, but she tries to be encouraging, despite the separation of church and state.

He's out there on the corner, waiting for her just like any other Sunday. Maybe a little paler than usual, but she thinks she remembers him looking pale when she dropped him off.

Under the weather. That time of year.

He opens the door, hops into the passenger seat, buckles the belt, and with everything he does, every movement of his hands leaves a trail of red on the surfaces they come into contact with.

Some mothers would scream right off the bat. Blood or no, red streaks on the upholstery are never a good thing. Not her. She wants to know if its blood or no. Of course, she isn't really thinking it's blood.

"What's that on your hand?" she says.

"Jesus blood," says the boy.

Blood confirmation. The rest of the mothers are screaming by now. Except for the really religious ones. Not her. She keeps her cool. No point screaming if it isn't his. Screaming only helps in an emergency.

"Get it out of my car," she says.

"I'd have to get me out to get it out," says the boy.

"What's that some kind of religious thing," she says.

He reaches out toward her, slowly, palms out to show her the blood on his hands, still drip wet and red.

"Out," she says.

He moves his hands to unbuckle his seatbelt.

"I'll do it," she says.

She unbuckles his seatbelt one-handed. He moves his hands toward the door's handle. She grabs him by the shoulder. He stops reaching. She leans over him, careful to avoid his hands, the blood on his hands, and pops the door open two-fingered to avoid the blood on the handle. He hops out and stands in the doorway.

"Go wash your hands," she says.

"It's Jesus blood," he says.

"I don't care whose blood it is," she says. "You're not getting back in this car with blood on your hands."

"I'm not washing Jesus blood off of my hands," he says, and slams the door shut, wasting precious Jesus blood on her paintjob.

For a moment, for several, she just sits there staring at him from the driver's seat. Then she drives off to teach him a lesson or something.

He awakens in a hospital bed.

If you can call it awake. His eyes are swollen shut, and his head is bundled so tightly in bandages and gauze that he can't hear a sound if there is a sound, and all he can feel is the pressure of the bandages and a searing pain that seems to emanate from somewhere within his own skull.

As for smell—the usual burning and salve.

There's no one in the room. He wouldn't know that there was someone in the room if there was someone in the room, but this doesn't make up for the fact that there's no one in the room.

Lying there, in the room, in the bed, in the bandages, it's hard to tell if this is the beginning or the middle or the end.

As his evening draws to a close, he makes a mental note.

1. Don't tell her it's your fault.

Better yet, 1. Call her now, and tell her it isn't.

He's in the car, driving home, but there aren't any payphones around here. There is, however, one on the corner a few blocks up, next to the sandlot that used to be a community garden.

He pulls up across the street from it, puts the car in park, leaves it running, jogs over, and only realizes there's no receiver after inserting the quarter. He pushes the coin return button, but it doesn't return his coin.

He looks around, down, and sees the receiver lying on the gravel in what used to be a pool of blood, what is now only a circle of somewhat darker gravel.

He'd told them it was broken.

He picks up the receiver, brings it back to the phone, and slips the coiled metal wire back into the machine. He puts the receiver to his ear. No dial-tone. He presses the coin return button again. No quarter. He pulls the receiver and the wire out of and away from the phone again. He raises the receiver above his head. He brings it down on the phone. Again. Again. The coin slot, the coin return, the cradle, the metal plate, the keypad. He does not stop until the payphone is badly scuffed and he is heaving.

He makes another mental note. Some combination of the other ones.

They get lunch after church.

"So what's the matter with this one?" he says.

She tactfully ignores his tactless question.

"He's an insurance salesman," she says. "Can we talk about something else?"

It's not a great restaurant, a diner really. They go there every week after church because it's not very far from church. Everything is stainless steel and formica. There are televisions in each of the four corners.

"Eat your food," she says.

They sit in the same booth every week. He sits on the same side of the same booth, and every week, the television in the corner opposite him seems to be resting atop her head. Bad eyesight or something. Loss of blood.

"I'm not very hungry," he says.

His eyeballs roll backward into their craters and he swoons. His face slides through space, backward, forward, side-to-side, finally coming to rest against the window that looks out onto the empty street.

He is unconscious. She is relieved.

A man with a face like a moon sees a woman in a long, dark blue skirt and a beige blouse escorting a man with [a club foot /a lazy eye/a gimp leg/ distended belly/ pox scars/ crooked spine/ buckteeth/ no teeth/ gangrene/ a goiter/ an eyepatch/ four digits missing/ blond hair/ brown hair/ red hair/ black hair/ gingivitis/chancres/ kinky hair/ alopecia/ wavy hair/ warts/ dimples/ elephantitis of the left leg/ right leg/ right arm/ left and right leg/ albinism/ chafed nose/ eyepatches/ no left leg/ hands/ a weak chin/ the kind of incontinence you can see/ freckles/ hypochondria/ a charming smile/ a toothy grin/ breasts/ a hunchback/ high cheekbones/ jaundice/ a symmetrical face/ burns that cover 100% of his symmetrical face]anything but a chest riddled with bullet scars out of a restaurant, a diner really. And gets religion.

A later night rendezvous.

The door is unlocked. He lets himself in, and shuts the door behind him quietly.

All the lights are off, but there's a window open, and he can see the messy apartment by the light of the silvery moon. Clothes left scattered across the sofa, the armchair, the floor. Half-full and empty takeout cartons on the coffee table and the kitchen counters.

Nothing unusual about any of that. But there is something unusual about the smell floating above the usual odor of rotten food and salve. It smells like burnt flesh. It smells like it usually smells when he leaves. It makes him wonder if someone has beaten him to it, if the man with the fucked-up face has been two-timing him.

He takes another look around and decides it's unlikely. There are no signs of struggle. Yet.

He walks over to the kitchen area, opens a drawer, finds it empty.

"Shit," he whispers.

He opens the drawer beneath it, the one beneath that, another. All empty.

He speaks aloud, though not too loudly. Loud enough that the man in the next room might—if he weren't such a heavy sleeper, sleeping even more heavily than usual, deep in puppy-love dreams—hear that someone was speaking in the kitchen area, but not loud enough to hear what whoever was speaking was saying: "You didn't think that would stop me."

He slides over to the stove, turns the dial for the front burner to high, waits until he hears the hissing as the smell of gas slips into the kitchen, turns the dial further and waits for the click to ignite the gas. The gas turns to flame, surrounding the burner corona-like.

He takes a takeout container from the counter, empties it onto the linoleum, and tears the corners, flattening it out into a vaguely flowery shape. He holds the flower by one petal, and slips the petal opposite into the flame until it too is flaming.

As the flame spreads to other parts of the flower, he lifts it above his head, pointing it toward the smoke detector on the ceiling. The smoke rises lazily from the flame. The ceiling is high, and the air is stagnant, but eventually the smoke detector detects smoke and releases its chronic howl.

He drops the burning flower atop the leftovers on the linoleum, and flattens himself against the wall behind him. He tries to block out the howl of the smoke detector, listening for movement in the next room.

He hears movement, someone throwing off the sheets and leaping from the bed. Someone running down the hallway.

Someone skids into the kitchen and sees a pile of burning matter on the linoleum. Rather than fill a container with water to douse the flames, he bends toward the flames, and as he does, the man against the wall pushes him from behind, shoving him toward the stovetop where he holds his face to the burner just long enough to make a point before making a quick exit.

He awakens in a hospital bed.
There's a face hovering above his, a face he doesn't recognize. His eyes are still full of sleep, and his brain is floating in the ether, and even this is not enough to account for how blurry this face is. He can't make out any hair, and all he sees are dark patches on the face where the eyes should be.

He knows better than to ask who he is.

His throat is dry and his mouth tastes like pure oxygen. When he speaks, his voice is lost somewhere between a whisper and a scrape.

"What do you want," he scrapes.

A dark patch appears in the face, where the mouth should be, and says: "A guy with your bad luck could use some life insurance."

The insurance salesman pulls a business card from his blue running suit, a white rectangle with a few dark spots in the middle, a few in the corner. He makes no move to accept it, and the salesman places it on his chest.

"It isn't bad luck," he scrapes.

"Ok, a guy with your luck," says the salesman.

"Luck either," he scrapes.

"Ok, a guy like you."

He tries to scrape another contradiction, but his throat is too dry even for that. He tries to gather some saliva in his mouth, but the glands don't seem to be working, the oxygen sealing them off. He coughs. That's all he can get out. Another cough.

The insurance salesman looks around. He finds a small plastic pitcher on the stand beside the bed, pours some water into a plastic cup about the size of a shot glass, places a bendy straw into the cup, and positions the straw at his lips.

He sips. He says: "What about you?"

"What about me?" says the insurance salesman.

His vision is starting to clear. He closes his eyes.

"A guy like you could stand to take his own advice," he says.

"I'm a fucking insurance salesman," says the insurance salesman.

How to respond to that. There is no response.

"Open your eyes," says the insurance salesman. "Look at me."

"I'm tired," he says.

The insurance salesman pulls a whole stack of business cards from his blue running suit and lobs them at his moon-shaped head. They scatter across his face, the pillows. Some of them trickle down to the floor. The insurance salesman leaves, but it's a long time before he opens his eyes again.

The method to his burns.
The fact is, there is none. Sometimes there are more and sometimes fewer, not that anyone notices from one operation to the next. His face is a map of chaos, and chaos is a constant, and when he opens his mouth, to yawn for instance, his face is a chaos with a black hole in its center, and this chaos is a yawn, too.

No one calls her.
She puts the phone back on its cradle. She buttons the top three buttons of her blouse and lets her hands drop to her sides. She thinks about getting away from the phone, the mirror. She stands in front of the mirror looking at the phone.

Maybe the ringer's off.

She thinks she might remember the phone slipping between her head and her shoulder at some point. It might have slid the switch from on to off ringer-wise. She lifts the receiver. Dial-tone. She checks the ringer switch—on. She switches it off, then on again, replaces the phone, lifts it. Dial-tone.

As she puts it back down, she catches a glance of herself in the mirror, her blouse. She glances at the spot of blood on her blouse, or stares at it. She remembers that she meant to buy some more stain remover before heading over to the hospital for what.

Might as well buy some more stain remover.

A little boy takes his time getting home.
Nothing so eventful as church this morning, but the freedom is exhilarating.

They are building a parking lot where the other church used to be, and when the breeze blows something can get in your eye.

Two mailboxes side by side—one for out of town and one for in.

The gray sky seems happy to be resting on trees shedding.

The time on the clock outside the bank says a different time than his watch and gives temperature readings in two different scales.

A nest of cigarette butts in a sewage drain.

There is a bee in the air, and you don't often see that this time of year.

Three cars drive by, and the drivers inside them are all listening to the same song, because the song is on a radio station.

If there is blood on your hands, you should not stick them into your pockets and then take them out and then stick them in again if you don't want the blood to get worn off.

A tall building that proves that the earth really does move.

The crows look as small as the bees because they're higher up.

A restaurant, a diner really, with an ambulance outside of it.

The cool wind makes him feel warm.

A dignified business man makes himself look ridiculous when he smoothes the sides of his hair while crossing the street and his arms look more stumpy with every repetition of the gesture.

Don't step on a crack.

The sound of cheers comes from a basement bar as he passes.

He catches himself putting his hands in his pockets just in time.

Girls even younger than him playing hopscotch and cussing.

He is not the only one who revs his bicycle or says giddyup to it.

Some of the people walking the streets are talking to a phone but some are just talking to themselves.

His mom may be worrying about him by now.

That man's singing sounds sad.

A man going into the store smells like his mom burned dinner.

He catches himself pulling his hands from his pockets—too late.

A fire alarm, somewhere behind him.

Could the wind have knocked that stop sign down.

Only take one newspaper per quarter.

There is an alley in this little city where a woman is asleep and you have to poke her six times with a stick before she wakes up and resignedly asks you to go away and even if you tell her that it's Jesus blood on your hand she will ask you just the same not to touch her.

Some cracks in the sidewalk just can not be avoided.

The sound of snores comes from a street-level bar as he passes.

A woman whistling with her hands in her pockets.

That man's singing sounds happy but out of tune.

A girl must be far from home if she can't hear her mother screaming that it's time for dinner.

A teacher, driving to a store—he knows because she's his teacher.

There are other kids he does not recognize who get to do this all the time, so as he passes them, he pretends that he does too.

Three people drive by listening to the same song because they are in the same car.

He spits on the ground and then looks around.

A priest a minister and a rabbi wait for the light to change at the corners of the intersection that he is not standing on and everyone solemnly acknowledges the others.

There are probably as many cats that don't have homes as do.

He sticks his hands in his pockets, then pulls them out, then sticks them in again, without thinking.

The man who lives next to the gas station brings pigeons to his stoop with stale bread, and when they have all been brought there, he throws a firecracker at them.

The smell of chicken makes his stomach grumble.

Some cracks you don't even want to avoid.

The everpresent temptation of gum on the sidewalk.

There are no quarters in the coin return of the payphone next to the sandlot, but the receiver smells like the man whose mother burned his dinner.

He wishes that this walk could last forever, but every step closer to home takes him closer to the end.

Staring at himself in the mirror, he hopes that this time it's all going to end.

Staring at himself in the mirror. He hopes that this time it's all going to end.

Who cares.

The skin beneath the bandages, if it can be called skin, feels like leather, the shiny kind. No, like the dream, who can remember how but the skin, usually on his arm, his hand, just ruptures, like trenchhand but less moisture, skin so soft and tissuey it can be scraped away by grazing fingernails. And as it splits upward toward the elbow, the meat inside is like cotton stuffing or the lobster in the tank at the grocery store, the injured one being cannibalized by the rest of them if that's the type of company he keeps.

It depends whether you're his face or his fingertips.

"Let's see what you look like this time," he says, and he almost giggles.

Because how is it going to look any

different this time. Sure it'll be different, but it won't feel different. It'll be different in that it'll technically look different, but then there's that thing about a brain can't absorb more than eight things at once, different things, from tectonic shifts to a tree falls in a forest, a national forest if those are the biggest.

That different.

He unfastens the butterfly clip, unravels the bandage, around his face and around.

Nope. No difference. He can already tell. Nothing you can do to a face when everything but nothing's already been done to it. That sounds like some sort of ending, but it isn't. That's the only thing we can agree upon. Shit.

The last of the bandage falls off into the hand that's been collecting the rest, and he can see the whole bare, fucked-up face in the mirror. He balls up the bandage and tosses it at the shelf.

It's too easy to anthropomorphize that face, to see the combination of rage and pain and despair, especially as the tears well from the rimless eyes. But none of it's really there. Except for the tears. Tears tend to fall when there aren't any lashes or lids to hold them up. Mostly he just wants it to end.

And there's a payphone he's supposed to try to use.

An acceptance of responsibility for this.

The room is empty. Not empty of a phone, a stand, a mirror, but empty of people, a person to lift the receiver of the phone on the stand and say hello should the phone ring, someone to stare into the mirror while being talked at.

Whoever left the room empty of herself turned out the lights on the way out, so the mirror has ever less to reflect as late afternoon becomes twilight and twilight night. The phone is a shade of light gray where once it was beige. And the ring, once it begins to ring, sounds somehow changed as well, less jarring, more of an echo, more than one or one-and-a-half rings before whoever is not answering answers and says hello.

It rings once, twice, three times, four before the tape in the answering machine begins to turn and whatever beeps beeps and the tape says: "You've reached such and such a number. Please leave a message after the beep."

Beep.

It doesn't sound like her voice. He knows it's her voice, but the machine does something worse than similar machines do to other voices, similar and otherwise. It distracts him for a moment from his intention of telling her that it's his fault.

He remembers: "Pick up if you're there," he says.

She doesn't pick up because she isn't there, or because she isn't picking up.

"Are you there?" he says. "Where are you? Why won't you answer?" he says.

Because she isn't picking up or she isn't there.

"I was gonna tell you something," he says. "It was that it was my fault," he says, "and that I thought of a way we could get this over with, so pick up."

The room is empty of a person to pick up the phone that it is not empty of. It is not empty of the turning of the tape in the machine, or of the voice coming through the speaker, changed in a way that isn't worth elaborating on and saying: "Fuck you."

Yes. Fuck you too.

He awakens in a hospital bed.

Her face hovers above his. He recognizes her face, despite the fact that his eyes are full of sleep and his brain is floating in the ether, because her face is the idea of her face, and her halo is a florescent light.

"You're up," she says.

His eyes still haven't adjusted to the light, to being awake. His eyes won't adjust to being awake. He lies there in the cloud that is him, enjoying the blur that is her, and the down of her face catches her halo just so, refracts it.

"I brought someone," she says.

She glides away, and is replaced by

another face, a face he doesn't want to recognize. It's more blurry than hers. He can't make out any hair and the eyes are just darker patches on his face.

His throat is dry, and his mouth tastes like pure oxygen. When he speaks his voice is lost between a whisper and a scrape.

"What's he doing here?" he scrapes.

A dark patch appears in the insurance salesman's face, where the mouth should be, and says: "A guy with your bad luck could use some life insurance."

The insurance salesman pulls a business card from his blue running suit, a white rectangle with a few dark spots in the middle, a few in the corner. He makes no move to accept it, and the salesman places it on his chest.

"It isn't bad luck," he scrapes.

"Ok, a guy with your luck," says the salesman.

"Luck either," he scrapes.

"Ok, a guy like you."

He tries to scrape another contradiction, but his throat is too dry even for that. He tries to gather some saliva in his mouth, but the glands don't seem to be working, the oxygen sealing them off. He coughs. That's all he can get out. Another cough.

The insurance salesman looks around. He finds a small plastic pitcher on the stand beside the bed, pours some water into a plastic cup, places a bendy straw into the cup, and positions the straw at his lips. He sips.

"Why'd you have to bring him?" he says.

She walks over to the insurance salesman and puts a hand on his shoulder. He can make out her hand, but beyond that, only an impression of her.

"Maybe it would be better if you stepped out," she says.

"Maybe it would be better if you stepped out," says the insurance salesman.

She leaves without a word.

"Get the fuck out of here," he says.

"That's uncalled for."

There's a throbbing in his head. At the same time, a feeling of falling, the weightlessness of gravity pulling harder than it should.

"Forget it," says the insurance salesman. "I'm tired."

His heart is beating so rapidly it's painful, and through the numb of the painkillers and the dumb sleep that accompanies it, his belly aches. He turns away from the head hovering so close that he can feel the heat radiating from it. He can smell its miserable breath.

The insurance salesman takes his big hands and turns his face back toward him. His eyes are clearing against his will, a mutiny of focus. He can see the salesman's face, his eyes, his wisps.

"Sometimes it seems like it'll never be over," says the salesman.

Tears well in the salesman's eyes, brim over missing rims and fall to his broad face resting there stagnant against its flatness.

"But we could do it," says the salesman.

And now his own tears begin to flow. They well up in his eyes and have nowhere to go. He squeezes them shut and the tears rest there on the lids.

"We could end it all right now," says the salesman.

The salesman tries to force his eyes open with his big hands. He resists. The throbbing in his head throbs harder. He'd rather not ask how.

"Any way you like," says the salesman. "Shake hands, go our separate ways. Or."

He's still squeezing. The salesman is still prying. He shakes his head back and forth but the salesman won't let go.

"No," he scrapes. "Help," he scrapes. "Somebody," he scrapes. "I don't want to end it."

So it doesn't.

TONY RAUCH

LOCATION:
Minneapolis, MN

STYLE OF BIZARRO:
A little bit of everything swirled together

BOOKS BY RAUCH:
I'm Right Here
Laredo
Now We Can Buy a Monkey

DESCRIPTION: Rauch's writing can be described as abstract, funky, jazzy; dream-like, and surreal. His fiction explores the absurd, the silly, the unexpected, the odd, the fragile, the subconscious, the strange juxtaposed against the banal, dreams, loneliness, isolation, regret, fears, impermanence, uncertainty, imbalance, a person's search for his or her place in an indifferent world, and general weirdness.

INTERESTS: Art, architecture, urban design, music, reading, creative writing, biking, cleaning, gardening, walking my dog Gilbert, museums, pro basketball, model railroads, sleeping, old stuff—mid-century modernism, 1950s and 60s stuff, almost anything imaginative and different. You know, the usual.

INFLUENCES: Dr. Seuss, Donald Barthelme, J.D. Salinger, Richard Brautigan, Kurt Vonnegut, Jr., Roald Dahl, Charles Bukowski, Franz Kafka, Leonard Michaels, Antoine de Saint Exupery, Robert Coover, Steve Martin, Barry Yourgrau, Mark Leyner, Adrienne Clasky, Lydia Davis, Etgar Keret, D. Harlan Wilson, Stacey Richter, George Singleton, Diane Williams, Rod Serling, L. Sprague De Camp, Ray Bradbury, Phillip K. Dick, Aurthur C. Clarke, Isaac Asimov, Charles Beaumont, Ursula K. Le Guin, History, Biographies, Music, UFOs.

WEBSITE:
www.myspace.com/tonyrauch

WHAT YOU'RE MISSING

So it's Saturday morning and I'm working on my flower bed when I have to go into the shed out back to get some fertilizer and a hand trowel. I open the door to find the trowel lying on the ground. I bend down to retrieve it and as I'm crouching down, I notice some big ants crawling on the floor in that random manner in which ants seem to find themselves wandering around. But these ants are kind of different—big and thick, as if from the jungle or something. So as I crouch, one of the ants suddenly stops and looks up at me. Then it stands up on its hind legs and flips its head back, as if its head is a hood or helmet or something. And who should be under that helmet? Why wouldn't you know it's a person! A little person wearing a tiny ant suit! I lean in closer to check the little person out, thinking it must be a tiny remote control toy or something. And who would it be wearing that wonderful little ant costume? Why wouldn't you know, but it's my ex-girlfriend, Larane!

I tell you, this is quite a surprise, but then she was always up to something. She'd really come up with some clever stuff alright. Anyway there she is, tiny and on the floor of the shed out back, dressed in a little ant outfit. So she nods up to me as my big fat mug is gazing down in wonder at her. Neither of us says anything for a moment. I mean, I am just frozen, marveling at this unusual situation. I'm so surprised to see her here at all, much less this way, that I only stammer a few short breaths and that's about it. Until finally I just go, "Hey, Larane, whatcha doin' down there?" and that sort of breaks the ice. That seems to do it.

"Oh, hey Chuck," she flips the head back, and it drops behind her and just hangs there like a hood, as if on a hinge. I guess it's not really a helmet, it's more like a cockpit windscreen, like in those old airplanes. Then she pulls her arms from the sleeves and the front of her costume sort of folds down. She begins to straighten her hair. I guess she wants to look nice, me being her ex-boyfriend and all.

"Larane, how'd ya get so small like that?" I peer down.

"Oh, yeah, that," she smiles and looks around at herself, "Would ya look at that. It's the darndest thing. Really. I mean, just look at me here."

"It's me isn't it? . . . It's all my fault," I drop to my knees, "Right? It's me? Right?"

"Yes, it is, Chuck. I mean, just look at what you've reduced me to here," she holds her arms out and chuckles jokingly. "Naw, Chuck, don't worry about it. This is all my doing. Totally my decision. This is my new thing. How you like it?" she twists from side to side, "Check me out. I'm teeny."

"It's me, isn't it? Oh what am I saying, of course it is. I'm a loser. A horror. A walking horror. An emotional horror show. All I do is upset people. It's all my fault," my head drops into my hands and my shoulders quiver. "I'm nothing but a clumsy bumpkin at life, constantly clanging into other people's feelings, befouling one and all, polluting, befouling. . . It's me. It's all me. . . Oh, I'm no good. No good at life. I shouldn't have never been born. Never ever. I mean, just look at me. I shouldn't have been mean to you. Maybe you could've helped me get a good job. Or helped me meet a great girl. I should've been more practical. I should've been nicer to you. You deserve better than to be treated that way. And now here you've come back to haunt me, to show me what a great new life you have. Haven't you? You've come back to haunt me, right? You're doing this to harm me emotionally? Aren't you? To get back at me?"

"Not everything's about you, Chuck. I got this way because they came to me and asked me to join them and I said yes. They're showing me a better way and now here I am, working for that better way. . . Chucky, why are you looking away from me?"

"It's hard to look at you. It hurts too much." I exhale in confusion.

"You can only get hurt by the things you love."

"I'm sorry. I made a mistake. I should've never let you go."

"The fact that you make a mistake makes you normal. You're not a loser. You're perfectly normal. Tragically, horrifyingly normal. That's the litmus test for normality right there - making mistakes."

"Do you feel that you need to repay some sort of moral debt or something? Huh? Is that what this is all about? More charity work? Another one of your 'projects?'"

"I s'pose we all have our own moral debts to repay, but no, that isn't part of it, or at least not for me. And man, do you look like hell, Chuck. I mean, really. Have you been sleeping in the trunk of your car or something lately, 'cause, dang, man, you look like you haven't slept in weeks. . ."

"Yeah, I been feeling a little run down lately, a little out of balance, a little out-of-sorts, now that you mention it."

"Looks like you're wearing a rented smile. I mean, where did you find that thing, along the side of the road or something?"

"O.K., that's enough. You always gotta lay into me, don't you?"

". . . and a borrowed expression. Did some down-on-his-luck bum lend you his face for awhile, 'cause yours just wasn't cutting it there? Huh? Did he feel sorry for you? Did he feel that you might need his face more than he did? Huh? Did he pity you? 'Cause that's what it looks like from down here."

This was rather odd, to see her so carefree and happy like this. To see her so limber, joking around, so loose, as if a great weight has been removed from her shoulders. Before, when I knew her, she was always on the dour and morose side of things. For example, at Halloween when the kids would ring the bell, she would answer by saying, "Trick or treat," and ask them for candy. That side of her never really bothered me much as I enjoy the sweets from time to time. But her picnicking in the cemetery on moonlit nights really creeped me out.

"It's because nothing I do ever works out. Right? That's it, isn't it?" I gaze down at the hard, dirt floor in realization. "That's why. I mean, it's not like I do things half way. It's just nothing ever works out. I'm no good. I'm just no good. That's all. I'm no good at life. No good at all. It's as simple as that. Please help me," I quiver and sob.

"No. No dear. It's nothing to do with you - my reduction, that is. . . And you have to complete your thought. You say, 'Nothing you do ever works out.' But really, what happens is that nothing you do ever ends up working out exactly the way you envision it in your head in the first place. And who amongst us can not say the same? You see, ideas change once those thoughts leave our bodies. You have a thought or idea in your mind, a perfect vision of things that gets changed once it enters an imperfect world. You just have to get used to that and recalibrate your expectations for the inevitable change. Once you move in this world there are automatic reactions. Once an idea is released into the atmosphere it instantly becomes distorted from its original features, taking on a life of its own and is subject to the forces around it. Once you have set it free from your mind, it's on its own and begins to grow in its own metamorphosis. You have given birth, but you can not control your baby once it is no longer yours, now forced to shape itself by the wind, the world, other people's perceptions, other people's will, and thus changes anyway. So no, dear, you're not a failure or loser as such. No, you're pretty average that way. Maybe you just need to plan things out in deeper detail or something. Maybe prepare more and see things through all the way to the end. Not as a control freak, but to try and maintain the shape of that original vision or idea. . . ."

"But, *we* failed."

"At least we tried. We got together at least. Don't get bogged down by your perceived failures. Learn from them and grow. Do you know how hard it is for people to get together these days? I mean, people are so busy and have their own view of what should be. It's hard enough to get them all to match up and jive and fit together toot-sweet. So, yeah, it didn't work out in the end. But just getting together in the first place is the hardest part anyway. So in that regard, we didn't fail. It's just in how you look at it, that's all. At least we accomplished the very hardest part. So that's at least something. Isn't it?"

"Well, isn't that just a convenient rationalization? An excuse?"

"Well isn't thinking you're a loser a convenient rationalization not to keep trying?"

"You're a treasure, my dear. A lost treasure. Please come back to me, for you soothe my bruised psyche," I plead as I lean closer to try and see her. She is maybe a quarter of an inch high now. Maybe three-eighths of an inch, tops. I keep squinting to try to see her clearly.

"Randal Von Westmeyer!" barks the neighbor. Every once in awhile I can hear him from over the fence and through the overgrowth of bushes that separates our two yards. It's just a quirky little thing he does. Now and then he calls out a random name, like an involuntary spasm or something. He's always done it. I've been too embarrassed to ask him about it, figuring it's all just a personal matter, as if it's his way of remembering old childhood chums or something, recalling an innocent time in his life to comfort himself, as if it were a reaction to all the comings and goings in his life, so many people slipping away and getting lost, so many times and places evaporating away, so many things changing on him without his permission. I think it's something he can't help, like it's just his way of dealing with things beyond his control. He just lets fly with random names. "Terry Nighberg! . . . Terry Nighberg!"

See, there one goes again.

"Silly, why are you squinting?" she asks.

"Because you're so hard to make out."

"Oh," she smiles in realization of the situation.

"I mean, come on, you gotta meet me half way on this one."

"Yeah, I suppose," she sighs.

I'm surprised that she's here, that she'd show up in my life again. I figure she'd find some big muscular jockey guy with a Trans Am and really work to rub it in my face. But she seems so peaceful now. Centered. At ease. Down to earth. She speaks so matter-of-factly. Her voice never wavers. I'm impressed with the calm that she radiates. It radiates into me and makes me warm and calm, absorbing any and all anxieties. "Why did you leave?" I finally grow the courage to ask.

"You were preoccupied and unkind to my needs. I guess I needed more attention than what you could offer at the time. I don't know, it just didn't work for me any longer. Maybe we took it as far as we could and that was it. There was no more left of it. . . . Plus you slurped your soup something awful. And I mean every damn spoonful. Slurrrrrp. Slurrrrp," she mimics, raising a fist to her mouth. "A person can only take so much of that."

"Well, I really like my soup. . . I realize that I'm imperfect. Incomplete. But you made me a better person. Just by being with me. You calmed me and gave me warmth. You made me feel like I didn't have to worry about anything, because no matter what happened out in that grotesque, distorted world out there, I would always have you and you would always be there to listen to me and cheer me up and laugh at my silly observations of things. I mean, I can only see and do so much," I plead, my brow furrowing. "I wish I was perfect for you. You deserve that. That much anyway. You deserve perfection. Absolute purity. Honestly, you really do. . . I wish I was perfect, like all those guys on television and in the movies and in print advertisements. The guys from the beer commercials, or even like the guys down at the lodge," I sigh. "Yeah, I wish I was perfect for you and could give you everything that makes you happy."

"Joyce Maynard!" Another disembodied call from beyond.

"Well, I could never really figure you out either, you know?" she sighs.

"Why would you want to? Why couldn't you just let things be themselves? Why couldn't you just let me be me, whatever that would be at any given moment?"

"Oh, I don't know. I guess I might have been all wrapped up in other superficial stuff back then too." She seemed to be apologetic. She seemed sorry things didn't work out for us. And I must admit that did make me feel a little better, like it wasn't all my fault.

"Well, maybe it's nobody's fault then. Some things just are what they are. Maybe we should try to move on. Start fresh," I reach to the ground and rub it a little, as if I were reaching out to her. ". . . Say, I been meaning to ask, how'd you do that to yourself?"

"Do what?" she squints up at me, the sun burning bright behind me.

"How did you get so small all of a sudden? If it's not too impolite or personal."

"Oh, it was 'The Orb.' This tight little shining ball of energy. I'm better off this way. This size. I take up less space. I need less resources. I'm better off this way. Happier. The Orb has made me happier. And they've shown me and told me of all sorts of things. You know, the whole Zen simplicity thing - 'don't focus on the bowl, focus on the light reflecting off the ripples inside.' 'Love the journey, not the outcome.' That whole angle on things," she explains.

"The Orb? Who is that?" I wonder.

"A glowing orb of light the size of a marble. Actually, there's two of them. One's referred to as 'The All.' We don't know what that one does. It just is. We think it just floats around and looks pretty. We don't know. It has such a force, such an energy. I was sucked right in and absorbed it late one night in my room while I was lying in bed. It just came to me and asked if I wanted to join it and I said, yeah, sure, I'm sick of this lame-o world, this tired old life. And then it entered my stomach and glowed real hot until the next thing I knew, here I was, this size."

"Really now?" I gush in disbelief. But how could I disbelieve, I mean, here she was, right before me in all her small glory.

"David Hageldorn! . . . Haggy! . . . Haaaageldooooorn!" barks another anguished cry from beyond as if searching, calling out to other days, lost days.

"Yep, really. And then I followed it and it showed and told me all sorts of things. It showed me a small, glowing, green plasma known as 'The substance' that allows a person to learn at a radically accelerated rate."

"You don't say."

"Yep. And it showed me these ghosts that can only be seen in the reflection of glass. And it introduced me to a delightful little curly haired fellow we all call 'Marty,' who's just super positive and a really nice guy to be around. Just a super guy. Really."

"Well, if he's any good at bowling, I'd sure like to meet him. Maybe we could all go out for a pint sometime in the near future?"

"And a heretofore undiscovered sponge-like organism that lives just underground and can travel all over just by oozing around. It's known as 'The Gump,' and exists in an undetectable squishy, blob-like state and occupies a footprint of about a square block of space that . . ."

"The Gump, huh. Yeah, I think I'd like to meet that guy too. He sounds interesting. Sounds like a right fun guy. Right there, that one does."

"Tucker Hingle... Tucker." This one was not a scream that called out to fate accusingly, but more of a tired, frustrated, out-of-breath whimper of an exhale.

"Man, Chucky, I tell ya, you don't

know what you're missing. We get around in these ant devices here. See. I mean, just look at me here," she spreads her arms apart, "I mean, they're actually little robots that look like ants to the human eye, but really it's just us, truckin' around in 'em, doin' our thing - like you guys peel around in your cars. Half of this robotic device opens up like a car door and you just climb right in, like a snug car seat, and just go. They're great bio-engineered robotic suits—temperature controlled, amphibious, strong. You can lift things. Move things. Heavy things. You can climb things. They're weather-proof. You name it, these primo baby's are loaded."

"Oh," I exhale, "That must be loads of fun." I'm trying to be more positive about things, more supportive for once in my life. "What do you eat? How do you live? If that's not too impolite of me to inquire?"

"Off scraps of food. You'd be surprised how many of us you could feed with, like, just a quarter of a doughnut."

"Oh. Sure. 'Cause you're, like, real small and everything."

"Brady Aldridge! . . . Frickin' Brady . . ."

"Yeah. We don't need much. . . . Don't ever worry about us. I feel good now. Really good. Like I never could before for some reason. Maybe it's because I'm free. Unencumbered. Free of all the crap in your world. I hope to evolve into a new form of purity. Maybe grow into a burning ball of energy like The Orb. Eventually I hope to melt down and liquefy and, you know, just totally let myself go. Hopefully seep down into it all and seek out that squishy blob, The Gump, and hopefully, if I'm good enough, pure enough, join the blob, the gang, the scene, to absorb it and be absorbed by it, to join that final naked finality. To finally be free of it all, to finally be pure - 100% free, 100% pure. To finally connect and join and belong and be together and contribute and move forward and evolve into that next thing that is waiting for us out there in that grassy field known as the future, to . . . It's the calm, the warmth, the everything, the gumption of it all, the audacity, the . . ."

"Tie your gumption to your rumption," I sigh, interrupting with a passive aggressive mumble, upset that I am about to lose her again, to lose her not to another guy or another place, but to a disturbing, sponge-like mass. "I don't think this is you talking, Larane, I think it's The Orb, or The All, or the gumption, or the substance, or whatever it is. I don't think it's really you. . . . Please. Please come back. Please. I miss you. I miss your warmth. Your dental work. Your tire rotating abilities. Please. Let's give it another chance. Relationships need time. They evolve. They go through stages. If only we could get to know each other better, you'd understand my situation and thought processes. Things would work out better this time. I'm sure of it. Now that I know how much I need you. How much you mean to me. I miss you. And I miss our enthusiasms. And I gotta tell you, I'm feeling mighty enthusiastic right now. . ."

"Kip Tuckerson!"

". . . Now that I'm lost here in this weird world of ours. Stranded. Now that I find myself lost in that dark, sticky morass of perpetually being single. Everyone else is paired off. And I'm the only one left. Alone. All alone. I'm nothing without you, Larane. I'm mist. Vapor. Invisible. . . . Maybe you just need a break from things. Maybe you're just stagnating, trapped, in a rut, and need to try some new things - mix things up a little. Maybe you could try some bioenergetics? Or some Reichian therapy? Gestalt therapy? Yoga? Natural foods? Erhard Seminars? I mean, come on - there's all sorts of stuff out there for you in the human potential movement. . . Why would you want to give in and be absorbed by me or anyone else? Why not be a free and independent you. Think for yourself. That's gotta be better than just being a small piece of anything else. Right?"

"Tuckerson! . . . Tuckerson! . . . Oh God, Tuckerson!"

"No, Chucky. I really don't think

that's going to do it. Not this time. I'm sorry. Relationships shouldn't seem like work. They should grow and evolve naturally. Like how it is with The Gump. You, fine sir, are like work to me. Constant upkeep and general all around maintenance. . . I'm very sorry. But I've moved on. I don't need attachments or relationships anymore. I don't need to be big or to be a big shot. I don't really even need a body anymore. All I feel I need is the warmth and energy of The Gump. I can't wait for it to absorb me. So that I may join it and ooze along under the ground in peace and harmony with nature and everything, the way a mushroom-like mass should. I can't wait to be a part of something that's bigger than myself. To belong. To be warm and involved."

"Well just where did you meet this spongy Gump? Do I know him? How did you find out about him? Really, he's just a guy. Just like me, right?"

"Well, it's not a 'him' really, but more of an 'it' or a 'what' in that The Gump isn't gender specific in any way. It just is. As for finding it, The Orb sought me out, sensed my melancholia, my discontent, my detachment, my disconnected state, my ambivalence, my restlessness, my trepidation, my angst, my unbalance, my emptiness. It came to me late at night, woke me, and told me of a better life, a more pure, complete existence in The Gump. I think I could feel it coming too, like for days there was this sweet smell in the air, like perfume."

"It's a trap! A trap! Don't believe it! You belong with me! You belong up here with me, breathing the fresh air, thinking for yourself, going to ball games, rotating tires," I yelp in a slobbering whine, "We belong together. You and me. You don't need The Gump, and it doesn't need you either. Not at all. Not in the least. Not like I do. It could never appreciate you or love or need you the way I do. Be careful, Larane. This organism sounds more like a cult to me. I mean, if you have to give yourself up like that. Surrender yourself. Let yourself be defeated. Do you know how many people out there only want to tell you just what you want to hear just to use you? Who only want to spread dirty lies about others. To use you for their gain. To separate you from others. To manipulate you for their own needs in some smarmy way. To absorb you into themselves. Do you know how many? Most of them. Lots of them. Lots and lots of them. So how can you trust this Orb? How can you trust The Gump?"

"I just know, that's all. I know by the warm, comforting feeling inside they give me - just knowing that they're out there and that they care for me gives me peace. And I want to join that peace and be a part of it and have it as a part of me. They make me feel good. They make me feel good about myself."

"They're just telling you what you want to hear. Complimenting you and then trying to separate you from others, from yourself. . . Yeah, that Gump thing, if he exists at all, sounds about as reliable as a puddle of stewed prunes."

"You don't need to lie to me to try and get me to stay. I don't like liars and it only makes you look bad. Lying will only push me further away from you. . . Besides, we never really meshed anyway. You're not missing a thing with me leaving. In time you will find someone else who compliments you and listens to you and makes you feel good about things. And it's not a cult. I'm giving myself up to it for a chance to join a more pure existence of comfort and acceptance."

"I'm missing you. I'm already missing your company, your support."

"That's nice to hear. I appreciate your honesty, but you were never a good fit for me anyway. Remember that time I was watching the neighbor kids and I asked you to teach them about monkeys and you thought I said 'money' and took them to that pool hall to hustle pool . . ."

"Simple economics, honey," I smirk, remembering that Dawn, the youngest, skinned a hobo for twelve dollars and treated the rest of us to ice cream.

"Jackie Davison!"

"You just need to get out there, Chucky. Throw yourself out there and join the world. Get out there and meet some new people. Give yourself a fresh perspective. . ."

"But I don't function well in large groups. . . . Or in groups."

"Sure you can. . ."

"We're so close. So close to growing together. Why the Gump? Why now?"

"Well, I don't rightly know. I guess, eventually, well, the way I figure it, eventually you gotta believe in something. . . . I have to go now. I feel The Orb calling me. I feel The Gump calling out to me, I feel its heartbeat in the wind, in the ground. There are negative forces out there, negative attitudes, defeatism, bad vibes that must be fought and kept in check. I feel the entities I mentioned need my help, my strength, my honor and integrity to help stop the negative advancement, help absorb them like a sponge, opportunities to broaden, freedoms to win. There is this negative force out there called 'The Goo.' The Gump is looking to build up mass in order to reduce the influence of The Goo. The Gump has fought it for years, but eventually had to retreat. And now it is my time. Mine and others. To join The Gump and make it stronger. Besides, I'm tired of this life, of always having to comb my hair and shave my legs. I mean, it's friggin' endless. I'm throwing it all in. I'm letting go, leaving for a better place. A place of peace and togetherness. A more restful place. A softer place of purpose and direction. Off to combat The Goo. Off to persuade a large, potato-like mass known as 'The Lump' and a stringy thing known as 'Hinkey-dinkey' to come and join us. To absorb all the negativity and churn it into a butter-like liquid to use to eventually process into things that will help feed, clothe, and educate the disadvantaged."

And just then, in trying to process the events of the last few moments, it finally came to me. I finally realized that my problem in the past had been that I never said, 'please don't go' to anyone. That must be it, the magic words to prevent the unpreventable. I think in the past I probably just stood there and pouted as they left - just stood there so angry at life that I stubbornly refused to move or take any action at all, too mad to do anything. I had *refused* to do anything, as if in a state of protest. Man, that was so stupid of me, to play it cool like that, to get mad, to let my emotions get the better of me. I mean, if you have the rug pulled out from under you a couple of times you might think 'why even bother trying anymore.' You too might lose confidence in your ability to hold something close to you, or lose faith in life itself. And now, in realizing all of this, it just makes me so sad. Sad and lost and empty, knowing that it is helpless, that another really great something who made my life richer and more interesting and fun and easy and safe and filled is slipping away from me again. Again.

My mouth moves several times, until finally I utter, "Please don't go," in just an exhale of a whisper to myself, as if trying out the idea of actually *doing* something. "Please don't go," I practice, looking to see if the very air itself would somehow spoil the words, would somehow ruin my chance at affecting some measure of change.

"What's that, Chuckie . . .?" she began, "You know . . . I just . . ."

"Pleasedon'tgo," I spit, pronouncing it as one single word, interrupting her again.

"It's too late for that now, you see I can feel myself already melting away."

"But you're still right here."

"I know, but inside I can feel myself leaving, turning to mist."

"You look the same."

"I won't for long. Once The Gump digests you, well, then you're The Gump."

"Please don't go," I sigh, "I need you here in my life."

"You're not listening to me."

"Yes, I am."

"When you give advice, I think that you're not listening, only that you're meddling. You see, I just need some 'me' time, I guess. Some alone time. Some time away from it all. Like a few decades. . . . And you need to learn how to live without . . ."

"Please don't go," I mouth. She claims that I don't know what I'm missing, but believe me, I already know what I'm missing.

"It's all up to me now. This is what I feel I must do. . . . I have to go now. I feel them calling to me. . . . I'll see ya around." And with that she reaches around herself and flips up the back of her ant suit machine, throws her arms into the machine's arm sleeve things, drops down on all eights, and scuttles off, joining another group of ants in the corner and mixing in until I can't recognize which one is her anymore.

I don't know if any of what she told me will turn out to be true or not, but I can tell you this - I sure miss her. Now more than ever. Now that she's truly gone. And that's truth enough for me - heavy, painful, and stinging.

This entire episode has only hardened my opinion that I've been spending way too much time preoccupied with the frivolous and unmeaningful - light bulbs and shoelaces, and not enough time on meeting new and interesting people, making new connections with others, so many people just coming and going in life, too many of them lost to the mists and shadows of time. I mean, I should join a bowling league or a chess club or something. This entire episode has only heightened my fear that I really don't understand this life at all. It's all just a vast mystery. And all too slippery and elusive for me to grasp.

"Marvelous Marvin Hennigan! . . . Marv! . . . Marv Hennigan!" A glorious, celebratory bleat from beyond. Not sad. Not this one. This one is happy. A happy celebration of a long lost someone.

And I look down in defeat and close my eyes and whisper, "Larane," to fate. . . I guess I haven't yet gained the strength to cry out.

BIG HEAD

My wife looks over to me. Startled, she gestures her knife in my direction, "Honey, your head is growing," she squeals in surprise.

"What?" I say, lowering my fork.

"Look! Just look at yourself!" she gasps, cupping a hand over her mouth.

"Yeah, Dad, your head's bigger," my daughter leans inquisitively. "Does it hurt?"

"What? I . . I don't know," I gently place my silverware down onto my plate and slowly raise my hands to my face, touching my head - the top and sides and back. "Really?" I feel around. "I can't feel anything."

"Yep, that melon a yers is a swellin'. No doubt about it," my daughter studies me, her eyes narrow. She continues chewing.

"Do you feel alright?" my wife looks concerned.

"I think so," I respond, still touching my head, trying to gauge its size.

"Maybe we should leave," she whispers.

"Our food just got here," I shrug, nodding down to my plate.

"Yeah, Mom, I'm starved," my daughter swallows, her eyes not leaving my head.

"But your cranium," she furrows her brow.

"It's really getting bigger," my daughter squeals.

"It is honey. Oh my, it's really growing. Swelling," my wife frowns.

"It's gross, Dad," my daughter continues staring at me, then she looks over to her mother. "Let's get outta here." Then she looks back to me. "Before someone I know sees."

I continue patting my gourd. I want to stay at the restaurant. My wife and I are worried about our daughter. We're concerned about her eating habits. We suspect she hasn't been eating. Or sleeping enough. Or maybe she's sleeping too much. We don't know. We just suspect something. We don't know if this is a phase that she'll grow out of or something deeper. They say if your kids aren't eating, it may be a problem with their parents that is manifesting itself within the children. Maybe she senses something in our marriage, something missing, something wrong in our relationship. Maybe she is being affected negatively by something, some outside influence. Me and my wife keep graphs, and scales, and we chart everything we can think of, her movements, her company, her habits, we take turns following her around, hire a detective, things like that.

"Oh," I say, feeling around. "Oh my, this could be bigger," I stand up. "I better get to a mirror, check this thing out." I turn and walk briskly through the crowded restaurant, holding my head, trying to squeeze it back down. I move swiftly. Luckily no one notices. I quick-step down the hall to the bathroom, holding my head, pushing it in my palms, rushing to a mirror, any mirror. I bull my way into the men's room and stagger up to the sinks and look up.

They were right.

My head is bigger.

Quite a bit bigger.

Maybe if you didn't know me you wouldn't really notice right off, but this thing is becoming quite a melon. It looks all puffy and inflated. It is definitely bigger than most heads, getting out of proportion with my shoulders and the rest of my body - getting out of proportion with society. This is unacceptable. This surely won't do. To be different. So different. So cruelly, cruelly different.

Is it something I ate? Something in the potatoes maybe? Radon? Is it radon gases leaching in through the floor slab of the basement, its invisible stink poisoning my genes against myself?

Why me? I begin gasping. This couldn't be happening, not to me. I just made "Associate" at the firm. Finally, after years of sucking up, I had a title, a coveted little title.

I have to stay calm. Calm for myself. Calm for my family. I'm sure it's nothing, just a touch of the flu or something, just a reaction to something in the food. "Oh no," I utter under my breath, leaning in close to the mirror. "No. No. No," I rub my head with both hands. "Not me. Not here. Not now." I spin and dash out. "I've got a big meeting tomorrow."

I tell the matron to get my family, tell them to meet me out front. I run to the car.

On the way home I have to hold my noggin out the window. By this time it simply won't fit inside comfortably while I drive.

"Oh, gross, Dad. Groatie groatie groatie," my girl shrieks, looking away. "It's ballooning, Dad. It's ballooning."

Once in the garage, I run straight to our bedroom. The largest mirror in the house is in our bedroom above my wife's bureau. I huff out-of-breath, crouching to fit my face in the mirror. "Oh, man, it's bigger. It's bigger," I whisper. "What am I gonna do?" My head is enormous by this time - as big as a large t.v. —monstrously distorted mouth, gigantic ears, big googilly eyes, all flopping wearily on my shoulders, bogging me down.

"What should we do?" I turn to my wife as she runs for the door.

She stops and clutches the jambs with both hands to steady herself, then she catches a look at me. She just stands there trembling and shaking her head. Then she brings her hands up to cover her mouth again. Her knees weaken.

My daughter catches up to us. "Oh, my God, Daddy," she stomps her foot. "Come on Daddy, get outside. Get outside. Before it's too late," she waves.

I try to move, but my head is just so gosh darn big and heavy now. It totters monstrously on my now puny shoulders - teetering me this way and then rolling back again that way as I stagger to balance under its weight - staggering to the door, stepping forward and back, side to side, trying to even out and distribute the load, desperate to balance the crushing weight on my shoulders. "Oooohhh," I steady myself, watching my head growing in the mirror. I simply can not look away - a giant, comical pompadour forming, my knees buckling.

My wife screams as my head begins to crack the plaster of the ceiling. Stunned, she staggers back a step or two.

"Ow," I complain, my now stubby arms reaching up to try and rub my fantastic head. "That hurts." But I only reach the sides of my puffy, inflating cheeks.

"Come 'ere, Daddy," my daughter holds out her arms from the hall. "We've gotta get you out of here," she huffs out of breath from the panic. "Let's get you outside," she bends at the knees and claps her hands as if calling an unintelligent puppy. She drops to her knees and slaps the floor with her palms.

I lower myself to crawl out, but my neck gives out, flopping like a limp noodle, slamming my head into the wall next to the door. The momentum of my big, goofy head thrusts me forward, my head bounces off the wall and flops to slam on the floor. "Ow." I push with all my might, bulldozing my big head to the door.

"Come on Daddy, come on," my daughter slaps the floor in encouragement. "You can make it!"

But by the time I get there it is simply too late. I am out of breath and can't squeeze through. All I can see is floor. Just carpet. "Get a doctor," I wheeze, "Get a doctor," I pant, flailing my arms as if trying to swim my way out the door.

My daughter turns and runs. I don't think she's running for the phone. It feels more like she's escaping in terror, abandoning me here like this. My wife just stands there hopelessly. Out of the corner of my eyes I can just make out the bottom of her quivering legs.

They must've been out in the driveway waiting for the ambulance. Surely they heard my screams as my head began working its way through the siding, creaking and bulging like a baby bird cracking to split through its egg shell.

AT THE SHOE STORE

She's been in before. She's young, like him. She lounges comfortably sideways on a chair and gazing in the other direction, as if she has no bones, just spread out there as comfortable as can be, as if sitting is easy for her, as if just 'being' is her natural talent and one true gift to the whole entirety of existence, as if the best, most casual sitter in recorded memory. She wears the same black gown, long evening gloves, curls flowing from an avalanche of long black hair. Very noticeable - simple, yet elegant. But nothing is ever good enough for her.

"You wanna see something really good, huh?" The young proprietor exhales in exasperation. "Well how 'bout this, this good enough for ya?" In last-straw frustration he pulls off one of his pinkies with a loud "snap" and raises it to his mouth and begins to play it like a flute: "Twee tweedily-deet tweedily-dee diddliy deet paw-weeeeee."

"Yeah, that's cute," she shrugs unamused and looks about as he snaps his pinky back on with a muffled "pop."

"Oh, I suppose you could do better?" he says as his ears blow out a thick stream of large bubbles that smell of lilac.

"Yeah, well smell this," she turns and unzips a tiny zipper in her back which reveals a pale violet sky of dazzling luminous pink clouds.

"Not bad, but try this on for size," he offers as he unscrews his arm, lets it dangle nonchalantly in his other hand braggingly for a dramatic moment, twirls it like a majorette with a baton, then raises it to his lips and blows into it, trumpeting an apocalyptic thunder: "Bumbpa Bumpa-ba-bump-buda-pum."

"Well done," she smirks a slight smile, mildly impressed. "But try this." Slowly she opens her mouth - wide as a mid-sized, yet affordable car. It produces a funny stretching sound, like a swelling balloon. And suddenly a herd of cat-sized elephants roars out, diving to the carpet in a great gray fleshy stream, hitting the red carpet on stride and stampeding wildly into the back room.

His head follows the little thundering herd as the elephants kick up a long cloud of dust, finally curling around to disappear into the storage room. "Nobody's 'sposed to go back there you know," he says as his thin head strains on his pencil neck.

She just stares at him impatiently.

He looks back at her and thinks for a second. "Hhmmm, well put this in your pipe and smoke it," he loosens his belt and squats, lowering his felt pants just slightly, not enough to be lascivious in any manner, but enough to gain sufficient access. He squints his eyes, furrows his brow, and forces a ridiculously long, thin, purple balloon out of his behind and onto the floor. It curls up at the end as it makes its way 30 feet across the carpet, finally curls to form a fifteen-foot-tall circus balloon rabbit. He looks behind and watches, finally pinching it off with his razor sharp sphincter. "Whew," he wipes his brow in exertion as he rises to lift his trousers, which look as if they were from another era and didn't belong here at all.

His pants give her a momentary discomfort, her ears turning into tiny dancers that jig on each of her shoulders.

Pretty impressive, he thinks.

"O.k., I've got to get going," she exhales, "I guess I'll just take the black pumps," she shrugs in disappointment, weakly pointing at several boxes on the floor. The dancers hop back onto the sides of her head, returning to the form of her ears once more.

Later, on his break, he sits alone in the back room, drinking his formaldehyde and thinking about her—thinking and thinking and concentrating—desperately trying to draw her back.

THE EGG

I roll over in the morning to find a giant egg next to my bed. The egg is fantastically huge — the size of a small car, but clearly and unmistakably an egg.

After a while I hear a small peeping and fluttering at the window. The shades are drawn, and I just lie there. Eventually the little bird at the window begins pecking at the window pane, as if knocking, as if trying to get in, as if the large egg belongs to him.

I really didn't know what to do. My life to this point has not prepared me for such an event. Should I touch it? I don't think I could roll that thing out the door. I'm not sure it would fit. And it looks *very* heavy. Maybe I'll just leave it there and wait for now. It appeared out of nowhere, maybe it'll disappear on its own as well. More fluttering and scratching against the window - the little bird trying to get in. I roll back over and close my eyes and yawn. The way I figure it, these kinds of things have a way of working themselves out. I mean, these types of things happen to everyone from time to time. Don't they?

I forget about the giant egg until later that morning when I walk out my door, off to start my day. That's when I notice, across the narrow street, the giant egg resting on top of the neighbor's front stoop. The egg is still the size of a small car. It's just teetering there on the top of the steps. I stop to watch in curious wonder. And just then that egg slowly rolls to tumble down the stairs and onto the sidewalk, then into the street, gaining momentum. The rolling sound is tremendous—like a bowling ball on the wood floor of a long hallway. I watch helplessly as the egg rolls down into the street, its speed building, the thunder of its roll growing.

The great egg crosses the street and slams into a brownstone right in front of me and cracks open like a twisted car wreck. It just crumples and splits down the middle, just the way you'd expect a giant egg to crack open.

I'm stunned. All I can do is just stand there frozen and watch as an old lady leaps from the wreck and staggers up the street.

And I'll tell you, it is a heartbreaking sight.

THE STENCH

I come home, step inside, set my briefcase on the floor, lift off my hat, draw in a breath—and that's when it hits me. Wwwoooooffff. I draw in a stinging, mossy smell I have never before encountered. It is a thick, pungent, stagnant lake, sweaty gorilla kind of tangy, swirling fog of rotting vegetables stench. "Whoa, boy," I cough. "What in the name of Mother Goose is that?" I gag.

My wife steps from the hall and gestures in a neighborly manner, as if to present a new guest. She puts her other finger up to her mouth in the international "Ssssshhhh" symbol. She is wearing some type of inhaler mask - something she must've gotten from a storage locker out in the garage—from when the painters were here—some type of yellow, cheap, strap-on, plastic de-stenching device. I shrug and hold up my palms in the "What gives?" pose. She points, poking her hand at the couch and furrows her brow at me.

I turn my head to where she's pointing. Sitting there on our couch watching t.v. is a great big hairy beast. He is huge - eight feet tall at least. His thick, shaggy brown hair is matted and snarled. And the stink. Worst stench ever. A crippling fog. "Oh, man," I mouth, bending at the knees dramatically.

"Where did *that* come from?" I cover my nose with my hand.

My wife shrugs, "Just wandered into the house. I think it was warm," her voice is muffled behind the breathing apparatus. "You know how hot it's been." Her voice is a strange whistling wheeze.

The beast turns its big shaggy brown head to look at me.

Whatever it is, it's an ugly mother, that's for sure. I stand and nod to it in a friendly greeting, then tilt my head to look at it one way, and then another. I step forward, hang my hat on the top of the coat rack without looking, and step across the living room and sit down on the couch, settling in next to the brown, raggy beast. I look him over. Gnats buzz about him. He holds a glass of water on his leg. At first glance, in proportion to him, it looks like a glass of water, but it's actually an entire plastic pitcher of water.

I nod and smile. The beast gazes down on me blankly, then turns his head back to the t.v. before us. A wilderness movie is showing - forests and mountains and streams and meadows and bears and everything, just as this area used to be before we rode the glaciating wave of sprawl out to cover it all.

After a while I nod. "Yeah," I exhale heavily. "It's been hot." But the beast doesn't say anything, doesn't even move. "Really hot."

Later in bed, my wife and I argue quietly. "We can't let 'im stay here," I whisper from behind my plastic breathing mask. "We can't live like this." My whisper is nothing more than a thin, distant, tinny muffle. Even though it was lying on the cool cool concrete floor of the basement laundry room, in the crisp coolness of air conditioning, I could still taste its sharp, stinging odor. We even put pillows up against the duct grills along the floor so as to not have the air conditioning draw up its crippling soupy fog of stench.

"Maybe we could cut its hair, give it a bath, hose it down?" my wife whispers from the breathing mechanism. "Soap it up?"

After a while, I just can't take it anymore. "I'll get the scissors," I roll over and drop my feet to the floor.

"Yep," my wife rolls out of bed too. "There's gotta be a solution to every problem," she shakes her head, the mask shaking in the darkness. "There's just gotta be."

We creep downstairs, tiptoeing, slowly peeking around the corner of the paneling. But it is gone. The beast has left. I step out from around the corner.

I feel weird now, disappointed. Sad. Sad that I have let it down—that I was given this chance, an opportunity to contribute and help someone out, and here I let it slip right through my fingers. Here I let it down.

I look around. The basement seems so very empty now. So lonely and ashamed in its emptiness.

My wife stands behind me. "Well, it's much cooler out now," she sighs, holding the big scissors.

And I picture him now, prowling the neighborhood, lurching down the empty streets, lurking in the shadows, heavy gaited, hunched, dragging itself in a sideways lope, thick matted hair, looking for an open door or window, looking for a nice, friendly couple. Looking for *nice* people, for *better* people. For people not like us.

I turn to my wife. "Honey, let's have children," I exhale and nod desperately, "Lots and lots of children."

AS I TUMBLE SOFTLY THROUGH THE SKY

I found myself in an old rowboat floating through the sky. I have no idea how I got here like this. I mean, how do you explain or interpret the unexplainable? I'm just here, in this soft floating dream machine.

The sky is an endless rolling expanse of cotton, streams of puffy clouds, waving strands, baby blue breeze and fresh air.

I see another old rowboat approaching through the strands of wiggling smoky mist. A man is sitting in it. He is wearing a brown suit and a tie. He is reading the newspaper and wearing a monocle. "Hey! . . Hey!" I call, waving an arm to signal him. "Hey, over here!" My voice echoes as if in a gymnasium. The man looks over. "I'm on my way to work," he says flatly, as if he did this everyday and didn't want to be bothered.

Another man drifts into view from out of the mist. He's wearing a baseball uniform. Several dots appear in the hazy distance. And then more dots beyond those. There seems to be more old boats in the fog of clouds, some gliding above me, others below.

Some of them get quite close as they sail on by. One has a mother with her son sitting next to her. Another has a cheerleader. One has a tiger. Another a policewoman who looks as if she needs a hug; another a mailman who needs reassurance. These are the people who populate our lives.

Now more rowboats, many in disrepair, in various states of decay, some with large holes and planks missing, some all but falling apart—a student who needs a compliment; a trumpet player who needs a breath mint; an out-of-work dentist; a lonely lawyer/lumber jack; a girl with a violin in her lap (she isn't playing it); a workman with a sledge hammer in his lap; a teenager who is actually laboring to pry his boat apart board by board; the man in the suit again; a gymnast doing a hand stand; a man sitting still, his head tilted back, looking straight up with a lighted grill balancing on his chin; a woman standing, balancing a large t.v. on her head; people balancing things; sudden iconography; these are the people in our lives.

"*Where am I going*?!!" I call in distress to the man in the suit as he sinks away. I am distraught. I wave my arms. After a brief pause, the man turns and lets his paper flop down into his lap. He drifts further away. He is watching me with a sad look on his face. He sighs as if the answer couldn't be found in the newspaper. "I don't know," he reports dryly, calmly turning back to his newspaper as boards begin to drop from above.

SOMETHING, ANYTHING

"A big mitt," an intense little man insisted as he stood before my desk. I didn't even hear him come in. But there he was. Slowly I raised my head from the worn science fiction paperback resting on my elevated knee. He held up his hand. And my eyes met his hand in perfect timing as each were lifted. He stretched his arm across the old desk and put it right up into my face. He held it there for a dramatic moment. "A big mitt," he whispered as he withdrew his stubby little arm.

I looked him over for a second. I looked him up and down, or what I could see of him from behind the desk. I looked him in the face. Then I reeled my arm around, out of the big center drawer, out from beneath the desk, swung my legs down off the desk, sat up, and reached my arm across the top to tap him on the chest with an old clipboard.

"This," I tapped a hollow tap against his stocky front. "Fill it out," I whispered in equal drama. Then I tilted my head secretively to the mismatched collection of folding chairs in the corner.

The fading walls blinked from the neon sign outside in the dark drizzle. The timid multi-colors were worn and stained. They peeled fingernails of paint-like skin, shedding as if to hope to blossom into something different, something new, into something, into anything. It was as if the walls were trying to peel off their past lives. You could tell they'd tried over the years to cover them up, here and there, but each wall's soul tended to shine through the cracks, their true selves fighting their way out of the muted hues as I sat late at night with that room's souls peeking through at me and those lonely lost souls that wander in here, somehow finding their way to me in the middle of deep dark dripping nights to scribble and scratch and peck onto the army surplus clipboards, pouring out their dreams, searching to be something other than what they were.

Dreaming.

Flipping the cable access channels as perfect bodies and perfect lives flash across the faded walls of their lives deep in the night with that big old channel clicker, searching for our cleverly hidden commercials on dead-of-night channels few late night people would ever find. I'm still amazed at how we pull 'em in, at how we manage to somehow reach out through time to these desperate people, as if contacting them by some secret code. They find these obscure, secret channels and somehow manage to stumble across those invisible personal ads in over-the-counter magazines wrapped in crinkly brown bags, sold by ragged old men who limp with wounds that they lie about how they got in the war. Brown paper bag lives. They bag 'em up and dump 'em in my lap up here in this obscure office up in the corner of the night, and I get paid for it. But me, I guess I'd rather be drunk in front of the t.v. myself sometimes. It ain't a bad life though. It ain't a bad life at all, I guess, being a receptionist for the doctor.

He was set up in a big hospital out east, but got himself disbarred and ended up here. It was a great idea. Ingenious even. The seeds were already planted in each of them by our advertising culture, planted by you and me, on playgrounds and on school busses. Yeah, the seeds were already there. They just needed somebody to come along and water them, for someone to come along and activate 'em. The fish were already lined up, just waitin' to jump in the boat.

The small guy in front of me was a tight, fidgety ball of flesh and energy. A dense fist bursting at the seams with some dripping past molding his stocky frame as if the giant hands of fate were clinched tightly around him, gripping him in a constrained, throbbing life creeping around just inside of his own. Yeah, I see guys like this all the time. Somehow they seem to find their way in here, in the deep pit of night, and I tend to them. It's my job.

"A big mitt," he whispered, looking at his hand as he turned to find a chair.

Hoping.

The room sweated its pearls of shame as I thought about what had been here before the doctor moved in. Hhmmm, maybe a sleazy lawyer or some telemarketing real-estate scam held up by old card tables, cardboard boxes, and post office boxes. They set 'em up and they take 'em down, folding and unfolding. Yeah, we get all kinds of those cardboard lives in here too. The doctor has his people cast the nets and they hop right in. At first it was the usuals—all the ones you'd expect—housewives who want big breasts and receptionists who want little noses. Then men who want big calves and small butts and more hair in some places and less in others. Men who want clefts in their chins and men who want their clefts removed. All shapes and sizes of stuff. Aw, you know what I'm talking about.

Fill this out and get in line.

Yeah, I've seen 'em all.

And it's been nice, I must admit. To get to help people. Really help them. Especially with really deep dark difficult problems that no one else would be willing to touch or reach, or that they'd be too embarrassed to admit to others. It's been really touching to see their faces when they walk out, strutting proud and clean and pure, as if reborn, as if heavy weights had been removed. It's really touching to see their dreams finally realized. You could feel the years of shame lifted from their shoulders. They come from out of the long, dim hallway, walking lighter, breathing brighter, standing taller, with a new expression of relief on their faces. And the doctor does good work. He wasn't all about the money, but of changing—changing lives. So word began to seep out.

I tell ya, it started slow, but after a while they began to trickle in. You've got to find a market and specialize, I guess. By the look of them I'm sure it had as much to do with the places the doctor could afford to advertise, like that midnight lawyer, whispering in your ear, whispering promises of a better life (Hell, I just answered an obscure ad for night counter help. Seemed like an easy gig, a good way to avoid the hustle and bustle of all that daytime crap). Maybe it was the neighborhood - the obscure old brick warehouse, the multiple years of paint overlapping one another, the institutional gray metal receptionist desk, the wobbly mix of wooden and metal waiting chairs. A curious assortment that breathed "not authorized by the state" to me when I answered the ad. It wasn't these surroundings so much that drew me in as much as it was the crude sign on the wall

— "I can not do anything internal—only cosmetic." But boy was he wrong. Man, did he work wonders. I don't even think he realized how much he could accomplish. He was a magic man, a wizard, a shaman.

Trying.

The little man stopped and stood in front of a chair. He looked down at the smooth, creamy tile floor. Then he looked at the chair and sat down. "A big mitt," he mouthed as he began scribbling. I guess in his brief hesitation he was just mulling over his decision. I see a lot of that in here.

It's been O.K.. I sign for boxes and answer the phone, order stuff, make appointments, keep records, take out the garbage, never look in the plastic garbage bags. Never.

And you might think I'd be tempted to go in there myself, after working here for a while. And maybe I am just a little. And so would you be, believe me. The doctor does some fine fine work. Anyone would be tempted, watching these suppressed dreams rise to the surface. You go see the shame lifted and then you tell me. You come in and see their faces. You'd be tempted too - maybe a new nose, new muscles, a new life.

Yes, I was a little tempted at first; I must admit it. But then we started getting them in. You would be surprised at the profound effect this parade would have on you. Night after night. I've got a friend who works in an emergency room, and you'd be surprised at the wrecks they get in. So you know where I'm coming from, being right here in the front row to watch that tight grip of fate loosened, prying away, wrestling those big hands of fate.

We live in a big city, and it hides its unique people pretty well. Somehow they have their own underground, their own vibe. I can feel it. It's not really something that you talk about, or ask for, but they do travel, sending themselves through those unheard of publications and invisible late night channels. You can tap into it.

And you know, I don't see it as a matter of aesthetics. I really don't. You may on the surface at first, but it's deeper than that. It's about freedom really—the freedom to control your own destiny, about shaking off past expectations and constraints—emotional, physical, psychological, whatever. It's also a matter of prosthetics. That's how I see it. It's a matter of evolution. The next stage. Natural evolution. Searching out. Reaching. An extension of yourself—trying to grow, evolve out of your own skin, your own possibilities—stretching it, tugging at your limitations, trying to unravel that invisible cocoon that you were born into, trying to crawl out of yourself. Someday everyone will go into places like this, like going to the barber. You'll see. Maybe you'll be one of the first. Maybe one day I'll see you in here, standing in line, looking away from me in shame.

I mean we all use prosthetics, augmenting what we have - wearing sunglasses, reading glasses, hair pieces, hearing aids. Each of us. We all reach out, stretch ourselves farther and farther to grab onto the future and give it that one good tug to try and pull it closer to ourselves, to reach out of our own constraints, reaching to grab the future and choke it. We use pencils and hammers and screwdrivers and telephones and answering machines and clickers to help flip the channels late at night so we don't have to get up, each of us searching, leaving our sweating jobs and homes and lives and names and identities and expectations, drifting into the darkness, creeping into the darkness like bats.

More or less of this or that, hiring a lawyer, hopping in a car—it's all prosthetics, man. We want to reach and extend, control time, wrestling fate, fight hidden inner demons, fight our own limitations. We heed those late night whispers drifting in the darkness from the magazines and televisions. Who utters these secrets? Who wants you to do this and think that? Who's controlling you, what you think, what you want? Those whispers seep out of who knows where and peek at you, they stare at you from some unknowable darkness, tap you on the shoulder, reach out to poke you. They call out to you. They call you out.

No one would be able to trace them back to those staggering behemoths, those pharmaceutical or cosmetic bats, lumbering out there, whispering to you, getting a grip on you, trying to remote control your life. Believe me, I know. I've seen it first hand - up close and personal. And it ain't pretty. Ho no. It took me a long time to realize that, a long time to own up to it. I can hook you up to your deepest, hidden, creeping desires. I can free you from them. I can loosen their grip on you. For I know that hidden late night vibe. In living in the late of night for so long, I can now see into the shadows, into cracks and crevices that you wouldn't even know were there. Butcher shop. Get in line. Maybe we all just want to be other people for a while. Those whispers open you up. I hear it all night long in the breeze of the alley just outside the window. I hear it all night long because I live inside of it now. And so do you, you just don't realize it yet.

"I want a longer tongue."

"I'd really dig another arm. One that comes out from just under my left one."

"I need some really long arms. . . And I mean *really* long ones. Like a half dozen on each side of my body." ("Sleeve" was the name on the application).

"I always thought one really huge breast would be really nice. One big melon, right in the middle of my chest. I could wear a knapsack around my front to support it. Oh, and I'd like it nippleless, please. Maybe shave a spot on top of my head and put it up there. That way I could comb my hair over the top of it when I want to hide it from strangers."

"Can you make it so I can secrete a toxic venom?"

"Can you fix it so that I can see in the dark?"

"I'd like my ass crack completely removed." They stand before me, fidgeting with hope, wringing their hands. "No, wait. Wait. On second thought, I guess I'd like my ass crack lengthened. Run 'er all the way up my back. Up and around my neck if you can, please."

"Can do" and "No problemo," I chirp and shrug as I hand out the clipboards.

"Please make it so my face is really really tight," she says standing before the desk with her hands on her cheeks, pulling, stretching her skin back skeletally to her ears.

"A dick. . . . Another dick. . . . I'd like another dick."

"I need more eyes. . . Maybe some in the back of my head. . . A couple at least. . . That possible?"

"I'd like a large set of bat wings affixed to me, so I can fly."

"Fingers. . . I need more fingers," a tall skinny freckled gentleman exhales in a low grown of a voice. "Run 'em up my arms. . . . Let 'em wiggle."

Perhaps it's just the next logical step in our evolution—custom bodies.

I call the doctor's connections and they deliver the goods—the spare parts. I don't know who they are or where they get them. I don't ask. I don't even want to know. Some guys in lab coats show up holding coolers and I sign 'em in. And they take 'em down the hall to the back room. And that's all I want to know.

Believing.

I heard a door gently close down the hallway. Then the soft footsteps on the stained tile floor. Slowly the little man shuffled from the birthing cannel-like hall. He emerged from the darkness, gradually growing into the light of the lobby. He appeared from the womb and was reborn. He still seemed like a tight little knot of a person, somehow getting squished by a far off voice, squeezing him in its vice. But he was different. That's for sure. You could sense it somehow. He walked a little slower, stepping carefully, deliberately, as if taking it all in. He walked lighter, almost with a slight bounce in his step. There was also a new sort of calmness about him, a sense of relief, as if he was ready to get out there and tackle some unseen demon, as if he was ready to wrestle fate, to break its grip, to take it on in a fair fight for once.

Suddenly there was a glow about him, a shine that you could feel, as he gradually began to realize that this wasn't all just some kind of dream, as he slowly took it all in, realizing that he was indeed a changed person.

A skinny lady in the corner stopped scribbling and looked up as he shuffled. He was different. He was a new man. "Looking good," the lady whispered and winked and gave him a thumbs up.

You see, much of the time they have that look about them—that new look like they've just won the lottery, but are also sort of cautious about it all, as if still woozy from the anesthetic, as if they don't quite believe it just yet, as if they fear it might all just wear off in time.

And there you are, just sitting around and thinking it's not possible. But it is. And there you are, believing it's not our place. But it is. It's in our nature to tinker with things, to try and adjust it all to our liking. There you are, convinced that it's running against fate's fickle will, running contrary to the cards we were dealt, to how fate wanted it to be, but you'd be mistaken. I mean, why stop at wearing reading glasses or taking aspirin? Why stop wearing clothing? Why stop adjusting and augmenting? Why not really reach out for it all, really go for it, go the distance, be brave and fight what we are all constrained by—ourselves. Why not reshuffle those cards you were dealt and change what is changeable. Why not mold and remold until we achieve our own versions of contentment? Why sit back and be passive? Why not take action against it all? Why not bully back? Why not strive for the best? Why not fight through what we are?

The little man stopped to nod politely to the thin lady, then he took a step forward, turning to nod in gratitude to me as he slowly sauntered by, proud as can be, a restrained joy bursting within him. I stared impolitely at him as he sort of casually half-waved with his massive hand, this really big super huge massive slab of a big giant hand. It glided out the door as big as your head, as big as your life, but bigger.

His stocky steps faded, gently bouncing against the back stair and off the walls to snap back to me, echoing down the hall as the door slowly closed. I swiveled my chair around and looked out the window, down to the corner where the back door met the alley and then the street. The drizzle formed a vague dark mist of night. Eventually he stepped into view and scurried under the hard light of the street lamp, swinging his big, heavy mitt at his side. He hopped up on the curb and stopped at the corner, his breath leaking out from behind his back in a fog. It popped like a series of bubbles in the cold air as he puffed. He faced the night, facing his new future, staring down his destiny, opening that book of time with the shadow of that mitt the size of his head.

He fumbled with his drab jacket. I figured he was buttoning it, as if he was having trouble with it. His hump of a back was to me, obscuring my view from above. Maybe it was the cold affecting his grip, or maybe he was adjusting to his new big paw, getting used to it, the new proportions, the new size and shape, the new feel, the newness of it all. But he was opening that book - that new book of fate, and instead of bombast, only a wide expanse of silence drew in a breath.

He pulled something out of his jacket. He flapped it like a large hanky to unfold it as he stepped off the curb. He started from the street lamp and into the drizzly darkness. It was a big glove, a bit mitt. A huge glove, like a flag of victory. He held up his hand, and then extended it out to the world as if to show fate he was about to take it on one-on-one, to wrestle it, pry that grip away, fill those big shoes that had clomped and echoed in his mind for years, big shoes to fill, no more little guy. He brought that big flap of a glove up to his hand and slid that thing on, proudly wiggling that big flabby piece of meat into that mitten as he strutted into the darkness.

I suppose you're wondering what I think of all of this. And I'll tell you, because I see their faces, it's really quite simple—let 'em shine, I say, let 'em shine.

Bizarro books

CATALOGUE – SPRING 2008

Bizarro Books publishes under the following imprints:

www.rawdogscreamingpress.com

www.eraserheadpress.com

www.afterbirthbooks.com

www.swallowdownpress.com

For all your Bizarro needs visit:

WWW.BIZARROCENTRAL.COM

BIZARRO BOOKS CATALOGUE – SPRING 2008

Introduce yourselves to the bizarro genre and all of its authors with the *Bizarro Starter Kit* series. Each volume features short novels and short stories by ten of the leading bizarro authors, designed to give you a perfect sampling of the genre for only $5 plus shipping.

BB-0X1
"The Bizarro Starter Kit"
(Orange)

Featuring D. Harlan Wilson, Carlton Mellick III, Jeremy Robert Johnson, Kevin L Donihe, Gina Ranalli, Andre Duza, Vincent W. Sakowski, Steve Beard, John Edward Lawson, and Bruce Taylor.

236 pages $5

BB-0X2
"The Bizarro Starter Kit"
(Blue)

Featuring Ray Fracalossy, Jeremy C. Shipp, Jordan Krall, Mykle Hansen, Andersen Prunty, Eckhard Gerdes, Bradley Sands, Steve Aylett, Christian TeBordo, and Tony Rauch.

244 pages $5

BIZARRO BOOKS CATALOGUE – SPRING 2008

BB-001

"The Kafka Effekt"

D. Harlan Wilson

A collection of forty-four irreal short stories loosely written in the vein of Franz Kafka, with more than a pinch of William S. Burroughs sprinkled on top.

211 pages $14

BB-002

"Satan Burger"

Carlton Mellick III

The cult novel that put Mellick III on the map... Six punks get jobs at a fast food restaurant owned by the devil in a city over-populated by surreal alien cultures.

236 pages $14

BB-003

"Some Things Are Better Left Unplugged"

Vincent Sakwoski

Join The Man and his Nemesis, the obese tabby, for a nightmare roller coaster ride into this postmodern fantasy.

152 pages $10

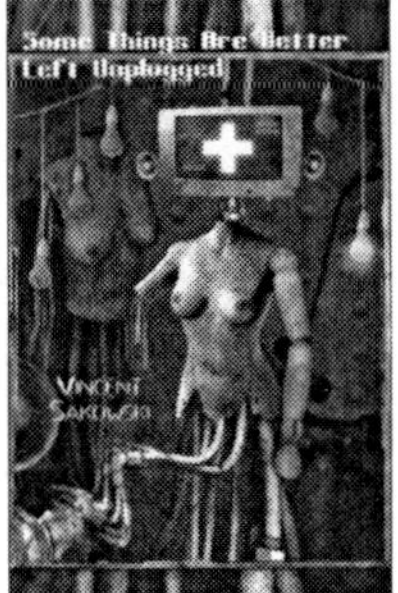

BB-004

"Shall We Gather At the Garden?"

Kevin L Donihe

Donihe's Debut novel. Midgets take over the world, The Church of Lionel Richie vs. The Church of the Byrds, plant porn and more!

244 pages $14

BB-005

"Razor Wire Pubic Hair"

Carlton Mellick III

A genderless humandildo is purchased by a razor dominatrix and brought into her nightmarish world of bizarre sex and mutilation.

176 pages $11

BB-006

"Stranger on the Loose"

D. Harlan Wilson

The fiction of Wilson's 2nd collection is planted in the soil of normalcy, but what grows out of that soil is a dark, witty, otherworldly jungle...

228 pages $14

BB-007

"The Baby Jesus Butt Plug"

Carlton Mellick III

Using clones of the Baby Jesus for anal sex will be the hip underground sex fetish of the future.

92 pages $10

BB-008

"Fishyfleshed"

Carlton Mellick III

The world of the past is an illogical flatland lacking in dimension and color, a sick-scape of crispy squid people wandering the desert for no apparent reason.

260 pages $14

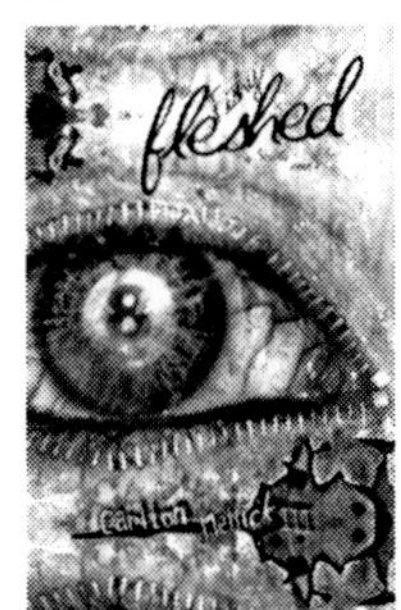

BIZARRO BOOKS CATALOGUE – SPRING 2008

BB-009
"Dead Bitch Army"
Andre Duza
Step into a world filled with racist teenagers, cannibals, 100 warped Uncle Sams, automobiles with razor-sharp teeth, living graffiti, and a pissed-off zombie bitch out for revenge.
344 pages $16

BB-010
"The Menstruating Mall"
Carlton Mellick III
"*The Breakfast Club* meets *Chopping Mall* if directed by David Lynch."
- Brian Keene
212 pages $12

BB-011
"Angel Dust Apocalypse"
Jeremy R. Johnson
Meth-heads, man-made monsters, and murderous Neo-Nazis. "Seriously amazing short stories..."
- Chuck Palahniuk, author of *Fight Club*
184 pages $11

BB-012
"Ocean of Lard"
Kevin L Donihe/ Carlton Mellick III
A parody of those old Choose Your Own Adventure kid's books about some very odd pirates sailing on a sea made of animal fat.
244 pages $14

BB-013
"Last Burn in Hell"
John Edward Lawson
From his lurid angst-affair with a lesbian music diva to his ascendance as unlikely pop icon the one constant for Kenrick Brimley, official state prison gigolo, is he's got no clue what he's doing.
165 pages $14

BB-014
"Tangerinephant"
Kevin Dole 2
TV-obsessed aliens have abducted Michael Tangerinephant in this bizarro combination of science fiction, satire, and surrealism.
212 pages $11

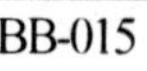

BB-015
"Foop!"
Chris Genoa
Strange happenings are going on at Dactyl, Inc, the world's first and only time travel tourism company.
"A surreal pie in the face!"
- Christopher Moore
300 pages $14

BB-016
"Spider Pie"
Alyssa Sturgill
A one-way trip down a rabbit hole inhabited by sexual deviants and friendly monsters, fairytale beginnings and hideous endings.
104 pages $11

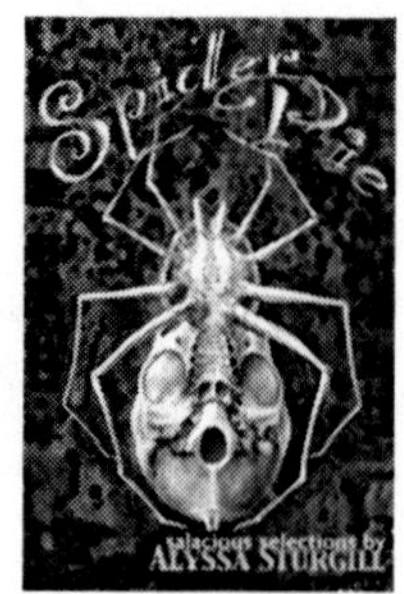

BIZARRO BOOKS CATALOGUE – SPRING 2008

BB-017
"The Unauthorized Woman"
Efrem Emerson
Enter the world of the inner freak, a landscape populated by the pre-dead and morticioners, by cockroaches and 300-lb robots.
104 pages $11

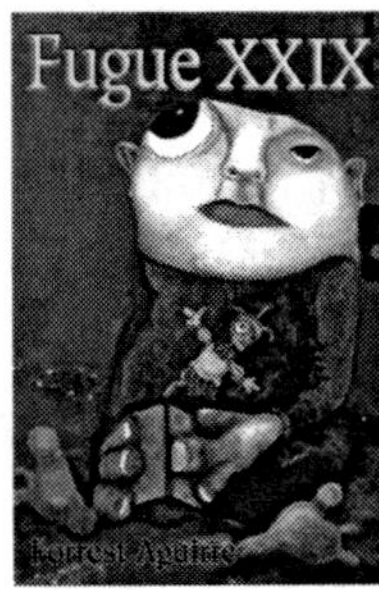

BB-018
"Fugue XXIX"
Forrest Aguirre
Tales from the fringe of speculative literary fiction where innovative minds dream up the future's uncharted territories while mining forgotten treasures of the past.
220 pages $16

BB-019
"Pocket Full of Loose Razorblades"
John Edward Lawson
A collection of dark bizarro stories. From a giant rectum to a foot-fungus factory to a girl with a biforked tongue.
190 pages $13

BB-020
"Punk Land"
Carlton Mellick III
In the punk version of Heaven, the anarchist utopia is threatened by corporate fascism and only Goblin, Mortician's sperm, and a blue-mohawked female assassin named Shark Girl can stop them.
284 pages $15

BB-021
"Pseudo-City"
D. Harlan Wilson
Pseudo-City exposes what waits in the bathroom stall, under the manhole cover and in the corporate boardroom, all in a way that can only be described as mind-bogglingly irreal.
220 pages $16

BB-022
"Kafka's Uncle and Other Strange Tales"
Bruce Taylor
Anslenot and his giant tarantula (tormentor? friend?) wander a desecrated world in this novel and collection of stories from Mr. Magic Realism Himself.
348 pages $17

BB-023
"Sex and Death In Television Town"
Carlton Mellick III
In the old west, a gang of hermaphrodite gunslingers take refuge in Telos: a town where its citizens have televisions instead of heads.
184 pages $12

BB-024
"It Came From Below The Belt"
Bradley Sands
What can Grover Goldstein do when his severed, sentient penis forces him to return to high school and help it win the presidential election?
204 pages $13

BIZARRO BOOKS CATALOGUE – SPRING 2008

BB-025
"Sick: An Anthology of Illness"
John Lawson, editor
These Sick stories are horrendous and hilarious dissections of creative minds on the scalpel's edge.
296 pages $16

BB-026
"Tempting Disaster"
John Lawson, editor
A shocking and alluring anthology from the fringe that examines our culture's obsession with taboos.
260 pages $16

BB-027
"Siren Promised"
Jeremy R. Johnson
Nominated for the Bram Stoker Award. A potent mix of bad drugs, bad dreams, brutal bad guys, and surreal/incredible art by Alan M. Clark.
190 pages $13

BB-028
"Chemical Gardens"
Gina Ranalli
Ro and punk band *Green is the Enemy* find Kreepkins, a surfer-dude warlock, a vengeful demon, and a Metal Priestess in their way as they try to escape an underground nightmare.
188 pages $13

BB-029
"Jesus Freaks"
Andre Duza
For God so loved the world that he gave his only two begotten sons... and a few million zombies.
400 pages $16

BB-030
"Grape City"
Kevin L. Donihe
More Donihe-style comedic bizarro about a demon named Charles who is forced to work a minimum wage job on Earth after Hell goes out of business.
108 pages $10

BB-031
"Sea of the Patchwork Cats"
Carlton Mellick III
A quiet dreamlike tale set in the ashes of the human race. For Mellick enthusiasts who also adore *The Twilight Zone*.
112 pages $10

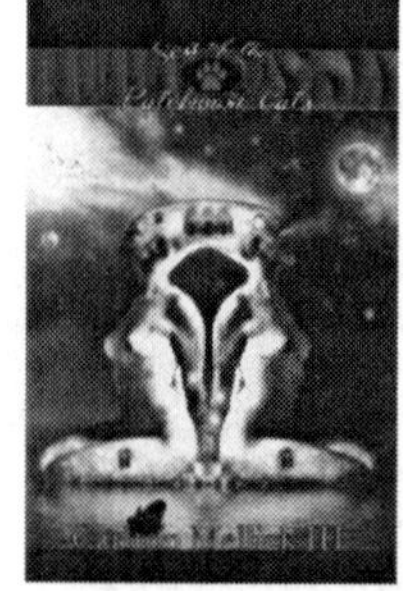

BB-032
"Extinction Journals"
Jeremy Robert Johnson
An uncanny voyage across a newly nuclear America where one man must confront the problems associated with loneliness, insane dieties, radiation, love, and an ever-evolving cockroach suit with a mind of its own.
104 pages $10

BIZARRO BOOKS CATALOGUE – SPRING 2008

BB-033
"Meat Puppet Cabaret"
Steve Beard
At last! The secret connection between Jack the Ripper and Princess Diana's death revealed!
240 pages $16 / $30

BB-034
"The Greatest Fucking Moment in Sports"
Kevin L. Donihe
In the tradition of the surreal anti-sitcom *Get A Life* comes a tale of triumph and agape love from the master of comedic bizarro.
108 pages $10

BB-035
"The Troublesome Amputee"
John Edward Lawson
Disturbing verse from a man who truly believes nothing is sacred and intends to prove it.
104 pages $9

BB-036
"Deity"
Vic Mudd
God (who doesn't like to be called "God") comes down to a typical, suburban, Ohio family for a little vacation—but it doesn't turn out to be as relaxing as He had hoped it would be…
168 pages $12

BB-037
"The Haunted Vagina"
Carlton Mellick III
It's difficult to love a woman whose vagina is a gateway to the world of the dead.
176 pages $11

BB-038
"Tales from the Vinegar Wasteland"
Ray Fracalossy
Witness: a man is slowly losing his face, a neighbor who periodically screams out for no apparent reason, and a house with a room that doesn't actually exist.
240 pages $14

BB-039
"Suicide Girls in the Afterlife"
Gina Ranalli
After Pogue commits suicide, she unexpectedly finds herself an unwilling "guest" at a hotel in the Afterlife.
100 pages $9

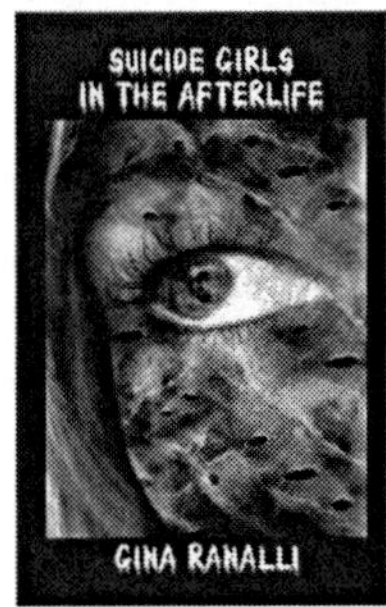

BB-040
"And Your Point Is?"
Steve Aylett
In this follow-up to LINT multiple authors provide critical commentary and essays about Jeff Lint's mind-bending literature.
104 pages $11

BIZARRO BOOKS CATALOGUE – SPRING 2008

BB-041
"Not Quite One of the Boys"
Vincent Sakowski
While drug-dealer Maxi drinks with Dante in purgatory, God and Satan play a little tri-level chess and do a little bargaining over his business partner, Vinnie.
220 pages $14

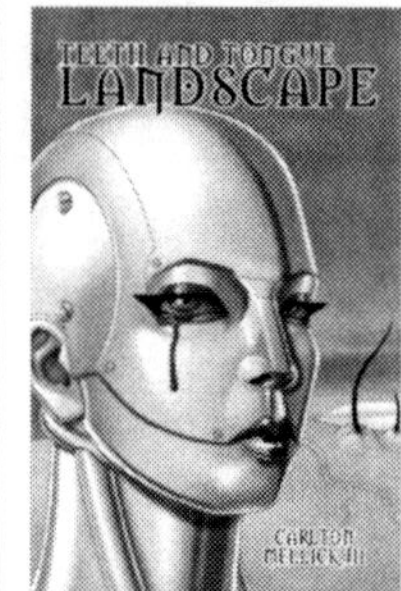

BB-042
"Teeth and Tongue Landscape"
Carlton Mellick III
On a planet made out of meat, a socially obsessive monophobic man tries to find his place amongst the strange creatures and communities that he comes across.
110 pages $10

BB-043
"War Slut"
Carlton Mellick III
Part "1984," part "Waiting for Godot," and part action horror video game adaptation of John Carpenter's "The Thing."
116 pages $10

BB-044
"All Encompassing Trip"
Nicole Del Sesto
In a world where coffee is no longer available, the only television shows are reality TV re-runs, and the animals are talking back, Nikki, Amber and a singing Coyote in a do-rag are out to restore the light
308 pages $15

BB-045
"Dr. Identity"
D. Harlan Wilson
Follow the Dystopian Duo on a killing spree of epic proportions through the irreal postcapitalist city of Bliptown where time ticks sideways and ultraviolence is as essential as a daily multivitamin.
208 pages $15

BB-046
"The Million-Year Centipede"
Eckhard Gerdes
Wakelin, frontman for 'The Hinge,' wrote a poem so prophetic that to ignore it dooms a person to drown in blood.
130 pages $12

BB-047
"Sausagey Santa"
Carlton Mellick III
A bizarro Christmas tale featuring Santa as a piratey mutant with a body made of sausages.
124 pages $10

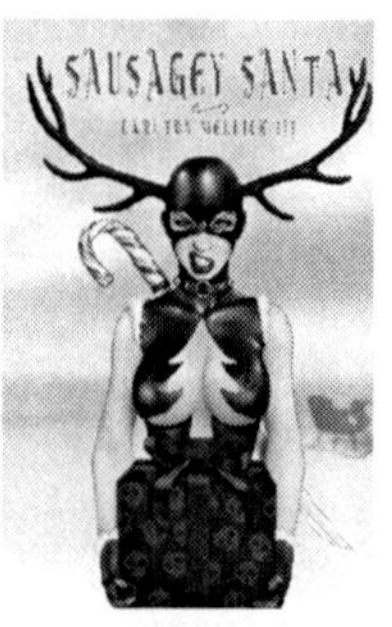

BB-048
"Misadventures in a Thumbnail Universe"
Vincent Sakowski
Dive deep into the surreal and satirical realms of neo-classical Blender Fiction, filled with television shoes and flesh-filled skies.
120 pages $10

BIZARRO BOOKS CATALOGUE – SPRING 2008

BB-049
“Vacation”
Jeremy C. Shipp
Blueblood Bernard Johnson left his boring life behind to go on The Vacation, a year-long corporate sponsored odyssey.
160 pages $14

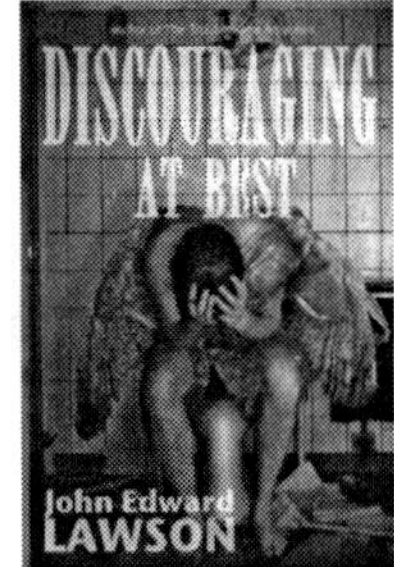

BB-050
“Discouraging at Best”
John Edward Lawson
A collection where the absurdity of the mundane expands exponentially creating a tidal wave that sweeps reason away. For those who enjoy satire, bizarro, or a good old-fashioned slap to the senses.
208 pages $15

BB-051
“13 Thorns”
Gina Ranalli
Thirteen tales of twisted, bizarro horror. Illustrated by Gus Fink.
240 pages $13

BB-052
“Better Ways of Being Dead”
Christian TeBordo
In this class, the students have to keep one palm down on the table at all times, and listen to lectures about a panda who speaks Chinese.
216 pages $14

BB-053
“Ballad of a Slow Poisoner”
Andrew Goldfarb
Millford Mutterwurst sat down on a Tuesday to take his afternoon tea, and made the unpleasant discovery that his elbows were becoming flatter.
128 pages $10

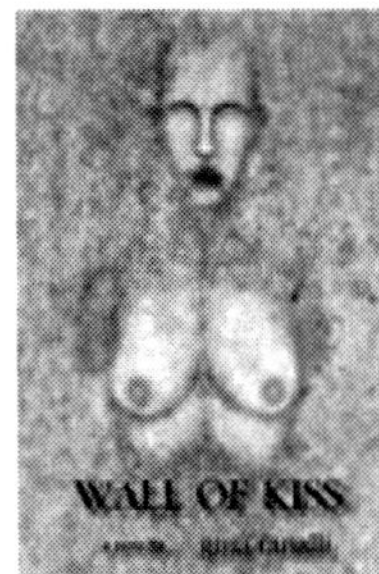

BB-054
“Wall of Kiss”
Gina Ranalli
A woman... A wall... Sometimes love blooms in the strangest of places.
108 pages $9

BB-055
“HELP! A Bear is Eating Me”
Mykle Hansen
The bizarro, heartwarming, magical tale of poor planning, hubris and severe blood loss...
150 pages $11

BB-056
“Piecemeal June”
Jordan Krall
A man falls in love with a living sex doll, but with love comes danger when her creator comes after her with crab-squid assassins.
150 pages $11

BIZARRO BOOKS CATALOGUE – SPRING 2008

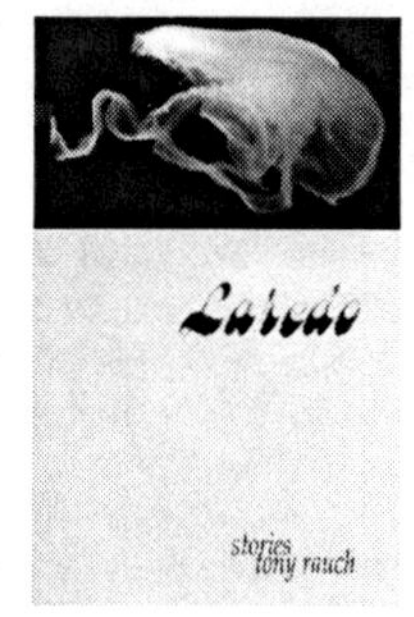

BB-057
"Laredo"
Tony Rauch
Dreamlike, surreal stories by Tony Rauch.
180 pages $12

BB-058
"The Overwhelming Urge"
Andersen Prunty
A collection of bizarro tales by Andersen Prunty.
180 pages $12

COMING SOON

"Adolf in Wonderland" by Carlton Mellick III

"House of Houses" by Kevin L. Donihe

"Super Cell Anemia" by Duncan Barlow

"The Ultra Fuckers" by Carlton Mellick III

"Cocoon of Terror" by Jason Earls

"Jack and Mr. Grin" by Andersen Prunty

ORDER FORM

TITLES	QTY	PRICE	TOTAL
		Shipping costs (see below)	
		TOTAL	

Please make checks and moneyorders payable to ROSE O'KEEFE / BIZARRO BOOKS in U.S. funds only. Please don't send bad checks! Allow 2-6 weeks for delivery. International orders may take longer. If you'd like to pay online via PAYPAL.COM, send payments to publisher@eraserheadpress.com.

SHIPPING: US ORDERS - $2 for the first book, $1 for each additional book. For priority shipping, add an additional $4. INT'L ORDERS - $5 for the first book, $3 for each additional book. Add an additional $5 per book for global priority shipping.

Send payment to:

BIZARRO BOOKS
C/O Rose O'Keefe
205 NE Bryant
Portland, OR 97211

Address

City State Zip

Email Phone

Printed in the United States
117174LV00004B/212/P

9 781933 929620